The Tapestry of Us

Lily Pickard

FT
Pbk

ISBN-13: 978-1-78292-486-9
ISBN-10: 1782924868

PART ONE
AFTER YOU HAD GONE

CATE

It's kind of like looking in a bathroom mirror steaming up from hot beads of water squeezing from the showerhead. On the glass there's a very faint outline of your face, hovering, and if you really squint you might be able to see a bit more, perhaps a dark shadow. But really the outline you can see is more like a ghost – you're not really there. That pretty much sums up how I feel these days. A ghost. Lost. Trapped on earth, biding my time.

I'm standing in the kitchen, pouring boiling water into a cup, watching the teabag being sucked deeper into the liquid. I place the kettle back on the bench, open the top drawer and reach in to take out a teaspoon. I stand still, spoon poised in my right hand. I count to ten and dip the spoon into the murky brown water to salvage the teabag. I turn around, take four steps and open the cupboard door below the sink, dropping the teabag into the garbage bin. I watch the bin lid swing back into position, walk three steps and take a carton of milk from the fridge. I pour the milk into the hot water, watching white coil into brown. Then I just stand rooted to that spot on the kitchen floor, staring at the white glossy tiles lined in perfect rows on the wall above the bench.

Twenty-nine days ago, the phone rang and the conversation, or rather the words that were said and my silence in reply, has been swirling through my body ever since. Those words have been wrapping themselves tightly around my lungs making breathing difficult and strangling the blood from my heart at such a rate that sometimes I catch myself spreading a palm across my chest to protect the saddening organ inside.

Now I sleep in a foetal position. When I'm out, sometimes I involuntarily drop to the floor. I know when it's going to happen, I feel myself sliding down the wall and watch as people's faces around me slowly distort and then quickly turn away.

I guess sleeping wrapped in his favourite T-shirt, the British racing green one with the white motif on the sleeve, will soon stop. So will the constant need to bury my face deep into the fibres of that shirt, frantically trying to smell one last scent of his aftershave and to touch the fabric that would have fallen on his beautiful skin.

God, there's someone at the front door. Automatically I stoop below the bench top. It's probably Laura thinking that she should show she hasn't yet given up on me and can lure me out of my hazy bubble. Her persistence has been unflappable – I will give her that. It's as though she's signed up to a 'Frequenting Grief' programme where the more times you visit a friend in need of cheering up, the more points you earn to purchase a lifetime of happiness. That's another thing, lately I feel an overwhelming sense of bitterness, especially about other people's happiness and my own misfortune. Knuckles wrap against the front door again. I suck my breath in between clenched teeth.

"Cate, come on, I know you must be home. Why don't we go for a walk? The fresh air might do you some good," Laura's voice barged through the door, an intruder storming my cocoon.

A walk in the fresh air, she must be joking. At the moment I can't do the walk to the letterbox, let alone a walk in public. I know this because I've tried already. It was the seventeenth day following the phone call. I thought I may have been able to just about make it to the shop – living on the stale air hanging in a heavy mist throughout the house, a bottomless cup of tea and the bottles of red wine I opened every day in an attempt to numb the pain were all starting to wear off. I had rummaged through the drawer in the hallstand searching for my sunglasses before gingerly opening the front door. I stood there for at least a minute, breathing deeply and counting to ten. "OK" I told myself, "On ten, lock the door, walk to the gate, open it and put one foot in front of the other and walk down the street like a normal person." But that's just it, I wasn't normal anymore, nothing would ever be the same again and the hurt that caused was unbearable. Slowly though, I got to the letterbox and made the mistake of deviating from the deal I'd made with myself by opening the letterbox. Inside were two white envelopes, the top one windowed with the name and address of the intended recipient printed in bold type. One look at the name and I froze. My heart started to beat like it was about to pop right through my breastplate and land at my feet. I felt myself sliding and I knew I had about thirty seconds to make it back inside the house to avoid collapsing in a heap at the gate for the paperboy to find me.

"Alright, well you know it's only going to be a matter of time before I decide to use my key and come in there and get you…I love you," Laura whispered through the door. I heard her footsteps tread carefully down each step leading from the verandah, pausing momentarily on the concrete path scorched from yet another day of a bleaching Sydney summer, before the gate eventually creaked on its hinges. Then I knew I was safe until at least tomorrow evening.

The day of the phone call had started off like any other. That's the funny thing about a tragedy; all is in its place, nothing out of the ordinary. In fact, at the time, it's highly likely you're even feeling a bit smug about your life. One of you leaves the house as usual with the other never even guessing that will be the last time you'll ever see each other. Imagine if you did, what would you do? To know your little arms got to squeeze his waist one more time. To have one last look into those eyes, one last thumb pushed across his eyebrow to adjust the faint hair.

My mobile phone ringing and vibrating on my stomach wakes me. I must have dozed off on the couch. Thank God, I haven't been able to sleep properly for the last twenty-eight nights. Dr Penfold had prescribed sleeping pills and valium. For the first five days, I gladly gobbled the valium like a greedy child, but soon discovered no pill could cure the pain and sadness twisting at high voltage through my body. I reached down and clicked the green button on the phone.

"Cate…" It was my dad's voice, gentle and husky.
"Hi."
"Sweetheart, I was just ringing to see how you went today…"
"Hmmm?"

"Oh, honey we thought you were heading back to work today."

"Today?"

"Maybe we got it wrong."

"Wait, what's the date?"

"It's the second."

"Oh shit."

The next morning I am lying in bed. I have been watching the alarm clock click around each hour for the past four hours. For the last eleven minutes I had challenged myself to close my eyes and count the seconds in my head to see if I could time my counting exactly to when the clock clicked over to the next minute. I was putting off calling work, I wasn't ready to make excuses for not showing up yesterday, but mainly I didn't think I could manage listening to first the receptionist and then my boss trying awkwardly to piece together some words that wouldn't upset me or sound off-hand and uncaring.

I dialled the number. After three rings our receptionist answered cheerily: "Good morning Hertz and Wells". I quickly sat up and swallowed hard before attempting "Hi", which must have sounded like a scratch into the receiver.

"Good morning Hertz and Wells…"

"Larissa, hi it's…"

"Cate, is that you?"

"It is. Yes."

"Oh…oh Cate, I am…we are so sorry…"

'Yes I know thank you, the flowers were very kind…"

"Well it's nothing…but anyway how are you?"

I was twisting the corner of the sheet between my thumb and index finger with such grip that the colour had drained from my thumbnail.

"You know…I am doing OK," I lied. "Listen I was wondering if I could speak to Garry, if he's in yet?"

"Of course Cate, I'll put you straight through, listen Cate if there's anything…"

I knew what was coming next, people feel so helpless and I know they genuinely want to try and help. Every conversation is punctuated with pretty much the same standard phrase: "If there's anything I can do, anything at all please let me know. It doesn't matter what time of the day or night it is and you think you need something, just call." After hearing it a few times, I have started to see the funny side of it. For instance, if one of my friends were a brain surgeon and I decided I needed a new box of soft, aloe vera tissues to dry my throbbing eyes – I imagined calling them on their mobile phone in the middle of an operation. Of course, they would oblige, rip off their gloves and make a dash for the swinging metal doors, calling behind their shoulder: "Nurse, fill in for me would you. I have to source a box of aloe vera tissues."

There was a dead silence for a few seconds while the phone connected through to Garry's office. It was answered on the fourth ring. I had rehearsed a speech in my head and decided if I could just buy myself another couple of weeks' grace, I would make a pact with myself – no crying before lunch time.

"Hello Cate, how are you doing?" Garry asked softly. "I'm kind of OK. Listen Garry I am really sorry, I think I was meant to come back to work yesterday and to be honest, I completely forgot. I can't believe that I did, but I did and it wasn't until my dad phoned in the evening to see how I was that he reminded me that I was meant to start back at work and I hadn't even remembered…" I was talking a mouthful of words a second.

"Cate, it's OK, it's OK. Don't you remember you and I chatted about this when I was leaving your place last week? I really thought it was too early for you to come back to work…after all that's happened and what you must be going through. So we agreed to play it by ear for a few more weeks and catch up around the twentieth and decide on a date then."

"We did?"

I was staring at the sheet corner, which had dropped out of my grip and laid a crumpled white on the pillow. I could remember talking to Garry when he arrived unexpectedly one evening last week, my parents were still here. Garry had looked awkward, sitting on the edge of the couch, one foot pointing towards the door and sipping on a beer my father had given him. The beer was a brand we didn't buy.

I remembered looking at Garry, but my mind was set deep in a Sunday afternoon late in summer. The sun prickled our backs as we sat on the veranda. We had friends over, we were talking about a wedding we'd been to the weekend before – the groom looked like he was going to throw up at the crucial moment. Tom went inside to get more beers. When he came out he had rolled a freezing bottle on my back. I had squealed jumping off the railing and grabbing his arm as I landed inches from the outdoor table stacked high with empty beer bottles. Tom held the bottle firmly on my back while I squirmed and yelled, "Get it off!" He told me if I stayed still he would. Reluctantly I stood still, ever so lightly Tom rolled the bottle over my shoulder and onto my chest, with the glass resting on my chin, he whispered: "I love you, you little squealer." I had smiled at him.

"Cate, are you OK?" Garry's voice was nervous on the other end of the phone.

"Yes I am. Sorry. God I had totally forgotten that, we talked about it at the front door didn't we? After Mum and Dad had gone to the shop?"

"That's right. Listen try and get some rest and don't worry about work, we can manage."

"Thanks Garry, I really appreciate it." I quickly hung up the phone, stayed in bed and let the tears spill hot over my cheeks, itching as they rolled down my chin. Already I had broken my pact with myself – it was only 8.54am.

Later that day I am sitting on the back step smoking a cigarette. Even though I don't really smoke I found the packet when I was drifting through the house from room to room. Much of my time these last few weeks has been spent moving silently around the rooms of the house, pausing at the doorways to just stare emptily into the spaces. This morning I had been leaning against the doorway of the sunroom looking at the coatings of dust which had gathered on the windowsills and at the curtains which hung in mourning bending and straining the rods. The chairs sat silently, their cushions slumped like tired old men. I walked over and sat down on the chair closest to the back door, crushing its cushion to my chest and watching the water dropping from my eyes seeping and spreading into the fabric. It was as though the entire house was creaking with the pain and loss I felt. I pushed my blurry, watery eyes around the room letting them rest on the art deco dresser we had found abandoned on the street one evening when we were walking home from dinner at our local Thai restaurant.

I stared at the dresser drawer, trying to think what might be inside. Slowly I got up and walked over to it, fingering the brass handle shining wearily on the drawer. I remembered Tom had cut his finger when the screwdriver slipped as he was replacing the drawer handle. I let my finger rest on the metal before opening the drawer to find it revealed little more than a few old bills, a couple of pens and the packet of cigarettes. I have no idea who the cigarettes belonged to because neither Tom nor I were smoking these days so guessed they had been left when we had friends over for a barbeque the weekend before Tom...I clutched at the cigarettes like a thirsty explorer who had stumbled across a watering hole. Giving the packet a shake, the sound of light paper rolls bumping into each other gave me all I needed. The box of matches sitting on top of the fridge was now in my hand. I had to get outside.

Going out the front had not been an option, it was too easy to be seen and I didn't want to be seen. So now here I was on the back step, nestled down low in the garden, a packet of matches and a cigarette packet that wasn't mine lying beside me on the step. I had only taken a few puffs, instead letting the cigarette burn low, the ash dropping lightly from the end and fluttering into the air.

The garden had overgrown. Weeds sprouted up from the soil in the once tended flower beds. The mint in the herb garden had gone wild, drawing long tentacles up towards the sun while the lavender buds dropped to one side looking like weary heads hanging low in grief. Even they knew Tom had gone. I looked away from the mass of purple to the leaves lightly blowing across the path. It was turning into a wasteland out here. Tom had loved the garden. On the weekends he would go for a surf early in the morning, always around six o'clock. An hour or so later he would shake the salt from his hair while collecting the weekend newspapers, two takeaway coffees – a short black for him and a skinny cappuccino for me – a couple of fresh croissants and be on his way home. I was always still in bed, stretching and yawning, blinking as the sunlight came splintering through the curtains Tom was pulling back with far too much energy for that early on a Saturday morning. Then we'd sit out here in the garden together, just the two of us reading the weekend newspapers, sipping on coffees and brushing pastry flakes onto the grass.

If I had known the horrendous misery cunningly lying in wait for me, is that how we would have still spent our Saturday mornings, casually sitting out here pretending we had all the time in the world. Why didn't I touch his beautiful face. Let my fingers stick and snag in the salt crystallising in his hair or even just lightly touch his elbow. I needed more. More of everything. More of one thing. Just more.

I had to do something. I no longer felt like just sitting here all alone on the step, crying the day away. I wanted to move my body and expel some energy so I could exhaust myself. Properly tire myself out so I could sleep, so I wouldn't have to think anymore and be unconscious in a deep long slumber. Then when I wake up, another day would be gone or at least some more time would have passed which surely would start to make the pain duller and weaker. Surely.

Suddenly I was up and in the house getting the broom from beside the fridge and furiously sweeping the porch steps. I sneezed as the leaves and dust blew up and into my nose. By the time I reached the fifth and final step my eyes were watering and I was constantly reaching up to wipe my nose with the back of my forearm. As I saw the steps become cleaner, I felt an overwhelming sense of satisfaction which only made me want to press harder on the broom, sweeping in long firm strokes. Leaves and dust continued to spiral upwards into the air, catching at my hair, eyes, nose and mouth. As quickly as it had all started, it finished. Brushing feverishly at a stubborn stain on the bottom step the broom handle slipped in my hand. A splinter caught and slid under a layer of skin. I dropped the broom and stared at the tiny piece of wood which had worked its way neatly into my palm. It didn't hurt. I prodded at it with the edge of my fingernail. Even the nail jabbing at the skin didn't seem to strike any pain. I pressed the nail deeper into the flesh, waiting for a pain sensation to message a nerve that there should be some pain starting to register somewhere in my body. But still nothing. I felt no physical pain at all. I threw my head back and stretched my arms out towards the sky letting out a long, low piercing noise – standing all alone on a Wednesday morning in a beachside backyard sometime during my sad sweltering Sydney summer.

LAURA

I had already knocked on the door twice, the house was silent, but I knew Cate was inside, hiding from me again. The part left out of the saying: "A friend in need is a friend indeed," is when that particular friend doesn't want your damn help. I sighed, watching the mirrored needles on Cate's wind chime sway in the sunlight and gently clash. "I love you," I whispered through the firmly shut door.

Opening the front gate, I noticed a man across the other side of the street holding a cardboard box. When he saw me he smiled awkwardly and looked quickly down at the box in his arms. I smiled back at him, squinting from the sun. Driving off, I caught him in the rear vision mirror, watching my car leave Cate's street.

"Still no luck, I'm going to have to give her a few more days," I said pushing a chunk of blonde hair behind my ear.

"And if that doesn't work, then what do we do Laura?"

I was on the phone to Isobel, Cate's and my best friend since university. We'd met her in the university bar one Thursday night. The only two vacant barstools were either side of a girl with a face of thunder angrily ripping the corner off a drink coaster. It was Isobel. Cate and I had looked anxiously at one another, silently conversing with our eyes as to whether we should ask this angry girl if we could possibly move the empty barstools that were either side of her together. I did another quick scan of the bar heaving with sweaty undergraduates clutching plastic cups of flat beer. Swarms of bodies were pressed together in conversations yelling over the top of the indie sound projecting from four straggly-looking guys strumming instruments on stage, while the rest swayed in tangled unison to the music. Giving up, I shrugged my shoulders at Cate's raised eyebrows and stepped forward to ask the lone girl on the barstool if anyone was sitting on the ones either side of her. At first I didn't think she had heard me as she kept tearing at the coaster, adding tiny twists of mangled cardboard to a pile next to her glass. Finally she looked up, her eyes were swelling with water that she quickly wiped at with the backs of her hands and shook her head.

"Are you OK?" I asked hesitantly. She twisted her bottom lip and nodded.

"Are you sure?" Cate asked softly.

"Yeah, yeah. It's nothing. I am just being an idiot," she said, eventually shifting her focus from the coaster in her hand to look at us. Cate and I must have been staring at this girl as she nervously darted her gaze to the floor before slowly meeting our eyes again, "Seriously. I'm fine," she said defiantly while gripping the crushed coaster. I knew I was staring at her face. Even with eyes filled with water, they were gleaming emerald, flicking up at the ends like a cat. Her nose drew a perfectly straight line to two full red lips, while sheets of honey-blonde hair draped from a middle-part framing her face. I tugged self-consciously on my own blonde hair, matted and knotted from swimming in the ocean. The self-conscious tug on my hair is a habit I fall into around Isobel, even now, eleven years later.

Cate perched herself on one of the stools, "Do you want a drink? My shout. I'm Cate by the way and this is Laura," she smiled, gesturing to me.

"Sure. Why not? I'm Isobel," she said attempting a smile, "I'll just have a beer. I don't care what sort."

"OK," Cate said, frowning at me while I stood clumsily beside the stool, clearly undecided about whether to move the stool over by Cate, or just sit on it where it was with this stranger perched between us. Cate continued to frown at me until I awkwardly sat down on the square of cracked black vinyl, leaving the stool exactly where it was.

"Are you sure you're OK?" Cate said to Isobel, handing out three plastic cups of beer and clearly not self-conscious about how she looked while she spilled drops of beer down the front of her T-shirt. Cate's long dark hair was slicked back in a ponytail which showed her fresh face, free of make-up, with big hazel eyes that always seemed to look like they were smiling.

"Yeah. Yeah. It's stupid really. I just found out my...boyfriend has gone overseas. Just like that, he didn't even tell me. Apparently he's gone backpacking. Why does everyone have to do that, it's so...so..."

"Common and unimaginative?" I chipped in.

Isobel cracked a smile, "Exactly!"

"Well no one wants to go out with common, unimaginative people. Let me guess, did he take off to London and is now living in Earl's Court along with every other bloody Australian who's apparently experiencing the world and meeting people from different cultures?" I quipped. Isobel smirked and nodded. "And predictable too. Good thing he's gone then," I said, taking a sip of beer.

"But if he's your boyfriend, and you didn't know he was going away, that's pretty bad," Cate cut in gently.

Isobel twisted her bottom lip, "Well, we weren't exactly going out by the time he left. We had been. Going out. For ages," she faltered for a moment before continuing, almost whispering, "but then something kind of happened and, umm, we lost touch, I guess. I took a year out of university and now I've come back and he's, well he's gone backpacking apparently. I haven't seen him for ages anyway, so I don't know why I am so upset. Stupid, really." Isobel shrugged and started to pick at the edge of her plastic cup. Cate and I exchanged a nervous glance, we were all silent for a minute while the air hung heavy with cigarette smoke around the three of us, "Let's talk about something else," Isobel said suddenly, sitting up straight and shaking her hair from her face.

And the tactic of shifting the conversation in a different direction, deflected away from herself – one of Isobel's greatest tactics that I now know like the back of my hand – is how she got Cate and I forgetting the conversation and instead laughing at the drunk couple leaning against the bar next to us. The rest of the night dissolved into loud laughter and empty plastic cups of beer as we all slowly grew drunker. The three of us excited about finding a new friend in that easy way you tend to be able to at university, it's only years later that you discover a simple ease with strangers is a rare event and even rarer is turning them into lifelong friends. So, looping our arms in a drunken sway to a bad cover of Beck's 'Loser', courtesy of the indie band, along with the discovery that Isobel and I were in the same history elective class, sealed our friendships. Who knew then that we'd all be dealing with a death when we hit our thirties. A loss so harrowing, for Cate especially, that at times it feels like the grief is going to swallow our gorgeous friend whole.

Since Tom's funeral, Isobel had somehow gotten away with instructing from the background, while I was repeatedly sent to the frontline to try and persuade Cate to at least open her front door. I must admit once it was apparent Cate was slipping, really slipping, Isobel had told me upfront she didn't feel strong enough to coax Cate out of her haze. At the time I had thought Isobel a coward. But as the weeks started to heave over, I realised I was more annoyed that I didn't have the foresight to allocate myself Isobel's self-appointed position first.

"Well *we* are going to have to do something about it. After all, wouldn't *we* want someone to help us if *we* had just lost the love of our life?" I snapped.

Silence. Isobel's greatest defence and yet another one of her tactics for winning over friends or boyfriends caught off-guard.

"Isobel?" Silence. "Issy, come on. I need some support here, I have been practically stalking Cate and it's not working." Still silence. "Issy…"

"Do you think she is seeing a counsellor or therapist or something?" Isobel finally asked quietly. The best way to deal with one of Isobel's silences was to plough right on with the conversation as soon as she gives a tiny bite of a reply.

"I hope so Issy, but from what I can see she hasn't left the house. So, unless Cate's getting home visits, I can't see that she would necessarily be seeing anyone for help, no, which can't be good in any case."

"Hmmm," Isobel replied. I knew Issy so well and guessed she would be twisting her bottom lip down toward her chin, considering what I'd just told her.

"Should…should I perhaps go around to Cate and Tom's…" Isobel stopped short at the sound of Tom's name.

"It's alright Iss, it's only natural we're going to mention Tom. He was such a good friend to all of us… and with you…" I let the sentence hang in the air, unfinished. I thought of Tom, his floppy blonde hair dropping in his eyes. The way he would stand, his head tilted, absorbing a conversation. "It will be alright Iss, I promise we'll sort something out. Cate knows we love her."

"Yep," Isobel replied, the cut of my earlier words now obviously healed over.

"Listen, I hate to do this, but I gotta go, I'm running late," I said.

"Oh."

"You'll be pleased when you hear why I have to go."

"Yeah, why?"

"Because I have a date."

"Oh Laura, who is he?"

"No one you know."

"Laura!"

"Bye Issy, gotta go…" I said smiling broadly as I hung up the phone.

ISOBEL

I lay on the couch trying to concentrate on a documentary playing on the TV about something I didn't really want to know anything about. I had been flicking through channels for the past twenty minutes or so and had landed on the beginning of whatever this documentary was. I thought about Laura on a date with some random guy who must be new on the scene. I imagined her trying on all different outfits until she finally settled on the first one she had tried on. Knowing she was running late, she would have kicked the clothes strewn across her bedroom under the bed so everything looked presentable in case she got lucky later in the evening. If he came to collect her, Laura would have practised a casual smile before opening the door and then pretending she had to collect her bag from another room. Then, turning on her heel she would take deliberate strides with a slight swing in her hip up the hallway, the poor guy would be standing there watching her athletic figure sporting a neat arse disappear into the bedroom. The thought of this scene forced a smirk to my face.

Outside it was starting to get dark, the long shadows had all but disappeared leaving a greying light drifting half-heartedly through the gap in the lounge room curtains. A few streets away I could hear the sounds of the sea playing a gentle rhythm with its waves onto the sand which most people found to be a calming sound, but for me it was a stark reminder I lived on my own. When the noises of the day had quietened for the evening, that sound engulfed the flat, taking over my head while I lay in bed at night trying desperately to shut off, to sleep, and not have to think.

Mostly, I didn't mind living on my own. It was my choice after all. One too many stinging relationships helped me make up my mind once and for all that I should try living on my own. I wasn't in my twenties anymore either so the thought of sharing with a flatmate, for me, was now absolutely out of the question. I had too many beautiful pieces of furniture, artwork and just generally nice things that I was no longer willing to have at the mercy of a random stranger and their late night stumbling interludes picked up in the pub somewhere between the fifth and sixth drink and whatever else they had put up their nose or swallowed. Besides I had a good job in art dealing, earning good money, so really I didn't *need* someone living with me. But tonight I was feeling *alone*.

My mind wandered then to Cate. I imagined she too would be home alone, not by choice though, probably crying. A pang of guilt hit me. I hadn't really seen her or even spoken to her properly since the funeral. God that was a bloody awful day, so hard, so difficult, so...just thinking about it now produced a surge of panic rising and swelling in my stomach. Laura seemed to be taking the reigns, looking for ways to drag Cate back to normality, but Laura would wouldn't she, after all. Her phone calls wanting me to help, do my bit, be a support, were still persistent because she just doesn't get it. No one gets it. Everyone has different ways of dealing with loss, Laura even says that herself. So why she just doesn't get on and let people deal with things the way they want to deal with things, instead of recruiting everyone – well me – into her way of dealing with things, which is to try and bloody fix everything all the time, is beyond me.

Maybe I should call Cate, see how she's doing. Show her I am still here and that I do really care, because I do. Really care. But the thought of having to engage in conversation and think of something comforting to say was terrifying. I have never been very good at knowing what to say and something as big as death, well what could I say that would possibly make Cate feel even a fraction better, to make her feel there could be the faintest hope when she woke tomorrow morning that the daylight hours of consciousness might be slightly less painful than all the other ones she has just endured without Tom. I had no idea what to say to her and if she started to cry that would make everything much worse, I really wouldn't know what to say then. I would end up saying the wrong thing, I know I would, or I would stay silent and hear her crying all by herself in the dark with Tom haunting every room. I looked around the empty flat, sometimes I feel like Tom is hanging around in my space, scratching at the layers, silently willing me to do something.

'Fucking hell,' I said out loud, reaching for the packet of cigarettes sitting on the coffee table. I tapped one out of the packet, lit the end and took a long slow drag letting the smoke suck deep into my lungs, my head rolled back on the couch as I exhaled white in winding curls up towards the ceiling.

My left foot was tapping vigorously on the floor. I took another long drag hoping the tobacco would calm my body down. Still my foot tapped. I pressed a fist to my leg to steady it. Still my foot continued to shake under the pressure of my clench. 'Fucking hell,' I said out loud again.

I stood up and went into the kitchen to retrieve the bottle of vodka from the freezer. I didn't bother with a glass instead sucking furiously on the bottle. The cap had dropped to the floor rolling along the tiles while the cigarette dropped ash in small piles. The vodka was cold. The liquid laced my mouth and throat, hitting the pit of my stomach like a punch. I pulled the bottle from my mouth, coughing and shaking from the direct hit of alcohol. My lips were numb. I shook my head and winced. 'Fucking hell,' I said out loud for the third time. The room started to spin. I closed my eyes, steadying myself on the fridge. My hand was still gripping the vodka bottle as I licked my lips, wincing at the remains of alcohol still sliding through the creases in my lips. I felt sick and raced to the bathroom, flipped open the toilet seat and heaved up clear liquid. My pulse was racing. Another surge of ghastly clear liquid hit the toilet. I felt completely crap for a good few minutes, just letting my head hang slightly above the bowl, every now and again raising a limp hand to push my hair back off my forehead. Finally when I thought I wasn't going to be sick anymore, I yanked myself up and shoved my hands under the cool running water in the basin and splashed my face, taking in a big gulp of water, gargling and then spitting it out. I closed my eyes not wanting to face myself in the mirror. I couldn't – more like I wouldn't – look at myself in the mirror lately. Closing my eyes though was making me unsteady. I prised them open, immediately regaining my balance, but the shock of my reflection staring back at me almost knocked me right off balance once more.

Large black rings hung in heavy sacks under my eyes. My cheeks were gaunt and drawn. 'Shit. I look like shit.' I chastised the face hanging in the mirror. 'Fuck it,' I flicked the bathroom light off and went in search of the cigarette packet.

CATE

"Would you love me if you found out I was an alien?" Tom asked.

"Which planet are you from?"

"It doesn't matter."

"Well, depends what you looked like."

"Would you turn me in?"

"Who to?"

"The authorities…"

"Absolutely, if I thought I could make some cash out of you."

Laughing Tom grabbed the belt loop on my jeans and drew me into his chest. I drank in his smell.

It was day thirty-seven following the phone call. I was flicking through our CDs when I came across a post-it note stuck to the front of one – Tom's handwriting was scribbled across the yellow paper. I felt pins and needles spread across my earlobes and down my neck. I studied the writing, looking at the curl of the "y" and the straightness of the "t". I peeled the post-it note off the CD cover and held it close to my chest. Little reminders of Tom like this kept taking me by surprise. It's strange how a scribble on a bit of yellow sticky paper can prove someone's existence. I had never examined his writing before and imagined what a handwriting decoder might say: "The writer is a man. The curl of the "y" makes him sensitive and emotional while the straightness of the "t" indicates strength and protection…he will die young. His lover will be forever heart broken and angry that he dare leave her without saying goodbye, that he ruin their link and let her roll onto his side of the bed every night, weeping silently that his warm, strong body will never lie next to her again".

Suddenly without even knowing what I was doing, I picked up the CD and hurled it across the room with such a force that I surprised myself. A corner of the plastic case clipped the wall above the couch, leaving a grey dent.

"God damn you Tom. How dare you do this to me," I shouted across the room at the CD. "You're an arsehole, I don't want to be without you. It wasn't enough time, I'm not ready." I flung myself towards the couch, punching the armrest hard and fast. I picked up the cushions and swung one, two, three, four of them across the room, letting them land wherever the hell they wanted to. My arm, with a mind of its own, jerked forward to swipe a magazine off the coffee table, letting it collect a tissue box, TV remote control and my mobile phone on its way to the floor. My next victim was a happy, smiling photo of me and Tom on holiday last year – two smiling sun drenched faces – that had to go. I threw it against the wall. Of course the coffee table was asking for a good boot in the leg, so I crunched up my toes, lined my foot up and kicked the leg. "Jesus Christ," I screamed hopping around in pain, clutching my striker foot and cursing my life and the unfairness of it all at the top of my voice. Then I collapsed in one pathetic heap on the floor.

Sitting in the middle of the lounge room floor, panting and staring at the destruction around me, I waited for the tears to start welling in my eyes, for the throbbing lonely, sad pain to surge up from the pit of my stomach and fire like gun shots into my veins or for that long low noise to erupt from my throat. My body was silent.

The handle of the front door moved to the left. I stared and watched it turn right the way round. The door opened a few inches and Laura's head poked very slowly through the crack. I thought about dropping flat to my belly, snaking my way across the floor and into the bedroom to climb and hide in the cupboard. Manoeuvring silently around the debris I had just created would be impossible. It was too late anyway.

"Holy shit Cate, what happened?" Laura asked gently as she opened the front door completely and stepped carefully into the hallway. Laura was clearly startled. She probably thinks I've lost it completely I thought. Had I been left any longer, I would have been discovered years from now with matted hair, clutching a few stray cats, unphased by a family of pigeons nesting in the corners of the lounge room.

"Sweetheart, I know you'll be cursing me because you don't want me here inside the house...the cocoon you've made for yourself and Tom." Hearing his name said out loud made the hairs on my forearms stand to attention.

"But I can't bear to leave you here alone any longer. I have tried to stay away and let you come around your own way... but I can't do it anymore." Laura said inching towards me and ever so slowly lowering her body so it was level with my own slumped version on the floor.

I watched as Laura picked up the smiley, happy photo of me and Tom. In the photo, the wind was blowing my hair over Tom's face. He stood grinning between the strands, his green eyes looking straight into the camera lens. My fingers were grabbing at the flyaway strands. Our heads were pressed together.

Laura made a clicking sound at the back of her throat, sighing she reached for my hand. My instant reaction was to pull away for fear of starting to cry, but Laura grabbed my hand before I could and lightly kissed it.

"God, it's…it's fucked isn't it?" I muttered. Laura nodded, holding the back of my hand against her cheek. "Do you know I don't think I can even cry anymore? I just went absolutely mental because I found a post-it note Tom had written and for the first time since this whole bloody crappy thing happened, instead of crying, I just got angry."

"Bloody angry by the looks of things," Laura said softly, surveying the room. The back of the remote control had fallen off, two Double AA batteries lay on the floorboards like little tin soldiers. The cushions must have taken a few things with them on their one-way ticket to the floor, a vase of dead flowers was now on the floor, water running between the CDs and brown lilies splayed across the floorboards.

"What did it say?" Laura asked.
    "What?"
    "The post-it note."
    "Oh, it said: burn track five for Matty."

Laura looked down, touching her hand to her mouth, but I could see the corners of her mouth moving upwards, a smile spreading across her face. She looked up at me and started to laugh.

"What?" I demanded. But I knew exactly why Laura was laughing. It was laughable. The whole sodden mess, me included. For the first time in thirty-seven days, I could actually feel the corners of my mouth slowly turning upwards too.

"That's better." Laura said. "I…everyone's been so worried about you. I wish there was a manual telling us what to do, when you'd need us, when we should stay away and most importantly when you'd feel like a stiff drink. I mean I know you love a bubble, but I felt strange about bringing around champagne because it's hardly a celebration. But then in some ways it should be."

"Well, it couldn't hurt. I'm willing to give anything a go," I replied straightening up and folding myself into one of the over stuffed armchairs Tom and I had bought in a second hand shop down the coast two summers ago. Laura picked a couple of dead lilies off the couch, laid them on the coffee table before sitting herself down across from me. Normally when Laura's over, she slumps into the couch, straightens her legs over the coffee table and starts the conversation with a colourful, animated description of something that had happened that day. The story is always a tall one, hole-punched with exaggeration and Laura waving her hands about, usually with a wine glass in hand. But today Laura sat quietly, almost formally, studying me.

"Well usually around this time of day, I am curled up in a ball, howling my head off of course. So unless you want to join me in that, maybe we better have a drink," I said.

Laura smiled. "Is there a choice? We know which option I want. Let's both get on that floor now and start crying." Despite myself, I smiled for a second time.

"Right, this could be good, I'm not sure what's in here," I said opening the fridge door. On the shelves were two bottles of white wine, one three-quarters full, a quiche my mother had made – completely untouched – two soft tomatoes, a block of cheese and Tom's condiments – a few jars of pickles, tomato relish and Hot English Mustard. Little jars of colour I knew I would never be able to throw out. I shut my eyes for a second, sucking my breath in.

"You OK?" Laura asked. I could feel her coming up behind me, easing the fridge door open a little further. "Well minimalism is in honey," Laura exclaimed, looking at the white, yellow and red in the fridge. I reached for the opened wine bottle and pulled the cork out. A sour smell of over ripe grapes hit my nostrils. I replugged the cork and placed the bottle back on the shelf and collected the un-opened bottle.

With wine glasses and bottle in hand, Laura and I had picked our way through the debris in the lounge room and were now sitting on the veranda chairs; the afternoon sun was dropping, lazily blinking between the trees. I watched Laura as she wound the corkscrew efficiently into the bottle top and pulled the cork out smoothly. "Old habits die hard huh." Laura said pouring the wine into both glasses, slowing as she filled the second to ensure it was level with the first.

"How are you anyway?" Laura asked. I looked up from my wine.

"Well I guess I'm better than I was."

"That's a start."

"Yes."

I thought back to two days ago when I was standing in the kitchen trying to open a jar of olives. Without thinking I called out to Tom to come and help me. I caught myself just in time before the "m" squeezed out. I had stood still, the house was silent, a car drove up the street and it was at that instant I realised properly for the first time Tom was never coming home again. I held the jar trying to recall the last time Tom would have helped me to open something. Whenever it was, there was no way I would have had any inkling that time would be the last. I had foolishly gotten him to help me without even bothering to watch his left hand grip and tighten around the lid, his shoulder blade clench, his elbow rise.

"I get bogged down in minutiae," I said to Laura. "I try to remember every piece of Tom. Stupid things, you know. Like the bend in his elbow or the way he would pull a T-shirt over his head, which shoe he put on first. God sometimes I drive myself crazy with millions of tiny, pointless details." I could feel tears burning at the backs of my eyes. I took a long sip on my wine, holding the glass to my tongue and concentrating on the cold liquid clinging to my teeth and seeping its way down my throat. Don't cry. Come on Cate, you couldn't cry an hour ago, just keep it together, I silently told myself repeatedly.

"That's probably normal, whatever *normal* is in this situation," Laura said interrupting my silent chant.

"Probably, but the really shitty part is I can't see his face. No matter how hard I try to picture it, I just can't. I can remember all these things we used to do together and Tom being there. But I can't see his face."

"It will come back. Maybe it's your mind just trying to deal with things and being able to see his face might just be too much at this stage. The mind and body has some funny ways of helping us," Laura said gently.

"Yeah maybe you're right. Sometimes it would help to see him though you know? I want to be able to see him smiling at me, even if it's just in my mind. It might make me feel better. God anything to me make me feel better. I'm sorry Lau..."

"Hey don't be ridiculous, it's perfectly OK. I am hardly going to come around here and talk about the stimulating meeting I was in today am I? That's enough to send anyone over the edge. Besides you need to talk, it helps. So does throwing things around the room," Laura smiled and held my hand tightly.

"Do you remember his face?" I asked my friend. Laura's hand tightened around mine. Slowly she nodded her head.

"Yes I do sweetie and what a great face it was," she replied staring straight into my eyes.

"It was, wasn't it?" I smiled sadly, a bead of water running down my cheek. Laura was crying too.

"Sorry. I'm just so sad for you and probably for me too. I miss Tom too. God, dying really is a selfish thing to do isn't it? Leaves us mere mortals here on earth pining after them and crying on verandas for all the world to see. Not very productive is it?"

"Tom would probably love the fact two women were crying over him," I tried to laugh, but really I was looking down the far end of the veranda where he used to sit on the railing, drinking a beer to unwind after a long day at work. What I wouldn't give to see him there now as bold as life and laughing, always laughing.

For a long time Laura and I sat on the veranda loosely holding hands, watching people arriving home from work, going out again, heading to the beach for a swim before dinner. Normal everyday things people do when there is no enormous puffed up grey cloud of grief hanging over them. I watched them all, coming and going. Had anything like the death of the one person who they chose to love – really deeply love – out of everyone on the entire planet ever hit any of these people fair between the eyes and whacked the wind out of their stomachs. If it had, when was it that they were able to peel themselves up out of bed, shut the front door behind them, fix a smile on their face, and look to everyone else in the rest of the world – maybe even to themselves in that reflection staring back at them in the bathroom mirror every morning – that yes they were 'normal' again. When would that ever happen to me? What about all those people who that never happened to, still won't happen to. Those people who still double check the front door is locked with them safely inside in the silence, the deafening silence, where no one can see them and then take to their beds, pulling the crushed damp sheet over their heads and praying the world would stop or that they would never wake again.

My eyes shut. Completely silently I screamed 'Tom' inside my head, the sounds ricocheting around my empty body. My eyes opened slowly. Laura's fingers gripped tighter around my own.

We continued to pour the wine, sometimes exchanging a smile, mostly though we were silent, on the outside at least, on the inside I continued to scream my lover's name. Finally the inside wanted to get out. I started to cry uncontrollably and Laura hugged me so tightly I thought I would stop breathing. So the silence my body had temporarily allowed earlier this afternoon when I destroyed the living room was broken again.

After seeing me in such an uncontrollable state again, Laura had insisted on staying the night. Of course I had instantly resisted, but she eventually won. I watched now as she grabbed both corners of the pillowcase, shaking them violently, forcing the sack of feathers inside. It felt strange to have someone else in the house, of course Mum and Dad had stayed after the funeral, but that was different. The house had hung heavy with long silences, strained smiles and a carefulness we had never bothered with before. Tom's mother had been over a few times but her visits were awkward and too painful, neither of us wanting to upset the other one. Mainly I think she found our house as a way of still being close to Tom. While I made tea for us both she would disappear into another room and I would later find her stroking her son's coat hanging on the hook in the hallway or staring at a photo of him in the lounge room. Each time she would startle and apologise. Then the pain would become too great for us both and we would end up clinging to one another crying. Recently, though her visits had slowed, I think Tom's dad thought it wasn't good for either of us to be doing this to each other. Of course he was so upset that his son was gone he hardly spoke and launched himself straight back into work, all his talk of retirement no longer. He tried calling a few times, but his voice always stung with tears and creaks of pain at the end of the phone, neither of us had the heart to drag on another conversation when so much sadness hung all around us. "Maybe you could go and visit David, get away from things for a bit," I had suggested one evening during one of these painful exchanges with Tom's father. David was Tom's older brother who now lived in the UK. David had of course come home as soon as he had news that his baby brother had died, but had a job and a girlfriend he had to get back to across the other side of the world. I think seeing his parents hollowed of any life had been more than he could bear. He was grieving too and although David and I had only met a couple of times, once when Tom and I went on holiday in England and another when David came home for Christmas one year, we sought and clung to each other at the wake. Both of us had been drinking red wine for much of the afternoon, waving away plates of sandwiches and the shows of support and comfort constantly offered to us. It was their dad who came to our rescue and suggested we take a bottle and go and sit somewhere quiet so we could be left alone to talk. We both trod slowly, like an old frail couple, to the bottom of their parents' garden, dragging two garden chairs under a weeping willow – both of us half drunk and thinking it was very apt that we sit under this particular tree. David had been so kind and had even managed to make me laugh when he told me stories about them both as kids. Then as they got older, how they would go surfing together – just two brothers sitting on their boards, talking. David was so vivid in his descriptions, I felt like I was sitting on the end of Tom's board eavesdropping into teenagers' conversations. But the drunker we got the more David began to look like Tom and the more I wanted to caress his face until I became completely disoriented thinking I had dreamt Tom died which only sent me into a confused sobbing state. At first David had soothed me, trying to comfort me and make me smile, but when finally he couldn't hold it in any longer, David joined in my uncontrollable sobbing, his head in his hands and his shoulders shaking. The sound of a grown man crying like a child, to me, is one of the most upsetting sounds to ever hear. David only stayed for a few more days after that but we didn't see each other again. Without ever talking about it, both of us seemed to come to the conclusion it was better to let each other grieve silently.

Having Laura here now moving about the room, getting the bed ready for her to sleep in, reminded me of what it used to be like before anything had happened and it did make me think there might be some hope that one day I could feel like returning to some sort of life. "Hey you, come back," Laura said, watching me closely. "I'm here," I replied, folding the quilt back.

NICK

I had seen her from across the street. I could tell by the way she moved and held herself that something was not right. She had walked carefully down the front path. Even from where I was standing I could see her clutching desperately at her bag and biting her bottom lip. By the time I was in the car reversing down the driveway she was gone. I looked down the street but there was no one.

The next time I saw her, she was sitting on her front veranda with another woman. A wine bottle sat between them. As I shut the car door I noticed they were hugging. Although, she was more like clinging, her head buried deep into the other woman's chest.

I recognised the gesture instantly – grief. I rolled the car keys in my hand and walked inside, the image of those two women pressing into my mind.

ISOBEL

I knew Tom long before I knew Cate. Tom and I went to high school together. I'd had what I guess you would call a schoolgirl crush on him since about grade eight. Once we hit our senior school years, my silent perseverance finally paid off when Tom and I officially became an "item". I was head over heels, pathetically besotted. My mum worried about the gusto at which I obsessed over Tom. There was no doubt about it, I was in love – sneaking out of the house, tip-toeing down the street to meet him under the street light, under a milky moon and right under the noses of my sleeping parents. I had no idea what I was doing and neither did he, but we both knew it felt good. The kind of reckless good you can only feel as a teenager. Mum was petrified I would wind up pregnant and "crippled by my own stupidity" was the way she described it. My dad told her she was being melodramatic. But I knew she knew me too well. She had every reason to be alarmed.

We managed to finish school without a pregnancy, that had come later.

It was no coincidence Tom and I ended up studying at the same university. I had pretty much manipulated the outcome. My parents believed my interest in getting a degree had actually nothing to do with wanting to further my study and pursue a career. Although I would never admit it, in fact at the time I staunchly denied it and did a really spectacular job ducking and weaving my way around the topic like a pro footballer. I knew they were right.

"You're throwing your life away for a boy Isobel." My mother was slicing tomato and throwing red slivers into a salad bowl.

"I know that's what you think."

"No, that's what I know." She rested the knife on the chopping board to peel a boiled egg.

I could feel ripples of heat rolling in my head. I shifted on the kitchen stool and concentrated on a mosquito bite on my thigh. It was mid January, the cicadas had started their evening song and the smell of steak Dad was barbequing floated in through the kitchen window. I stared at the bite on my thigh and swallowed the argument I was about to spew out for the seventh time that summer. Four weeks later I would be arguing with Mum over the tins of tomato and tuna and the rolls of cling wrap she insisted I take with me to university three hours drive up the highway.

The day I told Tom I was pregnant it was cold and misty. I was gazing out the window of my university campus bedroom, watching my breath form a foggy patch on the glass. An essay I was proof reading sat on my lap. I had read the first paragraph at least five times because my mind kept wandering to what the look on Tom's face would be, to the "thing" growing inside my belly.

"Babe, are you in?" I bit my bottom lip at the sound of Tom's voice through the door. I held my breath before replying very weakly, "Yep." Suddenly Tom was in the room, his hands on my shoulders, leaning down and bruising kisses on my ear and neck. I could smell his breath was sour with beer.

"What's going on in here?" Tom said picking up my assignment and tossing it on the bed. He was straddling me now, the chair starting to over-balance. "Jesus Tom, what are you doing?"

"What does it look like baby?"

"Don't!"

'Why?"

"Because I don't feel like it, OK?"

"Come on baby, you've been cooped up in here all afternoon…"

"Yeah and you've been at the pub by the smell of things."

"Jesus, what's wrong with you?"

"Nothing," I screeched the word as though I was in pain. We both stared at each other and Tom stood up. I felt stupid, cursing myself for starting what I knew would turn into yet another one of our arguments. This was certainly no way to tell Tom what I had to tell him. I watched him open my bar fridge and pull out a beer. His eyes were on me the whole time.

"What the fuck is your problem Isobel?"

"You, you arsehole." I muttered.

"What?"

"Nothing."

"Bull shit, there's always something wrong. I've always done something wrong. It's like we've been married for fifty fucking years, not frigging uni students. You're so uptight it drives me crazy…so I've been at the pub, big bloody deal."

Tom was shouting now and I knew that if we continued in this way we would end up in a spiral of words ignited with such venom that he would storm out and I wouldn't hear from him for a few days – his way of telling me that I didn't own him. Meanwhile I would sweat and wonder if it was too soon to call, but this time was different – I knew I wouldn't be able to hang onto this secret for another day, let alone the time it took for Tom to decide he might talk to me again.

"It's not that," I said very quietly, watching Tom closely.

"Yeah right," he said taking another swig of beer.

"Please…"

"Please…please bloody what Isobel?"

"God you really aren't going to make this easy for me, are you?"

"What easy? What you want to break up with me…is it your turn this time?" Tom spat the words at me.

'Please Tom, I am not trying to break up with you OK?"

"Really?"

"Yes, really…"

My eyes were straining with tears. "Don't start crying now Isobel for God's sake. Don't try that on, it really isn't going to get you anywhere."

"Fuck you."

"That's it, I've had enough of this shit." Tom said opening the door to my room, the beer still in his hand.

"Yeah that's it, go on go. Should I just call you in nine months when it's time for you to be the proud, smiling dad?"

Tom stopped dead. "What did you just say?" he whispered, his back still turned to me.

"I'm pregnant."

"Is it mine?"

"I hate you," I breathed the words so quietly, even I wasn't sure they had come from me.

CATE

I leant my head against the window. It was still raining, it had been raining for four days straight now. The water running down the glass gave me a sense of comfort probably because it matched my mood. My finger traced a drop trickling down to the ledge, following it melting and disappearing into other drops until it become nothing individually beautiful anymore – just some water.

I tucked my knees up and stroked the cotton of Tom's T-shirt that I was wearing again for the fourth day running. I must have been wearing it since the rain had started. The days were still continuing to be a blur and I couldn't really remember anything significant I had done in what seemed like months. Maybe all I had been doing was drifting around the empty house with memories and snippets of snatched conversations – ones Tom and I had shared long ago – rattling around inside my head. The depression was still hanging around me like the last four long damp days which tapped relentlessly at the windows and brought my mood down to even further sinking depths, if that was possible. For a second or two I allowed my mind to wander into a tiny corner of normality, wondering if my depression was being made worse by my self-imposed exile from the rest of the living. Maybe wandering around this tomb was prolonging the agony and misery. Of course I knew it was, but admitting anything of the kind out loud felt like I was betraying Tom because my life would have to carry on without him. 'Without him', the two words stung, making me flinch. I leant my head down towards his T-shirt hanging in limp folds off my shoulders. His smell no longer lingered in the fabric. I twisted my hair around a finger, my hair had grown. Would Tom have ever seen it this long before, even when we first met I don't think it would have been quite this long. A fresh scene of two strangers on a bus looped in my mind. I allowed myself one slow sad smile. My head dropped, when would this end?

The sound of the postman dropping the lid of the letter-box startled me. I went to stand up but was quickly sitting back down on the chair, my foot was crippled with pins and needles. Wincing I tried massaging the blood back into the limp limb, just like Tom would have done for me, until finally my foot started to have some movement and felt like it belonged to my body again. Giving it a final shake, I stood slowly and balanced my weight on my other foot to make extra sure the pain had subsided.

I opened the front door to the rain coming down in sheets. For an instant I hesitated, but with shoulders hunched and eyes squinting against the water, I made it to the letterbox and bolted back to the safety of the veranda to open the mail. There were a couple of square envelopes with our address handwritten on the front. Turning one over in my hand, I knew both would be more sympathy cards. The news of Tom was still slowly meandering its way to people in all different pockets of the world. Some of the people I had received cards from I didn't even know, they had been friends Tom had collected like a magpie when he went backpacking around Europe after he had finished university. Some of these people had obviously felt very awkward about writing to me – from a few words on a sympathy card I could tell the words were chosen carefully but had still somehow managed to appear strained across the cardboard. Some had spelt my name with a 'K' which made me shudder. Sliding my finger under the glue of the first envelope revealed the sender to be a second, or maybe third, cousin I hadn't seen since I was a teenager so the words were quite neutral and thankfully didn't stir too much emotion in me. I picked up the second card. The handwriting looked familiar but many of the letters on our address had been blotted by the rain, making the ink run in long streaks to the edge of the paper. I turned the envelope over to see the sender's address, but it was blank. Once again I slid my finger under the flap to release the glue, but this time I snagged my finger on the paper and got a neat paper cut in the crease of my knuckle. Wincing, I sucked on my finger, tasting the warm salty blood seep into my tongue. Finally I got the card free of the envelope and opened it. There was no 'Dear Cate', 'To Cate', or even my name on it for that matter. The card simply read, 'I am so, so, sorry about your loss and pain. All my love, Isobel'. I read the words over and over, until the letters started to change shape. I looked out at the rain falling on the lavender in the garden. Isobel. It must be Isobel, 'my' Isobel. I am sure I don't know any other Isobel. Maybe it was a relative I had forgotten about. No. It had to be Issy. I frowned and sucked my breath in. The card didn't make any sense to me. Isobel had barely been in touch since the funeral. I knew she found it hard, of course she did, we all did. I do. A card was obviously an easier way to communicate and show she cares. I couldn't really blame her, but it didn't take away the pain of feeling Isobel was somehow making Tom's death her personal tragedy. I looked down at the card. Reading the words again was now starting to make me feel angry and bitter. I snapped the card shut and went back into the house. My finger was still bleeding.

BEEP, BEEP, BEEP, BEEP
   "Oh God, what is that?"
BEEP, BEEP, BEEP, BEEP
   "Oh Christ."

It was 7.21am. Tom had always set the alarm at odd numbers in a strange attempt to fool himself into thinking he was getting extra sleep. It was a habit I too have adopted, just so I can hang onto the little tiny pieces that made somebody be my someone – Tom.

With my eyes shut, I turned on the shower taps, jumping when the cold water spurted out. Slowly the warm water started to fall, warming the goose bumps on my skin.

It was my first day back at work and waking up to an alarm clock instead of tears was an unfamiliar feeling. I had already made yet another pact with myself before I drifted off to sleep the night before, that I would be as strong as I possibly could. Laura had arranged to meet me for lunch and she promised to write me a note if I couldn't face work in the afternoon. The seriousness in Laura's voice when she promised the note made me smile as I dried my body and searched for moisturiser. I reached right over a can of Tom's shaving cream, staring at it momentarily feeling my breath shorten. Come on Cate, get it together, the familiar chant clicking through my head.

As I zipped up a pinstripe skirt, I felt the fabric fall loosely on my waist and start to slip towards my hips. I looked in the mirror to see the skirt gaping where it should have been a firm fit. Slowly I looked up and noticed my once tailored skirt now hung and sagged. My "sorrow diet" as Laura called it – red wine, tea and a few slivers of cheese and crackers – had left my body hollow and hungry. The image staring back at me was not unlike a bag lady who had hit the jackpot in a clothing bin at the back of a swanky department store or a child clomping around the house, dressed in their mother's clothes.

Frowning I opened the cupboard to look for something that might fit a little better. Then suddenly I remembered that for the first time in months I was working to a timeframe. The clock beside the bed blinked 8.03. Quickly I found a belt and threaded it to the last hole, grabbed my handbag and ran out the door.

Just as I was shutting the gate, a man across the road was getting into a car. He looked up and smiled at me. I smiled back to see him raise his hand in a wave as he awkwardly sung out, "Have a good day." I smiled again, "God I hope so," I thought to myself.

LAURA

Isaw Cate walking across the park, her tailored shirt and skirt billowing in the wind. She was clutching her handbag, her elbow pressed firmly into the leather, her hand wrapped tightly around the shoulder strap. She looked thin and pale. Her dark hair was swept back in a ponytail, which swung from side to side and only accentuated her now hollow face. Even if Cate were a stranger, it would be plain to see she was unhappy.

"Hey you."

"Hey yourself," Cate said settling herself on the grass. We both leaned forward to kiss one another on the cheek.

"First, I'll give you Pitt Stop's famous number three sandwich and then you can tell me how your morning's been," I said, knowing I was sounding like a presenter on a children's TV program.

"Well," Cate started through a mouthful. "People are very, very, very sorry. In fact they're so sorry for something they didn't do that by 10am, even I was embarrassed for them and spent the rest of the morning trying to avoid anywhere that I might have to talk. So I was busting to go to the loo for most of the morning, sat at my desk with my legs crossed and picked up the phone, pretending to be deep in conversation, each time I caught sight of someone approaching. I can't tell you how happy I was to get out of there. I reckon if I don't go back, they'll all be relieved, me included."

Both of us smiled and bit into our sandwiches and then there was silence. "I'm sorry Lau. Let's talk about something else."

"Don't be silly, at least you can see the funny side of it. Have you heard from Issy today?"

"No."

Cate's reply was clipped and I knew I had chosen the wrong the question. How could I be so stupid, Isobel had been acting so strangely, barely calling Cate. If I mentioned anything to Isobel about Cate, she went quiet and did that twisted lip thing she does, making it very obvious she wants to change the topic.

"Sorry…"

"Don't be. For God's sake, of course we knew her and Tom had something going on before we even met either of them, but it was bloody ages ago and it's not like it was serious. It was a fling. Tom barely talked about it. It really pisses me off Isobel is acting like she's lost the love of her life… because he was the love of mine," Cate whispered.

At my desk that afternoon I dialled Isobel's work number. It rang out until a generic voicemail clicked in. I hung up without leaving a message. I flicked through my mobile phone until I found the name I was looking for and dialled the number on my landline.

"Hey it's Laura."

"Hey, good to hear from you, how are you?"

"Good. Listen I'm really sorry but I'm not going to be able to make dinner tonight."

"Oh really, why?"

"I kind of promised Cate I would see a movie with her."

"Oh. What does "kind of promised" mean?"

"Well OK promised. I saw her for lunch and it was her first day back at work and she was feeling really down, so I kind of suggested her and I see a movie together tonight."

"What about our plans?"

"I know, I'm sorry, I really am, but she's not doing so great."

"Does she know about us?"

"No I haven't told her yet."

"Well will I see you this week?"

"Yes of course, how's Thursday?"

"Good."

"OK how about I call you later and we'll decide what we're going to do?"

"Sounds good."

"OK well I have to go into a meeting, so I am going to have to go. I am sorry about tonight," I said, collecting my meeting file from the tray on my desk.

Sitting in the boardroom, with the blinds pulled down, a powerpoint presentation projecting onto the only blank wall and people around me arguing about market research results, I cursed myself. It was ridiculous that I had changed my plans to go to the movies with Cate. It's not like dates are hanging like apples from trees waiting for me to just pluck them off whenever I feel like it. Here was a guy I really liked and while it was certainly early days, I was pretty sure he liked me too. But instead here I am letting him hang ripe and blooming on the tree and if I kept postponing he would soon rot. I sighed out loud, my breath pushing my fringe upwards.

"So I see you disagree as well Laura," the client was looking at me across the table.

"Mmm, it appears I do," I replied, pretending to look for a pen in my compendium.

It was four Tuesdays after Cate had finally let me into her house. I had decided to drop into see her on my way home from work. When I pulled up out the front, I could already tell she wasn't home, but true to my newfound sense of duty I found myself walking purposefully up the front path. The smell of the lavender bushes Cate and Tom had planted along the line of the path percolated in the air. As I left the house, I plucked off a lavender head and rolled it tightly between my fingers, bringing my fingers up to my nose to draw in the smell.

"Hey."

I looked up startled to see a figure dressed in a business suit, with a very bright, almost garish coloured tie hanging loosely around his collar, sitting in the gutter across the street, an empty chip packet was trapped under his one highly-buffed shoe.

"Hello," I replied, recognising the figure to be the same man I had seen several weeks earlier carrying a box from his car into the block of flats.

"I've locked myself out," he said, smiling.

"Oh really, what a bummer," I said. 'Bummer'. I never use that word, why was I using it now with a total stranger and a good looking stranger at that. I looked at him more closely, his face was tanned, black hair hung slightly in his eyes and laughter lines formed around the corners of his mouth when he smiled.

"Can you call someone?" I said opening the car door.
"I was actually waiting for my flatmate to get home."
"Will he be long?" I asked.
"She could be all night, I think she was going out."
"Oh I see." He was standing now and brushing the seat of his suit trousers. "I'm Nick," he was saying, stretching his hand forward to shake mine. I swivelled between the body of the car and the open door, dropping the lavender heads onto the seat and wiping my palm over the fabric of my skirt to out-stretch my hand. "Laura". I said.
"Good to meet you Laura."
"And you."
"Is that your friend who lives there?" Nick said nodding his head towards Cate's house.
"Yes it is, but she's not home, or if she is, she might just be choosing not to answer the door. She's pulled that trick on me before today." My voice trailed off.
"Oh." There was silence.
"Can I ask you something that's probably going to sound a bit presumptuous?" Nick asked, shifting his weight from one foot to the other.
I felt my eyebrows shoot up and I consciously tried to pull them back down towards my eyes. "I'm not sure I like where this is going, but something tells me I should throw caution to the wind, so shoot," I replied.
"Shoot?" Nick repeated looking startled. "What, are you American or something?" Oh Christ, I thought, there I go again, another foreign word to my vocabulary, which I just

dropped into a conversation like it was as natural as getting out of the bed.

"No, I'm Australian, just like you, but I can see why you think I might not be after that comment, so perhaps just put me out of my misery and ask me what you were going to ask me, so it can be your turn to look like a dickhead."

Nick smiled, the lines around his mouth forming double curves.

"Well…since I am locked out and your friend is obviously not home, both our plans are basically wrecked for the evening, right?"

"Right," I said, unconvincingly.

"So, would you like to maybe go out for a drink…you know to take advantage of the situation we've both now found ourselves in…I mean…" I raised my eyebrows again. "Nick, thank you for saying that because I reckon you've successfully taken the spotlight off 'shoot'." I had to laugh as I watched Nick quicken his weight shifting from foot to foot, the chip packet now blowing down the street, and bite his lip.

"Touché," he laughed.

The sun dipped below the blocks of flats lined in neat rows along the headland at the north end of Bondi Beach as Nick and I clinked our beers together, initiating our second round of drinks. We'd managed to squeeze onto the end of a table, stained with sticky rings of beer, out on the balcony. The heat of the day still hung heavy in the air, smearing the horizon into the sea line. Nick's tie was completely removed now, shoved in his briefcase which was sitting in the boot of my car. Beads of sweat collected on the top of his lip that he wiped away with the back of his hand. I found myself unashamedly flirting with him. Looking up through my fringe, laughing like a wounded hyena at little things he said, which to a sane person might have constituted a broad smile, maybe even a light giggle – at a push. As for my conversation, it had gone to pot after two sips of my first beer. I continued to use words and phrases I didn't even know I knew, making me wince each time another foreign word spat out and sat like a sour piece of lemon in front of me on the table. Nick continued to smile and pick up on my choice of words, lightly teasing me and if I didn't know any better, he was flirting with me too, or maybe that was the beer.

"I see you're fairly persistent with your friend across the road from me, she's going through some big stuff huh?" Nick asked over the din of the pub.

I thought then to Cate and Tom. To a weekend a group of us had gone camping. Tom had put everyone's tents up and lit the campfire within the first hour of arriving. We had all laughed about him being a secret lumberjack and someone who didn't belong in his big city banking job. Taking a long sip of his beer, Tom had laughed, pulling Cate closer to him and whispered something in her hair. I remember this scene so vividly, like an old film playing in my head, because I had stared at the two of them and knew I had seen something very beautiful, but so simple.

"Yes she is, a completely rotten time actually. She is too young to have to go through all this and well...Tom...he was too young for this to happen to him. It's so bloody unfair for both of them," I let the sentence trail off, feeling water lightly trapping along the length of both eyes.

Nick took a sip of his beer and nodded slowly. "Yeah I know. I knew Tom, he was a nice guy, everyone liked him. I worked with him, he was really good at his job, was really going places."

My gaze fell to Nick's eyes, "You worked with Tom?"

"Yeah, only for a bit though, just before – well just before it happened. He told me about the place being up for rent that I just moved into. I was looking for somewhere near the beach so I could go surfing, and it's a great place, I love it. It's just weird to be living in Tom's street and now he isn't. God, you just never think something like that is going to happen to anyone you know. Not when you're our age, anyway," Nick swallowed hard and stared at the table at a spot between our drinks.

"I know," I nodded slowly.

"Yeah, we were just starting to be mates, a shared love of a coffee on the way to the office from the same place and surfing, of course. He was a cool guy, but going through a pretty rough time by the sound of it, so it's such a shame he didn't get that resolved before…" Nick cut himself short, he must have sensed me glaring at him.

"What do you mean?" I asked, still glaring at him, "What are you talking about, what rough stuff? He was about to get married and he looked pretty happy to me. I knew him really well you know?" I could feel my voice rising in defence of my friend. Who was this guy sitting across from me?

"Sorry, sorry Laura I didn't mean anything – as I said I didn't really know him that well, so I must have got my wires crossed about a conversation we had once."

"What did he tell you?"

"Nothing Laura, seriously I think I must have got my wires crossed as I said. Anyway, you seem like a great friend to his…"

"Fiancé," I cut in, sounding defensive for the second time.

"Her name's Isobel, isn't it?" Nick asked.

"Isobel?" I repeated slowly.

"Yeah, Tom's fiancé, the girl who lives across the road from me."

"No her name is Cate, why did you think her name was Isobel?" My skin was turning cold. Nick looked even more alarmed, turning a coaster over and over in his hand, I watched his Adam's apple rise and fall. He shifted in his seat and swallowed. I stared at him, suddenly feeling sick in my stomach. "Nick." I said urgently. He concentrated on his beer.

"Nick?"

"Yes?" he finally mumbled quietly.

"Why did you think Cate was Isobel, and why did you think Tom was having a rough time before he died?"

"Because…"

My heart was pounding now and my tongue had given over to that 'fat' feeling before vomiting.

"Because why?" I asked not even recognising my own voice and not caring if I no longer resembled the cool calm girl I was attempting to be earlier.

"Because. Oh God, I am really sorry, I shouldn't have said anything and now I am probably just making a mountain out of a molehill. Forget I said anything."

I gripped the glass, "I can't forget it. Please tell me what's going on. Cate is in bits and I don't know how to help her, so if you know something, anything, please tell me. Please." I didn't care that the trapped water was now escaping down my cheeks. My mind was completely preoccupied with whatever knowledge it was that this relative stranger was holding from me about my friend and my friend's lover. I was determined to get him to tell me what he knew.

Slowly I tucked my hair behind my ear before trying again, "Nick, please I am not going to say anything to anyone, I just have to know for me, for no other reason and no other person. OK?" I crossed my legs, knowing that my skirt was riding up on my thigh. Nick's eye line twitched to the bare skin before quickly fixing his eyes back on my face.

Nick sighed before starting to speak, "God Laura, I'm sorry. Look, I don't think I really know what I am talking about. Tom told me some pretty heavy stuff right before he, ah died, and well it's kind of been with me ever since because I don't think he would have been able to work it out in time. Shit, I really shouldn't be telling you any of this…"

And so, when this relative stranger finished repeating a conversation he'd had with my best friend's lover the day before he died, he looked up through his hair to a point somewhere above my head, unable to meet my gaze. I dropped my head into my hands, rubbing at my face, while the truth sunk like a stone to the pit of my belly and lay there cold and hard.

CATE

It was a late Saturday afternoon, maybe two or three months after Tom never came home to me when I finally built the courage to scrap open the door of Tom's cupboard. I just stood there, staring in at his jeans, his T-shirts, his jackets, his suits, his jumpers – just his. Ever so slowly I reached out my hand, stroking my fingers over the sleeve of a navy blue suit – he always looked so smart in this one. I had thought of burying him in this suit, I had even taken it from the cupboard the morning before the day of the funeral, but the faint smell of Tom's aftershave had fluttered around the room, making me hurriedly clip the hanger back over the rail to retrieve a different, less familiar suit, the grey one he had only worn once to his cousin's wedding. Now, I bent down and gingerly picked up one of Tom's heavily polished shoes, the left lace was still tied. I imagined his fingers twisting the loop and pulling the lace tight. "Oh Christ, I really can't do this," I muttered into the back of the cupboard, dragging the door jaggedly along its runners, making the timber jump to suspend awkwardly from the runner along the top of the cupboard door. Muttering again, this time with a "bugger", I fell against the half open door, breathing heavily and knowing water was travelling towards the backs of my eyes.

One of Tom's T-shirts lay crumpled on my side of the bed. I would sleep in it again tonight, just like last night, sobbing with the fabric knotted beneath my rib cage. I woke during the night, the alarm clock blinked at 1.54am. I lay there in the darkness, one half of the bed a deep, barren black. I rolled onto my side. Another strip of deep black hung like an entrance to a cave from the half closed cupboard door. I took the hem of the T-shirt and started to twist it between my fingers, the room started to swell with Tom's scent. I breathed in as far as I could, my chest rising, too scared to breath out in case the scent escaped me, leaving me all alone in the black.

For another twenty minutes or so I lay there blinking in the dark. Sometime around 2.30am I looked at the cupboard door, ajar. Turning on the bedside lamp, I slipped out of bed and heaved the wood across to reveal what I was too petrified to explore hours earlier. Tom's shoe with the lace still tied lay on its side, my hand rested on it while I looked into the blackness of the cupboard, my eyes blinking to adjust to the light. Finally I moved the shoe aside and reached for the shoe box right at the back of the cupboard.

ISOBEL

The waitress put my coffee down on the table in front of me. "Thanks," I muttered, but she was already clearing away two glasses from the table next to me.

The café was right in the middle of Sydney's Oxford Street, the part that still clung to the bright young things who hadn't migrated up the road to the huge shopping mall which had sucked the life out of this once vibrant shopping strip. The cafe and this part of Paddington was still a favourite for Laura, Cate and me. Regardless of what shopping mecca might have been drawing the crowds further up the city, we had chosen to cling to habit, still stopping here for a mid-shop break. Our order always the same – a skinny cappuccino for Cate, a latte for Laura and a double espresso for me. Sometimes we'd split a slice of blueberry cheesecake. I sighed now as I looked at the empty chairs around me and bit my lip.

Hesitantly, I gazed out the window onto the street, willing time to stand still. The city heat was blistering and bubbling the tar on the road. I watched as a mother with shopping bags straining from one elbow and a screaming toddler nestled in the crook of her other elbow battled through the sweaty Saturday morning shoppers. That's when I saw her.

She was standing across the other side of the street, waiting for the lights to change.

My neck and earlobes started to tingle. The nervous child in me reached for a clump of hair and started twirling it around and around my finger. The lights changed to green and I watched her step down off the footpath and start walking directly towards the café. Each step was careful and strained, like she was wading through a river. Her hair fell around her face and swayed in time to the wade of her steps, her tanned athletic legs cutting strong shapes from the bottom of faded cut-off jeans. I noticed my own hair then, wrapped blonde and tight around my finger. I could feel the blood pulsing through my veins while I sat there, frozen to the chair, each step bringing her closer to me.

Laura had been calling me a couple of times a day for the best part of a week, in total she had left seven messages, each one more urgent than the next. At first, I thought it was about Cate, so I hadn't bothered to call back. Then Laura's seventh and last message had spun the axis of my world into full speed.

"Isobel, hi it's me, Laura. Again. I know you're screening me and I don't want to do this over the phone, but since your not answering any of my calls, I am going to have to leave this message. I know Nick Bowmen, he used to work with Tom, and he seems to know you very well…" I didn't listen to the rest of the message, I had dropped my mobile and was dry-retching into the kitchen sink.

Laura and I clamped eyes through the glass of the café window. She stood still, clasping a vintage brown leather satchel to her shoulder with her face shaded red from the heat, looking in at me. Shoppers rushed past her, a teenager talking on a mobile phone jolted into her and kept going without even looking up. I watched as she turned and moved against the crowd. I heard the bell on the coffee shop door ring and watched silently as Laura pulled the empty chair out next to me. Her handbag now slouched across the back of her chair. Then finally I felt Laura take my hand and press it into her own.

"Do you want to tell me what's going on Iss?" she asked gently, pushing sweaty strands of blonde hair from her face.

LAURA

Despite the air conditioner whirring, it wasn't doing much to cool down the café, my hand was sweating as it clutched Isobel's, but hers seemed to be cold and lay like a limp fish in my palm. I searched her face waiting for an answer to my question. My friend looked pretty awful, like she hadn't slept for weeks. Her hair hung in yellow strings. Her big full lips, normally stained red, were all dry and cracked. A grey V-neck T-shirt gaped from her chest, revealing glimpses of a red bra, the lace lying limply at her breast. She was such a strikingly beautiful girl, but today she just looked damn awful.

"Iss…"

Isobel snatched her hand away from mine and shoved it under her thigh.

"What am I supposed to tell you Laura. It sounds to me like you already know everything."

"No. I don't. I want to hear it from you…"

"Don't you believe your boyfriend?" Isobel snapped.

"Jesus. You are impossible sometimes. I want to try and help you and you're treating me like I'm your enemy. Why? I don't get it."

"Because Laura I don't think it's going to make any difference what I say to you. God only knows what you've already told Cate."

"Nothing. I haven't told Cate anything."

"Why?"

"Because I don't know what the hell is going on. I have pieces of the puzzle but I have no idea how they fit together. More importantly, you're my friend and I want to try and help you."

"There's nothing to help."

"Really." I spat the word out of my mouth, knowing getting frustrated with Isobel was not going to get me anywhere. She would soon clam up, probably storm out of the café and that would be the end of that. I took a deep breath and tried a different tact.

"I'm sorry Iss. Try looking at things from my perspective. I start dating a guy who strangely happens to know not just Tom, but also you, and very weirdly doesn't know Cate – the person Tom loved and the person he lived with…"

"I know who Cate fucking is." Isobel hissed.

"Sorry. Of course you know who Cate is, but do you know how weird this all seems? It's like you have this whole other life…a double life almost…"

"Congratulations. You've worked it out. I think that's enough for today." Isobel said, gathering up her handbag. I grabbed her arm.

"Iss come on please. This is ridiculous. Don't go."

"I know you want to try and help me because you're my friend," Isobel said mimicking my voice and sounding like a whining child. "And let go of me." The man at the table next to us looked up from his newspaper, meeting my eyes, he quickly looked down and started to stir his coffee urgently.

"Iss. Please sit down." I pleaded in a whisper.

"What am I making a scene am I?"

The man with the newspaper turned the page and shifted in his chair.

"Let's go somewhere else. We can go back to mine where we can talk properly."

Isobel rolled her eyes. But that wasn't a 'no' so I sat waiting for her to respond.

PART TWO
Before

TOM

The beer was ice-cold and worked quickly to numb first my throat and then my chest as it made its way to my stomach. I took another swig, this time much bigger than the first which instantly sent fizzing liquid up into my nose and the back of my throat. Coughing, I set the beer on the bar and slapped my chest.

"You alright mate?"

"Yeah, yeah, I'm fine. Just went down the wrong way," I croaked to the bartender who was drying glasses at the other end of the bar. That was an outright lie, I was far from alright. My girlfriend appears to be a lunatic. Actually make that a pregnant lunatic. Christ, a baby. "Fuck, fuck, fuck," I muttered into the glass. There was definitely a time when I knew I had loved Isobel, she wasn't so mad, so crazy, so messed up then. But when was that?

Isobel was gorgeous, there was no questioning that. She was my 'type' of girl or so I thought. Her long dark blonde hair which swung lightly across her breasts when we had sex. Those feline eyes lightly closing and clenching as she got more and more excited. The way her body would arch under my own sweaty mass while her nipples tightened and strained. Her breath fluttering against the nape of my neck.

That girl could and would easily make me beg for more of her. There was a time, I could almost drink the way she smelt. She always smelt the same, some type of bitter orange oil that I could never remember the name of that she dabbed on her wrists, behind her ears and between her breasts. The smell growing stronger as it mixed with the faint odour of sweat and drove me wild. Isobel used to laugh easily then, throwing her head back, eyes shining. Her two front teeth were gapped slightly apart, about enough to roll a five cent coin between. The gap only contributed to Isobel's offbeat beauty and sense of fun and I found the whole package drop dead sexy. These days 'more' is most certainly what I have ended up with. More of Isobel's unprovoked outbursts, her rising insecurities and jealousy over everybody – my mates, random girls in the pub, in lectures, at parties, at the rowing club. Phrases like: "You're an arsehole Tom", "I know you don't love me" and "I saw you looking at her" are some of her select favourites.

That kind of girly shit I can handle, but it's all the other stuff she has started to wheel out that's gotten me worried. Even Christian and Sam, my two best mates at university since I landed on campus two years ago, have taken me aside (on separate occasions I might add) to have a word.

"Dude, I don't know how to say this, and you can tell me to bugger off, but what's going on with Isobel?" It was Tuesday night which meant Christian and I could only be found at one place – our college's poker night held in the campus kitchen. I had already lost seventy dollars, drunk five Carlton Draughts and was thinking about heading to the pub to blow some more of the one hundred and fifty dollars

I had borrowed from Isobel a few days earlier. I looked at Christian.

"Sorry mate you can tell me to piss off…" he offered cautiously, suddenly realising his comment may have come across the wrong way.

"No that's cool. Christ man, I don't know. I know Isobel's under a lot of pressure with her course and stuff…you know. Heaps of assignments due and shit, but she's starting to do my nut in." Christian raised his eyebrows at my response. I scratched the label on my beer and stared at my feet.

"Do you want to go to the pub?"
"Sure," I replied.

When we got to the pub I ordered two bourbons, we may as well ramp things up a bit. I had already decided on the short walk to the pub I wasn't going to my eight o'clock psychology tutorial in the morning. I think I'd only managed to make four of those tutorials this semester. With three weeks to go, I was within a beer's reach of failing the course completely.

Psychology was my 'wild card' elective to provide what I thought would be some easy relief from my economics subjects. I was poorly mistaken. Turns out, I don't have a head for psychology, understanding people is my weak point. Isobel was my living and breathing case in point.

"Cheers," Christian and I said, slamming our glasses together. The first gulp was sweet and kind of disgusting after all the beer. "Mate, I was trying to say earlier…about Isobel…" Christian was trying to attempt the earlier conversation again, this time choosing his words carefully, "don't get me wrong she's a great girl and all, I really like her and she's ah...hot you lucky bastard. But the other night, man…" I flinched. I wasn't sure how much Christian had actually witnessed of the 'other night'. Isobel had ramped her usual unreasonable behaviour up a few notches and she didn't fail to impress. She had clawed so aggressively and desperately at my T-shirt, the fabric was ripped by what could only be described as claw marks. Then punctuated the scene by calling me an arsehole before turning on her heel and fleeing towards the pub door, knocking shoulders with Christian on the way and sending his drink straight down the front of his T-shirt. Clearly startled, Christian had searched me out through the crowd, spotted the clawed fabric of my own T-shirt and tried to make light of the situation.

"Not sure who's worse mate," Christian yelled over the din of students warming up for a big night out on an early Saturday evening.

"At least she didn't draw blood with you," I said laughing uneasily. Inside I was freaking out. That was fairly mild for Isobel lately.

"Want another?" the bartender had finished drying schooner glasses and the tea towel was now slung across his shoulder. "Why not." I replied, draining the last of the flat beer from my glass. I watched as the bartender picked up a fresh glass and held it at an angle under the tap. Something cracked across my back. The barman dropped the glass, the sound of smashing filled my ears, blurring the scene for a moment, before the realisation that something had just struck my back – on purpose. "What the fuck…" I swung around on the barstool, my back already giving way to a low throbbing ache. There stood Isobel, clutching her hand with tears streaming down her face.

"It's been six freaking days you bastard. Six bloody days you haven't bothered to call me," Isobel was shouting in my face and grabbing her hand more tightly so I could see the veins in her fingers swelling a bruised light purple. The barman muttered "Jesus" as I heard him move to the other end of the bar to retrieve a dustpan and brush. I just sat there, staring at this woman in front of me. I had no idea what to say to her, she was right I hadn't called her, I didn't know if it had been six days, but knew Isobel would be right. That was six days of me not sleeping properly and recruiting anyone I could find to drink bourbon and smoke pot. There were so many things I wanted to say to her and feelings of strange sentimentality swallowing me whole. How could I ever phrase all of this into something succinct and heartfelt that she would actually believe and not throw straight back in my face as a lie? I also knew the longer I left calling Isobel the harder it would be to rise up and swim above my cowardice, so I stated the bloody obvious and said what I was feeling, literally.

"Did you just hit me?"

Isobel stared back at me, her eyes glistened with tears. She was shaking. The barman returned with the dustpan and brush, giving us both a look before he crouched down to sweep up the broken glass. Isobel didn't flinch, she just continued to stare at me with eyes drilling into my own.

"I'm sorry," I whispered. "Really. I really am. I have no idea of how to deal with this and here is not the place to do it. Come on." I said, taking Isobel's arm in an act of momentary madness, she was never going to come anywhere with me. And I was right. My touch was met with Isobel's stiffening body. "Please Iss…" Still she stood there, further stiffening her arm linked in mine and refusing to unclasp her

hand from the other which, minutes before had landed with
more force than I gave her credit for. Then without warning, Isobel slumped in a heap on the floor. Her blonde hair
splayed across her shoulders. Looking at her like this, I felt
pangs of regret stab me. 'I am an arsehole', I thought, 'she's
been right all along, who behaves like this? Why the hell
would she come anywhere with me?'

But she did.

Back in my room, I threw the pile of washing sprayed across
my bed onto the floor and gestured to Isobel, who was
standing at the door, to sit down. Gingerly she walked over
and sat right on the edge of the mattress. "Do you want a
beer?" I asked reaching for the fridge handle. "Do you think
it's a good idea to offer a pregnant woman a beer Tom?"
Isobel asked matter-of-factly. She was staring at the floor.
Immediately I cringed and snatched my hand away from the
handle. "Sorry." I whispered.

"Seems to be a lot of 'sorry' going on with you Tom, do you
even know what you're sorry for? Is it for getting me pregnant, is it for ignoring me for days or is it because you just
offered your pregnant girlfriend a beer?" I was silent.
　"Do we even love each other?" Immediately Isobel's
eyes snapped from the floor straight into my own. Still I was
silent. She started to twist her bottom lip, never leaving my
gaze.
　"Yeah…" I finally breathed.
　"Do you want to keep this baby Tom?"
　I paused, my hand resting on the handle of the fridge. I
really needed a beer, just something to take the edge off. I knew
I really needed to choose my words carefully, "We're so young.

We didn't plan it. What hope is this kid going to have, what hope are we going to have?

"You mean as a couple?"

"No. Why do you keep coming back to us and our relationship? I am sure you agree there is something a little more pressing going on here. I mean raising a baby. We're so young. We've got our whole lives ahead of us. How the hell would we ever get ahead? We have no money. We haven't even finished uni yet. Don't you want to get your degree and have a career and some sort of future, because I sure as hell do. This is not what I'd planned. I'm way too young to be a father. Christ, I am only a kid myself. Someone needs to be practical and I get the feeling it's not going to be you." The words came out too quickly and once I had started I couldn't stop, knowing that each and every word would be like bait dangling from the end of a hook to a hungry piranha. I was starting to breathe really heavily and desperately needed some air. I lunged towards the window and threw it open. Outside two guys I recognised from my rowing club were running along the path, pushing another guy in a shopping trolley. They were gathering pace and suddenly let the trolley go, sending it hurtling off the path and into scrubland.

"Wow the hits just keep on coming, don't they Tom? It seems like this would really ruin *your* life plans, which clearly don't include me." Isobel's words drowned out the laughter of the trolley guys. I balanced my palms on the window sill, for fear of really losing any shred of calm, and didn't turn around when I said, "Do you really want to push me to the brink, because that's where I am heading?"

"So our relationship has nothing to do with this, is that what you're saying? Because I am having a very hard time separating the baby apart from our relationship..." Isobel answered, totally ignoring what I had just said. The guys now minus the trolley looked up towards the window, maybe they had heard me.

I tried again, "That's not what I meant. I meant, I *mean* we need to decide what we are going to do about this now Iss…the you being pregnant bit I mean…"

"The YOU being pregnant bit." Isobel roared. "I just got pregnant all by myself did I? Don't speak to me like I've got a disease that a course of antibiotics can fix. It's a fucking baby Tom and it's YOUR fucking baby." Our words were bouncing off walls and hiding in corners. Isobel was doing that thing she does with her bottom lip which I knew would be followed by endless silence.

I took a deep breath and walked very carefully towards where Isobel was perched on the edge of the bed. Ever so slowly I sat down next to her and to my surprise, she didn't flinch when I took her hand. "Please Iss, calm down and we'll try and work through this together, OK? We can't make any rational decisions while we're both so emotional and upset. I think both of us are saying things we don't mean and we're having a hard time trying to understand where the other one is coming from." Isobel nodded slowly. Finally, a positive breakthrough.

"I'm scared Tom."

"I know, so am I."

ISOBEL

I studied Tom's face as he sat next to me on the bed, holding my hand. It was such a familiar face, I felt like I knew every crease and pore. His dark hair flopped into his green eyes, he was obviously too scared to shift the strands that kept catching in his lashes. Since I had known him, Tom's jaw was strong and angular, making him look like a man rather than a boy, and gave his face a rugged outline which was now shaded with a blanket of dark whiskers. My eyes traced the shape of his tanned neck to his broad shoulders and big capable arms, years of rowing and surfing had built them up to naturally lightly flex even when he was doing something that didn't necessarily involve exertion.

I felt panicked he was sliding away from me. Reaching out to him was like trying to glide through honey. All I wanted Tom to do was put those arms around me and tell me everything was going to be alright, but the deep burrowing feeling that he didn't love me anymore was swallowing me whole – making me act like a crazed woman. I thought back to the night in the pub when I had ripped his T-shirt. I remember seeing the look on his face and feeling everyone's eyes on me. But no one had heard Tom spitting through clenched teeth that I was driving him away and everyone agrees I am crazy. Well why not let them all see how crazy I am and so I grabbed his shirt, dug my nails into the fabric while he tried to pull away from me. The sound of the material tearing and the look on his face startled me. All I could do was flee.

I was fighting the urge to flee again. It had taken all my strength to keep my feet planted on the floor and grip the edge of the mattress to stop myself from springing up and shooting out the door before Tom had even turned around from the window. With him now holding my hand and looking at me, confused and hurt, I could barely help myself from melting into the mattress. I wanted to curl up in a tight ball and drift into a long sleep so I wouldn't have to confront any more of these feelings.

"I'm tired of fighting Tom. I just want us to make a decision and see it through," I muttered into his chest.

"I agree." His words fell softly on my hair.

"Good, well that's a start."

It had been two weeks since that day in Tom's room. University had broken for mid-semester and I had left my room this morning, running down the frosty path pulling a trolley bag behind me to catch the train back to my parents. I had seen Tom a few times since then. In those first few days he had called me every day, sometimes I picked the phone up, but mostly I let him leave a message. So I hadn't said good-bye to Tom or even told him I was going away. We spoke yesterday morning and I told him I would be going to the doctor at the end of the week to 'discuss options', he had offered to come with me. The fact it was an offer had really pissed me off. I had wanted him to be decisive and tell me what time he would be coming to get me and sit there holding my hand through the appointment. During our last telephone call, a first year student had been hovering behind me waiting to use the phone, so instead I pushed my tongue up into the roof of my mouth and whispered I would call him and then hung up. "All yours." I had said sarcastically as I brushed past her elbow.

Looking out of the train window at the city rushing past me, I rested my hand on my belly. The morning sickness had started a few days ago. As I felt the rise and fall of the train tracks push up through my belly, it made my whole body shake with nausea. I tried to fix my gaze on a point on the seat in front of me, but this only made me feel worse. I closed my eyes and slowly drifted off to sleep, when I opened them the countryside and the smell of the ocean had replaced the grey tall buildings of the city. I smiled knowing I was getting closer to home.

"Hello Darling," Mum chirped as I slowly stepped from the train. "Dad's waiting in the car and he's double-parked so we better hurry up. Here. Give me your bag." Mum took the handle and was rushing up the platform in front of me. I hurried to keep up. "Come on sweetheart."

"I'm coming Mum, for God's sake," I panted at her back.

By the time I arrived at the car Mum had already put my bag in the boot and was hopping in the front seat. Dad smiled at me, reaching over to open the back door.

"Hi Dad," I said.

"Hi Iss. Did you have a good trip?"

"Yeah it was fine. I slept for most of it."

"The best way to travel I think. How did your exams go?"

"Yeah I only had two the rest were assessment tasks. I won't know for a few weeks. They'll send the results home."

"But you think you went OK?" That was Mum who I knew would be tallying up the fees in her head.

"Yeah I guess. It's always hard to tell."

Mum swallowed hard. Dad's eyes flickered in her direction.

"How's Tom doing?" Dad asked. The sound of his name made me shudder. "Fine," I said curtly.

Silence. The sound of the car rolling along the road.

"We're having lasagne for dinner," Mum said, turning around in her seat to smile at me. Thinking about the cheese coating the top of the lasagne made my stomach heave. "Sounds great Mum."

My bedroom still looked like it did when I left it to go to university two years ago. The maths text books and novels I had to read for English sat in a pile in a box next to the cupboard. I was never very good at letting things go. I dumped my bag and looked at the collage of photos I had pinned on the wall. Each photo had been painstakingly selected and arranged like a special exhibition in my own personalised portrait gallery. Tom was in almost all of them. I peered closely at one of him and I the summer we had gotten together in our last year of school. We were at the beach, Tom's legs were tangled around mine, both of us were wet from a swim with Tom's surfboard resting on the sand in the background behind us. I studied his face, he looked happy – although I couldn't make out the expression in his eyes because he was squinting from the heavy midday sun. I remembered that day, we had only been together for a few weeks. That morning I had come to collect him in my mum's shopping car, as Dad called it, beeping the horn out the front of Tom's parents house. It was hot, very hot, in the low thirties. The backs of my thighs were sticking to the seat, clinging and stretching as I tried to rearrange them. Tom had come running down the front steps, yanking the front door behind him, waved to me and then disappeared around the side of the house. When he re-emerged, he was carrying his surfboard.

"Hey," Tom said leaning inside the rolled down passenger window.

"Hey," I replied.

"This isn't going to fit is it?" Tom asked looking in the back seat and then back at his surfboard. "The roof?"

"How?" I asked.

"Maybe better in the back, we could roll the front seat down, sit the board in diagonally and I could sit in the back. It works. I've done it before."

"OK, sure if you think it will fit."

That's how we travelled the 10 kilometres to the beach where we were meeting our friends. Me driving, Tom in the back with the surfboard sliced diagonally down the middle between us. All four windows rolled down and singing with gusto to 'Hot in the City' playing on the radio's 'Saturday Sounds of Summer' show.

"Isobel, dinner's ready," Mum yelled up the stairs.

"OK, be there in a second," I yelled back, lightly touching Tom's young summer face before snapping off the bedroom light.

The dinner table was set and Mum and Dad were already seated in the same spot they had always sat at the table – Dad at the end and Mum sitting to his right. I took my place across from Mum. "How much do you want?" Mum asked balancing a huge slab of lasagne on a serving spoon. I looked at the cheese dripping and at the red of the meat wedged between the layers. The pungent aroma slapped at my nostrils. My stomach heaved as I slid my chair out from the table and raced to the bathroom. Mum's knock on the bathroom door was perfectly timed with my dry-retching echoing into the toilet bowl.

Mum and Dad both watched me carefully as I sat myself very slowly back down at the dining table. I looked at Mum and then Dad. "There's something I think I need to tell you," I said as carefully as their looks, knowing what I was about to say would change everything.

I'll never forget the look on Dad's face or the way Mum's hand shook holding the salad server. "Why?" was the word that finally broke the silence. In my own mind I didn't know why. I didn't know why I had decided that having this baby was the right thing to do or that my life would forever be pegged – in more ways than the obvious one – around the decision I would make as a twenty-one year old.

TOM

"I don't know I haven't seen her," Isobel's friend, Melissa, yelled above the din of the bar in the city we went to when university had finished for the holidays. "Seriously Tom I am telling the truth. You know Iss is a free spirit, she does what she wants. Maybe she went back home for the holidays."

"Yeah maybe…"

"I can give you her parents' number."

"No I have it. Thanks anyway."

What the fuck was Isobel playing at? I had lost count of the number of times I had tried calling her. I had also been to her room banging on the door three times now. The third and final time, the guy who has the room next door, I always forget his name, peered around the edge of his own door and told me I was a dickhead and to give it up. His name was probably Unhelpful Prick.

I had a right to know when the doctor's appointment was and I should be there too. Christian and I had talked about little else over beers, over spliffs, always in his back garden and always with Christian breathing out "Oh man" and doing that nervous shaking leg thing he does. But I knew all too well what the 'Oh Man' meant. It meant, I am glad it's you and not me. I am glad I don't have a girlfriend or if I did that's she's not a nut or a *pregnant* nut.

"You know mate." It was Christian talking. We were sitting in his back garden again. Discussing the matter at hand – again. "If she's not answering the door, it could be one of two things. One – she is there and doesn't want to answer the door because she knows it's you. Or two – she isn't there and has buggered off and hasn't told you." Great. I was getting life advice from someone who thinks stating the fucking obvious is helping. Christian hadn't thought of the third option though and it was the one playing most on my mind. Isobel had done something really stupid, mainly to punish me. Christ I couldn't live with any of that guilt. What was happening was big, but her doing that…I couldn't bear to think about it. I hadn't even had the guts to raise it as the third option to join Christian's startling first two observations.

"…Or mate….she's…" I looked at Christian. OK he has thought about the third option. "But she wouldn't Tom… she might have been a little crazy lately, but she is a smart girl…she…mate, I'm sorry that was a really stupid thing to even suggest and…oh…shit, I am not trying to put ideas into your head. Sorry, sorry. I'm an idiot. I am sure she went back home to her Mum and Dad's or something. Do they know?"

"Dunno." I replied. My parents didn't know. I thought we could just sort things out quietly between ourselves and then no one else would need to know.

"Maybe she's at her parents and she needs some advice. You know girls and their mums." Christian said sliding open the glass door to go in and get another couple of beers for us.

Isobel's mum has never been my biggest fan, she'd tried to discourage Isobel and I from going to the same university. I was glad Iss had applied and we'd both got in. Sometimes people find the person they're meant to be with early in life, others find them later and some never find them. Back then

I thought Isobel and I had been in those lucky first few. I was really cool with that. It was always Isobel and Tom, Tom and Isobel. Even the first year at uni had been fine. We both went through our teething of a new environment together. I always had someone to talk to. She laughed and listened easily. I can't pinpoint where this beautiful girl started to unravel. Exactly when she started to become paranoid, when she got uptight about everything I did, when her face distorted to give that wounded look and she stopped listening. Some days I wanted to shake her and scream into her face – to break that look to hunt down where my girl had gone. Other days, I told myself I was young. I was wrong. This was not right after all. I needed to get out there and that would mean cutting this girl free. But whenever I went to do it, I never had the courage or I would see the old Isobel flicker across this girl's face and I couldn't bring myself to cut her memory out of mine…not just yet anyway.

"Here." Christian said, flicking the crown off a beer bottle and passing it to me. "May as well get wasted while we solve the problems of the world. Always provides some more clarity I find. Although the same can't quite be said for my economics exam. Jesus Christ I know I've fucked that baby up…and you think you've got problems." Christian said laughing.

"Shit. You're right. I'm a self-absorbed bastard aren't I?" I said laughing. "You can always re-sit that little fucker – wonder if I can re-sit the night I managed to sow some Tom seeds around a bit."

"Make love not war hey mate?" Christian laughed into his beer.

"Something like that."

Later that night I was half drunk and slightly stoned, stacking tins of corn onto the shelves of the fifth aisle at

Woolworths. Working the night shift meant I was paid penalty rates and was worth staying on in the university holidays for some extra cash. I had my walkman on and listening to the music helped pass the time before I would have to go back to the store room and collect the tinned beetroot.

Of course I had tried calling Isobel several times that week. The first time I called, I was sweating so heavily with nerves my hands had slid down the receiver, almost making me drop the phone as it was answered at the other end. In my head I had already pre-empted the abuse I thought would be hurled down the line from Isobel's mother, but it never came. For the rest of the week, each time Isobel's mum told me Isobel wasn't home at the moment and no she didn't know where Isobel was or when she would be home. Strangely, I thought I could detect a hint of sadness in her mother's voice. I thought she would be rejoicing that Isobel and I seemed to be finished. I was also safe in the fact Isobel mustn't have told her parents about the baby because there was no way her mum would be able to speak to me without demanding I get on the next train to sort the mess out.

Earlier that evening and slightly pissed and stoned from drinking in the sun for most of the afternoon with Christian, I had dialled Isobel's parents' phone number again. Her mother answered by reciting their phone number. Why do parents always do that? It had made me smirk, but I quickly lost my nerve and hung up. My walkman clicked to the next track, it was a Crowded House song. The first lines of the song scratched into the headphones – 'the guilty get no sleep'. I wasn't smirking now.

It was well after midnight when my shift finally finished. I had agreed to stay on for another couple of hours to help unload dairy goods from a truck which had just arrived in the dock. I needed the extra cash. As I left the building, fresh cool air stung my face, seeming to flush clarity and sense through my foggy brain. I decided as soon as I got home I would call Isobel and tell her – or more likely her other self – I was going to get the train to her parents the next day. I picked up my speed, walking to the bus stop with a purpose. Two of the streetlights were out which made the night even darker. I walked quickly. "Shit" I yelled, stumbling on a bottle which rolled across the path somewhere in front of me. I narrowed my eyes hunting for where the bottle might have stopped so I could step around it. Then everything went black.

ISOBEL

"OK Isobel, you can pull your top down again now thank you and take a seat." My belly was covered in goose pimples from the draught slipping through the open window in Dr Robinson's surgery. Dr Robinson, the same Dr Robinson who had delivered me 21 years ago, smiled warily at me as I slid off the examination table and eased myself into the cracked red leather chair across from her. She knotted her fingers together and rested them on the desk. I wiped my palms backwards and forwards along my thighs.

"You OK Isobel?"

"Yeah, yeah I'm fine." I said very unconvincingly.

Dr Robinson re-phrased the question, "How are you feeling?"

My eyes burned hot with water. "Scared" I squeaked.

"Understandable. Are there things you perhaps need to talk about with the baby's father?"

I took a deep breath and gripped my fingers together and stared at the swirled pattern on the carpet, the swirls seem to be turning into Tom's face.

"Yeah probably." I finally answered, still staring at the carpet.

"Does he know?"

"Yes." My reply was quick and clipped. I stared harder, willing the water threatening to burst the banks of my eyelids to calm. Dr Robinson untwisted her hands and reached for a pen from a cylinder advertising a pharmaceutical product on the desk. Next to it sat a jar of jelly beans. As a child, I had been given a sweaty handful of the sweet bright colours following my tetanus shots, chickenpox diagnosis, broken finger and every other cough or cold I had contracted from all the other spluttering kids in the classroom. Now here I was being diagnosed with *pregnancy*. Somehow I didn't think my bravery this visit would be rewarded with jelly beans. If only it were that simple.

I thought about Mum pacing the aisles of the supermarket on the pretence of buying some groceries for dinner, while her only child sat listening to news we both already knew.

Of course Mum had wanted to come into the appointment with me. I had yelled 'No' for the final time last night while we sat in the lounge room. Dad was watching a documentary about a mining disaster somewhere in Asia. Mum kept looking across at me to where I sat huddled like a small child on the couch. It was like a silent conversation was volleying back and forth between us. Finally I couldn't take her looking at me with her mouth full of unsaid words any longer and hissed 'No' at her across the leather of the couch. The word hung like a sting in the air before it pierced Mum, reddening her face and making her eyes glisten. Dad looked up from the TV.

"You're impossible," Mum shot back before stamping out of the room. I watched as her feet left imprints in the carpet.

"You *are* impossible Isobel. Can't you see your mum and I care about you? We're worried sick. Yet it seems you're determined to make a huge decision on your own and you haven't thought about any of the consequences, or for that matter the effect it might have on your mum and me – the people who love you."

"So it's all about appearances is it Dad? Mum won't be able to hold her head up to all her cronies at bridge…"

"Isobel. That's enough. Think about what you are saying, but more importantly doing. You are behaving like a selfish child."

I untucked my feet from under me, trying not to cry. Dad continued to look at me for what seemed like hours. I knew he wasn't finished.

"I think it's time we talked about all of this – like adults – instead of tip-toeing around each other like we have been for the past week. I also want to know where the hell Tom is." Dad's voice rose at the mention of Tom's name. He slapped the remote control on the side of the armchair to make his point.

"Leave Tom out of this."

"Don't be so bloody ridiculous. That boy has a responsibility. I never would have thought he would be such a coward, but he has proven me very wrong. I am so disappointed I can't even begin to tell you. I have a good mind to drive up to that campus and drag him back here by his ears."

I rolled my eyes.

"Don't you dare roll your eyes at me. I tell you, he's very lucky his parents have moved back to Sydney because I would be around there demanding some bloody answers. I would be telling them exactly what I think of their son."

I heard Mum's footsteps come back down the stairs. She stood in the door way, clearly having regained her composure and now stared at me like a hunter sizing up their target.

"He has tried to call Ray." I couldn't believe it, Mum was defending Tom.

"Well trying to call is just not good enough." Dad spat.

"Yes I agree, but I think it's been made all the more difficult for him because Isobel refuses to talk to him or she hangs up on him." Mum turned to look at me. "In fact, the way you're behaving Isobel, it makes me wonder if

Tom even knows." Wham. Right on target, I was hit straight between the eyes.

"Why are you siding with him? I'm your daughter." I wailed like a child.

"Well your behaviour makes me wonder…"

"Of course he fucking knows…"

"Isobel!" My father hollered across the room.

"No let her go on Ray. We might actually get some truth here. I can't stand what she's doing to us any longer. This ridiculousness is killing me. I have absolutely had enough and I want it to stop right now, do you hear me Isobel?"

"Why are you being so awful to me?" I was crying now and furiously pulled at my cheeks where the tears were running down. "This is the hardest time in my life and you are being awful to me, even, even taking Tom's side. I can't believe it. I really can't believe it."

If I was honest, I didn't really know what I was saying. Their questions were perfectly valid, but a white sheet of anger fluttered so strongly in my face I couldn't be reasonable. I knew I wanted to hurt them and sticking to the decision to have the baby would do just that. Since telling my parents, that first night when I arrived exhausted at the train station, that I would indeed go through with the pregnancy, my stance had started to crack and creak under the strain of their whispered propaganda campaign. Both Mum and Dad seized any signs of my weakness, coaching me gently and carefully about how hard it would be to be a single mother, honing in on me losing all my independence, not to mention my youth. Their words had started to grab a hold of me, but I hadn't wanted to let them know that. Instead I kept quiet, changed the subject and shook my head when Mum mouthed 'Tom' holding her hand over the phone receiver. Now their true colours had burned brightly, boiling down to a faint, soggy mess. They were only worried about themselves. My doctor's appointment was booked for the following morning at 9.30 and I knew what my final answer would be to the choices Dr Robinson presented me.

"Honey..." Mum had moved to sit next to me on the couch, her arm hovered on my shoulder. "Please honey, we hate seeing you so upset. We are just so worried about you and we lost our patience, that's all. We're sorry OK? I don't have to come in with you to see Dr Robinson, but would like to at least drive you to the appointment OK?" Her hand now rested on my shoulder. The lounge room was silent. Eventually I nodded. Dad sat up slowly in his chair and asked if anyone would like a drink. Mum nodded and he left the room. I stared at the TV, the documentary had finished. The credits ticked over on the screen.

Dr Robinson was speaking gently again as she wrote on a notepad. "OK Isobel, well I will certainly respect your decision but would suggest, if you are on speaking terms, that you do talk to the baby's father first before making any final decisions. Perhaps you should come in and see me together. Here." She said passing me a piece of paper. "This is the name and number of a counsellor who is very good at dealing with these sorts of things. She will be able to talk to you at length about the various options and what to expect, basically help you make an informed decision that's right for you. I think it would be really helpful for you and...perhaps the baby's father to see her. I can make the appointment for you if you like."

"No I am fine thank you. I can do it."

"OK then. Well that is really all for now. Please make an appointment with Jessica on the way out to come back and see me next week, so you have enough time to see the counsellor. Take care Isobel."

I smiled thinly at the receptionist wearing a name badge with 'Jessica' printed in white type as I made my way straight past her to the door, scrunching Dr Robinson's referral into the cotton of my jeans pocket.

TOM

There were muffled voices somewhere off in the distance. A bright shock of light hit me in the face. I knew it wasn't the first time light had struck me because its harshness seemed faintly familiar. A squeaking sound rotated closer to me. I blinked, trying to peel my eyes open. Pins and needles yawned and stretched their way up through the base of my neck and ended in an intensely dull throbbing ache across the back of my head. My eyes fell closed again, I don't know for how long. The squeak got closer. A ruffling sound, maybe a curtain blowing in the breeze, I thought, half-heartedly trying to unlock my eyelids. Finally my eyes opened and this time stayed put. A figure dressed in white stood in front of me. I blinked, trying to focus. The figure was smiling at me, at least I think it was a smile and I think it was a figure.

"Ah you're awake." The figure was talking to me.

I watched as the talking figure came closer to where my head was resting on something soft, it must be a pillow.

"How's your head?" The mention of my head reminded my body to send the dull ache into overdrive. My eyes drooped closed from the pain.

"It's OK, you probably need your rest." I heard footsteps walking away from me.

"No, wait. Please wait," I stammered and the footsteps stopped. I tried desperately to open my eyes again. My right eye gave in first and then my left slowly took the lead of its mate.

"What happened?" I managed to put the words together.

"Don't you remember?" asked the figure.

"No. Not really."

"It appears some of the city's finest decided your wallet would look better in their pocket and knocked you over the head for it. Lucky for you, someone you work with had just finished their shift, found you and called an ambulance straight away which brought you to the hospital, which is where you obviously are now. You've been unconscious for a few hours, but you should be fine."

"What time is it?" The figure, which I assumed correctly must have been a nurse, plucked the watch from the chain hanging by her breast. "It's about 6.30 in the morning. So you have been out for the count for quite a few hours. I wouldn't worry though, all your vital signs are fine. We knew you would come round in your own time, but think you might have a pretty bad headache for a few days."

"Yeah it bloody hurts."

"Well just make sure you get some rest. I think we may be keeping you in overnight just to make sure everything is OK, but the doctor will be able to confirm that when he sees you later this morning. Is there anything I can get you?" I thought for a moment. I was starving, I felt like I hadn't eaten for days and then remembered sitting in Christian's back garden furiously stuffing potato chips into my mouth to fuel the munchies brought on by the endless spliffs we had sucked back all afternoon. The pieces of a complicated jigsaw started to come together as I remembered what we had been talking about – Isobel was pregnant. I broke into a sweat, feeling the beads bauble across my shoulder blades and seep into the starched white hospital sheet. My forehead grew damp and my tongue swelled.

"Are you OK?"

"I think I am going to be...." Too late, I threw up all over the hospital blanket, in full view of the blurry nurse. "I'll be back in just a tick," I heard her say as the curtain blocking me from the rest of the other casualties swung to the left to let her through.

Later that afternoon, I was cleaned up and had been moved to a ward full of complaining patients. I was dozing from the heavy-duty pain killers being pumped into my body when I became conscious of someone looking at me. Slowly I opened my eyes to see Christian's head peering around the side of the curtain.

"You alright mate?" Christian asked.

"My head bloody hurts."

"I bet," Christian replied, pulling the curtain aside to scrape a worn vinyl blue hospital chair closer to the bed. "Here, I bought you these," Christian said handing me a brown paper bag.

"Geez mate you didn't bring pot into the hospital did you?" I looked at him, aghast.

"Don't be stupid, they're grapes."

"Grapes?" I was puzzled.

"Yeah, isn't that what you're meant to bring people when they're in hospital? I didn't think I would be allowed to bring you a packet of smokes."

"Thanks mate." The smile spreading across my face was killing my head.

"Yeah well I don't know, I don't really visit people in hospital, the last person I visited was my gran and she was non compos mentis anyway so I ate the chocolates I bought her because she wasn't allowed to eat anything sweet apparently.

Anyway, you can say thanks, I am missing my shift at the Arms to see you and I need the money. I'm dead broke at the moment because I spent all I had on the pot you and I managed to consume the lot of yesterday. Now I don't even have a nice spliff to keep me company."

"Thanks mate...really and a visit to the hospital as well, I am touched."

"They got you on morphine?"

"Nah just heavy-duty pain killers."

"Oh tough luck, morphine would have been cool, especially if you could self-administer."

"Yeah. How'd you know I was here?"

"Ben, the bloke who always wears rugby shirts, found you, we're in history together, knew you and I were mates so called me to tell me what happened and where you were."

"Thank Christ he came along, it was freezing last night. Man, could things get any worse for me?"

"I've called your parents too and your mum is on her way to take you back to theirs for the rest of the break."

"Oh Christ, things just did get worse. Bloody hell, now I am going to have her all over me wanting to know where Isobel is and why she's not here. Great."

"Sorry Tom but I thought I should let them know. Something really serious could have happened to you."

"No, no it's cool. You did the right thing. Didn't try Isobel too did you?" Christian raised his eyebrows and shook his head.

The following afternoon I was sitting in the passenger seat of Mum's car heading north on the highway towards the city. Mum hummed tunelessly to a song I vaguely recognised playing on a country radio station she had managed to find the frequency for. Every now and again she strummed her thumb on the steering wheel and tried to snatch looks at me from underneath the rim of her sunglasses. For most of the journey I pretended to doze off. The sun winking through the trees which lined the roadside helped to close my eyes and keep them closed which suited me fine. A couple of times Mum asked if I was comfortable and feeling alright. My replies were small nods of the head or a mumble. This seemed to satisfy her, so she wound the volume dial around a couple of clicks and I rested my head against the seat until the trees thinned and the grey wash of concrete grew fat in my eye line.

The first few days back at home went by with me sprawled on the couch watching pirated videos my brother, Damien, had apparently bartered for in Thailand on his way home from his backpacking adventure across Europe.

As far as I could gather he had spent most of the time holed up in a flat share in Earl's Court smoking weed with nine or ten other Aussies. Since arriving home a few months ago he had moved back in with Mum and Dad and got a job as a labourer on a building site in the city, both of which were meant to be temporary, but Damien didn't look like he was planning on leaving either in a hurry. I could tell my being home was cramping his style by the snarls and grunts he passed in my general direction every time he wandered past the couch on his way to the kitchen to eat Mum and Dad's food sitting in Mum and Dad's fridge. Damien and I still fought like schoolboys and I had been the recipient of a good thump across the calves as he pushed my legs off the couch so he could reclaim his throne and his crown in the Cooper Empire. Mum's insistence on cooking my favourite meals, plumping up the pillows behind my head and avoiding any topics of conversation which could fork down the road which would lead us to Isobel weren't helping my cause in Damien's eyes either.

Besides occupying the couch I also claimed the fridge, swinging the door open and closed to watch the light wink on and off at me. I wasn't hungry, my appetite had waned since I was belted over the head, so all of Mum's carefully planned menus of roast chicken, pork chops and bangers and mash with her special onion gravy poured expertly over the entire plate's contents went to waste as I nibbled around the edge, watching Damien out of the corner of my eye almost inhaling his food, thanks to the non-stop physical labour his job demanded while he eyed my overflowing plate. For the last four nights I had mouthed 'fuck off' at his vulture-like eyes, in the end he always won, smugly picking at the carcass of my roast chicken while I helped Dad stack the dishwasher.

The fridge was where I was again now, standing barefoot on the cork tile, swinging the door with my foot a few inches forward and then a few inches back. Staring into the fridge and not feeling at all hungry, it was hard to tell if my lost appetite was down to the overbearing strain I felt about the whole Isobel business or if staring aimlessly into the big white crevasse was just etched into my DNA – crazy pregnant girl-friend or no crazy pregnant girlfriend. It's what I used to do every afternoon when I came home from school, when I had been surfing with the boys, after a night out or the first thing I would do when I got inside Isobel's room at uni. Bloody Isobel. Her fridge was always so meticulous, dairy products on the top shelf, booze on the second shelf and chocolate in the door. I leaned my head on the cool of the metal and stared at a carton of milk. Milk. Babies. Bloody Isobel. A wave of nausea washed over me. I leaned my head closer inside the door willing the cool air to calm my body.

"Do you want to go for a surf?" I peered over the top of the door to see Damien leaning against the cupboard, swinging a set of keys through his fingers.

"Yeah why not." I replied.

There's something trance-like and overpowering about the ocean which changes the behaviour of those who dare swim in or ride her, well at least for the Cooper brothers anyway. Damien and I had always been able to shove our differences and stupid brotherly quarrels aside, letting the warm water of the Pacific glide, slippery, over our wetsuits and boards as we sat quietly way out past where the waves broke, patiently waiting for the next set of heaving ocean to push our bodies into the movement which would catch a curve of liquid all the way to the gritty sand. All that waiting usually meant a hell of a lot of thinking and it was out here where we forgot we were competitive brothers and just talked about stuff.

"What's going on?"

"What do you mean?" I asked Damien, running a fingernail through the board wax.

"You know what I mean."

I felt a surge of water rise under my board.

"Isobel mate, that's what I mean. I've heard you on the phone late at night, when you don't think anyone can hear you. Well I can hear you and it sounds like you guys are fighting, actually it sounds more like you're getting the silent treatment because all I can hear is your voice...a lot. You talking into the dial tone or something?"

"No."

"But you know how I really know something's wrong?"

"How?" I muttered, really not wanting to hear the answer.

"Because Mum keeps telling me not to bring up Isobel..."

"How does Mum know what's going on I haven't even said anything to her?"

"Ha. So there is something going on, I knew it."

I let out a deep sigh and started a quick calculation in my head to weigh up the consequences of telling Damien what was really going on. Despite the fact we had been stalking around each other like two angry tomcats staking out our territory, we were brothers and we looked out for each other. I'd want Damien to think he could trust me with something and help me out, the same as I knew I could trust him.

"Mate she's just a chick, she's not your wife, she's probably a girl who has run her course with you. We grow up, we get older, we outgrow people. It's as simple as that. Don't beat yourself up over it, it's just life, it's just what happens." I looked across at Damien, he sat so comfortably on his board, rising with the tide as it rose and flattened again beneath him. He was squinting in the late afternoon sun as he looked at me waiting for a response.

"I wish it was that simple," I said finally.

"Has she met someone else?"

"No."

"Have you?"

"No."

"She's not umm..."

I gripped the board and waited for the dreaded word, the same word Isobel and I had so expertly managed to avoid in the snatched angry phone calls I hosted in the downstairs bathroom when the house was silent with sleep. Two days ago Isobel had finally agreed to come to the phone, she didn't say much, but it seemed like she was listening and softening into my words. At least she made some sort of a soothing noise when I told her I had been mugged and ended up in hospital.

"You can say it Damien."

"Pregnant?"

I nodded my head. I heard Damien suck air in between his teeth.

"And you're sure it's yours?"

I shot a look at my brother which left no doubt the baby was mine.

"What are you going to do?" he asked carefully.

"I dunno know mate. The whole thing is so huge. Isobel kind of wants to keep it and that just freaks me out."

"Keep it?" Damien squawked in surprise.

"I know, I know. Actually no I don't know, I don't know anything. I am so confused and Isobel is acting so crazy. Even before this happened she was acting so crazy that I was thinking about breaking up with her. But now everything has changed and basically... I'm fucked."

"No you're not. But mate you have to decide what you want, you've almost finished uni, you've got your whole life ahead of you. You're a smart bloke, you're the one who was blessed with the brains and you've got to use them. But just so we're clear, I got the looks alright."

In spite of myself I laughed.

"Everything you're saying makes sense, except for the looks bit, and I know it's just plain stupid to even think about having a baby now and especially with Isobel..."

"Well man, you gotta tell her. It's your life too and if you were thinking about breaking up with her anyway the last thing you should do is have a baby with her. It's no big deal these days mate, how many people can we name who have got someone pregnant, they've had an abortion and that's that."

"Yeah I know. But now it's me it seems different and everything seems really bloody hard. I know what you're saying makes sense..."

"Exactly it makes sense because it is the right thing to do. Look ultimately it's up to you, but if you want my opinion, I reckon you already know what you have to do and it's not play happy families with Isobel. Picture yourself in ten years time, do you want to be struggling with a ten year old who has strained you financially and you only get to see every other weekend because Isobel's taken off with some other bloke who this kid calls 'Dad'?"

I gripped my knees tightly under the board, shut my eyes and rubbed my fingertips at my forehead, Damien's words bounced off the edges of my skull. God how I wanted to shut the world out.

"Tom it'll be OK, whatever happens. What do you want?"

"I want for none of this to be happening," I said into the palms of my hands.

"Well it is mate so we are going to have to come up with some solutions before it's too late and your choice is made for you. It's not too late though is it?"

"No," I croaked.

"Right well you gotta tell me what *you* want so I can help you."

I pulled my hands down off my face and rested them on the board in front of me. There was something calming about looking at my fingers sticking white and crinkly against the wax and that's precisely when a moment of crystal clear clarity made me announce very calmly to my brother, "I don't want to be a dad. Not now. Not with Isobel. Not ever with Isobel."

Damien paddled closer to me, the tip of his board glided lightly into mine. "Well you don't have to be. Ring her tonight and tell her you are going down there to sort this out because you are one half of this."

"You're right," I nodded, "You are bloody right." I said decisively.

Damien looked over his right shoulder. "You'd want to start paddling there's a massive set coming through and it's got my name on it." With that, Damien's arms started to paddle and build momentum. I watched as my brother tucked his knees up beneath him and stood upright on top of the board to ride a beautiful curve all the way into the beach. The sun was starting to drop, I too looked over my shoulder and seeing a build of water began to paddle.

Shrugging off my wetsuit and standing under the shower at the beach, I dipped my head under the water flow and shook the salt out of my hair. I felt determined, finally like a man who made a decision and taken charge of his life. Sitting in the car waiting for Damien to get a case of beer I still felt determined. Slugging back my third can of beer, I was feeling particularly determined. Then standing in the hallway, dialling Isobel's parents' number I felt slightly less determined and prayed her mother would not answer the phone. For once things seemed to be going my way as Isobel's husky voice cracked a 'hello' into the receiver.

"Iss, it's..."

"I know who it is."

"How are you?"

"OK."

"Listen Iss are you somewhere you can talk. I...I want to come and see you."

"When?"

"Tomorrow, I...we have to sort this out." My throat was dry, it was very hard to swallow.

"Hmmm."

My palms were sweating.

"Tomorrow Iss. I want to come tomorrow, are you going to be there?"

"I don't think you need to."

"Yes I do," I was trying to remain calm.

"I *really* don't think you need to," Isobel repeated.

"Iss..."

"It's too late."

"What, no it's not too late we have to sort this out."

"No, I'm telling you Tom it's too late."

"What? No it's not. I don't understand what you're saying."

"I'm saying it's too late because it's already done."

"What, Iss, you're starting to freak me out. What's done? What are you saying?" My throat really had dried up, I couldn't swallow at all and I had started to pace across the carpet.

"I'm saying it's done Tom. I am saying I took care of what you saw as my problem and it's finished."

I was starting to gasp for air, I leant forward and heaved open the front door, cool air rushed into the hallway like an unexpected visitor.

"Iss..."

"Oh for God's sake Tom, do I have to spell it out? I had an abortion."

The word stung me.

"What, when?" I was feeling dizzy, the dull ache in my head which had sat relatively silently for the last few days now struck a strong beat and I clutched the wall to steady myself.

"This morning Tom. I had an abortion this morning. I am feeling very tired and I want to go to sleep now."

"Why, why didn't you tell me?"

"I thought it was what you wanted."

"Yes but we didn't even talk about it. I spoke to you last night and you didn't say anything."

"Because I knew it was what you wanted and you weren't going to be here. I'm tired I want to go to sleep."

"Iss please. Fuck. I don't know what to say. Are you...are you alright?"

"I'm fine. Really I am." Isobel's voice was soft, the old Isobel flickering lightly down the phone line. I thought about her hair, it always smelt like fresh apples or maybe it was pears, it was so long since I had bothered to stop and breathe her in. My crazy, crazy Isobel. It was the way she said those last few words that I sensed something had shifted, she sounded strong. What I sensed was this was it – everything was finished, not just the pregnancy, but us along with it. My stomach churned and I felt my pulse slow to a low strum.

"Are you there Tom?"

"Yeah. Yeah I'm here. Shit I'm sorry Iss."

"I think we should just have a break from each other Tom. I've been doing a lot of thinking and I am going to defer uni and go back next year."

"Really?"

"Yeah." Isobel's voice was still gentle.

"God I'm sorry Iss."

"So am I. I am so, so sorry Tom. Please remember I really am." Isobel's voice was still gentle, that girl I once knew flickered sharply out when I heard the phone hang up at the other end. A gust of wind slammed the front door shut. I dropped my head onto the wall and let the phone receiver drop down with my arm.

ISOBEL

My back was aching. Nothing new, it always ached these days. I shifted trying to get more comfortable. A ladybird landed on my bare foot which was lying lazily on the sun lounger. Someone told me once ladybirds were good luck so I let it dance across my foot and up onto my big toe even though it tickled like crazy. I need all the luck I can get. Finally I couldn't take the tickling anymore, flicking my toe back and forth made it float off. The little speck of black and red landed on the veranda railing in front of me. My head dropped back with my eyes blinking in the late summer sun, my hand drifted over the swell of my belly to rest on my thigh. Oh the swell of my belly. It was only a matter of weeks until the baby was due. I longed for this wretched little alien to be out of me, but I didn't long for my life starting again.

I reached for the notepad and pen which lay on the table next to me. I had tried several times to write this letter, but I was never really able to find the words. I rolled the pen between my fingers and drew my knees up to rest the notepad on them. The swell of my belly obstructed most of the paper. I adjusted my knees and tilted the pad at an angle so a small sheet of white poked out from under stretched skin. Gently I tapped the pen on the paper and began to write, strokes of blue caressed the fresh page.

Dear you,

I doubt you will ever know me, but at the very least you should know I am your mother. I am writing this while you are not yet born. I am hoping you will understand why I have done what I have done because when I lay eyes on you, I don't know if I will be able to explain myself properly, so it's best I do this when I don't know you at all.

I brought you into the world, but that is where my duty ends. Two people who will love you very much, in fact they already love you because they want you so much, are going to be your parents. I don't know them and they don't know much of me except I am young, healthy and would be messing up my life if I kept you – my parents' words, not mine little one.

Your dad was my high school boyfriend, we were together through some of university too. We're not together now, but God I love him. I cry a lot and get so frustrated that I have to throw and punch things. I don't really know what happened, it's so hard to explain how I'm feeling sometimes and sometimes when I do it scares people, really scares people. Somehow and somewhere it all went wrong between us. I guess what I am trying to say is, I grew slightly crazy. I don't mean literally, or maybe it was or is, but I became so jealous and angry I drove him away. I drive everyone away little one, even you it seems.

Your dad knows about you, well at least he did to begin with, but then I lied a terrible lie and now that's what he believes is the truth. He doesn't know he's living a lie and one day that lie might walk straight past him in the street and he won't even know, or maybe he will see someone he thinks is familiar, he will do a double-take, shake his head and keep walking a lie.

Late at night when I can't sleep because you're squirming and kicking and punching to get out, I rest my hand on you to try and calm you. I hope you can feel the warmth and the tenderness of my hand through my skin and then your skin. Maybe your body will remember my touch as you grow and when you feel sad, well that's what I tell myself anyway while my tears drop silently onto the pillow. Sometimes though little one, I don't know who I am crying for.

I try really hard not to wonder how you might look, if you will inherit your dad's gold hair or my green eyes. If you will get my fiery temper that drove your dad away or if you will get the look your dad gets when he is sad and confused because he doesn't understand me. But most of all I wonder if you will smile easily, something I haven't been able to do for a long time.

Promise me this little one, when you arrive into this world, you will go easily and you won't cause a fuss, crying out for the body which you blossomed in.

Then I stopped writing, my leg had gone to sleep, I shook it, grimacing as the blood started to tingle through my veins. I was glad for the distraction because I really didn't know how I was meant to sign off a letter like this. I had just continued to write and found the words came easily, I wasn't really making the connection that what I was writing was intricately knitted to the baby inside me. But now sitting here with the pen hovering above the page I felt numb and I think it was maybe for the first time. Up until now I had spent my energy being bitter and wanting to punish Tom so badly – for what I don't really know. I am ashamed to admit even to myself that I didn't care about any of the consequences or had even thought about the consequences, even in the last couple of months when I have had nothing but time to keep me company since my mother had bundled me and my expanding reminder to stay with my aunt in the mountains.

I looked down at the page, it's not even a page, it's a letter to my child for God's sake, the child I will never know and whose existence I have lied so callously about. I swallowed down hard and decided this was no time to give myself a sentimental pep talk. What is done is done and that should be that. So why were the tears dropping onto the paper and smudging the ink? I breathed out deeply.

"Isobel are you out here?" I heard my aunt Jean's sing-song voice as the French door from her bedroom swung open onto the veranda. "Oh you are. It's nice out here at this time in the evening, it's always been a favourite place of mine to sit and think." My aunt must have caught the look of panic spreading across my face as she quickly but gently added, "But too much thinking can harm you, some things are better left alone. What are you writing?" she asked looking at the pad balancing on my knees.

"Nothing really," I replied, clicking the top of the pen so the nib slid back inside.

"I might have said it's not good to think too much, but bottling things up can make things worse, so writing's good."

"Hmm well I don't know what's good anymore."

"I know you're scared sweetheart..."

"And stupid."

"Don't be so hard on yourself. Plenty of people have done much worse things than this and plenty of people will continue to do a lot worse."

I looked out across the garden and up into the mountains, the haze of eucalypt smudged the sky against the setting sun. Everything seemed so peaceful and somehow so much bigger than me, I was nothing more than a speck in a gigantic universe, so how could one decision, or lie, I make change the course of the sun setting behind the mountains, stop the water rushing in the creek at the bottom of the paddock or halt the crickets singing their evening ritual – it couldn't and that's what I had to remember. What I would remember when I woke up in the middle of the night clawing for the lamp switch or catching my reflection each time I passed the mirror in the hallstand.

"Would you like some dinner?" My aunt asked, standing up slowly. "It will just be salad I'm afraid, I'm too exhausted to do anything else. Besides it's too warm really to eat anything else. We could eat out here on the veranda if you like. I'll just bring everything out and make the salad on my lap."

"Sure that sounds great," I said smiling at Aunt Jean who was now over halfway down the veranda, making her way back into the house. I closed my eyes until I heard sounds of her struggling at the door with the dinner things. Rocking myself forward on the sun lounger I was able to very slowly ease myself onto my feet. "I'm coming," I yelled out.

"You'll do no such thing, stay where you are I can manage," my aunt yelled over the top of plates and cutlery being laid down on the dresser in her bedroom. Her elbow was the first to peep out of the house as she wedged herself backwards through the doorway, carrying a chopping board, an array of mixed vegetables and a sharp kitchen knife.

"Here give me some of that."

"Isobel, please darling I said it's OK. Don't cut yourself," Aunt Jean said levering open the crook of her elbow to release a bag of tomatoes into my grip.

After Aunt Jean had made another trip back inside to collect the plates and remaining cutlery from the dresser, we sat together, her dropping the chopped vegetables into the big white salad bowl, stopping every few minutes to take a sip of her white wine. We had sat in silence, letting the sounds of the early evening colour our listening. She picked up a ripe pear and regarded it in her hand. The way she turned the fruit in her palm bruised the young skin. I stared at the pear. Aunt Jean turned the fruit once more and balanced it on the chopping board, slicing a sliver off the pear edge.

"Do you feel like you have been banished up here?" she asked softly. I stared at the pear flesh resting on the wood and bit my lip.

"I like being here with you," I finally answered.

"That's not quite what I asked Iss," Aunt Jean said, drawing her eyes up to meet mine.

"Yeah I bloody do. Haven't exactly fit into Mum's grand plans have I?"

"Well you know your mum has always been somewhat, let me see, what's the word, Victorian, in her outlook."

"Don't you mean unreasonable and a snob?" Aunt Jean smiled at this.

"She only wants the best for you, you're her only child and I suppose she has muddled her way through, hoping it was for the best. I knew something like this would be too difficult for her to cope with because she loves you too much. It takes a strong person to admit that. And I think Iss that's why you're here, out of pure and simple love."

"Oh so it's not because the sight of me in that small town in full view of the bridge crowd would just be too much to bear."

"She's hurting for you..."

"Well she doesn't have to." I snapped. My aunt slid her arm across her chair and patted my elbow.

"Your mum thinks you think you have to go through all of this by yourself when you don't and..." she trailed off.

"And what?" I asked, twisting my lip and staring hard at my aunt.

"Nothing."

"No you were going to say something, what was it?"

"Nothing darling I wasn't going to say anything."

"Please tell me," I whined like a small child.

"Sweetheart it was nothing, I have forgotten."

"No you haven't!" The pitch of my voice sliced through the calm evening sounds carrying up from the garden and the paddocks. Aunt Jean twitched in her seat. "I'm sorry I didn't mean to shout," I said more quietly, as gently as I could.

"It's fine and it's none of my business so you have every right to get angry," Aunt Jean replied without looking at me. "I just don't understand where Tom is that's all. He always seemed to be someone who was reliable, dependable and now when things are at their most difficult, well he's just disappeared completely."

"No one knows anything," I spat the words out, feeling my anger spike up inside me again.

"No you're right Iss, no one ever knows the whole story about anything. People only ever let you see what they want you to see. We all have secrets we hide even from the people we love the most."

I nodded, swallowing the anger down to a light simmer. "Nothing's simple or as it seems," I replied quietly.

"Are you trying to tell me what's happened to Tom?" Jean asked very slowly, pausing her chopping, to study my face. She bit and twisted her lip in the same way I do. I looked at her lips, it was just like looking at my own reflection in a mirror, that's who I got my own mannerism from, I had never before noticed Mum or Dad do it. As a child and even a teenager I was forever being told not to twist my lip 'like that' because Mum knew it was a warning sign I was about to explode into a ball of anger and frustration. Now watching my aunt do something so familiar to me, struck something inside me, I rested my hand on my belly.

"Yes. I have really fucked this up and it's too late I can't undo anything."

"I'm sure it's not as bad as you think." "It's worse." Jean smiled and slid her hand between my belly and palm, locking her fingers in tightly around mine.

"You'll hate me."

"Impossible."

"Tom doesn't know." I whispered. Jean continued to look at me, her grip firmed.

"I'm not sure I know what you mean," she replied quietly.

I didn't say anything.

"Iss?"

"I lied to Tom...to everyone." My eyes frantically searched the veranda rail for the ladybird, all I could see was chipping white paint. The little beetle had gone and the memory of who my aunt thinks I am was about to go too.

"Tom doesn't know the baby exists, he thinks I had an abortion, I told him I had an abortion and I don't ever want him to ever find out the truth. Mum and Dad don't know any of this, they think Tom and I have broken up and he wants nothing to do with the baby. I have let them think all of this. The lie has gone too far and I can't reverse it." I couldn't bring myself to look at my aunt. Her grip loosened slightly. I watched as some colour started to drain back into her knuckles, my eyes fixed on the ironed-out folds of her skin stretching over the bone underneath. We sat in silence, both of us considering the words which had spewed, surprisingly effortlessly, out of my mouth. For me, the confession was a fog lifting from my shoulders, my head felt clearer. Aunt Jean shifted in her seat, putting the chopping board and its contents on the table in front of her and turned right around to face me, her knees moved in close so they pressed against the metal bar of the sun lounger. Finally she took both my hands in her own and squeezed tightly, looking straight into my eyes.

"Well," Aunt Jean breathed out, "Your secret is safe with me." She smiled, undid her fingers from my own, flattened out the crinkles which had gathered in the fabric of her skirt, slowly stood up and walked down the length of the veranda. The ladybird landing on the railing in front of me was timed perfectly with the sound of the old wooden door sighing shut behind Aunt Jean.

The days bled into hours which bled into the minutes my baby would be born. Aunt Jean stayed true to her word and we never spoke of what I told her that evening on the veranda, instead we moved around each other like a practised couple dancing a slow waltz. Mornings were slow and lazy, eating breakfast and reading in the shade of the veranda. Afternoons we walked down to the creek at the bottom of the paddock, me becoming slower by the day supported by Aunt Jean's arm looped through mine. On reaching the creek, Aunt Jean brushed away stray twigs to stake out a suitable sitting spot to spend the afternoon dozing under the leaves of gum trees and dipping our toes into the cool water sliding over the pebbles lying on the creek's bed.

Then one day, as silently expected, our routine was interrupted by the first of crippling cramps dragging my insides down towards the floor. For a moment I was paralysed with white pain shaking the breath from my throat and forcing me to grip at the doorframe with a newfound strength. Breathing out a shallow breath I wondered if I should call out to my aunt or whether I would be better to stay alone for a while, never liking someone to fuss over me when I'm sick. I usually preferred to lie alone on the cool tile of the bathroom floor, resting my head on a rolled up towel waiting for the nausea to pass. I knew I couldn't do that this time, instead I needed to sit or squat. Yes. Squatting would definitely be better, much more comfortable. My gaze clocked my bed sitting unmade in the middle of the room, that's what I would do, just make my way to the lump of soft and squat against it. Sweat prickled my hairline. A metallic taste iced my mouth. Cautiously I navigated my way to the bed and crouched down on my knees with my arms draped across the bedclothes just as another body numbing shock of pain released itself across my belly. I tried to concentrate but the darts of pain were coming quickly and intensely, much faster than I remembered being told in the pre-natal coaching classes Aunt Jean and I had gone to during the last month. I hadn't even felt those first few 'twinges' the nurse had described, smiling reassuringly at a sea of nervous faces as she pushed a doll through a plastic vagina to demonstrate the birthing process.

I heard the back door open and close, my aunt's footsteps padding across the linoleum on the kitchen floor. The old 1960s fridge door creaked open and then hesitated. "Isobel," Aunt Jean called out. I breathed out a shallow breath, petrified the baby would come if I dared breathe more deeply. "Isobel?" Aunt Jean called more urgently. The fridge door squeaked closed.

"In here." I said, my voice barely dancing past my lips. By now the sweat was trickling down my back. I closed my eyes lightly and when I opened them Aunt Jean was standing in the doorway, staring at my slumped body with her mouth rounded into a perfect 'o'. "The baby's coming," is all I managed to say before she was rubbing my back and cooing in my ear to remember my breathing and that everything was going to be alright.

"I'm scared." I whispered into the warm, soft flesh of my aunt's inner arm.

PART THREE
AND THEN THERE YOU WERE

LAURA

The room was heavy with cigarette smoke and loud with office workers expelling the stress of the week into their glasses. I arched my heels up to stand on the tips of my toes, giving myself a better position to scan the sea of faces for Cate. A guy with his tie half knotted lurched towards me with a full glass of beer, spilling a finger's worth of froth down the front of my shirt. "Sorry love. Long lunch," he stammered reaching out to brush the milky froth from my breast. "Do you mind?" I said angrily, picking his wrist away from my breast and placing my elbow neatly into the pit of his stomach as I nudged my way past to dive deeper into the throng of drinkers. Now I was barely able to move and could feel my shoes sticking to the floorboards while my handbag wrapped around something that wasn't me. I turned to retrieve the sack of leather which I could see had worked its way around the leg of a barstool and at that moment caught a flutter out of the corner of my eye. Thank God, it was Cate waving and motioning me towards a table she had miraculously found. She had dropped her hand-bag onto the spare stool beside her, claiming my spot to sit.

"Here. For you." Cate said pushing a glass of red wine across the table.

"Thanks, you're a lifesaver." I smiled, hoisting myself up onto the barstool and rubbing at the damp spot Cate's lip gloss had left on my cheek from her kiss hello.

"Have a good day?" Cate asked.

"Same old, same old and you?" I replied.

"Yeah not bad all in all. Glad it's Friday though." Cate answered, swallowing down a gulp of wine.

"Oh yeah," I answered into the bulb of the wine glass, my mouth already filling with another lot of spicy liquid.

After another two swallows of wine each, the pair of us slumped back on our barstools, sighing out loudly like two old men creaky with age. Cate looked at me and burst out laughing.

"Glamorous pair aren't we?" Cate laughed.

"Absolutely sure to pick up some fine young men fitting of our company," I laughed back.

"In here?" Cate looked at me, mock-mortified, crinkling up her nose.

"Well you never know your luck in a big city."

Cate smiled broadly, straightened her back and brought her elbows to rest on the table in front of her.

"Pete hasn't called back, so here I am again meeting you – not that there is anything wrong with that I hasten to add – on a Friday night when I could have been having red hot steaming sex somewhere," I sighed.

"What, with a guy who hasn't called you back? How exactly were you going to trap him into bed?"

"I have my ways," I laughed, sipping my wine.

"Black widow springs to mind Lau. For now though my friend, you are going to have to put up with me for a couple of hours –"

"A couple of hours? Why, where are you going?"

Cate tilted her head slightly, picking up a section of hair to twist it between her fingers.

"Cate, are you really deserting me?"

"Not right now, but I do have to be somewhere in a couple of hours."

"Where?"

"Where what?"

"Where do you have to be?" I asked staring straight at her, trying very hard not to smile.

"Somewhere –"

"Cate!"

"What?"

"Where do you have to be and 'somewhere' is not the right answer."

"OK." Cate replied, clearly enjoying the game she thought she was the master of. Slowly she picked up her drink and took a good long, exaggerated sip. Very carefully she placed the drink back down and licked her lips.

"You're a cow," I said, it now being absolutely impossible to hold my smile back.

"Am I really?" Cate answered, raising one eyebrow and twirling the stem of the wine glass.

"Yes you bloody are and you know you are."

"Hmm."

"Cate!"

"What?"

"Please let's not go down that route again. Just tell me that you have a really hot date and that's why you are leaving me."

Blotchy marks had started to rose the skin peeking out from the v-shape of Cate's shirt. She grabbed self-consciously at her top, tugging the cotton across her chest. Satisfied Cate let the fabric drop and continued to twirl the stem of her wine glass, smiling as she kept her gaze firmly on the table. I studied her child-like grin which invariably made me smile even wider. Cate was effortlessly stunning, but in an unconventional way. She had a strong jaw line and a nose which hung at a slight wonk at the bridge, but neither was enough to deter anyone's gaze from the whole package that was purely and simply Cate. Her hair was as glossy as the magazines she read and her eyes really were the windows to her soul – bright and alert. She smiled quickly and laughed easily. Her laugh sounded as though it had travelled from the ends of her toes, up through her body, collecting its strength from her organs before finally making its noisy and unmistakable entrance out of her mouth and into the atmosphere. Everything seemed much funnier when Cate was around. Everything just generally seemed better. She dished out evenly measured advice to her friends like small packets of pills which could be chewed or swallowed whole. Mostly she dragged people to her, effortlessly, unknowingly but always absolutely. She was exactly the same sitting here right now in her business suit trying to fool the Friday night drinkers that she was a serious career-minded young lady, until they saw her half un-tucked shirt, as she was sitting in the university bar downing beer and shots of tequila before announcing she was heading back to her room to write an essay which was due the next morning. Cate was purely and simply Cate, no matter what armour she chose to wear.

Cate liked to keep herself to herself sometimes and I was fine with that. We have known each other too long for me to take it personally or even to think about it anymore. So I guess that's was why when she had told me she could no longer make the movie her and I had planned to see earlier in the week, I didn't really ask any questions. But now that she was telling me she wasn't hanging around for any longer than a couple of hours, I couldn't help but feel a small paranoid surge rise up inside me. Strangely though, sitting here at the bar together the paranoia was spreading into a much deeper thinking, convinced she was hiding something from me. Cate turned the stem of her glass around and around. We had been best friends for too long for her to think it was OK not to tell me what was going on. I re-adjusted the sling back on my shoe. I had to press her. Find out what was going on. Cate looked up from the table. I shifted on the stool.

"So I guess this means you are going to cancel us going to the beach together tomorrow too does it?" I asked, trying to act cool.

"No." Cate replied, genuinely smiling.

"OK good." Nice work Laura - that made her spill the beans. I silently groaned inside my head.

Cate laughed and leant right over the table. "I'm killing you aren't I?" she whispered suggestively like I was some lover she was trying to lure. I shook my head. "Yes I am. Go on admit it."

"Alright you bloody are and you know you are. Happy?" I said, screwing up my nose for extra effect.

"Yes I am, thank you." Cate smiled dropping back into her seat and holding out her shirt to blow down her front. "Phew, I thought we would never get to second base baby." Both of us threw our heads back and laughed, not like two old men this time – more like elegant hyenas. It was what was needed to break my opponent.

"OK, I have met someone –"

"Whoohoo," that was me, too late for acting cool and pretending I didn't care.

CATE

"You're fantastic."

I looked up from the book I was reading to see a guy about my age standing in front of me. The sun was streaming through the window making it quite difficult to see. I blinked and attempted to shut one eye to block the bright light from my vision, trying to make out if the comment was directed at me. I'm not great at winking so was very conscious of my skin wrinkling and folding around my eye, the lid not closing completely over the eye. The guy continued to stand in front of me. I put my finger in the fold of the book to mark my page and cupped the other hand around the side of my face, shielding the sun off my face.

"I said you're fantastic." He was looking straight at me as he said it. I turned my head, snatching a look at the woman dressed in a business suit sitting across the aisle, she was looking at me, then at the man and then back to me again. She half smiled and shrugged her shoulders in my direction before turning back to the magazine resting in her lap and pretending whatever exchange was about to take place she had no part of. The whole bus seemed to fall silent and I could feel people watching us and probably thinking 'thank God he didn't pick me'.

"I'm sorry?" I managed to say.

"I said you're fantastic," he repeated, very sure of himself and a bit too loudly.

"Right," I replied very uneasily. OK he's crazy and lucky me he's managed to pinpoint me out of all the people on the bus to harass. The bus jolted forward as it pulled away from the stop. I looked back down at my book in a vain attempt to pretend he wasn't there thinking perhaps he would go away if I ignored him and his fishing for attention. The hem of his trouser caught my eye. It was navy blue with a freshly ironed crease dropping neatly over a highly polished black shoe. 'How crazy could this person be?' I asked myself. I tapped the edge of the book and reluctantly drew my eyes up the length of his trouser leg, navy blue all the way to the black belt, crisp white shirt, tanned neck and face. He motioned to the seat beside me.

"I said you're fantastic because you are going to be good enough to move your bag so I can sit down."

Instantly I flushed red and hot. My chest prickled.

"Oh." I replied. Startled, I grabbed at the gym bag to pull it across my lap, completely forgetting the book was in my hand until it dropped onto the floor and I watched as the page I was reading disappeared back into the hundreds of other slivers of white.

"Thanks," he casually replied, sitting himself down onto the seat before leaning forward to collect the book from the floor. "Did you have a bookmark?"

"No," I replied gingerly taking the book from his hand.

"So you don't know which page you were up to?"

"No." I couldn't look at him. I was too embarrassed and humiliated. I could feel him looking at the red blotches spreading across my neck. I prized open the gym bag and made a feeble attempt to stuff the book in the top. The zipper snagged the first few pages. The book was too thick to slide in down beside the trainers.

"Do you want a hand?"

"No thanks." I continued shoving. "Ouch." The zipper caught the skin on my finger and blood rushed quickly to the surface.

"You OK?"

"Yes." I said looking at him and letting a smile peek out from my stern exterior. I started to laugh. "Excuse me."

"Yes?" he answered sitting up straighter and inching slightly towards the edge of the seat. He seemed pretty eager this one.

"This is my stop," I replied with all the confidence I could muster which thankfully made the woman with the magazine smirk so I had managed to gain a little composure after all.

"Oh right. Sorry." He said swinging his legs around into the aisle so I could get past. Clutching the gym bag with my book spewing out between the sharp teeth of the zipper, I strode with my head held high and my shoulders back to the front of the bus and stepped off. Turning to my right onto the footpath I tried desperately not to turn around and look back. My willpower lasted all of about two seconds as the bus wove back into the traffic I let myself have one glance back into the bus where he was sitting. Whoever he was, he was smiling straight at me.

TOM

Ireef my shirt cuff back and check the time – just after 6.30. If I run I might just about make it to six-aside football. I haven't managed to get out of work anywhere near on time lately. The big deal we've been working on has sucked up all my time and energy, if we pull it off we'll be laughing. It will be one of the biggest deals the bank has ever been able to strike and I know the bonus coming my way will be well worth the fact I haven't been able to have a social life of any sort for the last few weeks. Weeks, what am I saying it's been more like months, years even. I know we are getting fairly close to pulling it off because my boss hasn't stopped whistling *You're simply the best,* which is his payday theme tune. It's around this time in a deal when the confidence literally comes whistling out of him. God I'm tired though. I could really do with going home to bed instead of football. The guys will kill me if I don't turn up again this week, they had to forfeit last week because not enough of the team turned up. But that's what you get when you think it's a good idea to make up a team mostly of professional guys who are all in banking or law. Money makes the world go round and for most of the team divorce seems to be as sure as death.

I shift my weight from one foot to the other, watching the little light indicating the lift dropping floors. The doors slide open and I am pushed further to the back of the cramped little box as more people pile in. A familiar looking guy from one of the lower floors nods 'hello' to me and then squeezes himself between two people in front of me. Two women are bitching about someone who never puts the refill bottle on the water cooler. Four, three, two, one and the lift doors open. I stand, pretending to be patient, as other people slowly file out in front of me. I let one of the water cooler bitching women out before me and now I am able to make my mad dash. I hitch my sports bag up onto one shoulder and slide my way across the highly polished floor in reception, wave my ID pass over the scanner, bolt out the double turn style doors and spill out on to the street. Fuck it's hot. I haven't been outside all day. Breakfast was a coffee at my desk at whatever time it was that I arrived this morning and lunch was a snatched sandwich on my way between meetings in the building. At least it's not dark yet.

I check my watch again. I am going to be late. I am literally sprinting now, picking my way through the rush hour crowd. I almost crash straight into a guy talking on his mobile. I hear him swearing at me as I continue my sprint. People are stepping aside and turning around to see if there's someone chasing me. The shoulder straps on my bag are welding themselves into my skin. It kills. I try and shift the weight of the straps but my sweat and shirt are keeping them right where they are. It kills. I am almost at the traffic lights now, the red man is still blinking. Bugger, I need to get across the road. I look up and down the street, there's traffic coming in both directions and a taxi is speeding up. I won't be able to make a break and cross the road before the cars get there. I will have to wait for the green man. The bloody green man. I am standing at the lights. People are filling up around me, I jostle my way to the front so I am standing on the edge of the gutter. Staring up at the red man, willing him to turn green. Come on. Come on. Finally the traffic is slowing. Stuff it I am going to go. I wedge my thumb up underneath the shoulder straps on my sports bag and race across the road. Christ those shoulder straps hurt.

I can see the bus I need to get on in front of me slowing as it prepares to pull into the bus stop. I have to get on that bus, I speed up. Now my legs are killing me. How am I going to play football tonight when I can't run any further. I need to sit down. I reach the bus. A few people are standing in front of me so I wait my turn and that's a good thing because it gives me a chance to catch my breath. I step onto the bus and dig my pass out of my pocket, thread it into the machine and start scanning the rows for a possible seat. There's one near the back. I weigh up the competition, a girl in a school uniform who was in front of me in the queue has spotted it too. Stuff her, I am older and I am absolutely knackered. I am going to get that seat. I edge past her. My sports bag hits someone in the head. 'Sorry'. I get to the seat and there's a bag sitting on it. That's rude. The bus is packed and someone thinks it's fine to give their bag a seat. I look across the seat to the owner. She's clearly oblivious and is reading a book. "Excuse me". No answer. She continues to read. "Excuse me". I catch the eye of a woman sitting across the aisle, she's rolling her eyes at the girl with the bag on the seat. "Excuse me," I repeat for the third time. Still no answer. Is this chick deaf or something? I try a different tact, clear my throat and say fairly loudly and very confidently, "I think you're fantastic." Blue eyes snap up from the book and lock straight into my eyes.

It's two days later, I find myself in a book shop staring at a rack of bookmarks. I have picked a few up and turned them over in my hands, but haven't really been impressed by any of the selection so have quickly placed each of them back in the holder. Most of them have fluffy animals, mainly cats and dogs, with quotes printed across the front. I don't really know what I am looking for but have already decided it's not the fluffy animal type of bookmark. None of them feel right. I am buying a bookmark for someone I don't even know. Someone I have seen on a bus once and whom I had a very brief, some might even say rude, exchange with. There's no guarantees I am even going to see this person again, but for some reason it feels completely right to be buying them a bookmark. I pick up a fifth bookmark, this one is purple leather with a quote in simple black writing across the bottom, 'Dance like nobody is watching.' It makes me smile. I hang onto this one, give the rest of the rack one last glance, and then walk with purpose to the counter. The cashier hands a bag to the customer in front of me and then turns her attention to me. '$3.95' the cashier says taking the purple strip and slipping it into a paper bag. I stuff the receipt into my trouser pocket and carefully fold the paper around the bookmark so the strip of leather fits neatly inside, tuck the package into my breast pocket and hold my hand there for a second to check it's not going to fall out before pushing the door open to fold myself into the throng of sweaty shoppers swarming up and down the street.

CATE

Excited anticipation has been bubbling up into my throat. My heart has been thumping that little bit extra each time I step up onto the bus and take my seat, pretending to be like every other commuter on their way home from work. But really I am half-heartedly reading a book with one eye on the door each time the bus pulls into a stop willing today to be the day he is going to get on the bus. I thought I saw him yesterday when a sharp suit strode confidently down the isle, his face was obscured by another suit in front of him. As they got closer I could feel my face growing red and the familiar prickle of skin rushing its way across my chest. I gripped the book, bit my lip and willed it to be him even though I didn't really have a clue what I would do if it was. Would he even recognise me? What if he has a girlfriend? These thoughts were getting ridiculous. So was the spontaneous daydreaming where I found his face swimming around my mind. The guy in front pealed off, taking a seat a couple of rows further down the bus which left me staring expectedly at a face I had never seen before. Instantly disappointment popped the bubbles of anticipation one by one. I slumped lower into the seat and silently cursed myself for these uncontrollable ridiculous thoughts along with the growing anticipation and excitement I was getting from the opening of a bus door. It was unlike me to be so irrational, thinking one tiny scene in a lifetime of strung-together scenes was going to be some sort of turning point in my life which, when I looked back, would lead me to think it made me, me.

Now though, I was looking for someone else. I was sitting in a cafe waiting for Isobel and Laura. I had managed to get a table by the window and as the late afternoon sun cast long shadows in shards across the table I watched the door, eagerly willing each swing of the wood to announce the arrival of my two friends who were both always notoriously late. I should learn, I told myself, never to be punctual as I am always left waiting by myself for those two, pretending to be busy and preoccupied with something or other, but really just waiting. Today I had forgotten to bring a book so found myself rustling through the compartments in my bag to find something to entertain me while I waited. All that greeted me were layers of receipts, empty chewing gum packets, a pen which had leaked all through the lining of the bag turning it a garish purple, my purse, keys and a few bits of long-forgotten eye shadow which I had now unwittingly stuck my finger inside and felt the powder gritting under my fingernail. I hunted around for a tissue but of course couldn't find one so was left to wipe the offending glittery powder off with an old receipt. The paper caught at my skin so I screwed it up and threw it back inside the bag. I looked at the other customers who were all sipping on coffees or herbal teas. Many had ordered cakes and I watched as two women my age shared a massive wedge of chocolate cake. Between snippets of hushed conversation, each of them studied each other carefully to assess when it was polite for one of them to casually pick up the fork resting on their side of the plate and stab at the sponge which lay like a dead carcass between them. My eye caught the outline of a figure hunched over one of the tables towards the back of the room. Their back was facing me. Mostly I could see a hand with twisted knuckles, reminding me of knots in an old tree trunk, reaching out every now and again raising the teacup to their lips and placing the cup back down onto the saucer in very considered movements. I shifted slightly in my seat to get a better view and saw the person was alone. There was something about that figure, an old lady, yes I could see it was a female, just sitting there alone like that having a cup of tea with seemingly nothing but the busy doors of the cafe's kitchen swinging open and closed with each order. Seeing people on their own, especially old people eating on their own has always upset me.

I shifted back in my seat and turned to look out the window trying to shake the image of the lonely lady out of my head. Maybe she was waiting for someone, I tried to tell myself but the frail hand wrapping around the teacup kept coming back.

I hated being alone, I always have. As a kid I had thought being alone indicated independence, so I would insist on walking home from school in the rain instead of being collected by Mum. I'd even refuse offers of lifts home by other mothers who had come to collect their sodden children standing under a mass of upraised parka hoods at the school gate. I'd pull my own hood up over my ears, hunch my shoulders and squint my eyes ready to set off determinedly in the wet, arriving home to find Mum rolling her eyes while she handed me a towel, telling me I would catch a cold and be in bed for a week. Apparently then I would 'know all about it'. I never have known what exactly 'all about it' actually meant, 'it' in particular confused me and in my own funny way made me all the more determined to stomp through the puddles alone just to see if I could always outwit and beat the dreaded 'it'. But really I never wanted to be by myself and by myself in the rain was even worse. I just wanted to prove I was independent.

Just then the cafe door swung open and through it burst Laura, clutches of shopping bags straining at her fingers and wrists. She caught sight of me waving and weaved her way between the tables.

"God," Laura sighed dragging the chair opposite me out from under the table to slump her weight down into it. I watched as her shopping bags fell to the floor like weary soldiers surrendering in the face of defeat. It made me smile as I thought of the chocolate cake now devoured by the two women sitting near me. Laura poked the bags swiftly with the point of her stiletto ramming each further under the table and out of her way and mostly into my way. Lightly I edged the bags sideways with my foot.

"Sorry, I know I am late – again," she was saying now. "It's been one of *those* days," rolling her eyes and making sure she placed extra dramatic emphasis on the word *those*.

Suddenly she was stretching across the table to kiss my cheek. "How are you?" she asked, her face only a centimetre away from my face.

"Good thanks. And you...apart from being late again?" I smiled.

"Yeah, great. Just exhausted from all this shopping, it really takes it out of me you know babe?" Both of us laughed. "What are you drinking?" Laura asked, lurching backwards into her chair and picking up the menu.

"Oh nothing yet I was going to wait for you and Isobel before I ordered anything, which means I could have ended up totally parched," I smiled cheekily at Laura. "Where's Isobel anyway?"

"Oh she's not coming. She did call me though. I was in a change room trying on bras, so basically naked, when she called. Just as I went to answer the phone I noticed a sign saying 'CCTV cameras in operation in this store' and suddenly I thought of two fat disgusting security guards sitting in a room somewhere monitoring – more like, well you know what I mean – and leering into the ladies change rooms. So I really wasn't taking in what Isobel was saying I just wanted to get out of there you know? So I cut Isobel off pretty quickly and of course I stuck two fingers up at the sign before exiting the change room. Filthy bastards."

"So there was a camera in there?" I asked completely accustomed to keeping up with Laura's disjointed story-telling methods.

"God I don't know. But it's the bloody principle of the thing isn't it? I mean surely that's illegal. Invasion of privacy or something I am sure. Perverts. Filthy bastards," exclaimed Laura very loudly and perfectly timed with the waitress stopping at our table asking us what we would like to order.

"A wine," Laura said, looking at me with raised eyebrows.

"I'm sorry, we are not a licensed premises. We do have herbal tea though." Both of us tried unsuccessfully to stifle a laugh.

"Maybe, give us a minute then," Laura said turning to me, "Should we have something a little stronger?"

"Like a wine you mean?"

"Yeah or..." Laura paused, "Or maybe something even stronger like a whiskey, I don't mind though it is still the afternoon after all. But that means we will have to go somewhere else."

"Sure why not. Except what are you going to do with all that?" I said looking down at the bags of shopping now lying dead at Laura's feet.

"Oh we won't be out forever. It's only the afternoon isn't it? I can just take them with us, we'll have a civilised wine and then go home. How does that sound?"

"Yes, I say yes to that!" I said diving under the table to retrieve a handful of shopping bags. It was only a matter of seconds until we were out the door and walking down the street when suddenly I remembered the lady sitting by herself inside the cafe. "Wait a sec," I told Laura as I turned and walked quickly back up the street. I stopped at the cafe window and peered inside. Many of the people had emptied out or were collecting their things to leave. I could see the waitress who had served us, she was clearing one of the tables towards the back of the cafe. I could see another one of the waitresses sitting sideways on a chair at one of the tables, her legs were outstretched towards the middle of the room and she was laughing. My eyes traced across the table to her companion and I could see it was the lone woman. She was laughing too and patting the waitress' hand. Relief swept over me. I turned on my heel and made my way back towards my friend who was standing waiting for me further down the street. When I reached her, Laura looked expectedly at me.

"I thought I left something behind," I said, "I didn't though."

"Oh good. The Albert?" Laura asked, shifting the bag straps up over her shoulder.

"The Albert," I confirmed, linking my arm through hers and setting a determined pace.

About two hours later both of us were sipping on our third wine, forgetting it was going to be a couple of drinks at the most as the sun slowly dipped lower in the sky. Now the sun had all but gone. Low dimmed mood lighting had been switched on along the bar, drawing long shadows over the faces of people ordering drinks. The Albert was beginning to fill up with the city's bright young things out for the evening. Heels became higher and shirts were tucked in. Laura and I were sitting in a favourite spot towards the back of the main bar where the bar stools changed into old leather-worn couches. An empty peanut packet lay discarded on the table in front of us, both of us stretched back into our lounge chairs. I was twirling the stem of the wine glass between my fingers.

"Should we call Iss and ask her to come and meet us?" I asked Laura, looking up from the glass.

"Yeah sure. You calling her or am I?"

"I can," I replied, reaching into my bag to hunt around for the mobile. Pulling the phone out, I selected Isobel's number and hit the 'call' button. The phone rang out for quite a long time, I was just getting prepared to leave a message when Isobel picked up.

"Hi there!" Isobel yelled into the receiver. In the background glasses were clinking and people were talking, chattering and laughing all around her. I pressed my finger into my ear. "I'm still out with Laura and we wanted to see if you would like to come and join us, but it sounds like you might already be out."

"Oh I am, but I can come and meet you. Where are you?" Isobel screamed back down the phone.

"The Albert."

"Where?"

"The Albert," I repeated, slowly like I was talking to a small child.

"No I know that, but where in The Albert? I'm in here too – at the tables up the front by the windows. But don't come to me..." Isobel was whispering now. "I am on a date and it's not going so well, he's just gone to the bar, so when he comes back I will finish my drink, make my excuses and come to meet you."

"OK babe. But we can't stay in here though if your date is in here too."

Laura had leaned forward, trying to press her ear into the phone to listen, but was laughing, watching me talk to Isobel.

"Tell her you can all come back to mine. We can get a pizza," Laura whispered in my ear. I nodded.

"We can go to Laura's Iss. Come and meet us there, we're going to go now. But we'll go out the back so your date doesn't see us OK?"

"Perfect. See you soon. Shit gotta go," Isobel hissed into the phone and promptly hung up.

Less than an hour later Isobel and I sat on Laura's couch, both of us clutching the wine glasses which Laura had slopped generous glugs of pinot into before heading into the kitchen in search of the pizza delivery menu.

"So, are you going to tell me who this date was this evening?" I asked Isobel casually before taking a very long sip of wine. The trick with Isobel was to pretend you didn't really care if she answered your question and then just wait silently until she decided to unfold slowly. I started to wonder just how many tricks Laura and I shared silently between us to unlock Isobel and her secrets. We always seemed to be managing her like a delicate egg – nurturing and protecting the thin membrane she occasionally limply threaded around us. There were times when Isobel would disappear for a few days, it would be impossible to get hold of her. She wouldn't return calls, the receptionist at her work would say she was in a meeting, even though you got the distinct feeling she wasn't, and if you dropped by her flat no one came to the door. Of course Laura and I had talked about this from time to time – probably more to make sure Isobel was also ignoring the other one to confirm it was nothing personal or something one of us had unwittingly done to upset her in some way – but usually we ended up putting it down to 'just what Isobel is like'. Neither of us ever really took any offence and that is probably why our friendship with Isobel never really waned – we tended not to ask questions and she tended not to offer any answers. It would be quite nice to be like that. The one people pussy-footed around instead of the 'pacemaker', the one who always works out the solutions and rearranges plans so they fit into other people's.

I watched now as Isobel tucked her leg beneath her, starting to twist her lip. I fiddled with the base of my glass. In the kitchen Laura was pulling drawers open and slamming them closed, obviously the pizza menu was continuing to allude her.

"It's no one special, you know how crap I am with guys Cate," Isobel finally said. The sound of her voice barely sliced above the kitchen noise so I only really caught some of the words she said. I looked at her, turning the disjointed words around in my head until I was able to string them together into something that made sense.

"No you're not, you just won't settle for second best that's all. There's definitely nothing wrong with that," I replied confidently, hoping my response would fit.

"True, but I do think giving a guy literally two drinks – and believe me they were fast drinks – to prove himself is a bit harsh, even by my standards."

I smiled. "Well maybe he was really boring and two drinks was being generous. You've done your bit for charity tonight so don't worry about it." Isobel looked up at me and smiled.

"He *was* boring." She nodded.

"Who's boring?" Laura came back into the room holding a well thumbed pizza delivery menu.

"It was on top of the fridge wasn't it?" I said pointing at the paper in Laura's hand. "Yeah," Laura replied, looking puzzled. I rolled my eyes. "Anyway who's boring?" Laura asked again.

"Iss' date tonight," I replied not catching myself in time to realise Isobel could easily stitch herself back up and that would be the end of the conversation. But to my surprise

Isobel continued where I had left off, seemingly relishing the attention as she twisted a few strands of blonde hair around her finger and become animated about the size of the poor guy's eyebrows – like two hedges apparently. The three of us cackled like witches around a cauldron and I couldn't help but feel sorry for the guy. He was probably completely taken with Isobel, they all are. It's that mass of blonde hair and those big almond-shaped eyes that soon draw them in. The way Isobel looks seems so stereotypical of a heroine in a fairy tale, but it's true, guys are always taken with her and women stare at her. Despite all that, there's also something very timid and frail about her. When I first met her she reminded me of a little sparrow. She sat delicately on the edge of chairs and her words were constantly measured and considered. But when she becomes angry about something or someone, I've seen how her posture and almost her whole form take on a new shape, it's sharp with edges you don't want to get snagged on. Laura and I had branded these moments 'Iss Fizz' and although we both agreed it was purely an affectionate nickname for our friend, neither of us had ever told Isobel that we called her that. In fact Laura and I had never even discussed telling her or not telling her, it was more like an unspoken rule that we never mention the nickname to Isobel, along with the tricks we had learnt to get our friend to open up.

"I think I need to go," I said slowly.

"Where?" Laura asked.

"Home. I am slightly pissed and I really want to go for a run in the morning."

"Run-schmum. It's only early and it's the weekend and we haven't even ordered the pizza yet."

I was rubbing my eye. My contact lens had been slipping around inside it for the last few minutes and it was really starting to bother me. My lips were feeling dry and cracked.

I could see a reflection of myself in the window glass and decided it wasn't really very pretty. My lips were definitely stained red from the wine and I am sure my teeth were striving to be the same colour. I was definitely going home.

"No really Lau, I am going to head off. I can't drink anymore and I do want to get up early and do some exercise, I feel like I haven't done any for ages. Plus I am pretty sure I am looking pretty revolting."

"Who cares how you look?"

"I do. Seriously I am going to go, are you coming?" I said looking at Isobel and standing up.

"I'm pretty hungry and I probably haven't has as much to drink as you two..."

"Good," that was Laura. "Sit down Cate. Come on let's just have a girly night."

"Oh God, alright," I replied. "I'm going to go to the loo though. I am allowed to do that aren't I?"

"Yes!" Laura and Isobel replied at the same time.

I shut the bathroom door behind me and turned on the taps to splash cool water on my face. That felt much better so I just let my hands and wrists hang in the running water for a bit. I looked up and stared at my face in the mirror. I looked every bit as dishevelled as I thought. Drying my hands on a towel hanging next to the basin, I noticed red wine splashes across my jeans and tried to rub at the stains with the towel, but the wine was dry. I smoothed my hair down and rifled through Laura's cabinet for some moisturiser. I found an expensive brand and slapped it on my face and headed back in the lounge room. Laura was on the phone, ordering the pizza. Isobel looked up and smiled when she saw me come back into the room. "Better?" she asked. "Better," I replied sitting down next to her and reaching for my wine glass. Laura hung the phone up. "All ordered," she said settling down into one of the arm chairs. "Oh you look so much better babe," Laura laughed looking at me. "Oh fuck off," was my reply. "Charming," Laura laughed again.

"Right well I have been interrogated about my love life, so it's time you both divulged yours," Isobel announced, refilling her wine glass and offering the bottle to me and Laura.

"Null and void I'm afraid," Laura said taking the bottle from Isobel. I looked at the floor.

"And you my love?" Isobel nudged me with her elbow. I continued to stare at the floor. "I'll take that as a 'yes' then I think. Come on you're among friends here Cate."

"Well it's kind of stupid..." I started. Both Isobel and Laura leant forward. "No really, it's dumb..." I tried again. "I kind of feel stupid even saying this."

"Cate, you're killing me. Tell us!" Laura whined.

"It's nothing. Seriously it's absolutely nothing..." "Is it someone from work? Oh God you're not having an affair with your boss are you? Cate!" cried Isobel. "Or that guy in IT who we met at the pub that time? Oh no Cate." Laura chimed in.

"No!" I yelled at Laura, mortified she could even think I would like creepy Alan.

"Well who then?" Laura demanded.

"I don't know..."

"Yes you do!" they both cried at the same time.

"OK well I do know, but I honestly don't know his name, or actually anything about him." I took a long sip of wine and grimaced, why was I still drinking I asked myself. "He's some guy who was on the bus that's all," I finished and took another sip of wine.

"Oh," Laura and Isobel replied in unison again.

"Well you asked and I am telling you the truth and now you're disappointed."

"Has he spoken to you?" Isobel asked.

"Kind of..." "What did he say?" Laura asked, clearly regaining her eagerness.

"Oh God, this is really embarrassing..."

"Tell us," the pair of them shouted.

I stared at them both. "Are you two sharing the same brain today? How come you keep saying the same thing at the same time? It's starting to freak me out."

"Come on, don't change the subject, we want to know what bus boy said to you," Isobel smiled rolling the glass around in her hand.

"You're going to be disappointed again – and it's really embarrassing."

"Doesn't matter," Isobel said.

"He asked me to move my bag." There was silence and then both of them starting laughing. "I told you!" I yelled above their hoots of laughter.

"Is that it?" Laura asked. "Pretty much..." I replied. And they were both off again, laughing. I couldn't help myself and started to laugh too. "He's good looking," I protested above the racket. But it was too late, the pair of them were in hysterics all over again. Isobel patted my thigh. "Bless you," she said through ripples of giggles.

Laura winked at me and started to laugh again. I rolled my eyes at them both. "Where's that wine bottle?" I asked.

"Empty," Isobel answered.

The doorbell rang and Laura was up answering the door and looking for change to pay the pizza delivery guy. Isobel went into the kitchen in search of more wine. I leant back into the couch and allowed my mind to steal a glimpse of the guy from the bus. I smiled and waited for both my friends to come back into the lounge room with the pizza and the wine.

LAURA

The room was heavy with cigarette smoke and loud with office workers expelling the stress of the week into their glasses. I arched my heels up to stand on the tips of my toes, giving myself a better position to scan the sea of faces for Cate. A guy with his tie half knotted lurched towards me with a full glass of beer, spilling a finger's worth of froth down the front of my shirt. "Sorry love. Long lunch," he stammered reaching out to brush the milky froth from my breast. "Do you mind?" I said angrily, picking his wrist away from my breast and placing my elbow neatly into the pit of his stomach as I nudged my way past to dive deeper into the throng of drinkers. Now I was barely able to move and could feel my shoes sticking to the floorboards while my handbag wrapped around something that wasn't me. I turned to retrieve the sack of leather which I could see had worked its way around the leg of a barstool and at that moment caught a flutter out of the corner of my eye. Thank God, it was Cate waving and motioning me towards a table she had miraculously found. She had dropped her hand-bag onto the spare stool beside her, claiming my spot to sit.

"Here. For you." Cate said pushing a glass of red wine across the table.

"Thanks, you're a lifesaver." I smiled, hoisting myself up onto the barstool and rubbing at the damp spot Cate's lip gloss had left on my cheek from her kiss hello.

"Have a good day?" Cate asked.

"Same old, same old and you?" I replied.

"Yeah not bad all in all. Glad it's Friday though." Cate answered, swallowing down a gulp of wine.

"Oh yeah," I replied into the bulb of the wineglass, my mouth already filling with another lot of spicy liquid.

After another two swallows of wine, the pair of us slumped back on our barstools, sighing out loudly like two old men creaky with age. Cate looked at me and burst out laughing.

"Glamorous pair aren't we?" Cate laughed.

"Absolutely sure to pick up some fine young men fitting of our company," I laughed back.

"In here?" Cate looked at me, mock-mortified, crinkling up her nose.

"Well you never know your luck in a big city."

Cate smiled broadly, straightened her back and brought her elbows to rest on the table in front of her.

"Pete hasn't called back, so here I am again meeting you – not that there is anything wrong with that I hasten to add – on a Friday night when I could have been having red hot steaming sex somewhere," I sighed.

"What, with a guy who hasn't called you back? How exactly were you going to trap him into bed?"

"I have my ways," I laughed, sipping my wine.

"Black widow springs to mind Lau. For now though my friend, you are going to have to put up with me."

"The perfect date I would say," I smiled at Cate.

After university, the first jobs Cate and I had got were only a couple of skyscrapers apart, so it was easy to meet up after work for a drink. If one of us was having a bad day in the office, we'd ring the other, both make our excuses and dart down the lifts and into the street, the pair of us passing a cigarette backwards and forwards while one of us re-told the story which had just taken place. The other agreed profusely that the whole thing sounded completely unjust and whoever was at the butt of the problem needed to 'get a life'. Whichever one of us was holding the final centimetre of rolled paper, sucked back the very last shell of tobacco, threw the cigarette down and stamped on it with a high heel. The one having the better day would tell the other 'don't let the bastards get you down,' we'd laugh and then sprint off in opposite directions, limping under the pain of ill-fitting high heels. I loved that we could do that because in some ways it was still like being at university and even though we now dressed in uncomfortable clothes and earned marginally more money, I wasn't ready to be a grown-up. Frankly it scared me. Being at the bottom of the heap at work had also scared me. Endless photocopying and being asked to make the tea for meetings proved three years at university and a marketing degree was only really a ticket to walk through the firm's doors every day and that was it. I was fast learning doing marketing in a law firm was exactly what I thought it would be – boring. Cate and I had laughed at the creativity I had applied to answer questions in a very stressful interview situation, forcing myself to look straight into the eyes of three very stiff suits sitting across the boardroom table from me. During the interview I was so intent on impressing them that I'd lost focus of that fact I would actually have to work at this place if they gave me the job. Cate had started her job in a PR company two weeks before I went for the interview. It was a corporate PR company and we had laughed about her having a job so serious she needed to tuck her shirt in properly all the way around her waist. My shirt was firmly tucked in now too, so firmly I sometimes had trouble breathing and often found myself scratching furiously at the waistband of my skirt grabbing the cotton fabric in bunches away from my skin.

"You alright Lau?" Cate asked, placing her wine glass back on the table.

"I need a new job," I replied drearily twirling the stem of my own glass around, making the wine slosh dangerously close to the top of the glass.

"Well what's stopping you? You know you aren't cut out for marketing a bunch of lawyers, why don't you do something more creative. Go work for an agency with cool brands and people who wear trainers to work and all look about twelve years old."

I spun the glass more quickly.

"See how creative you are?" Cate laughed grabbing hold of the glass right after a small puddle of red liquid splashed onto my hand. "Seriously though, I think if you are unhappy you should just look for something else. You tried it, you didn't like it and that's that."

"That's that?"

"Yes, why not?"

"What about you then?" I asked, licking the wine from my finger.

"Leave my job do you mean?" Cate looked at me startled.

"Yes!" I replied. "You don't like yours either do you?"

"I don't love it but I think I should stick it out a bit longer. Get some more experience and then maybe I will look for something else."

"But you're telling me to change jobs and I have been at mine for less time than you have been at yours," I said, stamping the wine glass down.

"True Lau, but you know we're different. I am much more risk averse than you. You will be able to wow another company despite what experience you have. I just...I just wouldn't have the confidence to do that. I would have to back it up with experience to prove I could do it," Cate finished, sounding more sure of her decision the more she spoke.

"What, and do an Issy?" I smiled, raising my eyebrows. Cate raised her eyebrows too and started to laugh.

Isobel had managed to wrangle a job with one of the top advertising agencies in the city, despite having no experience apart from the required number of hours working as an intern all of us had to do as part of our undergraduate courses. Beautiful people are more likely to get what they want, Cate and I had both learnt that in our one and only semester of psychology.

"Why not?" Cate said defiantly.

I took a long slip of my wine, draining the glass. "You're right you know?" I said standing up and reaching for my handbag, "I can do it and I will. I am going to quit that bloody crappy, stuffy job and make a new life as a crazy creative who gets to work in an office with a basketball court in the middle of it..."

"A basketball court?" Cate looked puzzled.

"Well hasn't Isobel's office got a swimming pool in the centre?"

"Think you might find it's a fish tank."

"Hmm, well it's a bloody big fish tank. You sure it's not a lap pool? Anyway do you want another drink?" Cate nodded.

"Same again?" I asked sliding off the bar stool, reaching for my bag as Cate continued to nod enthusiastically.

ISOBEL

Warm, stale breath falling in long streams across my shoulder gently shakes me awake. Slowly I open my eyes and see a rush of blonde hair. It wasn't my hair, it was too short. Sweat dribbled down between my breasts, it felt hot and itchy on my skin. I rolled over, dragging the sheet with me to wipe the sweat. It was so hot in this room. I propped myself up onto one elbow, fanning at my body with the sheet and reached across to edge the window further open. The wood stuck and strained against my hand. Quietly, I inched closer to the window, propelling my body up and grabbing the window frame with both hands to yank it up, rattling the glass and shaking the wood. Horrified at the noise, I looked down to the person sleeping soundly beside me. He stirred slightly, shoving a hand under the pillow. A slight breeze fell through the window and blew strands of his hair in whirling shapes around the top of his head. I stared at him until I was sure he wasn't going to stir again and then balancing my knees on the pillow I looked out across the street to where the beach met the lower edges of the cliff faces. The rocks stood glistening and defiant against the constant smothering of water crashing over them. Their smooth surface made for perfect sunbaking when the tide was out. It was easy to slide into the water like a seal when you got too hot or for surfers to launch into the water to paddle out to the waves. A few surfers were already sitting on boards a long way out from where the first surge of water, which would eventually turn into a white, foamy mess, began. The water was fairly flat and there didn't seem to be many waves this morning. A car drove by and I was suddenly conscious of my naked body propped in the window frame. I flopped back on the bed, my arms stretching out behind me, dropping wearily off the edge of the mattress. I sighed and bit my lip – what the fuck had I gotten myself into now. Again. I rubbed at my face and clamped my eyes shut tight. Carefully I rolled to one side and swung my legs over the side of the bed, looking over my shoulder to ensure my companion was still asleep before padding silently to scoop up my knickers which lay crumpled like a small meringue on the floorboards. Slinking the fabric up onto my hips, I trod gingerly across the hard wooden floor hunting for the rest of my clothes. My companion slept on. Two finger-printed wine glasses sat on the dresser, the stain of my lipstick laced one of the rims. I felt slightly ill and my head was thumping. Where the hell was my bra.

"What are you doing?" His voice made me jump.

"I've got to go," I mumbled, not daring to look at him.

"No you don't. Come on, come here. Come back to bed."

"No I can't, sorry," I replied still searching the room for my clothes.

"Yes you can. It's Saturday you don't have to go to work, Saturdays are for sleeping in," he persisted. I couldn't be bothered answering, I just wanted to find my clothes and get out of there. As far as I was concerned last night was last night and was over and just because I wanted something, or rather someone, last night did not usually translate into the same wanting in the morning. This was now the morning.

Finally, there it was. My bra hooked over the door knob, a dangling reminder of the night before that I clearly no longer wanted otherwise I would still be in bed or at least

answering this idiot back. He was still talking or really pleading for me to come back to bed, but I was shutting that out
and was only interested in clipping my bra back on so I could
shove my top on and leave. Just as I snatched the bra off the
handle, two arms criss-crossed around my waist, dragging me
backwards. My heels slid so quickly across the floorboards it
caused a strip of goosebumps up through my legs. Both of
us landed with a thud on the bed, a tangle of sweaty arms
and legs with me struggling to stand up again. "Let go," I
shouted. His grip tightened and became more forceful, an
ankle wrapping around my own in a knot. "Don't...get off
me..." I tried spitting the words out between gasps of air.

"Babe, come on. Stay in bed..."

"NO!" I screamed, my voice bouncing off the walls and
splintering back down onto our limbs. The shock in my voice
startled us both, our bodies momentarily lay still. His grip
loosened enough for me to shove my elbow into the hollow
of his chest and lever myself up in a crowbar-like manoeuvre.
I stood in front of him, we stared at each other.

"I was only mucking around Isobel. Jesus..."

"Fuck off," I yelled back, trying to swallow back tears and
hastily hooking my bra around my rib cage.

"What the hell just happened there? Jesus Christ, you're
crazy," he looked up at me from a crumple of bed sheets.

I closed the front door to the sound of the shower running.
The sunlight hurt my eyes. Shielding my face with my palm, I
looked up, there was barely a cloud in the sky. I waited for a
car to pass before crossing the road to stand on the edge of
the cliff top to gaze out to sea at the surfers. There were more
there now, just bobbing up and down in the water like seals
sunbaking on strips of rock. There was something quite peaceful about standing here, looking at the water. I wanted to stay
here forever, well at least until I had managed to calm down.

My breathing had returned to a more normal rate, along with my heart which was now rising and swelling in my chest like it should.

I blinked hard thinking of the look which had swept over his face. It was the same expression as most of the guys I had been out with, bewilderment veneered in fear, looking at me like I am some sort of crazy woman and frantically searching my face for a sign that I am actually joking. I'm not joking though, I never am. Even as my voice is ripping through the air and I am clearly so angry I could turn violent any second, I can't control myself. I am watching this person – me – growing more and more manic until I am too weak to suppress her, to buckle her down and make her shut up.

I turn and look back at the house. He is obviously very wealthy. The house sits grandly hugging the rocky cliff-face. Walls of windows stretch along the front and wrap around the sides, giving three-hundred-and-sixty-degree views of the beach. The place is whitewashed crackling under the harsh sun. I think I see movement at one of the windows and suddenly remember that I shouldn't be here, standing across the other side of the street staring back into the house where I have just terrified the poor guy who lives in there. He's probably on the phone to his mates calling me a 'bunny boiler' or worse calling the police because he thinks I am mad. I will probably never bump into him again anyway and I certainly don't plan to call him. My mind wanders to the scrunched up bit of paper with his number scribbled onto it discarded somewhere in my handbag. Looking down at the clothes I had on yesterday makes me feel even worse. I really need to get out of here.

I drop my head and start to walk quickly along the footpath back towards the direction of the city. In the distance I can see a taxi rounding the corner. The sun is too bright to be able to tell if the light is on or off. I slow my pace as it comes closer and at the last instant I can see the taxi is available. Waving my arm and stepping out onto the road, it has to swerve to miss me. Jumping onto the back seat, the driver peers at me through the rear view mirror. "You alright love, I nearly hit you."

"Yeah I am fine," I lie.

As I unlock the front door I can hear the phone ringing. I hesitate for a moment deciding whether or not I want to answer it. At the last second I decide I feel like company and run down the hallway to pick it up. It's Cate.

"Where have you been you dirty stop out?" her voice crackled serenely down the line.

"Huh...oh I've been out," I replied, now thinking I wished I hadn't picked up the phone.

"I know. I dropped around this morning on my way home from a run and Heidi said she hadn't seen you and thought you didn't come home last night."

I frowned and looked around the doorway into the lounge room to see if there were any signs of my flatmate being home. The house was silent, Heidi must be out now. A flicker of anger crossed through me. Bloody Heidi needed to get her own life and stop meddling in mine.

"Anyway," Cate was still talking, "Laura called and she finally heard she got that job so we thought we might go for a drink later this afternoon to celebrate, so I'm ringing to see if you want to come too."

"What job?" I asked, completely confused.

"THE job Iss. The one she has had the world's longest interview process for, the marketing agency one, at umm, God what's the name of the company again, I keep forgetting..."

"Oh right, that's great," I replied pretending to be excited for her, but the truth was I was scratching my brain trying to remember any conversations around Laura changing jobs.

"Buzz," Cate said.

"What?"

"That's the name of the agency Laura got the job with. Buzz. I knew it was something to do with bees."

Just before six, I was pulling on a pair of jeans and deciding which top to wear to the pub to meet Cate and Laura. The phone had rung a few times that day and I knew it was more than likely going to be the guy from last night, so I hadn't bothered answering it. I vaguely remembered giving him my number, weirdly the correct number, somewhere between the pub and his house before I even took his on that crumpled bit of paper still sitting in the bottom of my handbag. I also remember thinking whether I should change the last digit as I recited the number to him, but at the very last moment said 'seven' which is of course correct. The phone was ringing again now and I could hear Heidi scampering across the floor to answer it. The person at the other end had hung up by the time she reached it, so this only confirmed my suspicion it was him. "Who are you avoiding now?" Heidi asked, slinging herself onto my bed. I looked at her over my shoulder from the cupboard.

"No one." I casually replied, pulling a hanger out of the cupboard to hold a black slinky tank top up against me.

"Yeah that looks good," Heidi said nodding at the top. I pulled it up over my head and let the material drop down, smoothing the fabric and looking in the mirror to see Heidi staring at me.

"What?" I asked her, not turning around.

"Just wondering which poor blighter is going to fall terribly in love with you this evening, only for you to break his heart..."

"Oh fuck off," I said, surprising myself at how harshly the words seemed to drop from my mouth and the look on Heidi's face confirmed my tone had hurt her. "Sorry. I didn't mean for it to sound like that. I am just tired, not enough sleep because I was busy conquering all mankind last night." I laughed, trying to lighten the mood, but inside I was feeling queasy and empty. An image from last night entered my head and wedged itself there waiting for my attention. It was the guy, Dave I think that's his name, snatching looks at me from the other side of the bar. I knew he was looking at me, but carried on pretending to ignore him, immersing myself in a conversation with my colleagues and letting my hair fall so it half masked my face, knowing full well the effect this tiny action had on men. It was pathetic. I was pathetic. Sure enough he got the courage to make his way over to where our group was standing. I pretended not to notice him edging his way around to be closer to where I was standing until it was almost impossible not to notice. One by one, the girls I work with dropped out of the conversation and started to stare until it was just me still talking – to no one it would seem. Finally I had no choice but to look up and straight into his eyes which were the colour of black velvet, the kind you could only find on a well-made dinner suit from the 1960s. "Hi," Rebecca, one of the junior account managers said confidently, pulling her shoulders back to stand taller. This made me smirk and stirred my competitive streak to wake and sit bolt upright. I lowered my face to just the right angle so my eyes would have to look up and into his. But I needn't have bothered he was already mine, hook, line and sinker. He moved closer to me, almost standing on Rebecca in the process – who to give her her due was standing her ground – but was now at risk of toppling over if she didn't give him some space. The look on his face showed all his cards and I got an instant flash forward of what would happen later that night. It seems I wrote the script yet again. I let him buy me a drink and then another, both of us continuing to make polite conversation with my colleagues. Slowly they started to peel off until it was just the two of us and many drinks later and then the inevitable, 'your place or mine.' I shuddered.

"OK I'm off. Have a good night," I said to Heidi, leaving her still sitting on my bed as I closed the front door carefully behind me. No men, friends only tonight, I promised myself as I walked down the street towards the bus stop.

TOM

"It's pretty much heaving in here too mate," Robert, one of my work colleagues yelled across the bar at me. It was Friday night and pay day – a beautiful combination. It's a shame everyone else in the city was experiencing the same combination. The bar we usually went to a couple of doors down from the office was too crammed to even get into. Even at 5 o'clock – we'd given ourselves an early mark – people were spilling out onto the street with glasses of beer and wine. Four of us from my department had stood like schoolboys on the sideline waiting to get the 'subs' call from the coach telling us we could replace one of our team mates and charge onto the field. Our ties were already released and we danced from foot to foot, looking anxiously, watching for signs that people were actually leaving until finally someone – I think it was Robert – made the call that we should find somewhere else to go.

"Yeah alright," I answered, shoving my wallet further down into the back pocket of my suit trousers. One by one, we turned and headed off down the street. "Does anyone know where we're going?" I asked.

"A pub. Any pub. Give me a pub," one of the other guys, Simon, answered. Even though Simon's comment wasn't all that amusing, we laughed, we all laughed. It was Friday night after all and we were all in a good mood and keen to shift the stress of the week.

We found another pub further down the road, one I had been to a few times before and because it was nowhere near as busy as the first one, we decided to pile in. Robert and I got the first round of drinks and had now managed to squeeze our way through the crowds to find a relatively clear space right in front of the row of windows. It was a warm evening and the windows were the concertina-style that everyone seemed to love these days, opened right up, bringing the street into the pub. A warm breeze was blowing on my back and the beer was going down very well and that's when I nearly missed seeing her, or at least I think it was her. I had just turned around to lean forwards into the street from the wide, low window ledge so I could sip my beer in the breeze, Simon was next to me and telling me a story I had already heard before. I watched as a pair of legs in a skirt just above the knee walked purpose-fully down the footpath. My eyes naturally trailed up the body, stopping briefly at the open V of the blouse before finishing at the face. The face looked familiar. It *was* familiar. "Geez she's gorgeous," Simon was saying, diverting from his story to look in the same direction as me. Both of us stood there in silence until my brain confirmed it was who I thought it was and man-aged to get a message to the rest of my body to slam itself against the wall inside the window. I banged my head lightly against the hard brick, breathing out slowly so the front of my hair blew up in small strands. It was Isobel. It had to be. Crazy Isobel. No one else looks like that. Fucking Isobel. I stepped gingerly forward, peering around the open window to grab another glimpse to make absolutely certain it was her. She was gone. Simon was taking a long slug of beer and looking at me curiously.

"I know her...well used to," I said by way of explanation.

"I wouldn't mind knowing her mate and if that was me I would have hurdled the bloody window so fast I would have been nothing more than an airborne blur of lust," Simon said laughing.

"Not if you knew her mate."

"And how do *you* know her?"

"We used to go out..."

"Jesus Christ, Mary and Joseph and the three wise men thrown in. Why the hell did you let that one go? Or was it when she had bucked teeth and glasses."

"No, no she pretty much looked like that. We were at uni. Well we were also at school together and the romance continued on into the first couple of years at uni and then... then, umm stopped I guess," I replied, wishing I hadn't even gone into this much detail about how I know Isobel.

"Just stopped. Just like that. What happened Tom?"

"Nothing happened. We grew up and broke up. She dropped out of uni, I finished and then went overseas for a couple of years and lost touch that's all."

"I'd be getting back in touch if I was you, or maybe I could do it on your behalf mate. It's a tough ask but I am clearly happy to put myself on the line for you. That's what friends are for after all," Simon was laughing again.

"She's crackers but if you like things a bit mad well I am sure it would be a match made in hell," I answered dryly, swirling the last bubbles of beer in my glass and downing the liquid.

CATE

I felt like I was going to die of thirst. Sweat was running down my front and I could see the shape of my sports bra firmly outlined on my T-shirt. Maybe a grey T-shirt wasn't the best one to wear for a run in this heat. I had arranged to meet Laura at the playing fields near my house where she was supposed to join me for the second part of the run up around the hills and back down to the beach. I frowned and tried to concentrate on finding a tap and Laura, in that order.

Games of six-aside football stretched across every pitch with players – donning bibs in varying colours of awful – running in all directions and squinting from the setting sun. It was going to be impossible to find Laura in all this as neither of us had specified exactly where we were meeting.

I could see someone leaning forwards and what looked like water dropping onto the ground in front of them. It must be a tap. Injected with a new surge of energy I picked up speed in the direction of the tap. The person drinking straightened up, even with her back to me I could tell it was Laura. A messy dark ponytail with a slight kink twisted to just between her shoulder blades, strands of hair not quite reaching the hair band fell in fuzzy tumbles. I pinched Laura on the bottom, making her squeal and jump at the same time.

"Oh it's only you, for a minute there I thought I had gotten lucky," she said, familiarity washing over her face.

"Move over babe, I am desperate for water." Leaving the tap running, Laura stepped aside and I dashed straight into the flow, cupping my hands and lapping it up like a thirsty dog. "My, that's lady-like," Laura exclaimed, laughing.

"Come on we have to keep running," I said looking up at her, water dripping off my chin. "Nah, I'm knackered and can't be bothered," Laura replied, lowering herself to the ground and starting to take off one of her trainers. "No way, what are you doing...put that back on," I said, trying to shove the shoe back onto Laura's foot, but she was wriggling and scrunching her toes up in frantic awkward movements there was no way I would win. "Lau!" I whined, dropping her shoeless foot to the ground.

"I've got us a better offer," she replied defiantly, untying her other shoelace.

"What?" I asked, still standing and putting my hands firmly on my hips.

"My friend from work, Mike, is playing out there somewhere," Laura said sweeping her arm over the entire expanse of the playing fields, "he is almost done – I saw him at half-time and he has asked us to go for a bite to eat with him and some of his team mates when they're finished the game."

"Like this!" I said, looking down at my running clothes and shaking my head. "No way Lau."

"Oh come on it will be fun. Mike's gay so he won't care."

"Then I would say he probably cares even more..."

"It's only to get fish and chips and take it to the beach. Besides we have cooled down now so there is no point running any further. And," Laura looked up at me, cocking her head to one side and raising an eyebrow, "because we have already done some running, our metabolism will still be burning at full tilt so those fish and chips won't even hit the sides." Laura was one of the most brilliant people I knew for ability to convince.

"Oh alright," I finally said, rolling my eyes. "But what am I going to do about this?" I said pointing to the definite bra outline on my T-shirt.

"Mike's gay..."

"So you keep saying," I said rubbing at the sweat. "Are they all gay?"

"Don't know. I doubt it." I rolled my eyes again.

The game was over, I had met gay Mike and I was now walking at half a pace behind the pair because trying to walk three-abreast on the footpath meant I had to keep dropping back each time someone came from the other direction. Finally I had given up and just stayed back, half-listening to their talk about work and pinching at my T-shirt to blow lightly on the wet patches of sweat all the way until we are standing in the queue at the fish and chip shop. Mike had already sent a couple of the guys to get wine and plastic glasses from the bottle shop next door. Apparently someone else has a cork screw on their key ring. Laura had already announced she thinks this is 'genius'. All I think is that everyone can see the outline of my bra and am praying the other people who drove on ahead of us right after the game are gay too and then I won't care so much about how I look. Giving up on blowing at the sweat I have now switched to smoothing the cotton of my T-shirt over my chest willing for the outline to disappear. Laura looks at me and says in what is barely a whisper that I look like I am fondling my breasts. This makes Mike turn around and smile in our direction. 'Thanks', I mouth to Laura who is giggling and standing on tiptoes reaching to pick a menu out of the stack wedged in a highly polished aluminium box standing on the counter. She starts leafing through it and is asking Mike what he thinks we should get. It's one of those fancy fish and chip shops where you choose the type of fish you want, the type of marinade you want it basted in and whether you want thickly cut wedges of potato or old school thinly cut French fries. I am not very comfortable with all this decision-making around what should be a very simple choice. I would much rather just choose regular old-fashioned fish and chips, straight out of the deep fry. Laura turns around, "You happy with lemongrass and chilli as the marinade and some potato wedges?" she asks me. "Yeah that sounds great," I reply, relieved the decision has been made for me.

We place our order and shuffle our way through other customers arguing over ginger beer or spring water to stand on the street while we wait.

"You really can't see it Cate, it's fine."

"What?" I ask Laura.

"Your bra!"

"Oh," I reply, I had managed to momentarily forget about the sweating bra problem and on being reminded immediately started to tug at the bottom of my T-shirt in an attempt to pull the fabric off my body. Laura started to laugh again and turned to talk to Mike.

A group of about five guys were coming up the street towards us. As they drew nearer they all broke into broad grins, one of them carrying a plastic bag bulging with bottles waved. Mike's hand shot up and waved too. "Hallelujah, the booze has arrived!" Mike yelled down the street. All the guys were dressed in shorts and T-shirts and were obviously Mike's team mates. As they got closer I tugged even harder on the bottom of my T-shirt. None of them looked gay to me. They all looked more like blokes who spent much more time on their surfboards than they did in sequins. In fact they probably thought a sequin was the second part of a movie or book. This thought made a crooked grin form on my own face which was met with a broader grin from one of the approaching men. I smiled properly and promptly got embarrassed feeling the familiar prickle of red start to spray across my chest and up my neck. Swallowing, I looked down at my T-shirt and muttered 'hi' as Mike introduced everyone. Laura nudged me lightly in the ribs, "Should we go and see if the fish and chips are ready?" she whispered, grabbing hold of my hand. I followed with my arm tangled around my friend's while Laura yelled back over her shoulder that we were collecting the food.

"He's cute," Laura announced when we were safely inside the shop again but still a bit too loudly for my liking. I quickly snapped my head back in the direction of the street to make sure no one could hear her. I frowned and pretended I didn't know what she was talking about. "Oh come on," she persisted, "that guy made a beeline for you and you did the red blotchy freak out."

"He didn't make a beeline for me," I said scratching at my neck.

"Yes he did."

I shook my head. "The lady doth protest too much," Laura announced stepping around two teenagers holding hands to make her way to the counter to retrieve our food. Clutching recycled cardboard trays of fish and chips neatly arranged in pretty patterns, we shoved our way back through the crowd of customers to where our little party was standing and made our way to the beach. By the time we got there, a few swimmers were left shivering in the shallows desperate to milk the last rays of the sun while young families packed up sodden towels and carried howling children to the edge of the water to wash sandy feet. We found a good stretch of sand flattened by a day of sunbakers still enjoying the last rays of low light clipping and winking between the buildings.

I yanked my trainers off and stretched my legs out on the cool sand. "Drink?" I looked up to see the beeline guy holding a plastic cup of white wine out to me. "Thanks," I said, taking the cup and drawing a long, slow sip. The coldness of the wine made me shiver. He looked at me, raising his own cup and said "Cheers". I squirmed slightly embarrassed again that I should have waited. "Cheers," I replied feeling the prickle of the red blotches begin again.

"I know this is going to sound like a line, but have we met before?" he said quietly not wanting the others to hear his words, or my reply when I said 'no'.

"Umm..." I vibrated the sound between my lips trying to make it look like I was contemplating what he had just said to me. I stole a long exaggerated look at his face, the curve of his eyebrow, the high cheekbone, the strong jaw line. Then down to his forearm which was tanned with golden hair lightly dusting his skin.

"Possibly," I tried.

"No really you seem very familiar," he said, sitting down next to me.

"Maybe I look like someone you know and you're getting confused," I offered.

"No I don't think so. I have never seen anyone who looks like you..." he stopped himself and looked as embarrassed I had already felt twice since meeting him.

"Thanks," I smiled looking up to see if anyone else had heard. Laura was chatting to Mike and the other guys were all talking about work.

"How do you know Mike?" he asked changing tact swiftly.

"I don't. My friend Laura works with him."

"Laura?" he looked confused. "Yes, my friend over there," I said pointing to Laura who was now showing Mike how to do a handstand. "The show off," I giggled, reaching for a chip.

"Oh yes of course. Sorry I am pretty bad with people's names. I'm Tom by the way?"

"Are you going to remember mine if I tell you?"

"Yeah, I am going to try really hard to concentrate," he nodded.

"I'm Cate," I smiled into his eyes. Nice green eyes, a flicker of familiarity.

"Cate?"

"Yes with a 'C'."

"Cate with a 'C'," he repeated. I cringed. I don't know why I said 'with a 'C' – I don't think I have ever said that before to anyone. Here come some red blotches. I rubbed lightly at my chest and stabbed the recycled wooden fork into the lemongrass and chilli marinaded fish, wrecking the display.

"You might also need one of these," Tom said handing me a matching recycled wooden knife.

"Thanks. But I hate the feel of these things, it makes me permanently have the shivers and my teeth chatter," I said sticking the knife and fork into the sand. "I'm going to be uncouth and eat with my fingers. I hope you don't mind but I am starving and I can't use those wooden ones, especially when the wood hits my teeth," I begin to shudder just thinking about it.

Tom starts to laugh. "I've never heard of anything like that before. That's fantastic," he says. I frown at my fish, the word 'fantastic' rolling around his mouth like that. I have heard it said exactly in that way before, with exactly the same voice. I am sure of it. I narrow my eyes.

"Say that again."

"Say what again?"

"Fantastic." I say.

"Fantastic," he repeats, looking very confused and I can feel the sand shift slightly between our bodies.

"No not like that," I say, "say it like you said it the first time."

"Fantastic!" Tom tried again, it was a better attempt but it still sounded a little bit too forced. My frown deepens as I keep trying to place the word and more importantly Tom. He refills his cup and holds the bottle out to me. I hold my cup out and watch as the wine nears the rim.

"Oh my God," I almost shout. Tom jolts back and nearly sends his cup hurtling across the sand. He catches it just before a blob of wine spills out. A couple of the other guys stop talking to look over to us. "What have you done to her Tommy?" One of them shouts out. Tom raises both hands in the air, "I'm innocent," he shouts back laughing before they turn back to their conversation. Laura is holding Mike's legs as he balances on his hands.

"The bus. You're the guy from the bus," I say, staring straight at him, completely sure of myself. Tom's eyes narrow and he looks out to the water. I sit silently for a moment, hardly believing that it is the guy from the bus now sitting beside me. After all the feeble searching I had been doing each time I climbed on board the bus on the way home from work, willing his face to strike familiar among all the strangers and every day there had been nothing. If this was him sitting here now, which it clearly was, I realised I hadn't really remembered what he looked like so maybe I had already scanned over his face and not known. Slowly Tom turns back to me, his lips making a broad smile across his face. He seems to smile a lot and I decide I really like that about him already, he makes me feel comfortable.

"Yes..." he says slowly. "I remember now, of course. That's why you're familiar. See I wasn't trying to pull a line on you."

"Oh," I reply, letting the sound slip tightly out from between my lips and showing my obvious disappointment. I tuck my legs up underneath me, trying to regain a bit of composure and look as though I am OK with that.

"Well I didn't quite mean that...I didn't mean it to come out the way it must have sounded," Tom tried again, shifting a few centimetres closer to me. "But yeah, I do remember you, you were the girl who *kindly* took her bag off the seat so I could sit down," Tom smiled.

I half-smile back at him, remembering the ebb and flow of our first meeting. I reach up to my chest, lightly fluttering my fingers across my skin exposed by the V neck of the T-shirt but there are no obvious signs of the familiar red blotches. Instead my skin is smooth and cool from the early evening salt air. This makes me smile again.

"So you were running this evening, not playing football I take it?" Tom says breaking the silence.

"Yes, I was running to meet Laura at the playing fields so we could continue running together but we seem to have gotten a bit side-tracked and here we are eating fish and chips on the beach instead."

"Could you run home from here?" Tom asks.

"Yeah I could, it's not far, only a few streets away."

"Maybe I could run with you?" Tom says quietly into his shirt sleeve. His chin is resting on his knee with his arms wrapped around both knees. I glance at him sideways and see a flush of red lightly colouring his neck, but it disappears as quickly as it came straight back under the tan.

"Sure," I answer quickly. Once again I reach up to feel for red blotches, but still there's nothing. I take a few

mouthfuls of fish and a long slug on the wine. It tastes good
and I nod when someone else offers yet another refill.

"Maybe we better walk though," I say to Tom.

As the light fades to a dark grey and then finally sur-
renders to black, we gather up the discarded bits of our pic-
nic and shuffle feet back into trainers. Apart from a couple
of fishermen flashing torches to bait up their hooks at the
rocks at the northern end of the beach, we are the only ones
left on the beach. The streetlights flicker on sending long
streaks of low orange light across the sand. Laura comes over
to me and wraps her arm across my shoulder. "Had a good
night?" she whispers in my ear. I nod, "How about you, show
off?" I ask her laughing. "Yep. See this was a much better
idea than running. You might have even bagged yourself a
potential husband," she replies, hugging me more tightly
and twisting her finger into my ribs.

"Laura!" I hiss into the darkness. Giggling, she lets her arm
drop from my shoulders and then reels me back in to whisper
in my ear, "Is lover boy walking you home?" I roll my eyes at
the same time that Tom asks if I am ready to leave. Even in the
dark, I can see Laura pursing her lips and trying not to laugh.

"Shut up," I say in her general direction.

TOM

It can be weird when you walk next to someone you don't know. Keeping in almost perfect stride next to Cate with a 'C' that first night, to me felt like there was static crackling in the gap between our two bodies, energy fusing us at the elbows. Our feet only fell out of step when I jogged between the traffic to cross the road, leaving her standing under a streetlight, one foot out in front jiggling on the edge of the gutter while she waited for a bigger gap between cars to cross over and join me. She wound the hem of her T-shirt in a tight, neat knot as car lights streaked past, long flashes of orange and red curling around the sweep of the road and up the hill away from the beach. Suddenly she was beside me again and we fell straight back into step. She had long toned tanned legs with small patches of sand sticking between the creases of skin stretched over the kneecap closest to me. Her shorts fell mid-thigh and that was the point my eyes kept drifting back to each time I thought she was gazing into the shop windows. When our wrists scraped lightly, I flexed my fingers, stretching the palm hoping for another fumbled touch of skin. I decided there and then she was gorgeous and I would have to start doing some fast thinking and talking to make sure that this wouldn't be it, that I would see her again.

We had just turned off the main street and into a quieter strip of road where darkness fell with a heavy thud around us, gone were the lights glowing from shop fronts and busy restaurants, now it was just a few orange glows flickering in living room windows and the rich smell of someone's backyard barbeque bending through the evening air. The pressure of not knowing how long I had until Cate was going to tell me we had arrived at her house stacked like rows of bricks backwards and forwards, building higher and higher inside my head. She was still talking and I knew I was answering and throwing back conversation. I must have also been doing quite a good job at masking the various rehearsals of different suggestions for meeting up again going on inside my head because Cate was laughing at something I had said. I think I said it, maybe she was laughing at her own joke. I smiled uneasily in response.

"Well this is me," Cate said slowly, tugging more furiously on the hem of her T-shirt.

"Oh. Right," I weakly responded. The bricks continued to layer higher in my brain. Cate was biting on her bottom lip, looking anxiously at me and then to the block of art-deco apartments standing limply somewhere midway down the street we had turned into. Neither of us said anything for a long thirty seconds or so, but everyone knows when you are in this kind of situation it feels like ten awkward minutes have passed. Finally I had the courage to break the silence, "Do you live by yourself?" Quite a good stalling tactic I thought.

"No, I live with my boyfriend," Cate answered blankly. My body slumped and I quickly picked it up to look her straight in the eyes. Jesus Christ, maybe I got all the messages completely wrong. I'm an idiot. I quickly decided to change tact and play it as cool as possible so she wouldn't think I was trying to come onto her. Bloody lucky I hadn't opened my mouth to suggest meeting up again, I would have looked like a complete twat. Suddenly there was a hand – her hand – grabbing at my forearm and she was giggling and saying something, red lapping at her neck and face. The warm wash of embarrassment flooding my ears was making it difficult for me to hear or even register what she was saying. She was still laughing. I wished she'd stop.

"I'm joking!" Cate said. I was looking at her, obviously not convinced because she kept repeating the words again.

"Yeah I knew you were," I managed to exhale confidently, rolling my shoulders back to stand a little bit straighter and taller. "And since you don't live with your boyfriend maybe we should see each other again..." the words dropped out of my mouth before I even had a chance to engage brain, I had totally gone off script and not rehearsed any of those words. My audience though, was giving me the reception I wanted – a broad grin and a very certain reply of 'yes' started the clapping inside my head and an encore of 'that would be great,' got a silent standing ovation.

CATE

I was lying on the couch, pressing the buttons on the remote control, watching as the TV channels flipped in response. My mind was definitely somewhere else, I felt like a flock of nervous butterflies had been released and were crashing around inside me trying to flutter and flap their way to freedom. I let the remote drop to the floor and hooked my right index finger into the crease of my left and started to count – dabbing each finger on my left hand with a fresh memory until I had made it around to my little finger so many times I had lost count – a record of the number of times Tom and I had seen each other since that first night at the beach when he had walked me home. I calculated more than three months had passed, and in that time I had been learning the language of someone else. Tom liked eating toast in bed, couldn't take a bra off with one hand, trailed his fingers across his cheeks when he was concentrating, wore glasses to read thriller books and breathed on my neck when we slept. These to me were the first few words of our own language. The thought made me smile as I stretched my arms out behind my head, interlocking my fingers and arching my back before settling down into the fabric of the couch. The flat was silent. Now here I was, lying on the couch looking out the window, imagining an airplane lifting higher and higher into the clouds, heading south until it was nothing more than a black dot hanging in the sky.

At dinner five nights ago, Tom had looked up from the food in front of him and set the fork down very carefully on the side of the plate. Every action seemed exaggerated and considered. I remember the butterflies starting to flap their wings in slow motion as I swallowed a mouthful of rice and drew my eyes up to meet his. "Something pretty amazing has happened," he started. I smiled encouragingly, terrified at what he was going to say next. "I have got this great opportunity with work." I nodded. "Anyway, they're really keen to open a Melbourne office and I've been asked to go and help set up, bed some clients in that sort of thing. It's a great opportunity for me." I nodded again, trying for a smile. "So they want me to go down next week, initially for a couple of weeks for some meetings and then after that it would be more longer-term."

"That's fantastic. Congratulations," I tried those words for size and now they sat between us on the table next to the salt and pepper shakers. Tom was nodding. "Thanks," he mumbled and picked up his fork and then dropped it back down onto the side of the plate and looked awkwardly at me. I didn't know how to react. I was suddenly jolted back to a reality I had been avoiding. In the big scheme of things, this was all still very fresh and new. After all, a few months with someone are just that, a few months. Despite the rushed moments of pure heat between us, the easy conversations and laughter, maybe our history together wasn't long enough for either of us to figure in long-term plans. Apart from one of Tom's work friends we had run into one evening when we were out for dinner – I think his name was David and he had stood for no longer than a minute at our table, smiling and extending his hand when Tom introduced me as: 'This is Cate' – neither of us had met each others' friends. It was a subject which hadn't come up all that often. We seemed to be in a perpetual state of that ridiculous honeymoon phase that romantics like to wax lyrical about, where we can't get enough of each other, naked mainly, and we certainly don't want to share each other with anyone else, it's more the 'selfish' phase I think. Besides all of that, Tom usually worked fairly late every evening, arriving on my doorstep at around 10pm, tie half undone and half a smile as I stepped aside to let him into the hallway, grabbed his belt hooks and dragged him into the bedroom. Before 10pm and for parts of the weekends, I was still hanging out with Laura and Isobel. Tom was still quite separate to all that. Neither Laura nor Isobel really ever remembered what Tom's name was because we always referred to him as the 'bus boy'. Laura of course prodded me about when I was going to introduce her to 'bus boy', but I had mainly gotten away with any premature introductions as she was so busy with her new job that many of her evenings and weekends were spent at events or entertaining clients. Isobel too had switched jobs and was working at a small art gallery in one of the trendier areas where everyone wears black all the time, chain smokes and nurses a latte all day until it's time to pop the cork on a champagne bottle. She had asked if I wanted to bring 'bus boy' along to the opening show of a new artist they had just signed up, but Tom was working late. Laura and I had gone together, both dressed head to toe in black, snatching glasses of cheap fizz off the trays balancing precariously on the finger pads of scrawny waiters – also dressed in black – trying every now and again to catch Isobel's eye to smile and nod encouragingly. It was clear the gallery's curator was smitten with Isobel, even with his wife standing like a long streak of a painters' brush in the corners of the gallery talking loudly and throwing her head back to trill a laugh above the din of the evening, his eyes followed the line of Isobel as she moved about the floor, kissing cheeks and lightly touching people's elbows as she brushed past them. "How long until he makes a pass at Issy do you think?" Laura whispered into my ear, raising her eyebrow in the direction of the curator. "Probably already has," I muttered, smiling in his direction. "Don't look at him Cate, he'll know we're talking about him," Laura said pinching my waist and gliding a hand across a passing waiter's tray to pluck another champagne flute.

I rolled onto my side on the couch to retrieve the remote control off the floor and tried to concentrate on whatever was on the TV. Instead my mind jumped straight back to Tom and I having dinner a few nights before, picking up right where the memory had been interrupted by Isobel and her curator last time.

I remember looking at Tom across the table from me, the shadowy light drew a dark patch along one side of his face. He was running a hand through his hair, I wanted to reach out and run my hand through his hair, but now it seemed like something might have shifted between us, maybe the beginnings of a small chip breaking off the side. I tried picking up my fork to keep eating, but ended up just swirling patterns on my plate and watching as the blades slid around the china. "There's been talk of it for a while, but nothing had ever really been finalised until this week, so now it looks like it's all systems go. That's the way we usually work anyway," Tom was looking directly at me and I looked up from my plate to continue nodding. "I reckon I will have to move down there for about six months or so – it's not permanent Cate. I'll come back to Sydney for sure. I love it here. The surf is too cold in Melbourne." We both laughed, although I think mine was forced. "Anyway, I got you something," Tom said reaching behind him to pull a folded brown paper bag out of the breast pocket of his suit jacket which was slung over the back of his chair. The arms of the jacket were slumped like the person wearing it had deflated. Tom handed the thinly folded paper to me. I must have looked puzzled as I took it from him. "Open it," he smiled. I unfolded the paper and a neat crease sat down the centre, fanning the two halves of the paper bag out like wings. Still looking at Tom, I slid my fingers inside the bag, I couldn't feel anything so I carefully edged my fingers deeper inside until I could feel a thin strip of what felt like leather. I pulled it out between two fingers. It was leather, deep purple in colour with gold lettering: *Dance like no one is watching*. I must have read the words about four times, a puzzled smile cracking at the edges of my mouth. "You don't know what that is, do you?" Tom asked, smiling.

"Yes it's a bookmark. I think. Isn't it?" I replied. Tom nodded.

"Do you remember that day on the bus? When we first met. Ages ago." Tom said. I bit my lip. "Hmm," I answered, nodding slowly but knowing my brows were knitting together and it was obvious I didn't know how that embarrassing scene was connected to a bookmark. "You dropped your book on the floor. You didn't have a bookmark and you lost your page." I looked back down at the bookmark, rubbing my thumb on the suede and smiled, "Yes I do remember." I genuinely did remember. "I love the words. I think they're from a poem or maybe a song, I can't really remember," I said. "Yeah I can't remember either," Tom said gently, reaching his hand across the table, crumpling my hand and the bookmark inside his. "Would you come to visit me in Melbourne?" I started nodding again.

Now Tom was on a flight to Melbourne. This time it was only for a couple of weeks, but who knew what would happen when it was for much longer. I rolled onto my side and let my feet drop to the floor to shuffle my way to the bedroom where my handbag was draped on the edge of the bed. I reached inside and pulled out the bookmark, it still had the crumples in it from where Tom had wrapped his fingers around mine. I yanked at the edges a bit, trying to straighten it out a bit, but decided I liked the creases better.

ISOBEL

The nightmares had started again. Last night the one where there's a baby crying in a cot at the bottom of a cliff visited me somewhere in the hazy, smudged grey light right before dawn. I gripped at the bed sheets, twisting and turning them in a half-conscious state, desperate to scream out for help, my throat constricting and running dry with the repetition of one soundless word. Finally my arm sliced across the pillow, slapping the wall, shooting me straight into consciousness and breathing big gulps of air, eyes wide open and heart racing against the sounds of the early morning commuter traffic sliding its way towards the city.

In the kitchen I drank big plumes of water with the radio turned up loud. I had flung open the window and waited for the soft breeze to suck itself around me. Water dribbled down my chin which I hacked at with the corner of a tea towel. Maybe I should go for a swim before work.

I looped a bow around the back of my neck, tugging at the lycra to make sure the strap of the bikini top wasn't digging into my skin, shut the front door behind me and made my way to the beach. The rubber of my thongs slapped on the hot concrete and then sunk into the sand as I stepped onto the beach. Yanking the thongs off, my eyes squinted against the sun, the day was already warming up. It felt like summer had been so drawn out, it was hard to imagine a cold wind whipping the waves. Standing on the edge of the water, I let the cool rush of liquid slide over my feet and then ran at full-pelt into the sea. I duck-dived under a wave and opened my mouth to let the salty water rush in, spraying it out between my teeth as my face raised to the surface. I imagined a miniature water fountain balancing on the sea. Rubbing at my eyes until they focused, I looked up and down the length of the beach. People jogged along the water's edge, surfers stood in the foam with boards tucked under their arms, a stream of cars headed east to the skyscrapers that seemed to almost join hands, encircling the office workers for the day. All was as it should be. I let my feet plant down into the sand and started to make my way in towards the beach, feeling my body tense and rise up against the tug of the water. As I made it clear and onto the beach, I saw the edge of a baby leave me – for now. I couldn't go on like this. This city was too small, there weren't enough distractions. By the time I was reaching for my towel, rubbing it down the length of my legs, my mind was hatching an escape plan. The only other person in the world who might understand why I needed to escape from a country that scorched my mind and wouldn't let me forget the past was Aunt Jean. Later that evening on the phone, Aunt Jean was as gentle and supportive as she always was with me. Even though I knew she loved me and knew things about me that no one else did, or would ever know, I still sensed her treading carefully around her words, letting pauses of silence fill our conversation with a steady rhythm that made me feel safe. It was Aunt Jean's way of making sure the fleeting decisions I fluttered like confetti down the phone line were really going to send me in a forward direction – away from the birth of an unknown child. My child, the same one who still played silently at the edges of every conversation I had with her.

"You should go in search of discovering what makes you happy, my darling," Aunt Jean's words spun a warm yarn around me and my decision was made.

"You're what?" that was Cate talking over the top of her book. We were sunbaking on the beach. It must have been the Saturday after I had been swimming earlier in the week and then had the seed of the idea confirmed by Aunt Jean. The only problem was, Aunt Jean wasn't quite aware of all the intricacies of my entire plan.

"I'm going to London," I said surely, almost triumphantly.

"When?"

"In a month or so."

"So soon! For how long?" Cate rolled over onto her belly, balancing the book in her palms. She was about to fold the page corner over, but seemed to hesitate, letting her fingers hover for a moment before reaching inside the back cover to produce a bookmark, which she slid between the pages and closed the book shut.

"I don't know...maybe for a few months, years. I'm not sure yet," I answered, trying to sound casual, like my mind had been made up that this is what I was going to do.

"Wow. That's amazing. Good for you. I think it's a great idea, do it while we can, I say. Besides, we're only four or five years, or whatever it is now, out of university, so we have some work experience behind us. Hopefully that means we're more employable overseas, I don't know. So have you got enough money saved up, you know it's bloody expensive over there?"

"Yeah I've got a bit and I can work when I get there. I'll have a working holiday visa, and besides..." I stopped dead. I knew my plans were probably going to be too far-fetched for Cate to understand. She'll try to talk me out of it and I really didn't need that. Not now. Not when I had made my decision and however frightening I thought it was going to be, I had to go through with it. I just had to. Get. Away. Cate snapped her head up to look at me. I could see myself in the reflection of her sunglasses.

"And besides what, Iss?" she asked carefully.

I twisted my bottom lip and considered my friend. I let out a sigh. "You won't approve," I finally breathed out.

"I'm not your mother Iss."

"Thank fuck for that." I sat up, adjusting the bikini strap wound around the back of my neck. A red mark rubbed at my collar bone and a small patch of sunburn fingered in red and white dots across the top of my breast. "Could you pass me the sunscreen please," I dabbed the white cream into my chest, watching it disappear into the skin.

"Come on Iss. What's your plan? Just because I might not be as brave as you doesn't mean I don't support you. Maybe I even envy you – ever thought of that?" Cate looked a little hurt from my earlier comment. I cursed myself for upsetting her. She was so sweet. She always made me feel silently bad about my own shortcomings and I knew she would be more than slightly embarrassed – more like totally shocked – if she knew about some of the things I have done. But knowing Cate, she would be more hurt that she had somehow let me down because I didn't feel like I could go to her when I was in trouble, that I had been suffering in silence and she hadn't been able to help. How could she help, she doesn't know anything. The familiar rise and swell of guilt rippled. I flicked at the sand between my fingers. "You should never be envious of me. Seriously." I said decisively.

"Oh you're so hard on yourself Iss. We're young for God's sake, if we can't pack up now and take off to the other side of the world, when the hell can we do it, huh? Stop worrying about what you think I am going to think. I never usually think anything, as long as it makes you happy I don't care. I know you tell Laura some things and not me. I don't know why."

"What's Laura told you?" The words slipped out of my mouth defensively, my back instantly rising as my mind started to close up.

"Nothing! I just know, I can sense it. That's all. So please tell me what your other plan is for going to London. If you want to tell me that is."

"Of course I want to tell you –'", but I managed to stop myself there. I wasn't so comfortable with sharing everything. Well I guess this wasn't exactly everything and Cate and Laura would find out sooner or later anyway. "OK," I started slowly, "Do you remember that show opening you and Laura came to, it was for a new artist we'd just started representing?" I watched Cate nod. "Well, he and I have kind of been seeing each other." Cate smiled out of the corner of her mouth. "Yeah well, he – Julian – is going to go to London, and before you think anything, I am not going to London for him," I added quickly and Cate nodded again. "I...I want to go to London anyway, with or without Julian, it just so happens he is going there. To London. As well. He has a couple of galleries who are interested in him, so he wants to go and check it out. If he gets representation there, he will be able to make a lot more money than here and his work will be exposed to a much bigger market – an international market. So it's a really great opportunity for him."

"And what will you do?" Cate asked softly.

"Well I can maybe find work in a gallery or something. I do have some experience now and my boss has quite a good reputation and contacts all over the world, so I am sure he could hook me up with some people." I suddenly felt quite exhausted. This plan had been turning round and round in my head for the past few days and I hadn't really articulated it out loud before, not since mulling it over with Aunt Jean. I wasn't sure I was sounding that convincing until I looked over to see Cate smiling, she reached her hand out and squeezed mine. "Bloody good on you, it sounds really exciting. God, it will be amazing Iss. Imagine." I smiled back at her, a little trickle of confidence seeped in. Now all I had to do was tell Julian the plan, make him go along with it so my little white lie wouldn't be discovered or turn into another complicated lie I would have to live with. I already had one of those eating away at me, threatening to spew out in the still of the night, flecking across the faces of lovers and on the tip of my tongue when I had too much to drink.

"God everyone's leaving me..." Cate suddenly said, dropping her forehead onto the towel.

"What do you mean?" I asked, digging a big toe into her calf. Cate mumbled something into the towel. "What? I can't hear you babe."

"Oh, just you and the bus boy," Cate groaned, lifting her head to balance her chin in her palms.

"The bus boy? Why, where's he going?"

"To Melbourne," Cate answered, sounding like a petulant child.

"To live?"

"Yes. No. Oh I don't know. It's for work, to set up an office or something. We're at that point where it could go either way...and I really like him Iss." Cate let her face slide through her palms, hitting the towel face first again. "I've hurt my nose now," she said not lifting her head from the towel.

PART FOUR
BORROWED TIME

CATE

"**O**h I can't bear it!" My shoulders were cracking in desperation as I shifted my weight from foot to foot. I shut my eyes and bit the inside of my mouth, trying to steady my breathing. Tom squeezed my hand tighter, closing his fingers around mine. He seemed to be rooted to the ground, standing very still and sucking in his bottom lip. I watched his jaw clench and unclench. Tom was nervous.

"I need to put my hands over my ears, I don't think I want to listen," I whispered loudly, the couple in front of us turned around and laughed uneasily.

"You can if you want to," Tom said, kissing the top of my head. "It will all be over soon."

The auctioneer came out of the house, straightening his tie and clearing his throat. "Ladies and gentlemen, thank you very much for coming today. You would be well aware this is a highly sought-after property in a very desirable location..."

"Oh just get on with it," Tom mumbled, clenching my hand tighter. We were surrounded by people all wanting exactly what we wanted, this house with the veranda wrapping around the front and the letterbox hanging by one hinge on the fence. "That will have to be replaced," Tom had announced the first time we had viewed the property. The estate agent was already on the veranda twirling keys, looking for the one which would unlock the front door.

"I know, but I love it," I replied.

"What, the letterbox?" Tom laughed.

"No the house, look at the veranda. Oh, we could sit out here in the summer and I could plant...umm....plants along the path, here look Tom," I said pointing at the track of cracking cement leading to the house.

"Don't get too excited, it's not ours yet –" Tom lent his head into mine, lowering his voice, "Plus we don't want to show too much enthusiasm otherwise they will up the price."

"Yes I know, but –" Tom put his finger over my mouth.

Even the smell of layers of dust and peeling wallpaper littered with unrecognisable purple flowers greeting us in the hallway didn't put me off. Immediately I saw potential and imagined us in the house renovating it together. I had to have it. Actually we had to have it. I knew Tom was impressed because he kept grinning at me and giving my hand a little squeeze each time the estate agent turned to lead the way to the next room, yelling over the shoulder of his crisp grey linen suit of what his recommendations were for each room. "Look beyond the wallpaper. Look at the light coming in from these windows. These are original period features of course." He announced scraping a fingernail across the layers of paint stacked high on a mantlepiece.

"Well everything has a period doesn't it?" Tom said pressing a light switch on and off and getting no response from an elaborate fitting hanging in the middle of the ceiling. I stifled a smile while the agent laughed mechanically, quickly telling us we really must come and see the quaint room at the end of the hallway, a study perhaps, or a nursery, he smiled looking directly at my stomach.

"Idiot," Tom said under his breath. I had held my stomach in for the rest of the viewing, letting it out when we met up with Laura for a late breakfast.

"Over here!" Laura yelled, half standing while she folded a newspaper in half. Kissing us both on the cheeks, the three of us dropped into chairs. "Oh my God Lau, it was amazing," I said gripping the edge of the table with both hands.

Tom nodded, "But we're trying not to get too excited, as you can see," he nodded towards me. "It's definitely going to go to auction, the owners reckon they will get much more for it, and they will. Sydney is so bloody obsessed with an auction, ever since that tiny shed at the north end of the beach went for over a million a few years back. I think it was in 2001, maybe 2002, is that right?" Tom asked looking at me, I shrugged, "So looks like we'll be lined up with every other person in Sydney who can see beyond the wallpaper." Tom said leaning across me to read the blackboard with the day's menu scrawled in thick white chalk which was already chipping off.

"Well you could both be the lucky winners," Laura said.

"We have to pay for it Lau," Tom replied.

"Oh you're so practical," Laura laughed, patting his hand.

"Well one of us needs to be," Tom said, grabbing my elbow, "because if it was up to this one here, we would have already offered double the asking price..."

"And moving straight in and not sitting here agonising over whether or not it was going to be our house," I stated triumphantly.

"Yes and waking up in cold sweats every night because we have a mortgage that's going to take the rest of our lives to pay off," Tom answered, looking back over at the specials blackboard.

"And no furniture, not to mention you would never be going out again, poor as church mice the pair of you would be," Laura quipped.

"Hey, whose side are you on?" I asked, leaning into Laura's shoulder.

"Why are there sides suddenly?" Tom asked.

"So I can get what I want," I said simply.

Now here we were, standing on the street looking expectedly at the auctioneer, the house and at each other. The bidding had started. Poker-faced people around us were raising their hands or tilting the estate agents' pamphlet slightly above their heads. We had agreed Tom would do the bidding for us and would only go as far as the budget limit we had calculated and recalculated over and over again, combing through our finances at what seemed like endless meetings with the mortgage broker. Tom had just got another bonus which went straight into the budget for the house. The bonus was the biggest one yet.

I looked across at Tom now, standing to attention like a schoolboy about to be hauled into the headmaster's office. His jaw was still clenching and re-clenching, punctuated with deep breaths and eyes scanning the crowd gathered around us. I knew he would be weighing up the competition, plotting a plan in his head. I kept telling myself there was a reason he was so good at his job, his professional skills to stay calm under pressure would be what would get us across the threshold and into the house. My role in all of this would be to grip his hand, stare at the ground willing the house to be ours. So I stood there focusing on a clump of overgrown grass protruding out of freshly mown lawn feeling Tom's hand squeeze so tightly around my own that I felt the blood trapping in my forearm, pulsing uncomfortably. Stare at the grass. Forget the pain. Don't listen to the progress of the auction. Stare at the grass.

When I thought I had no other option but to withdraw my hand free of Tom's clench, Tom dropped my hand, wrapping his arm around my waist and lifting me high into the air, laughing. "It's ours babe. The house is ours," Tom was yelling into my ear, making it ring. I was clearly shell shocked as I stared into his face, watching his lips form the words and spreading into one of the widest grins I had ever seen Tom do. Finally my brain registered what was happening, tears spilled from my eyes, my cheeks stretched and hurt from smiling. I felt Tom's lips on mine, kissing me hard.

TOM

I had barely pulled up the handbrake when Cate opened the car door and was running to unlatch the gate. She stopped momentarily at the letterbox which was still swinging on its last hinge and tried to balance the tin box back into a more convincing upright position on the fence, as soon as she let it go it wobbled like a circus guy in a hire wire act. Cate laughed and continued running up the front path, turning to see where I was before jamming the key in the front door. By the time I had made it to the doorway I could see the outline of Cate standing halfway down the hall. Sensing me behind her, she started to run the length of the room, her red shirt trailing out behind her with her pony tail swinging from side to side.

I smiled at her outline, Cate was my outline and I loved her. "You know I still love this house Tom," Cate yelled from somewhere at the other end of the house. I guessed it was the kitchen. "That's lucky, because we own it now," I yelled back, starting to make my way towards her voice and frowning at the chips of paint flaking from the ceiling. I found her in the kitchen turning the sink tap on and off. "We have water...and clean water by the looks of it," Cate smiled triumphantly at me.

I grabbed her around the waist, she smelled fantastic, like Cate, it reminded me of apples. "What do you smell of?" I whispered into her hair. Cate turned slightly and raised her eyebrow. "I didn't fart if that's what you mean, that would have been you and as I can't smell it – yet – it means it definitely was you," she said, leaning further into me. "No you smell like apples, you always smell like apples but I can never figure out how you get to smell like that."

"I'm not sure that was beautifully put, but I think I get what you mean."

"Thanks," I whispered into her hair. "What do we think of this kitchen?"

"Not great, but it's ours and it will be fun to fix it up don't you think? God you better think that as that was the whole idea of buying this place, so we could do it up together. Remember?"

"Yes I remember," I said, letting Cate loosen her body from my grip. I watched her as she opened and closed cupboard doors, squatting the air with her hand as dust bellowed in great puffs from the shelves. "I do really love this place," Cate said.

"And I love you," I said twirling her around to face me. My fingers hooked into the belt loops of her jeans. With one movement, I hoisted her up onto the kitchen bench and was working denim down past her knees and then her ankles, until finally two blue fabric legs sat crumpled on the floor between us. Pressing my head into her collarbone, I winched her waist closer to me and felt Cate rise her hips against me. "God I love you," I breathed into her hair.

The first few months in our new house all went a little like that first day in the kitchen. By the time we had reached the end of the first week, we had managed to 'christen' every room in the house and I certainly wasn't complaining. The house was making Cate horny. Maybe it was the paint fumes, whatever it was I wanted to bottle it. We were bloody tired, coming home from work every night to paint, strip wallpaper, polish the floorboards or rip up carpet. I was usually stuck late in the office so it was Cate doing most of the work. A small light would be flickering in one of the rooms, the windows wide open to let out the paint fumes and in the centre of it all – Cate dressed in one of my old t-shirts and a pair of paint splattered jeans. Dinner was the pair of us sitting on the floor eating a takeaway or beans on toast with a bottle of wine surveying what Cate had managed to get done that evening and asking my opinion on what I thought of the wallpaper swatches she had bought home. Without even really being aware of it, we had slid into a domestic situation. I wasn't complaining about that either, I loved this woman. I had moved back from Melbourne for her, having to change jobs in the process which had actually seen me at a much better-paid job and a much bigger company where there were lots of blokes my age all working crazy hours and not minding each others' company, analysing our victories and our fuck-ups over a few beers at the pub around the corner from work. Cate wasn't a nag, she never seemed to get annoyed that I was going to be later than I thought or that maybe I wasn't pulling my weight when it came to renovating the house, even though sometimes I felt as guilty as hell. The guys at work ribbed me a bit about buying a house and looking like things were getting very serious with Cate and me, the thing is I guess it was and that didn't bother me either. Under normal circumstances – well before Cate – I would have run a mile and maybe had one eye trailing the room over the top of my beer glass, seeing who might be my target. But now, maybe it sounds corny, but I was just really happy with Cate so I hadn't even noticed that I had stopped surveying the room and was actually listening to what my mates were saying. The whole thing had sort of crept up on me I guess, nothing felt forced or made me feel like I wasn't ready. I wasn't really questioning any of it, come to think of it, and that alone felt good. The 'Domestic Goddess' they called me and that made me smirk because I knew I had something pretty special and all of the ribbing was stemmed from jealously, at least that's what I told myself.

"So when are we going to meet this beauty of yours, or is she not allowed out until she's finished renovating your whole place on her own?" Stuart, one of the guys at work, asked me over our second beer of the evening. We'd had a crappy day. We thought we were going to seal a major deal and had been working all hours for the past fortnight to make sure we pulled it off. Then, right at the last minute, it looked like they were getting cold feet, we got angry and called it a day. God only knows what tomorrow would bring, weeks of hard work for nothing.

"Oh I don't really think I need to put her through the agony of meeting you lot. Plus, as you say, she's way too busy painting walls and stripping floorboards to have the time. I've told her she's not allowed out until it's all done," I laughed, taking a long sip of beer.

"How long have you two been together?" Stuart asked.

"A few years," Stuart raised his eyebrows. "She's a very cool girl who also happens to be bery handy with the paintbrush," I said taking a big slug of beer and tried stifling another smile, but I know he saw the corners of my mouth turn upwards and my eyes dive into the depths of my beer in an effort to hide any more obvious shows of love for Cate.

A fork of lightning cracked the bruised sky as I ducked my head inside a taxi and shouted "Bronte thanks mate" into the driver's ear. Big thick drops of rain started to fall as the taxi sped across five-ways, barely stopping to give way at the roundabout and up through the streets of Paddington. I fished my mobile out of my breast pocket and called Cate.

The phone rang out and eventually went to her voicemail. I clicked the phone off without leaving a message and then instantly regretted it, what if she was caught out in this weather. I imagined her running along a damp street, rain pelting her crisp white shirt. Her shirt getting wetter and wetter and perhaps see-through...OK, yes see-through, perhaps very see-through. Things were starting to take shape in my trousers. Jesus Christ, what was I doing? What was wrong with me? I am in the back of a taxi, alone for God's sake. I looked into the rear-view mirror to see if the driver was watching me. He was watching the road, the way he was supposed to with passengers in the car. God what if he had been watching me? Right I have to think about something else and get rid of what is turning out to be quite an impressive erection before I get out of the taxi. I stare out the window and concentrate on a plastic bag trapped in the gutter under the gushing water. OK, nothing sexy about that. That's good. Breathe deeply, look back at the taxi driver, he's still watching the road. Finally the taxi turns into my street and I say, "Yep, just here after the 'For Sale' sign mate. Yep that's perfect. Thanks. How much?" I throw a wad of cash over the seat into a sweaty palm, tell him to keep the change and then I am out of the cab, up the front path and unlocking the front door. I throw my keys into the bowl in the hall and shout out to Cate. There's no answer. The rain is still belting down and my shoulders are soaked through from the sprint up the garden path, mainly to conceal my half-inflated erection. I make my way through the organs of the house towards a lamp glow. Cate must be in the sunroom, listening to rain pelt the tin roof. She loves that sound. She looks up as I step into the room, glass of red wine beside her and book in her hand. Her legs are slung over the side of a chair we picked up in a market on holiday down the coast last summer. She's gorgeous. She starts to open her mouth to say something, but I am already there. Placing my own mouth on hers and kissing her. I feel my trousers start to take shape again, but I am safely inside and Cate is raising her hips towards me and greeting my mouth with her tongue. Her eyes are closed and God I love her.

ISOBEL

My breath has spread into crystal drops freezing against the London air. I rubbed my hands together, blowing into them and encasing my nose into the wool of my coat sleeve. The air was so bitter it was almost impossible to tell if it ate boiling or freezing bites of my skin, there is such a fine line between the two extremities. Someone once told me the feeling of euphoria and sadness is so interlinked that it's why we sometimes cry when we laugh hysterically. Maybe it was the same with cold and heat. Stamping my feet in a bid to shake some feeling back into them, I was almost lightly jogging now, wriggling my toes backwards and forwards inside my boots. A stark fluorescent light hung from the bus stop making a neat square of artificial brightness. It was getting dark – very dark – people moved quickly along the street, coats pulled up around the tips of their noses, hats pulled right down so only a slit of skin dotted with two eyes looked out at the world. Despite the blackness, it was probably only coming up to five in the afternoon. It didn't matter how long I had lived in this city, it was five years now, the dense coldness and darkness of winter always still seemed to take me by surprise, like a short sharp slap across the face.

Sydney would be shrouded in darkness too. I imagined hot, sticky bodies rolling over in beds in the early hours of the morning, sleepy arms involuntarily swiping at mosquitoes while warm waves rolled onto the cool damp sand lacing the city's beaches. I could almost hear the waves and smell the salt air. I knew I shouldn't do this to myself. I should think about the here and the now. Sydney wasn't going to solve any of my problems. I was living in the liveliest city in the world. Cool Britannia and all that. I wriggled my toes again, there was still no feeling. That memory of Sydney still sticking heavily in my mind, sighing I pulled the iPod from my pocket and scrolled to find music to match my sombre mood. The new Amy Winehouse album, Back to Black, should do nicely.

Finally I saw the bus moving slowly up the Strand. Everyone at the bus stop took a step forward, dropping into single file as the bus pulled up. Swiping my Oyster card on the reader, I looked down the length of the aisle to find a seat. Dropping down into the vinyl, I rested my head on the window and watched as a pool of condensation built up on the glass. Outside the lights of the Strand, Charing Cross Station and Trafalgar Square rushed past, bringing long streams of colour running through the interior.

I was heading in the wrong direction. I was meant to be sliding my feet into a pair of stilettos, getting ready to smile falsely at a bunch of people who were, by their own admission 'cool' while I stood with a champagne glass telling them how wonderful it was of them to come. To come where exactly? To a dingy hole in the wall, deep in Soho to look at some disturbing black and white photography Dominic had shot over a series of drug-fuelled weekends. None of it even made any sense. I get that it doesn't necessarily have to, it's art after all, so it's all down to how the viewer interprets the piece. I had been curating some really questionable exhibitions for long enough to understand that concept, smiling smugly when it appeared my *understanding* of art had reached enough superiority to urge bankers with half-mast ties flapping against pinstripe suits to slide their black Amexes out of their wallets.

A woman in a red coat sat down beside me. I crossed my legs over one another. Dominic had been wearing that red shirt with the holes in it that I didn't like. I knew Dominic wore it for effect so he would look arty and interesting to potential buyers – the struggling artist act – he knew that I knew it was all an act. At first I had thought he *was* arty and interesting and then the more times I saw that shirt slipping down over his torso in anticipation for a show, the more I came to shudder, feeling my lips set to one side, tongue firmly pressed against the roof of my mouth, willing for him to fuck off. I had grown embarrassed to be attached to him, for people to think we were a couple. Very gradually I had started slipping around him, watching him out of the corner of one eye while I held a glass out for more wine and took small, calculated steps in the opposite direction, weaving my way into a throng of people so Dominic would always be left lapping at the edges.

I tried to locate the exact starting point where I switched from loving to loathing Dominic. I had been instantly attracted to him the first time I saw him sway into a New Year's Eve party, a bottle of champagne swinging from his wrist, his coat was undone and so was half the shirt he was wearing underneath it. I had turned my back to Julian. Oh dear, sweet Julian who had somehow agreed to let me follow him to the other side of the world only to have me pretty much use him as a flatmate and then as a springboard to flit into the bright lights and young things of London. That first time I saw Dominic was also the last time I saw Julian – not counting the awkward overlap of me posting the house keys through the letterbox when the door suddenly opened revealing a red-eyed Julian. He stood there staring at me and then said 'Why?' I had looked down at the mat which was thin and worn in the middle. I really didn't want to look up again, so I just stood there hanging my head, noticing how my shoes didn't fill the worn patch in the mat. Finally the door closed and I was left standing on the other side.

But now here I was with the person who replaced Julian and slowly but surely the shine was fading to a dull glimmer – again. I wasn't sure if my eventual loathing of Dominic had been like a sore tooth, slowly rotting reminding you of its decay only when you bite down into sickly sweet chocolate, caramel dripping from the lip, making you wince. Or was it that I just woke up one morning and the sight of his pasty back turned towards me, sheets wrapped between his legs, made me feel nauseous.

The funny thing is, tonight at the gallery, even after all the chaos of the afternoon, Dominic seemed vaguely tolerable. I'd been topping up my glass since about midday, watching as he argued with one of the gallery assistants, Richard, about the way one of his wretched photographs had been hung. Dominic had wanted a tiny black and white negative to be hung in the middle of the biggest wall, of course with nothing else around it. Richard explained over and over again that the gallery space wasn't big enough to 'afford him his luxury' and that would mean other works would be cluttered on the two remaining walls. "It will look shit. You won't sell anything you stubborn bastard," Richard delivered as a parting shot after he had slammed the hammer into the wall, leaving a hole of papery plaster flakes dropping onto the whitewashed floorboards, jammed a cigarette into his mouth and promptly walked out. I leant against the window, slowly draining the wine from my glass and watched as Dominic repeatedly sucked the insides of his cheeks in and then blew them out, fanning the plaster flakes across the floorboards. Finally he looked at me, "What the fuck am I going to do now?" he asked, looking like a child about to break out into a tantrum. I swirled the empty glass in my hand, "Maybe you could hang that little negative over the hole, although I don't think it's big enough," I offered, taking long strides across the room, looking for another bottle of wine. Even then, I didn't think I would just silently slide out the door, fold into the crowd and get on a bus.

Instead I had smiled at Richard when he came back in, smelling of stale smoke. "The guy might be talented, but he can be such an arsehole," Richard whistled in my ear as he yanked the last bit of cork out of the wine bottle I had been struggling with and slugged big drops into my glass and then into a dirty plastic cup he found on the make-shift bench. "He's not that," I remarked. "No, I know he's not an arsehole, I am just so fucked off with him. I should remember he always gets like this before a show," Richard said quickly, his eyebrows shooting up. "No I meant he's not even talented," I raised my eyebrows in response over the top of my glass. Richard looked at me for a few seconds, his eyebrows still arching in points towards his hairline and then slowly he started to laugh. He thinks I am bloody joking. I smiled, clinking my glass against Richard's plastic cup.

Back in the gallery, Dominic was talking loudly and falsely on his mobile phone. He winked at me as I picked up one of his rotten little photography pieces and pretended to size up where it would fit on the wall. Even though I winced, I still didn't think I was just going to leave. It was an important night for Dominic. I knew some serious buyers were supposed to be coming. He could make some good money tonight. I managed to surprise myself with a small twinge of pride as I held another one of the more bearable works out in front of me at arm's length, twisting it to catch the sunlight, and thinking I could potentially see why someone might find this appealing, talented even.

"Do you want it?" arms slid around my waist. It was Dominic. "You can have it, but it will cost you," the words slimed around inside my ear. I rested the picture against the wall, attempting to swivel my hips out of his reach. "Better you sell it to a willing buyer," I quipped. I felt Dominic smirk, his breath brushing my neck. I held my breath, feeling anger rise and drop like a stone into the pit of my stomach. Even then, I didn't think I would leave.

"Can we just hang these damn pictures up please? Where's Richard? Richard!" I yelled. Richard came out from behind one of the freestanding walls. "I'm here," he said. "Can we get this show on the road? I don't give a damn what Precious Balls over there says either. The pictures are being hung where I think they should go. End of story." I said sternly, taking command of the room. Dominic shot me a look and opened his mouth to say something, but saw the look on my face and shut it again. He reminded me of a fish, spiked to a hook, gasping for water. Just like so many times before now and so many men before now, I knew he had seen the fleck of a shadow cross through my eyes. I handed Richard the hammer and pointed at various spots on the wall where hooks needed to go. Dominic turned and slunk to the edge of the room, watching silently and biting his nails. Richard gingerly picked the hammer up off the floor and swung it lightly in his hand, careful not to make eye contact.

"There," I said, pointing to the freestanding wall, "come on Richard, we have to get a move on. Here, do you want me to help you?" I started to walk purposely across the room – for the second time that day – reaching out my hand to take the hammer from Richard. He was staring nervously at Dominic, who still stood by the window, now taking angry exaggerated puffs on a cigarette. "Oh don't worry about him," I said, nodding my head towards the pathetic figure by the window and taking the hammer from Richard, "if it was up to him we would be leaving people standing outside until midnight while we agonised over where one shitty little picture should go."

Suddenly there was a cracking sound behind me, a scurry of feet and before I could reach the hammer out of Richard's hand, I was being dragged down so my face pressed into the hard wood. My arm was pinned under my side and a heavy weight slammed down onto my waist. It all happened so quickly that it took me a few seconds to work out that the weight on top of me, making my breath come in short, sharp gasps, was Richard. I could see Dominic's trainers scuffed and grubby pacing backwards and forwards level with my eye line. Both of them were shouting at the same time, while I tried to struggle free, kicking my legs.

"You're fucking crazy," Richard was yelling, his weight sinking deeper down on to my hip. I had to get him off me, I couldn't breathe.

"No she's fucking crazy," Dominic yelled back, his pacing was getting more agitated.

"Don't even think about it," Richard bellowed, his arm stretched past my face, I could see his fingers lengthening and straightening, desperately grabbing at the floor like he was trying to pick something up. My eyes darted across the floorboards; the hammer was resting a couple of centimetres out of his reach. I wriggled more furiously and tried to scream, but all that came out were exaggerated gasps.

"I always knew the pair of you were fucking mental, but trying to attack her. Jesus Christ Dominic." I stopped wriggling and lay temporarily frozen. Finally I managed to gather all the pieces of shouting into one lump, then set about untangling the scene which had unfolded behind my back and why Dominic was now sitting on top of me.

"Please get off me, you're hurting me," I managed to whisper into the floor.

"Shit, sorry," Richard said, jumping off me like he had forgotten I was even there. I looked up from the floor, both men's faces stared down at me, the sunlight catching their hair making it look like halos were hovering above their heads. The irony of this made me smile. Richard looked confused. "Help me up, will you?" I said, extending my hand out to be folded into Richard's.

"He tried to bloody smack you one Iss," Richard said carefully, watching my face while he straightened my shirt and lightly brushed the dust from my jeans. "I'm sure he did," I said staring straight at Dominic. "Should we start hanging these pictures?" I forced a weak triumphant smile.

Even then, with my so-called boyfriend attempting to attack me without my knowing, like the true coward that he was, I still didn't think I would leave. Not that evening anyway.

It wasn't until a few hours later when the first lot of our friends had started to arrive, laden with Sainsbury's bags full of cheap wine and clear plastic cups, and Dominic had made a futile attempt at an apology that the idea of just leaving, walking out the door with my back disappearing down Lexington Street, was my answer. It was so simple, so easy and so beautifully obvious. "Hi sweetie," Rebecca, one of Richard's friends, lurched forward branding cool red lips onto my cheek, her nose was red with the cold. "Trouble here this afternoon I hear from..." she stopped, letting her words trail off choosing instead to nod towards Richard who was hanging the last two pictures on the far wall. I smiled tightly at Rebecca. "Business as usual I would say. You know Dominic."

"You OK?" she asked narrowing her eyes and giving my elbow a light squeeze.

"Fine," I attempted another tight smile.

"Yes, well I know what he can be like and I know it's not fun. I'm sure that you bear the brunt of it..." my smile vanished, Rebecca knew she had overstepped the line. Her face flushed red so it was now the same colour as her nose. She swallowed before continuing the conversation on a different track. "Tell me what I need to do. The space looks great, by the way, it always does. You always know exactly what to do. You have such a great eye Iss." My eyes swept the room and that's when I caught sight of Dominic. He was staring over the shoulder of someone I vaguely recognised, they had probably been to one of his shows, but Dominic was looking straight past them like they didn't even exist. He was watching the shape of Rebecca as she had turned from me to step back a few metres from the wall to admire one of his pictures. Dominic's eyes continued to watch her; the person had stopped talking and turned around to see what – or more like whom – he was looking at. Rebecca must have sensed she was being watched, she looked up and smiled at them both. I saw a pathetic grin form on Dominic's face. He disgusted me.

My mind cleared of all the debris and swirls of uncertainty and anger that usually bounced off its edges, leaving me with a new sense of calmness. Clarity at last. I walked behind the free-standing wall, now out of view of the rest of the room, crouched to find my handbag under one of the tables, collected my coat off the hook hanging on the door, slipped both my arms inside the fabric and buttoned it up. Carefully I turned the handle on the back door and found the cold biting my cheeks as I stood on the landing looking down the metal staircase leading to the back alley that would spill me out, first into the little alley, and then onto Lexington Street.

My heels clattered on the metal steps, making me wince and glance hurriedly over my shoulder expecting to see someone standing at the door, but no one was there. I dug my hands into my coat pockets, feeling the touch of leather fingers uncrumpling inside my palms and yanked the gloves out one by one, I shoved each onto my hands. Sinking my head against the wind, I turned into Lexington Street, making my way southwards, I disappeared into the dark folds of people until I arrived at the bus stop on The Strand where I boarded the bus.

The red light on the answering machine was blinking as I unlocked the door to the flat. Before even switching on a light, I pressed the 'play' button while I took off my coat and headed into the kitchen to make a cup of tea. My mouth felt furry and dry after the constant stream of cheap wine and champagne. A distant voice with a strong Australian accent spoke softly into the machine, "Oh, am I speaking to the machine?" I smiled recognising the voice of my Aunt Jean instantly. "Oh Isobel hello and hello...umm...Dominic. It's your Aunt Jean here Isobel darling. I hope you are not suffering the cold there too much. I was hoping to catch you, but you're probably out enjoying London. Yes." I smiled again, Aunt Jean was always so uneasy with the answering machine, always sounding like she expected it to answer her back and then seeming very confused when there was no reply. "Anyway, darling – Isobel – the reason I am calling you is because I wanted to see what you will be doing for Christmas. I mean I know you won't be home – here in Australia I mean – but I would like to know where to call you on Christmas Day, that's all." I stopped stirring the sugar into the tea. The adrenalin of leaving Dominic and the others in Soho was wearing off and now hearing my aunt's voice pushed the last tiny strand of adrenalin dangerously close to snapping. I gripped the teaspoon tighter, the sound of her voice hazy in the background like an old LP left playing once people had long left the room. "...anyway sweetheart, I hope you are well and smiling, of course. Just give me a ring when you can. Lots of love. Bye." The answering machine clicked off and the mechanical voice of the BT woman interrupted my link to the familiarity of my aunt and some sense of family, "End of messages." came the voice cold and unfeeling.

I released my grip on the teaspoon and watched as the silver hit the pottery. I didn't really know what to do next. The sense of purpose to leave Dominic without so much as a 'goodbye' had come so strongly, overtaking my thoughts and actions for the last few hours, now that I had seemingly arrived at my destination, I was at a total loss of what to do next. The sound of my aunt's voice only amplified my loss and startlingly took me back to another time and place where eucalypt hazed the sky, the sound of cicadas stung the night air and a frightened young woman, not much older than a teenager, sunk under the bed clothes punching her swelling belly. I could remember the fear burning a hole in the pit of my belly and translating into an anger I couldn't control or explain. There must have been times when my actions – mainly the cutting looks – and the words, the words that came hissing and spitting out of my mouth falling like hot embers at my aunt's feet must have disturbed her. If they did she never showed it. My Aunt Jean was always composed and seemed to understand, using measured sentences which never made me feel judged, but always protected. I could hear her on the phone to my mother, it would usually be late at night when she thought I was sleeping in the room off the hallway. I could only ever pick up every few words because Aunt Jean's voice was low in the receiver, pitching higher every now and again, but always calm, except for one night in late summer. It was just before the baby was born, my hair was hot and sticky against the nape of my neck, I had rolled over and twisted it into a knot high on top of my head. A thin slice of light cut under the bedroom door from the hallway and I imagined Aunt Jean sitting at the phone table, legs crossed with a wine next to her. It was a still, hot night so the bedroom window was open further than usual, I knew the front door which opened next to my bedroom window was open as I had hinged it to the hook on the wall so it wouldn't slam shut during the night and double-checked the gauze door was locked before going to bed.

Aunt Jean was talking to my mother on the telephone, her voice, usually hushed, was growing louder. I propped myself up onto one elbow, straining to listen. Even though I could only make out every few words I was starting to understand the gist of the conversation.

"She's a good girl. You know she is..." my aunt was saying. There was a long pause, "yes, but she has been like that since she was a tiny baby...that's no reason to punish or banish her... yes I understand she can get angry, but so can we all...I don't think she would be...violent, violent are you sure?...I've never seen it...with you...with Tom..." Then there was a long silence. I wondered if Aunt Jean had hung up or worse that my mother was still talking and Aunt Jean was listening – believing – what my mother was saying to her. I started to panic, I couldn't have my mother rip away the one person in the world who knew the truth about me, about who I really am and loved me anyway. I started to heave my body over the side of the bed. My feet touched the floorboards just as the light in the hallway snapped off. I sat frozen on the edge of the bed, my tummy bulging out in front of me like a swollen fruit. The bedroom door creaked open. I could feel Aunt Jean staring at me.

"You alright love?" my aunt whispered into the darkness.

"Yes," I replied softly.

"Do you want me shut the window, it could get cooler later on."

"No thanks."

"OK, well good night sweet child. Everything is going to be just fine..." her voice trailed off. I sat waiting for the shadow to move and the door to shut, but nothing happened. "Do you want to talk?" Aunt Jean finally asked. I couldn't answer. I heard her gentle footsteps across the floor and felt her weight sink down onto the mattress beside me. Her arm slid around my shoulders as she pulled me into the softness of her body. "I promise you everything will be just fine," she said into my hair.

Leaning against the kitchen doorway, I took a sip of tea, deciding what to do next. My eyes snagged on one of Dominic's cardigans slung over the back of the couch. I took another sip of tea, holding the warm liquid in my mouth while I tossed ideas around in my head and continued to stare at the cardigan. I had to leave the flat. I didn't want to be here when Dominic returned drunk and probably full of an array of other drugs, gloating over the over-inflated sale of that impossibly small photograph. The thought of his naked body sliding into bed next to me spurred me into action. I dropped the teacup on the kitchen bench and ran into the bedroom to pull the suitcase off the top of the cupboard. I opened drawers and cupboard doors taking arm-full after arm-full of clothes and jamming them into the case. I raced into the bathroom and emptied the contents of the top shelf into a plastic bag, pulled my dressing gown off the back of the door and zipped it into the bag. My passport. I opened the top drawer of the bedside table and found it under tissues and bits of make-up.

Wheeling the case up the hall to the kitchen with my passport curled in my hand I suddenly realised I had no idea where I was going. The red light was still blinking on the answering machine with Aunt Jean's message. I checked my watch, it was coming up to nine o'clock so that would mean it was about eight in the morning in Australia. I imagined Aunt Jean would be sitting on the veranda, eating fruit for breakfast and reading the *Sydney Morning Herald*, a piping hot cup of coffee beside her and Bessie the sheep dog lying lazily in the shade of the veranda step. I dialled her number and waited for the phone to connect. 'Please be there, please be home', I murmured. Eventually the phone was picked up and Aunt Jean was saying good morning and repeating her phone number into the phone. "Aunt Jean, it's me – Isobel." There was a slight pause before her voice came softly and happily down the phone line. "Isobel, it's so wonderful to hear from you darling." That's when I knew I had made the right decision. It was time to go home.

LAURA

I don't know what time it was, but the phone was ring-ing and it was disturbing my sleep. I half opened one eye and scratched around beside the bed with my hand searching for my mobile. I tried to read the screen to see who it was: 'unknown number'. I hesitated, it was probably the wrong number, but I was awake now so I may as well answer it, I thought.

"Hello," I breathed into the receiver.

"Lau, is that you?"

"Hmmm... who's this?"

"It's Isobel." Isobel. I sat up in bed, my elbow knocked over a glass of water on the night stand. "Oh shit," I said, watching water dribble between the cracks in the floorboards.

"Laura?"

"Sorry. Sorry I just knocked a glass of water over and it's going everywhere. Anyway, God it's so good to hear from you. How's sunny London?"

"Don't know," Isobel replied.

"What? Why, where are you?"

"I'm coming back Lau! To Sydney..."

"What? When? Why didn't you say you were coming back? Oh please tell me I haven't forgotten."

"No, no you haven't forgotten," Isobel said laughing. "It's a surprise, even to me."

I was standing at the arrivals gate, on tip toe, waiting to catch sight of Isobel. Everyone was anxiously watching passengers coming down the ramp, trailing their luggage behind them or pushing trolleys stacked high with luggage. They were all bleary-eyed off a long haul flight. That is, all except for Isobel. She came striding down the ramp in tight jeans and a T-shirt with the neck line falling seductively off one shoulder. Her eyes searched the crowd and no doubt the eyes of every guy in the crowd searched her. Isobel saw me and flashed a smile as I slid between the folds of people, stretching my arms out to give her a hug. She was skinnier than I remembered. I could feel the bones of her ribs poking into me as I hugged her. "That would be right, you are the only woman to go to London and not get disgustingly fat," I laughed as she gave me her hand luggage to carry. "So good to see," I smiled. "And you," Isobel said giving my shoulders a squeeze.

We had turned off the main artery road and were heading east around the outskirts of Centennial Park. The windows were down letting in the warm summer breeze. "God it's good to feel heat," Isobel exclaimed, tilting her face up into the sun from the open window.

"Is that why you're back, you missed the heat. Couldn't bear us having another scorching summer without you?" I asked, pressing down the accelerator as the lights turned green. Isobel was silent. I looked across at her and saw she was crying. "What's wrong babe?" I asked slowly, suddenly remembering the careful management of Isobel's emotions that is required more often than not. Isobel wiped at her face with the back of her hand. "Nothing, I am being silly. Just probably glad to be back and jetlagged. That's all," she said, attempting a smile. I nodded.

"I know Cate is looking forward to seeing you," I said, changing the subject. "She had an event or something on today so it was all hands on deck, otherwise she would have come to the airport with me. She's doing really well. Her job is pretty full on, but not as full on as Tom's..."

"Tom?" Isobel asked, bringing her face back into the car out of the sun.

"Yeah, her boyfriend."

"Oh, of course. Tom. What's he like?"

"I think he's great. They are really well suited and they seem really happy."

"Is it serious?"

"Well they have bought a house together, so I think it's pretty serious," I said.

"Hmm, yeah I guess so. What does he do again?"

"Banking. Don't ask me what type because I know basically nothing about that world. I know he works long hours, wears a suit and makes a lot of money..."

"But is a total bore," Isobel cut me off. I smiled, "You wish. He is actually really cool and funny and dare I say it good looking."

"Lucky Cate," Isobel said, with what I thought was a hint of jealousy. "It will be great to see her," Isobel finished quickly.

ISOBEL

I try to open my eyes, but they feel like old doors on rusty hinges, refusing to budge. Sleep takes over again momentarily and I let my mind sink back into a warm slumber. Some time later, much later I think, a light tapping on the door breaks me through the thin layers of unconsciousness. Lazily I respond to the knock with a 'hmmm.' The door inches open and Aunt Jean treads into the room holding a flower-patterned teacup and saucer I recognise as being part of my grandmother's wedding set. She smiles at me and sets the teacup on the dresser beside the bed before settling herself down onto the quilt.

"Sleep well?" she asks, smoothing the hair away from my face. I nod wearily and let my eyes close for a few seconds. "It's so lovely to have you home, Iss. It's been such a long, long time. You haven't changed a bit, maybe just a bit on the thin side."

"I don't think so. I am the same weight as when I left," I answer, sitting up and reaching for the teacup from the dresser, "You not having one?" I ask Aunt Jean smelling the aroma of freshly brewed tea, straight from the pot, swirling up from the porcelain.

"I've had my quota for today I think."

"Why, what time is it?"

Aunt Jean twists her wrist and checks her watch, "Goodness, it's coming up to six o'clock already. Even I thought it was earlier than that."

I blink a few times trying to remember the time zone I am in, "In the evening?" I ask her.

"Yes," she laughs and gives my leg a squeeze through the summer quilt. "Oh I have missed you Iss. I know we spoke on the phone while you were away, but it's just not the same as being able to see someone in the flesh and give them a big hug, is it?"

"No. I've really missed you too. It really is good to see you," I smiled, genuinely meaning the words.

"Do you think you might want to give your parents a call a bit later? I know they would love to hear from you."

"They know I'm home, I called them from Heathrow and told them I was coming back. I'll see them Christmas Day. That will be enough," I replied twisting the teacup around in my hand.

"OK, well I'm not going to force you into doing anything you don't want to do. So just do whatever you think is best. I know things are still a bit strained…"

"Strained! That's one way to describe it Aunt Jean. I would say irretrievably broken down. They haven't really bothered with me since the whole pregnancy thing and that was bloody years ago now."

"People are just different Iss, they react to things in different ways and I suppose it's almost gone too far for them, and now they just don't know what to do."

"Exactly as I said, irretrievably broken down," I repeated, swallowing hard. Aunt Jean used the pause to change tack. "So will you miss your friends in London? Tell me about living there, I really want to hear all about it," she said, taking the empty teacup from me and placing it carefully back on the saucer.

I thought of Dominic. As I was frantically trying to zip up the suitcase, stuffed to the brim with unfolded clothes, I had heard a black cab slowing to a stop out the front of our building. I held my breath for a moment, before slinking to the window and pressing my back against the wall to peer unseen out of a tiny gap in the curtain. The cab had stopped in the middle of the street and out spilled Dominic, Richard and Rebecca. I froze again, "Fuck it," I whispered into the darkness of the lounge room. It had taken a couple of hours on the internet to find an available flight to Sydney that was leaving the next morning that I could actually afford. Then, the earlier urgency of making the decision to leave had seemingly drained all my energy while I wandered aimlessly around the flat unable to decide what I could bear leaving behind for Dominic to get his grubby hands on. I flicked on the lamp in the living room and sprinted back to the bedroom to try and shove the suitcase under the bed. I could hear the main door to the building opening and the slow, drunken laughter of Rebecca. The suitcase would only go part way. I was on the floor now, desperately pushing at the case with my feet, but it wouldn't go all the way under the bed. Keys were fumbling in the lock of the door to our flat. All I could do was stare at the doorway of our bedroom while I tried pathetically to shove the bag into a space under the bed where it wouldn't fit.

"Oh Iss must be home," Rebecca said, "Iss," she yelled out into the hallway. I continued to stare at the bedroom door, open and waiting for them to find me shoving a packed suitcase under the bed. Richard was the first to appear at the door. He looked blankly at me sitting on the floor and then at what my feet were pressing up against. He was drunk and it took a moment for him to register it was a suitcase. Richard looked back at my face, "You alright?" he whispered, I could hear Dominic and Rebecca in the kitchen. I nodded before lifting my finger to my lips. He nodded in response. "Do you want a drink?" he asked. I shook my head and stood up.

"Help me with this, would you?" I said softly, trying to drag the suitcase out from under the bed, but Richard just stood in the doorway.

"Where are you going, Iss?"

"Come on, just help me will you? Richard. Please," I pleaded quietly.

"Is she here?" That was Dominic from the kitchen.

Richard and I stared at one another, "Come on!" I pleaded again. There were footsteps coming down the hallway and Dominic's figure closed in behind Richard. "Oh, so you are here. Nice of you to run off like that. Guess you also don't care that I sold the shitty little photograph for a ridiculous amount of money," Dominic said casually.

"Good for you," I spat back, heaving the suitcase up onto the bed to finish closing the zipper.

"What are you doing?" Dominic shoved past Richard and was now standing in the bedroom, glaring at the case on the bed. That pathetic T-shirt all artistically ripped and his skinny legs dangling out of impossibly skinny jeans, made me start to laugh.

"I'm leaving Dominic. How does that song go, *I'm leaving on a jet plane, don't know when I'll be back again…*" I started to sing.

"What? You're going to Australia?" Dominic asked, dropping his east London accent for his real, middle-class Cotswolds upbringing.

"Yes that's right, old boy," I replied, mimicking his authentic accent.

Richard had slunk away from the scene and I could now hear him speaking in a low, urgent tone to Rebecca in the living room.

"Fine, should I call you a cab?" Dominic said, his voice shaking.

"That's ever so kind of you."

"Fine. I will do it now. Heathrow is it? On a one-way ticket?"

"Yep and yep," I answered, finally getting the zip to go all the way around the suitcase.

Rebecca and Richard stood awkwardly in the doorway of the living room while I lumbered the suitcase into the hall. "Are you going back to Australia for Christmas?" Rebecca tried.

"No. For good, I think," I said, unwinding my house keys from the key ring.

"Oh."

"Yeah, so Merry Christmas and all that," I smiled, dropping the loose keys into the bowl by the front door. The three of them hovered in the hallway while I opened the door. "Come on, give us a hug before you go Iss. You can't just walk out the door," Richard said, grabbing my elbow. I turned and hugged Richard and Rebecca, "Good luck, yeah," she said into my hair. "Thanks," I muttered before firing one last look at Dominic who remained firmly rooted to the same spot in the hallway, staring blankly at me. Then I shut the door, walked calmly down the stairs to a black cab waiting on the street and only let the tears escape when I saw the first sign to Heathrow.

"No I don't think I'll really miss anyone in London," I now said to Aunt Jean, "I think I need to get up and have a shower or I will never sleep tonight."

"Alright then. I thought we might have something to eat out on the veranda, just like the old days..." Aunt Jean stopped, seeing my grip on the teacup tense and my eyes flicker. "Isobel, I'm sorry. I just meant when you were living here with me, no matter what the circumstances were for you being here, I just meant it was lovely having you here. The same as it's lovely having you here again now. That's all." Aunt Jean said quietly, watching my fingers loosen.

"It's OK. Don't worry about it," I replied, smiling tightly.

When Aunt Jean had gone to start preparing dinner, I let myself slip back down into the warmth of the bed, now slightly damp with sweat. Even with the blinds pulled down and a light breeze floating in through the door opening onto the veranda, the room felt humid, but I found it strangely comforting.

I let my gaze rest on the overstuffed armchair pushed at an angle in the far corner next to the door to the veranda. It was the same chair I had sat in so many afternoons, reading a book, waiting. Just waiting for the baby floating and swelling inside me to grow big enough to desert my body. And me. Forever.

My fingers stroked the dusty pink satin of the quilt. It was the same quilt I had clutched at, grasping big handfuls of twisted fabric, when I had felt the first heavy twinges of labour saturate me. Physical pain I now couldn't remember. Just then, my eyes began darting all over the room, taking in every piece of furniture, texture and ornament – every single piece was exactly as it was all those years ago when I was waiting. It felt like my body was re-absorbing all the anger and fear, but above all, the lie that had been harboured in this room. The image of Tom's face, trapped just as it looked the very last time I saw him fleeted through the mash of emotions the room pulled and tugged at until his face rested in the middle of the chaos inside my head. I guessed he now might have lines around his eyes and mouth, but those dimples piercing each cheek would still be there when he smiled. Does he still think of me? The last time I was in this room, I still could have been with him. It was my choice to end the whole thing, wasn't it? Wasn't it? I couldn't really remember the facts from the mantras I had whispered to myself over and over again, like some sort of prayer, in the half-light before dawn.

Where was Tom now? I had no idea where to even start looking.

CATE

I'm laying lasagne sheets onto freshly cooked mince. I take a long sip of wine before sliding the baking tray into the oven. Laura and Isobel are coming over for dinner. It will be the first time I have seen Isobel since she came home almost three weeks ago. She decided not to stick around in Sydney too long and left on a train the same day she arrived to visit her aunt down the south coast somewhere and spent Christmas there as well.

I turn on the stove timer and peer into the lasagne baking away. For an instant I screw up my nose thinking pasta perhaps wasn't the best idea in this heat, particularly straight after Christmas when I am trying to shift the little bulge which has started to pop out over the top of my jeans. I can feel it when I sit down. I suck my tummy in. Tom had seen me sucking in my tummy in front of the mirror last night. He'd stretched out on the bed with his elbow under his head, smiling and telling me I was an idiot, I looked the same, he couldn't tell the difference, he said. I wasn't convinced – even when he pulled me onto the bed, trying to pinch at the 'roll', exclaiming he couldn't feel or see anything. I was laughing so hard I fell off the bed and Tom fell straight on top of me. The events which followed took my mind off my new-found rolls. I smile now thinking about it.

The doorbell is ringing. I practically run down the hallway seeing two outlines cutting the shape of Laura and Isobel in the glass panels. I swing the door open and am hugging Isobel. We are laughing and shouting, none of our words are coherent and Laura is laughing and yelling 'what about me?' Then all three of us are hugging and jumping up and down and I can't quite believe we are all back together and Isobel is here in the flesh. I pull back to take a look at her. She is still beautiful, maybe even more so now because a few very faint lines have formed around her mouth. Her hair is a bit shorter with a long fringe. She looks skinnier to me. I immediately suck my tummy in for the second time this evening.

"Come in, come in," I am saying above the din which is still the three of us yelling at each other at the front door.

We're in the kitchen and I am pouring big glugs of chilled pinot into glasses. Laura is sitting on a barstool and Isobel is looking around the kitchen, picking up pieces of kitchenware Tom and I have collected over the years. "I really like your place," Isobel is saying.

"I know, isn't it great?" Laura says before I can reply.

"Thanks," I mutter, slightly embarrassed, feeling red rising on my neck.

"It's so grown up," Isobel says lifting the lid on a teapot.

"Well we are grown up now Iss..." Laura replies again before I have the chance. But I am thankful to Laura for replying, I prickle slightly feeling like that was a little dig from Isobel. I smile at Laura.

"Yes I know. I like it Cate, I really do. Actually I love it," Isobel says giving me a bright smile. "It's so good to see you both, you just don't realise how much you miss people until you see them again, do you?" Isobel says raising her glass in the air. "To wonderful friends," she says. Laura and I repeat it back to her and we all take a sip.

"I'm sorry I have been so crap at keeping in touch," Isobel says taking another quick sip. Laura and I look at each other. "Well I have been terrible too," I admit and Laura is nodding her head in agreement, "But you know that we're truly good friends because it only seems like yesterday that we saw each other – and the emotion at the front door," Laura is laughing and pressing her palm against her heart dramatically.

"Is it weird to be back?" I ask Isobel.

"Yes and no. Five years is a long time not to come home and it was so good to see Lau when she came over to London. I can't believe I missed you..." Isobel says looking at me. Tom and I had been in London for a week a couple of years ago when Isobel was in New York – something to do with the gallery she was working for and a new artist. She had been almost impossible to track down before our trip and I only got to speak to her the day we were flying out from Bangkok to London and that's when Isobel told me she wasn't going to be in town. The conversation was brief to say the least, our flight was boarding and she seemed agitated. When I switched my phone on again there was a text waiting from Isobel saying she was sorry, she loved me, along with the number of her boyfriend who would be happy to catch up with us. I never called him, I didn't really see the point, after all I didn't know him, he didn't know me and we were staying with Tom's brother.

"Can I take a peek around the house?" Isobel was standing up.

"Of course," I answer. "You would get the guided tour, but I need to sort this lasagne out. It's starting to look a little scary in here," I say crouching down to look inside the oven.

"And I have seen the place enough times, so I am going to fill up my glass," Laura pitches in reaching for the wine bottle on the bench top.

"That's cool, it's much better fun to open and close cupboards and rifle through drawers when you're on your own," Isobel is saying over her shoulder, she's already halfway down the hallway.

ISOBEL

I am standing in Cate's lounge room. I can hear her and Laura's voices in the kitchen. It's kind of weird snooping around Cate's house, nothing is really familiar to me at all. We used to spend so much time at each other's houses and I knew her old flat like it was my own place. We'd go there after an afternoon at the beach to drink very strong homemade cocktails on the balcony. Having an outdoor space was such a premium back then and Cate was the only one of us who did. Now looking around Cate's house I could see her life has continued on without me. Most of it is an eclectic mix of old and new. She's definitely got an eye for style and design. I try to remember if she was always like that, but nothing really sticks in my mind. It's obvious this is an adult's house with no children. Everything is in its place. I don't recognise any of the artwork on the walls, my thing is more urban art and Cate's taste looks to be more traditional. I notice a photo frame on the mantlepiece. I walk over to it and as I get closer I can see the photo inside is of Cate with a guy – it must be her boyfriend – Cate's hair is partly covering his face so I can't quite make him out just yet. It must have been windy when the photo was taken. I pick up the photo and stare at the two faces. They look so happy and so...so together.

A tingly feeling starts to erupt at the base of my neck. I suddenly feel very hot, the room is stifling. I stand there and stare at the photo. Logic tells me it can't be, what are the chances? How would I not know, Cate has been with her boyfriend for years – I think. The longer I stare at the other face in the photo, the clearer it becomes. It's Tom. Oh my God. It is Tom. *My* Tom. Seeing his face, years older is making my eyes well with water. My hand is shaking, the movement is distorting Tom's face. Maybe it's not him, I tell myself. Perhaps it is just someone who looks a lot like Tom. That happens. But then I remember that Cate's boyfriend's name is Tom. Tom who? What's his bloody last name? How could I not know what his last name is? Maybe she hasn't told me. The truth is, I haven't really spoken properly to Cate since I have been away and when I have it's been quick snatched conversations about my woeful love life and a few amusing postcards scattered through each other's letterboxes.

"Dinner's ready Iss," Cate is yelling from the kitchen.

"Coming," I am replying weakly, but I don't know if I am speaking out loud because I am wiping the water from my cheeks, carefully placing the photo frame back on the mantelpiece and trying to work out how I am ever going to muddle through the discovery of this relationship. I take another look at the photo before turning around and walking down the hallway and into the kitchen to my two oblivious friends.

TOM

Before I even unlock the front door, I can hear Cate and her friends laughing. Laura and her mate from England are obviously still here. Sounds like it's been a wine-filled night, I check my watch, it's 11 o'clock. I am knackered and stone cold sober.

Cate yells out as I open the door. "We're in the kitchen."

"Really, I couldn't hear you, I thought no one was home," I say, yanking my tie off and slinging it over a chair in our bedroom. I slip off my suit jacket and let it lie like a crumpled old man on the bed.

"Wine?" Cate yells over the sound of a cork popping out of a bottle.

"No I'll grab a scotch," I reply, making my way into the lounge room to retrieve the scotch bottle. I find a glass in the sideboard and pour a double measure. It needs ice. I walk into the kitchen swirling the glass and see Cate before I see anyone else, I kiss her on top of her drunken head. I'm smiling when I look up to say 'hi' to Laura and Cate's other friend. Cate has jumped up and is saying something, she's excited. But I can't hear what she's saying because I am staring at the other girl sitting in mine and Cate's kitchen. Laura is kissing my cheek, she smells of booze too. I try and smile in the general direction I think Laura is, but I am still not watching her or really clocking that anyone else is in the room besides – Isobel. Fucking hell.

I must look stunned. I can't say anything, all I think is that I need ice in my scotch. Cate is pulling at my shirt sleeve like a toddler who wants to show me her toy, but still I am staring at Isobel and wishing there was ice in my drink.

"This is Isobel," Cate is saying. I try and smile. Am I smiling? I don't know. I really don't know how to play this situation. Do I pretend I don't know her? No that's completely immature and would have been what I would have done when faced with the same situation when I was with Isobel. Yes, definitely immature.

I put my hand out to go to shake Isobel's hand. Another ridiculous move. What the fuck am I doing? Isobel is not helping me, she is just sitting there. Finally she gets up and makes the decision for us. "Hi Tom," she seems to breathe my name. I swallow. "Hi Isobel, nice to..." but she cuts me off.

"See me again?" she asks, red wine around her lips. Why did she have to say that word – *again*. I can feel Cate looking at me. "You two already know each other?" Cate, oh my beautiful Cate, asks. She sounds confused, scared even. So am I. I go to say something, but Isobel is quicker out of the starting blocks than me and answers before I can even open my mouth in protest. "Yes, we went to school together," she says casually.

"You're kidding!" Laura is screeching. My head is starting to hurt, I still need ice in my glass.

"That's right, small world," I say, still holding my hand out to Isobel who goes to take it but just stops short. "Oh come on, we know each other a bit better than that," she is saying. I must look like a rabbit trapped in headlights. I blink, a long hard blink. I'm thinking, 'why don't you just cut my balls off right now', but Isobel is smiling and saying, "Old friends should at least give each other a peck on the cheek...not a handshake."

I put my hand behind my back, I don't know why, it just feels safer there and then I lean my cheek in and basically do one of those air kiss things that I can't stand and try to hold my ground when a waft of Isobel's scent, bitter oranges, lifts into my nose. Her lips are impossibly red, her eyes are greener than I remember, but all her features are smudging together, she's starting to look like a Monet painting.

"I need ice," I say weakly and retire to the safety of the freezer. I stick my head inside the icebox for a bit and feel much calmer when I turn around and see Cate is smiling, pouring herself another drink and raising a toast to 'amazing coincidences'.

ISOBEL

I had been trying to act as normal as possible since I had picked up the photograph of Cate and Tom. I had even managed not to mention anything about it. Instead I told Cate how beautiful her house was and the three of us caught up on the last five years and laughed at old memories. Under the surface though, I was plotting to stay until Tom got home so I could see him, I guess. I wanted to see him. The image of the two of them together, so happy as a couple kept attaching itself to the front of my mind. I even went back into the lounge room to look at the photograph again on my way back from the bathroom – even though the bathroom was nowhere near the lounge room.

When I finally heard the key in the lock though, I started to lose my nerve at a very rapid rate, panic was washing over me. I'd had too much to drink and knew emotion would take over. So when Tom did arrive home there were torturous minutes of him wandering the rooms, his footsteps cracking on the floorboards and sounds of him pouring a drink in another room – that act alone made me feel even more isolated than living on the other side of the world – it was the sound of someone comfortable and so familiar with their home, their life. This was Tom's life...with Cate. I was struggling to keep the conversation going, knowing he was about to walk into the kitchen any second, so when I saw him standing in the doorway with eyes only for Cate, the tender way he kissed the top of her head, I knew he was content. I wasn't sure if he had ever looked at me like that. I sat rooted to the chair. Laura was excited to see him and there was such a familiarity among the three of them, it shifted my isolation further and deeper. He was about to see me, it could only be a few seconds until he saw me. Suddenly I thought, what if he doesn't recognise me. I wanted to vomit. But as soon as Tom looked at me, I knew he recognised me – instantly. His face, although a bit older, was transported back to another time and I knew he knew exactly who I was and knew *me*.

It was obvious he was awkward, really awkward. I would have to take control, to show him I wasn't the crazy person he thinks I am. His hand outstretching made the isolation plunge just a little bit deeper, but I brushed it off and said as confidently as I could muster something about us knowing each other from school. I had to get out of there as fast as possible.

CATE

I'm drunk. The ceiling is moving around and I want it to stop. Tom is lying beside me in bed. He feels warm and I can see the outline of his body under the sheet. He's glowing in the lamplight and this makes me smile. I have one leg slung over his. He seems to be asleep already and in a deep sleep. I guess he is really tired, he's been working so hard lately.

I close my eyes and Isobel's face comes into my head and I think how weird it is that she and Tom know each other. After all these years of being with Tom and knowing Isobel, two and two was never put together.

TOM

I am lying in bed, on my side, very still with my eyes closed. The taste of scotch is clinging in sickly sweet drips to the inside of my mouth, even though I've cleaned my teeth. Suddenly I don't feel tired at all, but I pretend I am asleep because I am avoiding talking about Isobel with Cate. I know I am going to have to eventually, how the hell am I ever going to avoid it, but I don't have to do it right now so pretending to be asleep is the immediate option I am going for.

The thing that I have been turning over and over is how honest I should be about mine and Isobel's relationship with Cate. Of course she is going to understand I have a past, but how do I tell Cate her friend is completely nuts, that the scar on my back is thanks to her friend clawing at me like a wild animal. Then there's the other thing, the pregnancy thing. Christ that was a near miss, how different my life could have been. I roll over onto my other side and grab Cate in close to me. Her breath smells of wine and there's the familiar smell of her perfume faint on her neck. Her eyes open slightly. "I thought you were asleep," she says sleepily into my shoulder. I hug her tightly like I am clinging to a life raft.

LAURA

I can hear Isobel tossing and turning on the sofa bed. I really should think about getting the springs oiled on that bed, it's so noisy and keeping me awake. It's hot in the bedroom, I get up to open the window a bit further and see the kitchen light snap on. Isobel is leaning against the doorframe, her back to me.

"You OK?" I say into the darkness of my room.

"Just hot. Go back to sleep," Isobel answers.

"Can't, it's too hot and I think I'm still really quite pissed," I say lying back down and shoving the sheet to the end of the bed with my foot. Eventually I start to drift off to sleep and somewhere between consciousness and falling off into the edge of slumber, Isobel and Tom's faces blur into my half dreams. Tom's face looks strained, almost alarmed, and I slowly realise it is the same look Tom was wearing in the kitchen tonight when he saw Isobel.

ISOBEL

I tried going to sleep on Laura's sofa bed for a couple of hours. My constant rolling and unravelling of my arms and legs sapped into the springs of the sofa, making them squeak and grind with every movement. So eventually I had given up and now I am sitting on Laura's balcony – seems all the upwardly mobile urbanites around these parts can afford an outdoor space these days. Not like when we got our first jobs out of university with the three of us standing, almost in single file, on Cate's balcony. That was the second time that particular image had bounced into my memory this evening. I think I have had enough memory triggers tonight, instead I stare out into the darkness. I can see the lights lining the promenade on the beach from here, occasional car lights stream along the edge of the water. It is peaceful, but I feel anything but.

I think about Laura asleep inside and I wonder what she would do if she knew how Tom and I really know each other. I was half tempted to tell her when we got back to her place, but as the wine started to wear off, my senses trickled in and I realised I should just shut up for now. There are so many complicated layers to this whole thing and where should the story start and end, because to me the story is still going. Somewhere out there is *my* child – mine and Tom's child. Cate's boyfriend's child. My eyes feel hot, water is beginning to sting the backs of them. I don't want to cry because I am not even sure who I would be crying for.

I draw my knees up to my chest and wrap my arms tightly around them. I will just stare out towards the sea for a bit and ignore the breeze cooling and closing in around my body. When I open my eyes again a slip of sunlight is breaking through a thundercloud. I can barely move my neck, it's cramped to one side and I have goosebumps running up and down the length of both legs. Slowly I unwind my neck and decide to go in and make coffee. I tiptoe back through the balcony door which I must have left open all night and very carefully make my way to the kitchen. Laura's bedroom door is half-open. There's no sign of life in there yet, catching sight of the clock in the kitchen I see it's not quite six o'clock, obviously way too early for Laura. The kettle has finished boiling when I hear Laura say, "You're up early." I swing around and see Laura stretching her arms above her head and yawning.

"I think the sun woke me up," I mumble, reaching into the cupboard for another cup. "Do you always get up at this time, it's not even six."

Laura yawned, nodding her head. "It took me a while to get to sleep, but once I dropped off I think I must have passed out, way too much wine," she said, taking the mug of coffee and wrapping both hands around it. "I really don't want to go to work," she muttered twisting her big toe into the floor.

"Well at least you've got work to go to," I replied, taking a sip of coffee.

"Enjoy it while you can Iss, I would love to have some time off and just do something totally different for a bit. It's so easy to lose perspective of the stuff that's really important."

"Like what?" I said, realising I had cut Laura off. Laura screwed up her nose, considering my question for a moment. "Hmm, like sleeping in," she finally answered. We both laughed.

"How's Cate's job going?" I asked.

"Good. I think. She seems to enjoy it and she's fairly senior now, gets share options and a bonus – all that kind of stuff," Laura replied draining the last of the coffee from her mug. "Of course Cate's bonus is not quite like what Tom would expect with his job. Bloody bankers," Laura continued, giving me a wink before pouring more hot water into her cup and holding the kettle out to me.

I took the kettle from Laura and started to carefully sift through words in my head hoping when they came out of my mouth they would sound casual, disinterested even, instead of what I really wanted to know. "Which bank does Tom work for again?" I tried, careful not to look at her, but watching the hot water stream into the cup.

"Hedges Bank," Laura said, short and sharp. I nodded, still not looking up from the cup.

"I can't believe you two know each other," Laura started, her voice carrying up towards the pitch she perfects when she's excited about something. I keep looking at my cup, waiting for more words to keep firing at me, spraying bullets all over me. "It's just the strangest thing, don't you think? Incredible really, I mean what are the chances?"

I continued to look into my cup, ignoring the familiar rise and swell of illness in my stomach.

"Hmm," I finally nodded, looking Laura straight in the eyes. "Well it was only at school and then, um a bit of uni – "

"University as well!" Laura jumped straight in, cutting me off. Her eyes were wide peering over the rim of ceramic.

For a second I lost my footing, "Yeah just a year – or two – maybe. Loads of people from our school went to that uni, so it was kind of no real surprise that Tom and I both ended up there." A blatant lie.

"Did you see each other at uni?" Laura asked.

"What do you mean?" I asked, perhaps a little too quickly and with a hint of defence. I wasn't sure of the context Laura was referring.

"Were you like Tom's girlfriend?"

I could feel Laura's eyes on me as I stirred my coffee. "Yeah, I guess, for a little bit. It was nothing very serious. I guess it was what was left of our high school relationship, you know," I said weakly.

"What was he like?"

"Tom?" I asked trying to buy more time, I wasn't sure I liked where the conversation was going, even though I knew there was no way I was going to be able to avoid it, with Laura, with Cate. Oh God, with Cate. I thought back to the evening before, her face was glowing in the candlelight, obviously the wine had made her cheeks a little rosier than usual, but she was beautiful and so happy with her life. Her eyes had followed Tom around the room, the way people who can't help loving someone do, and I couldn't help thinking all that Cate had come to know with Tom was now somehow on borrowed time. The knot in my stomach tightened. I didn't want to snatch anything away from my beautiful friend, but even now with the sun streaming through the window, Laura's bench tops gleaming white and impossibly bright, I know what I am feeling is not something I can just switch off. It's the same as when I decided to leave Dominic in London. The decision is made and I have to act on it, no matter what the consequences are and who gets hurt in my path. Perhaps if I just saw Tom again, when I am sober, I would feel differently. I would see how I felt seeing him without half the contents of Cate's wine rack floating around inside me and then make a proper informed decision about what I was going to do after that.

"Yes Tom – what was he like?" Laura said, pulling my head back into the kitchen. The room seemed even brighter. I was squinting and rubbing my forehead.

"Probably much the same as he is now. Only younger. I don't really remember," I lied.

"Oh," Laura answered glancing at the clock on the microwave, "Shit, I have to get moving. I've got an early meeting with some Yanks in town," she said placing her cup on the sink and making for the kitchen door. "I'm going for a shower. Help yourself to whatever you want," she smiled, squeezing my shoulders before disappearing.

I stood still for a moment, biting my lip and bracing myself for Laura to come racing back into the kitchen with another question. It wasn't until I heard the shower taps winding up the pipes into a creak and groan that I realised I was off the hook. *'Was that it?'* I thought. *'Was that the interrogation complete?'* It had never occurred to me that maybe people wouldn't really be interested, wouldn't really care that Tom and I'd had some sort of a past together. To them it was a long time ago and couldn't have possibly been serious because we were young. We didn't have a house with a wraparound veranda or a front door which closed on two people dressed in suits and kissing each other goodbye on the doorstep. No, we were just two stupid kids with a head full of future fantasies. Maybe they were right. Or maybe their naivety around the full extent of mine and Tom's relationship and what really happened between us meant they had no reason to suspect anything. Maybe it was only me because I knew I was the one carrying around the weight of the truth like a heavy locket encasing a secret lock of hair glistening gold for all the world to see. No one really had any reason to suspect anything. That, or I am a bloody good actress. The problem now was I didn't know how good an actor Tom was.

The shower turned off. I didn't feel like talking now. Slowly I leant my head around the side of the kitchen doorway and seeing the hallway was clear, bolted across it, into the lounge room and straight into the sofa bed, rolling over with my back to the door and pulling the sheet up over my head before Laura came in wrapped in a towel ready to ask more questions she'd thought up under a stream of hot water. Instead I heard the bathroom door open and her feet padding down the hallway to her bedroom. Within seconds the hairdryer was on and I closed my eyes listening to the sounds of her getting ready for work.

CATE

"Got you something." I smile, looking up from the magazine to see Tom standing in the doorway with a beach towel wrapped around his waist. Sand is clinging to his toes, his hair is damp falling in streaks around his face.

"What?" I say, watching him step into the sunroom and uncurl his fingers. Sitting on his palm is a brilliant white shell, flecked with electric blue. "It's beautiful, where was that?"

"On the beach."

"I know that," I say laughing. "Which end of the beach, north or south?"

"South," Tom replies stroking the end of my nose with the shell.

"Can I see?" Tom places the shell into my hand. I hold it up to the window and watch as the sunlight catches the blue flecks, making them almost transparent.

"Should we put it on the dresser?" Tom asks like an excited child who has just found a secret treasure.

"Maybe on the windowsill where it will catch the light?"

"Good idea," Tom says taking the shell from my hand, a drop of seawater runs down the length of his hair and lands on my bare thigh. Tom licks it off, smiling at me. "Do you want a beer?" he asks, his eyes just visible above my thigh. I nod my head and watch as he disappears into the kitchen.

"You've got a missed call on your phone," Tom yells from the kitchen.

"Yeah I know, I heard it ring earlier, but I couldn't be bothered getting up to answer it. Who is it?"

I hear the sound of the bottle opener clicking and two slow hisses of beer before Tom answers. "Um. I don't know, it's a private number."

Tom returns to the sunroom with a beer in each hand and my mobile phone clenched between his teeth. I frown as he drops the phone into my lap like an obedient dog. "Thanks babe," I say, wiping the spit off the screen.

"Want some chips or something too? I'm starving, the surf was still massive from the storm yesterday morning," Tom says, resting my beer on the windowsill next to the shell and leaving the room before he even waits for my answer. I'm not paying attention anyway as I am listening to my voicemail.

"Who was it?" Tom asks now back in the sunroom and stretching out in a cane chair to rest a bowl of chips on his stomach.

"That looks precarious," I say, looking at the bowl balancing awkwardly as his belly rises and falls with each breath. "It was Isobel," I answer Tom's question, taking a mouthful of beer.

"Oh, how's she going?" Tom replies, taking a long mouthful of his beer and sending the bowl crashing to the floor. The chips jump out like they are abandoning ship. We both stare at the bowl unbroken resting on its side on the floorboards. I raise my eyebrows.

"What a surprise that happened," I say going to stand up.

"No, no I will clean it up. Stay where you are," Tom says, jumping to his feet. "What's Isobel up to?" he asks as he crouches down to shove the escaped chips back into the bowl.

"I think she is on her way over – "

"Here!" Tom looks at me grinding a chip between his fingertips, small flakes of potato are falling like sawdust.

"Uh-ha."

"Right."

Tom's in the shower when Isobel rings the doorbell. "Come in," I yell. No movement at the front door, just the sound of the water running in the bathroom. "Come in Isobel," I yell more loudly, starting to stand up when I hear the door open. "I'm in the sunroom," I say as I hear footsteps coming down the hallway.

"Hey," Isobel says, swinging into the room with long golden legs stretching out from the bottom of cut-off jeans. She dumps her bag on the floor, leans over giving me a peck on the cheek and sits in the chair Tom has vacated. I can still see the outline of Tom's body crushed into the cushion as Isobel sits down. Isobel's leg crosses elegantly over the other as she slides her sunglasses up on top of her head and leans her head back on the windowsill.

"Oh I am loving the sunshine," Isobel says.

"Want a drink to go with that sunshine?" I say.

"Yes please!" she answers, twirling a long strand of hair around her finger.

TOM

The skin on my fingers was starting to shrivel, I had been standing under the stream of the shower for at least twenty minutes, straining my ears for the sound of the doorbell. In the end I didn't hear it, but eventually I could hear Cate yelling something from the back of the house and the sound of footsteps walking carefully down the hallway, straight past the bathroom, so I knew Isobel must have arrived.

I was wringing the face washer in tight, strong coils, trying to decide if I should call a mate and go for a beer mainly to avoid Isobel, when the bathroom door opened. "Hey!" I yelled out into the steam.

"It's only me, God," Cate replied laughing. "Who did you think it was going to be? Or more like *hope* it was going to be?"

"No one. I was just daydreaming and you caught me by surprise."

"How long are you going to be?" Cate asked, slipping her hand around the side of the shower curtain and stroking my leg. "We thought we might have a barbeque, you up for that?"

I swallowed hard and shook my leg free from her hand, turning my face into the water.

"Tom?"

"Yeah. Yeah, sure why not? I will be out in a tick." I managed to splutter through the water drops.

"Great!"

I heard the bathroom door click shut and rested my head against the tiles, water trickling down my back in fast furious gulps. "Jesus," I muttered into the steam. Of course I had seen Isobel a few times since she had first turned up in our kitchen like a bloody ghost sitting at the table and helping herself to our wine pretending she was a normal human being and not some weirdo who was going to crush me and my beautiful Cate. I really couldn't get the image of Cate sitting there, smiling and so happy to see her friend, out of my head. My wonderful, beautiful Cate who is so trusting of people and always taking them at face value, she is so ready to give anyone a chance and the benefit of the doubt. Her warm nature was one of the traits that first drew me closer to Cate. I loved that she wasn't bitchy and unsure of herself, like so many girls I had gone out with. Cate never played games. Even when it's awkward and nervous in the first throes of dating someone when you're never really sure if you are saying the right thing or the wrong thing, petrified you will be seen as too eager or not eager enough – never being able to get the balance right. That's what Cate did with grace and elegance; she got the balance just right every time and made me fall head over heels, embarrassingly in love with her. I had found it hard to fathom that there were no hidden agendas or game playing, but when I finally did work that out a few months into the relationship, I knew there was no going back. That was it. The ease of being with Cate was what everyone always talked about when they told you that when you found the person meant for you, 'you would just know'. A really bloody annoying phrase which I had always discovered seemed to drop out of the mouths of smug couples leaning into each other at the end of a long dinner party when the base of wine bottles patterned the starched white table cloth of the blessed ones. The single ones among us glowing heavy and bright with wine consumption having involuntary thoughts that after all the dishes were cleared of being able to roll into a soft, warm body who wanted you there breathing next to them. That same soft, warm body wouldn't wake up the next morning, hungover and blink blankly at your face.

The house – home – Cate and I had created together had lulled me into what I now knew was a false sense of comfort. It was too easy for both of us to come home after a long day at work, kiss each other, pour a wine and fold into a pair of warm, outstretched arms. Despite this picture of domestic bliss, Cate had remained independent. She took a painting course one night a week, went to yoga and caught up with all her mates, especially Laura, as often as she wanted to. Her beautiful ease meant Cate slotted into my group of friends like the strong stitch needed to hold the button onto my favourite pair of jeans. My mates all loved her and I knew a few of them sought Cate out for her advice, mumbling awkwardly with a beer bottle pressed against the side of their mouths protecting their sensitivity from spilling out amongst everyone, while Cate nodded returning the awkward staccato with low whispers of considered advice.

But I was as sure as hell not living and loving an angel here either. Cate could hold her own swilling back any poison of choice with the best of them. She could be over-sensitive, crying for what I think is no reason, which never fails to lift the lid on the memories of a crazy ex-girlfriend clawing at my back. It's obvious Cate is not a great fan of some members of my extended family, wrinkling her nose in their general direction at one too many Christmas functions while delivering a beautifully-crafted insult under her breath. In fact she's great with the insult delivery, my Cate.

The memory of Cate calmly talking down the phone at a boss – an ex-boss – with a very reasoned explanation of why she could no longer work for such a '*delusional, talentless money-robbing parasite*' any longer was delivered with just the right level of punch and effect. You had to really push Cate to end up on the receiving end of that kind of talk, but you knew once you got her there, she was bloody right. I remember being gobsmacked that Cate, usually so calm and measured, had it in her. I was so proud of her for standing up for herself after what seemed like months of Cate analysing and picking apart the seams of that particular work situation when finally something snapped and that was that.

The thought still makes me smile and reminds me of what a brilliant find my girlfriend is, and now, now there's an imposter – called Isobel – sitting in our life, ready to take swipes and chunks and pieces until there is nothing left, just like she did when her and I were together all those years ago. That easy pattern of making me go so crazy and with her own unpredictable craziness of a life turned into bitter exchanges punctuated by the claws of her fingernails running down the length of my back.

I was out of the shower now and rubbed a palm print of clear onto the mirror. My face was hazy staring back at myself like one of those old movies shot with Vaseline on the camera lens. Before I knew what I was doing some new power took hold and I punched the tiles next to the mirror. Jesus Christ that hurt, a sharp intake of breath as I felt the blinding white pain splinter through my knuckles, slowly turning to numbness. Very carefully I attempted to unravel my fingers, examining the smudges of red rising along the bone. Slowly I stretched the fingers in and out, willing the numbness to turn back into something else. I hope I haven't broken my hand, how am I going to explain that one to Cate?

I took a few deep breaths and tried to be rational. Even I had to admit the few times I had seen Isobel since she had sat in our kitchen, she seemed more stable. I guess she had gotten older and matured. I'd matured so wouldn't she have too? She has also seemed barely interested in me, making a few comments here and there, but never really referencing the past. That thought made me smirk at my crumpled fist. How could Isobel bring up the past knowing she was a lunatic and I could easily blow her cover at any time. I raised my eyebrows, considering this thought for a moment. It made sense, it was simple and uncomplicated and above all, it was logical. Isobel is many things, but stupid is not one of them. More than that, it was what I would do if it was me and this explanation certainly accounted for Isobel's seemingly normal behaviour around me. Maybe I had managed to work Isobel out after all. I shook my hand a few times feeling the ripples of pain ease slightly. I opened the bathroom window and watched the steam evaporate in great gusting swirls towards the open crack and allowed myself a smile coated with the tiniest hint of confidence.

CATE

"You must be a shrivelled up prune by now," I yelled out as I heard Tom open the bathroom door. No answer as our bedroom door shut carefully behind him. Isobel's eyebrows rose in spectacularly curved arches over the top of her wine glass.

"A grumpy prune, perhaps?" she laughed.

"A grumpy, deaf prune I would say."

"Anyone else coming over?" Tom asked as he walked into the kitchen, pulling a T-shirt over his head.

"Well Laura's on a date..." I started to say.

"Is she?" Tom asked, cutting me off as he turned from the fridge with a brown paper bag of meat in his hand.

"Apparently. We don't know who the lucky guy is though," Isobel said turning to Tom, "What about your mates?" she asked, standing up to take the bag of meat from Tom's hand. "What have we got in here?" Isobel said, prying open the bag and sticking her head straight into the paper. I watched as Tom took the bag back from her, almost snatching it.

"What about my mates?" Tom asked, dumping the bag on the bench and pulling a knife out of the wooden block.

"Are any of them coming over for this little barbeque we're having?" Isobel smiled, twirling the top of her wine glass with a finger.

"Don't know. It's pretty short notice and I haven't called anyone," Tom answered, slapping a steak onto a chopping board to trim the fat off the meat. He knows I hate the fatty bits. Tom seemed to be hesitating with the knife and then I noticed that his right hand was red raw, almost like the meat he was cutting, with tiny red lines criss-crossed along his knuckles.

"What happened to your hand?" I said, realising I was talking over the top of another question Isobel had fired at Tom in response to the fact he wouldn't be inviting any of his friends over.

"Huh?" Tom looked up at me with the knife poised limply between his palm and fingers.

"Your hand?" I repeated, taking the knife from him to get a closer look. Tom stared down at his hand while I turned it over in my own. He winced slightly as I touched the thin red lines of blood.

"Oh, I...just hurt it that's all," Tom said, snatching his hand away and rubbing it down his T-shirt before picking up the knife again to continue cutting the meat.

"It looks really sore. How did you hurt it?" I asked.

"Probably surfing," Isobel chipped in. I saw Tom half smile at her before slowly nodding his head.

"And you didn't notice?" I continued.

"Well yeah, it hurt a bit but my hand was in the cold water most of the time, so now that I am out and doing other things, it's obviously flared up. It's fine, don't worry about it. I think it's nastier than it looks," Tom smiled at me, stroking my nose lightly with his other hand.

I was in the kitchen finishing making the salad with remnants of leaves and some other ingredients resembling salad that I found floating around in the bottom of the fridge. Coupled with a bit of creativity from splashing and dashing drops from a few jars in one of the kitchen cupboards, we now had what looked like something quite impressive sitting on the garden table outside. I was looking for a fresh bottle of tomato sauce in the pantry when I caught sight of Isobel walking across the garden towards Tom who was standing at the barbeque with his back to her, expertly flipping a piece of meat over. He jumped and dropped the tongs when she tugged like a child at the bottom of his T-shirt. They both bent over at the same time to retrieve the tongs from the grass and clashed heads. I laughed to myself and continued hunting for the elusive tomato sauce bottle which I thought was lurking somewhere at the back of the pantry.

TOM

"Jesus Isobel, you scared the hell out of me," I said, nudging her clear of the tongs. She had fallen backwards after we had clashed heads and was now sitting on the grass laughing. Red wine stained her lips while her eyes had a washed glaze over them. *Excellent, Isobel is getting pissed, enter the crazy woman*, I thought to myself. I snuck a look back towards the house in the hope of catching sight of Cate to come and rescue me, but she had moved from chopping something at the kitchen window where I had seen her only a few seconds before and now was nowhere to be seen.

"Have you seen a ghost, Tom?" Isobel asked innocently looking up at me. Instantly the hairs stood up on my forearms, my injured hand started to throb.

"Very funny," I replied, turning back to the barbeque.

"Help me up please," Isobel's voice came in a giggling burst over my shoulder.

"You're a big girl, I am sure you can get up all by yourself," I answered, not bothering to turn around.

"Oh please," Isobel persisted.

I didn't answer nor did I turn around. Instead I decided to just ignore her while I willed Cate to come outside. The next thing I knew though, Isobel was standing beside me, very closely, taking the tongs from my hand, making it impossible for me to ignore her. I swung around, my elbow catching her rib cage, she stumbled and fell back onto the grass. "God, sorry," I stammered, bending down to help her up. "I didn't realise you were so close. You OK? I really didn't mean to knock you over. Sorry...sorry," I was stammering like an idiot. Isobel looked blankly into my face. Neither of us said anything for a few moments which seemed to stretch on and on like only those types of awkward moments can. Isobel kept holding my gaze. It was making me uncomfortable. Very uncomfortable. Eventually I had to turn away, I dropped my eyes to the grass and without returning my look to her face, I asked her if she needed me to help her.

"I've always needed you," Isobel replied very quietly without a hint of malice.

ISOBEL

Oh God, I felt sick. I couldn't believe I had just let those four words drop out of my mouth. I really don't even know where they came from, I just couldn't help myself. Obviously Tom's surprise equalled my own, he continued to rock on his haunches, staring at a patch of grass in front of my foot. There was only the tiniest flicker of what would constitute a startle from him, a small movement of the mouth, and then the words just hung in the air around us with the ghastly smell of the meat cooking on the barbeque coming in great gulfs towards me. I wanted to grab each word one by one, ravelling them back up like a big ball of wool and shoving them all inside a locked box never to come out again. But it was too late. Tom was slowly rising to his feet. Very carefully his eyes locked on mine, he watched my face, his temple flexing. I couldn't move as I sat fixed to the spot on the grass which was now feeling cold and damp. I wanted to get up and run as fast as I could out of Tom and Cate's garden, but now I had said what I said, it would be impossible for me to keep running away from Tom. He and I both knew the truth had finally spilled out.

"Don't do this Isobel," Tom said very calmly straightening his back before walking back towards the house leaving me alone in their back garden. I heard the gauze door open and close and then Tom speaking into the grey light of the house, asking Cate where she was.

It's later in the evening now and the three of us are sitting around a raw wooden table Tom has dragged from further up the garden to the patch of grass I had fallen onto earlier in the evening. I have one of Cate's cardigans hanging loosely around my shoulders, my bare feet feel cold against the dampness of the lawn, so I keep rubbing them together absent-mindedly hoping they will warm up. Tom has his arm around Cate's shoulders, like the perfect picture of a cosy couple, it's only his face which nearly gives him away. Tom's jaw is set hard against skin, every now and again he squeezes his grip around the wine glass in front of him before taking short, sharp gulps. He isn't really engaged in the conversation. Cate has been smiling and talking all night, but I can tell that she thinks something is up by the way she keeps snatching sidelong looks at Tom and then returning her gaze to me accompanied by crooked conversation and a nervous chatter which doesn't really suit Cate's usual calm exterior.

"OK who wants dessert, more wine?" Cate is asking Tom and me, looking back and forth between us. I shake my head and watch as Tom starts to stand up. "I'm going to put this stuff in the dishwasher," he is announcing, stacking our plates into the crook of his elbow and hooking the tomato sauce bottle between two fingers. Without another word Tom turns and starts walking towards the house. Cate and I are sitting together in silence. I twist the edge of a paper napkin between my fingers.

"I guess Tom is tired," Cate is feebly offering.

"I guess so," I say, smiling in an attempt to give my friend some sense of comfort. After all she isn't stupid; she clearly knows something is not sitting right. "Are you OK?" I start to say, then cut myself short, realising I don't really know where I am going with the question and certainly don't want Cate to start asking *me* any questions. Not tonight anyway, my guard is down and I am still feeling tense from my stupidity earlier when I was alone with Tom. His obvious uneasiness around me all evening was how he was deciding to deal with my little outburst. "I might go inside and help Tom with the clearing up," I am saying, instantly throwing myself into a more deeply fucked-up situation. What was I going to do, stroll casually into the kitchen, drape a tea towel over one shoulder and start humming the theme tune to *I Love Lucy* while I handed dishes to Tom to put in the dishwasher? A shiver ripples over my skin.

"I might sit out here for a bit," Cate is saying, pouring the last of the wine into her glass.

"OK," I reply, rising to my feet in what I hope looks like a very casual movement. "Can I bring you out some more wine?" I ask Cate. She is shaking her head with an easy smile spreading along her lips. "OK," I say quietly and follow the path to the back door.

Tom's head jerks towards the kitchen door as soon as I am just about to step over the threshold.

"I thought I would come in to help you," I am saying weakly.

"It's nearly all done," Tom is rinsing a wine glass under running water. I continue to stand in the kitchen doorway, unsure as to whether I should move any further into the room. My mouth is forming an 'O' shape in an attempt to reply a very straightforward, absolutely not-to-be-confused-for-anything-else 'Oh' to Tom's lack of use for me, but there is no sound coming out. Instead I twist my bottom lip and fidget with the hem on Cate's cardigan sleeve. Tom is rinsing the salad bowl now and is concentrating very hard on not turning his attention in any way to me. I take a very small step into the kitchen. Tom flinches slightly but is still not looking at me.

"Tom," I whisper. No response. "Tom," I repeat, this time a little more loudly. Tom turns the tap harder to the right, water starts streaming out in a strong thick flow, splashing out of the bowl, sending wet splats across his T-shirt. "Bloody hell," Tom is saying angrily, shutting off the tap. Finally he is looking at me. "What Isobel? What do you want?" he is saying, trying to control his voice.

"I...I'm sorry," I say very quietly.

"What for?" Tom says wearily, laying the bowl on the bench top and rubbing his eyes.

"For before."

"Before?" Tom drops his hands down from his eyes to grip the edge of the bench.

I nod before beginning again, "Out in the garden...for... for what I said to you. It was wrong and it just slipped out. I didn't mean to say what I said. I don't even know where it came from. It just slipped out and I didn't mean it. So I am sorry," I mumble the last few words quietly, ripping more furiously at the cardigan sleeve.

Tom shoots a look out of the window in the direction of where Cate is still sitting at the table by herself in the garden. "Did it really slip out or did you mean to say it?" Tom is still fixing his gaze out the window.

I took another step into the kitchen. "It did. The words just slipped out and I didn't mean them. Really," I bit my lip and willed Tom to look at me. "Really," I repeated more loudly this time.

Tom is hesitating.

"OK I believe you. Let's just forget it. It never happened OK?" he is finally saying, turning from the window and begins picking at the rim on the bowl.

"OK," I am saying. My head is involuntarily nodding.

"Good," Tom looks up, holding my gaze for a moment before smiling and sliding the bowl into the dishwasher.

TOM

I am pretty pleased with myself. Last night I had managed to diffuse what could very well have been the beginnings of a potential slippery slope with Isobel, just by acting cool and not getting all wound up the way I would have when we were at university. I smile to myself for finally understanding a tiny piece of Isobel and realising that I must have matured. Grown up and actually learnt something about emotions and crazy people like Isobel. I had even slept the whole night through without waking up like I have been, lightly sweating lying there in the dark wondering why I was awake. Usually I remember after a few seconds with the realisation normally producing a thicker film of sweat, but not last night. Last night was different. There was no waking up for a start. Then this morning when I did open my eyes just a few minutes before the alarm went off, that feeling of dread that usually washes over me, remembering that my crazy ex-girlfriend has snuck back into my life and now I have to stand guard, constantly watching her out of the corner of my eye, waiting for her to steal everything out from under me – well, that feeling wasn't there either. Had I really won the battle, so simply and so effortlessly? All it took was me not to react. That was it, it couldn't be that simple surely? But it seemed to be. That is, if Isobel's behaviour last night was anything to gauge this war on. I kind of pitied her, standing there in the kitchen clinging onto how I was going to react to her earlier unprovoked outburst. I had been trying so hard not to look at her, to make sure I kept my cool because I knew that any dent in my armour would have her pouncing.

But I know I did OK. She even apologised.

I smile to myself as I make a right turn out of our street and drive along the beach front on the way to work. The radio is on and I allow myself to sing – badly – to a song. I tap the steering wheel to the bass line. The light is changing to red and I press my foot lightly on the brake. Waiting at the traffic light I look at the beach. A nice swell is shaping a good set of waves. There are a few surfers down the south end bobbing around on their boards waiting for the little rise of water which gets sucked higher than the north end because of the rocks. I am watching as one of the surfers stands and catches a wave almost all the way to the shoreline, just before reaching the sand he drops off the board, shaking his head as it rises up out of the liquid.

The lights must have changed to green, but I have only just noticed as the car behind me is honking its horn. "Alright, alright, I'm going," I say into the rear view mirror. Rounding the bend I can still see the waves tumbling into shore. The road rises up much higher here. I have a habit of looking down onto the water which crashes into the cliff face on this part of the beach, the best waves usually form around this part. This morning I look down again, just like I do five mornings a week, squinting between the strips of metal of the low fence which runs the length of the road. Some good waves here today I can see, I might be able to run down with the board this evening if I get home while there's still some light. Afterwards I'll see if Cate wants to go to that Thai place near ours for some dinner. I smile again. Last time we were there Cate spilt satay sauce down the front of her which somehow fell straight down into her bra. She had squealed when the sauce hit her breast, the whole restaurant seemed to stop to stare at her. Cate had gone a deeper colour than the crimson paper napkin she was using to unsuccessfully dab at her boobs. I was no help I couldn't stop laughing. I was laughing again now with an ease I hadn't felt in a long time. Since Isobel had come back.

CATE

Islid my hand in between soft folds of cotton and silk until it touched a leather-bound Moleskine notebook, the same brand great artists and writers like Van Gogh and Hemmingway used to sketch and scribble the great shapes forming in their minds before they turned them into famous works of art and books. No such public greatness for me, just disjointed recordings of my feelings occasionally scratched onto the pages. I leave the top drawer, where I bury the notebook under obvious articles like knickers, partly ajar and sit back on the bed, straining my ears to hear Tom rearranging himself on the couch a couple of rooms away. Satisfied he is still reading a book in the lounge room, I start to flick through what I guess is a diary of sorts. I don't really write date entries, it's more snippets of thoughts, feelings, emotions which are expressed as chunks of writing, poems or sometimes even just a singular word. I am certainly not very regular with my thoughts, often going for large leaps of time between opening and closing the book. My last entry was over two months ago. At the time I thought it was going to be the beginnings of a poem, but re-reading the words stretching in sharp staccatos along the lines, my musings are more muddled, words that aren't really joined in a smooth flow of verse, sonnet or poem. It's to do with Tom, Tom and Isobel. I had written the words with a blurry head after she had been over at our place for a barbeque. I had sensed some sort of electricity between them. I can't say that it was the electricity of lovers, more zaps of energy fusing and sparking. There were moments where I had felt left out, like I was the friend over for dinner – not Isobel – and I was somehow intruding on two people silently feuding the way couples quietly battle it out over tense looks and clenched limbs when there's company skimming the edges of their personal lives.

Tom kept resting his hand on my thigh or moving his arm to encase my shoulders, like he was protecting me from a danger I didn't know about. At first I thought he was being affectionate, but as his grip tightened around me it wasn't so much affection, but more like he was clinging onto me, staking his claim over me and if I didn't know any better I would say trying to make Isobel jealous. I had never seen him act like this before; we were always so easy in each other's company.

I re-read the words on the paper.

And there you suddenly were as if from nowhere but a distant faint memory

> *Neatly folded away in my mind*
> *The sight of you, so bold, so brash, so real*
> *Slicing the memory folds open*
> *Exposed the folds lie, flick, flick, flickering*

And that was it, I usually date my entries – no matter what form they take – but this one is just lying bare on the page.

A fresh breeze blew through the window, blowing lightly on my neck. I got up and shut the window. The moon was hanging low just above the roof of the flats across the road, like a giant dollop of custard suspended in the sky. I touched the glass, running my finger around the shape of the moon.

Isobel hadn't been back to our house since that night. I had seen her but it was always somewhere else, the beach, a restaurant, her house or the pub after work. To me it seemed like she was slowly settling back into the groove of her old life here. She'd found work as a curator of a new gallery which was representing young urban artists and she seemed really alive when she talked about it. I admired the passion she had for what she did. My job was fine, but it wasn't who I was. I always felt like my work was just something I did. There are so many other parts to me. Just like there are so many different parts to everyone. Isobel once told me that you never really know anyone because people only let you see the parts of them they want you to see.

I hadn't really brought up with Tom what I must have been feeling that night and he never mentioned it. Thinking about it now, I realise he had returned to 'Tom' after that night. He had been so stressed with work, leaving early in the morning and coming home so late at night. By that time I was almost always curled up in a corner of the bed in a deep sleep when he finally dropped in beside me, lightly kissing my forehead before rolling over, only to wake up an hour or so later, sweating. Maybe this coincided with Isobel's return so I mistakenly joined the two events together. Now being reminded of these words I had hastily scribbled down through a film of red wine immediately after the door had clicked shut behind Isobel that night made me now think I had somehow overacted and read signs that weren't even there. My emotions blurred by wine reality.

I rested my forehead on the cool glass of the window for a moment before returning to the slump in the quilt on the bed. Picking up the notepad, I turned the page to a fresh sheet and let the pencil press down into the paper, imagining the tip crushing through the fibres. I wasn't sure what I wanted to write or about who so I just let the pencil hover for a moment longer until I heard Tom's footsteps on the floorboards in the hallway. I snapped the book shut and watched as his figure came into view, leaning against the bedroom doorway.

"What are you doing?" he asked, half smiling, swapping his gaze between the hard leather-bound book in my lap and the red rising on my face.

"Just writing," I replied, shoving the book back into the drawer.

"Original hiding place that one," Tom said, nodding at the chest of drawers.

"I know, I'm not the most creative person."

"I think you are," Tom whispered walking towards me and grabbing me around the waist in an easy, familiar embrace. I let my body sink into his, turning my head into the curve of his neck and shoulder. Tom smelt of a faint wisp of aftershave and sea salt. I breathed in deeply. "And I love you," Tom whispered into my hair before pulling me down onto the bed where our bodies became a knotted crumpled shape.

"Have you seen Isobel lately?" I'm at work on the phone to Laura who has caught me in the middle of writing a pitch for a new piece of business. I had picked the phone up on the second ring, relieved for the distraction.

"Umm," I twirl the end of a pen out of the corner of my mouth. "Um I think it was a week ago. She's called since then though. Well left a message on my voicemail. I called her back a few times but she never picks up."

"She never bloody picks up does she? She's always been the same and I guess she is definitely not going to change now," Laura was laughing.

"No I doubt it. Actually I was just thinking last night that she hasn't been to our place for ages, maybe a couple of months, but that can't be right, it seems far too long," I said clicking to the electronic calendar on my screen.

"Do you think she might feel uncomfortable around Tom?"

"Really?" I asked Laura, knowing I sounded shocked.

"Well maybe I am imagining things, but maybe Isobel feels a bit weird about hanging out with Tom. You've never gone out with one of her boyfriends before," Laura said laughing, "Has he ever said anything about it?"

"Who, Tom? No. Not really. There was only really the once when we first worked out that they knew each other but it was so long ago and Tom made it pretty clear it was nothing serious, a uni affair at best and you know what those are like!"

"Can't help you there I'm afraid, I *wish* I could remember but it was all such a haze darling." Laura giggled. "But seriously, Iss always does what Iss wants to do and she always lands on her feet, never her arse! And on the rare occasions she does end up on her arse, we have a small episode of 'Iss Fizz' and then the world levels out again."

"Yeah you're right. Listen Lau, I have to get going I have to get this proposal finished," I replied, removing the pen from my mouth to see fresh ink seeping from the nib. I rubbed at my lip revealing smudges of royal blue across my fingertips. "Oh no. Shit," I said.

"What's the matter?"

"I just got blue ink all over my mouth, I think," I kept rubbing at where I thought the stain would be. I imagined the ink staining my teeth, my smile a gash of blue.

"Delightful," Laura was laughing.

"Oh I know. I am meant to go to some work thing with Tom tonight. He and his team are being taken out for dinner because they've smashed some target or other, which would be lovely if I wasn't covered in blue ink."

"Listen I've got to go too. Tell me if you hear from Isobel and have fun tonight, old Bluey." I heard Laura laughing as she hung up the phone. I looked down to see four blue drops bleeding into the white cotton of my shirt accompanied by a thin line of ink running halfway down the length of my skirt.

"Great," I announced to myself and made my way to the bathroom where I assessed the damage to be even worse than I had anticipated. The Joker was laughing back at me in the mirror, ink smudged around my mouth, front teeth and even the tip of my tongue. My shirt was basically ruined. That stain wasn't coming out and there was no way it could be hidden.

```
Hi sweetie,
I've left you a message on your phone
but in case you don't get it, I am just
dropping you an email to say I don't think
I am going to be able to make it tonight.
Sorry. I am running behind with this
pitch, it has to be sent to the client
this evening, or so I have just been told.
But what's probably even worse than that
is the fact I have managed to spill ink
all over myself - all down the front of
my new white shirt. Everything on me is
now blue, even my tongue! So I would be a
major embarrassment to you anyway!
I'm really sorry. I hope you have fun and
see you when you get home, but I think I
will be asleep...
Love me xx


Hi babe,
So you're a blue tongue lizard huh? I'm
sorry about your shirt, I know you liked
```

that one, we'll get you a new one on the
weekend.
Don't worry about tonight, I think I am
going to be stuck at work for a while
myself, there's a few things I need to
finish off. I'll go for a bit, but would
rather see you.
Don't work too hard.
Tom xx

ISOBEL

It's getting late and I am feeling a bit tipsy. I watch as his hand stretches across the table, I know he is trying to find mine. He has been trying to do it all night, mostly I have managed to ignore him, concentrating on the conversations of the people dotted around the table. I don't really know anyone here very well at all, most of them I have only met tonight. I had only agreed to come as a last minute favour, to even up the numbers so he didn't feel left out. Why do couples always do that? Always feel that they have to even up numbers if their partner can't make it? Can't they go anywhere by themselves?

Anyway, he's doing it again, trying to get my attention. I am going to keep nodding at this woman in the ill-fitting dress. The cut is far too low for her, pushing her breasts out in wobbling waves over the edges of the material. I can see the crinkle of skin like fine crepe paper folding in and out of her cleavage as she cuts her food and raises the glass to two slashes of red lipstick. Prints of smudged lipstick scallop around the glass rim, looking greasy against the candlelight of the table. She has been flicking her hair a lot. The hair flicking has been amusing me for most of the evening as I know she thinks he is trying to make a move on her. She's totally misread the signals because it's my attention he is attempting to tangle up in his schoolboy game of 'crush'.

TOM

"You're not married are you Tom?" Nick, the new guy at work, is asking me as he leans across the table to shout above the blonde sitting next to me. I shake my head, "Thinking about it?" Nick continues. He is pretty forward this bloke, I hardly even know him. He joined the company probably about a month ago. He seems like a good guy but sitting next to him at dinner is the first time I have ever had much of a conversation with him.

"Maybe," I say, taking a sip of my wine.

"How long have you been together?" This guy doesn't really give up. Can't he see that I am looking slightly uncomfortable, that maybe I don't want to tell my colleagues and their other halves about my love life.

"A few years..." I start to reply before the blonde cuts me off.

"A few years! You won't be getting married anytime soon if you're as vague as that with dates, I am sure you don't even know when your anniversary is."

I am staring at this woman, she is a very loud talker, I can smell the stale scent of wine on her breath and the way she keeps twirling her hair with her index finger like a little girl is making me uncomfortable. She's been doing it all evening. Poor Dave, my work mate who goes out with her, maybe he is even engaged to her. I can't really remember, there seems to have been a few announcements of that nature made recently.

I loosen my tie before picking up the conversation with Nick again to change tack and deflect the line of questioning away from myself. "Are you married?" I ask.

"No. I find it usually helps if you at least have a girlfriend to pull something like that off," Nick answers.

"Heard of mail order?" both of us laugh and Nick raises his glass to me. I raise mine in response.

"Delightful you both are," says the blonde woman, shuffling her chair out behind her and muttering something about the powder room before swinging her bag over her shoulder and leaving the table. Nick slides onto the vacated seat, fills both our glasses almost to the rim, definitely not the 'done thing' in a restaurant of this ilk, clinks his glass against mine, splashing a pool of red wine on the tablecloth. "Cheers mate," we both say in unison.

ISOBEL

He has finally trapped my hand under the table. His hot sweaty palm is pressing down onto my own, crushing it. I try to slide my hand out, but he keeps pushing his down harder. He isn't even looking at me, he is continuing the conversation to his right. With my free hand I take a drink of wine and sit quietly for a moment, trying to decide what to do. Pins and needles are starting to spider along my fingertips where the blood supply is growing restricted. I whisper his name. His conversation continues. I stare at the back of his head, repeating his name more urgently now. Still he ignores me. The blonde woman is now paying attention. I know she can see our hands entwined on my lap, well his flattening mine against my thigh. I smile uneasily at her and ask where she got her dress. The slashes of red lipstick are moving, so she must be answering me, but I am not listening to her. I can only concentrate on my hand locked under a mound of flesh.

I am not even sure if the woman is still talking to me because I am so impatient to unleash myself from his grip that I turn back to him and without caring if I appear rude, tell him very loudly that I need to go to the bathroom. He swings around and looks at me, completely startled. "OK honey," he says in a tone you would speak to a child, half-twisting in the chair so his body leans into my shoulder.

"Your hand..." I start to say, but he is already looking down into my lap and releasing his grip. He stares for a moment at my hand, red and crumpled lying paralysed with the blood slowly starting to edge back into the fingertips.

"Oh God. I am sorry Isobel, I...I had no idea. I'm sorry." He looks mortified, how could he not know he was gripping my hand like his life depended on it.

"That's OK," I mumble, smoothing my dress as I stand to leave the table. In the bathroom, I flex the fingers backwards and forwards like a claw. As I am hoisting my dress up to reveal a blotchy crimson imprint of my knuckle on my thigh, the bathroom door swings open. It's the woman with the ill-fitting dress from our table. Dropping the fabric knotted in my hand, I smile at her.

"Are you OK?" she asks, staring at my dress as it drops back down.

"Yes I am fine thank you."

She positions herself in front of the mirror and runs her fingers through her hair. I turn around, set on opening one of the toilet doors and locking myself inside until she leaves.

"How do you know Patrick?" she asks, stopping me reaching out for the door so I have to turn and face her once more. In the mirror, her gaze shifts to me.

"Patrick..." I start to stammer, catching her eyes in the reflection.

"The guy sitting next to you, squeezing the crap out of your hand," she offers, her words echoing off the wall tiles.

I smile, "Yes I am well aware of who Patrick is and my hand certainly is too," I reply, waving my hand at her reflection in the mirror. "He's one of the investors in my art gallery."

"I see." A crisp reply.

"Do you?"

"Oh I certainly didn't mean anything by that. I know that he loves to show off with bright, young things. Sorry, I didn't mean anything by that either. I'm Gabrielle by the way," she said, turning to face me with an eye shadow compact clutched in one hand and her other outstretched to shake mine.

"Isobel..." I said extending my hand to meet hers.

"Oh I know, Patrick is smitten with you."

"How do you know Patrick?"

"He's my ex-husband," Gabrielle says, turning back towards the mirror to stripe make-up across her eyelids.

"Right."

"Oh don't worry, it's totally fine. All very amicable actually. Clearly we've remained good friends, despite his horrific taste in art." Gabrielle snapped closed the compact, flashing me a wide smile before opening the bathroom door and exiting.

"Right," I said to the door swinging shut, "How the fuck do I get out of this restaurant."

I rest my head on the wall feeling the cool tiles through my hair. Patrick never told me anything about an ex-wife, thinking about it Patrick never really told me much about anything. I had admired his confidence as he strode into the gallery one Thursday morning. I was just unlocking the door when I saw a tall well-dressed figure running across the road. It had started to rain, just a light drizzle from what seemed to be one cloud hanging purple and bruised right above the gallery. Fat rain drops collected on the footpath reminding me of crystals as they lay gleaming in sunlight streaming around the cloud.

"Wait," Patrick yelled out as I stepped inside and closed the door behind me.

"We're not open yet. We will be at eleven though," I replied through the glass, checking my wristwatch. "In about five minutes," I said, holding up my hand and stretching out all five fingers to illustrate the point. Patrick shook his head and knocked on the glass.

"Five minutes," I said more loudly, raising my hand again. "Maybe in four minutes now," I said smiling. He continued to knock more urgently on the glass. "For God's sake," I mumbled, giving in and opening the door. Patrick came striding into the gallery, but then like a wet labrador he became a blur of legs and arms flopping about shaking the water off his jacket and the damp out of his hair.

"Geez," I said stepping back to be clear of the spray.

"Sorry," he was laughing and pulling his arms out of the jacket sleeves. "Got a coat rack?"

"Not really. Here let me take that, I can put it in the storeroom for you. We're not quite open yet, as you know, so have a look around and I will be with you in a tick." I knew he was watching me as my stilettos clicked along the floorboards as I went to find a place to hang his jacket. When I returned he was standing in middle of the room with his hands on his hips studying a new piece of work which hadn't been hung yet.

"I'm impressed," Patrick said.

"With everything, or just that one you're looking at?" I asked, standing beside him.

"No everything," he replied without looking up from the artwork. He ran his fingers through hair that was greying at the temples. We stood in silence for a few moments.

"Tempted?" I ventured, nodding at the picce of work.

"What by?" he replied, shifting his gaze to look me straight in the eyes.

"The artwork," I answered, returning the fixed stare.

"Perhaps," he said nodding his head. "You don't have a clue who I am do you?"

I search his face for a flash of recognition, instantly praying this man standing in front of me wasn't going to be an ex-boyfriend who had somehow tracked me down. But there was nothing familiar about him – aquamarine eyes rimmed with long dark lashes and wearing a very sharp suit. I guessed he was about mid-forties.

"Don't look so worried," he laughed, extending his hand, "Patrick. Patrick Sutton."

"Isobel Taylor," I smiled, taking his hand. Suddenly I was filled with horror. "Patrick Sutton?" I repeated. He nodded.

"Oh God, I am sorry," I cringed.

"No need to be sorry," he laughed more loudly this time, gripping my hand tightly – even on that first meeting he was gripping my hand.

"Well it's slightly embarrassing," I muttered, trying to shake my hand from his grip.

"Not at all. You weren't to know Isobel Taylor."

"Well I should make it my business to know who my main investor is, and maybe not try and lock him out of the gallery until the general public opening time," I gestured at the door.

He smiled and asked if he could have a coffee.

I had never laid eyes on Patrick until that soggy Thursday morning in the gallery as he spent most of his time in London. All I really knew was Patrick had been convinced by the gallery's other investor, Peter Marchant that the gallery was going to carve a niche by representing edgy urban artists, a movement that was taking off across Europe and was slowly winging its way to Australia. I had been sold into Patrick as the curator and figurehead because of my experience and contacts in London and across Europe. We had come up with the gallery's name – Pop – on a drunken conference call at the opposite end of the day to Patrick in London. At the time we thought the simplicity of the name worked and somehow accurately represented what the gallery was all about. Since waking up the following morning with a thumping head and red wine crusting my lips, I wasn't quite so sure about the name. No one bothered to re-confirm anyone's sober feelings on the moniker that would hang above the gallery door, so 'Pop' became the name.

Patrick turned out to be engaging, humorous company who hung around for the whole day that first time we met. The weather and the weekday had meant business was slow so our conversation was only interrupted in miniature intervals by a few umbrellas shaking water and a set of high heels pacing like a caged tiger around the gallery before swiftly exiting.

We flipped the 'closed' sign over early, neither of us bothered that we could be missing evening trade, instead bunching together under an umbrella to find a table by the window in the Italian place across the street. That was how I met Patrick Sutton and would go on to meet nearly every night for six weeks, absorbed in each other with total tunnel vision. That was until my regular pattern which lies in wait for me like a predator waiting to pounce, reared its ugly head, making me want to push Patrick away. The long nightmares of a child's face flickering as a morbid backdrop in almost every unconscious hour had returned, so had the image I had been trying desperately to block out. Tom's face. The feeling of Patrick's body pushing against mine in the night made me want to scream, hit and punch.

Now here I was back in a familiar situation, agreeing to come to dinner because Patrick had asked me before I had scratched out my growing negative feelings to him. He hadn't wanted to come by himself, most likely because he knew his ex-wife was going to be draped at the table, satisfaction dripping like syrup from her pores.

I lifted my head from the tiles. I couldn't stand in the bathroom forever. I had been in here long enough now – Gabrielle would still get her satisfaction anyway. She was probably holding court, glancing every now and again at the bathroom door, smiling that it remained firmly shut.

I checked my make-up in the mirror, straightened my back and strode out of the bathroom back to the dinner party.

In those few short steps to the table, I had decided the only way to get through the rest of the evening was in the same way I had gotten myself through lots of situations like it and that was to make sure my glass was always full. Somehow I managed to make it through another two hours, even smiling sweetly at Gabrielle who chose to ignore our encounter in the bathroom.

Finally chairs were scraping back and people were shrugging jackets over their shoulders and I followed the trail of diners out onto the street to hail a cab. When one pulled up, I silently cursed myself as I let Patrick fall in beside me. I didn't want him to come home with me, but I was too drunk to argue. Throwing a rug over Patrick where he had slumped in an alcohol-induced slumber in the corner of the couch, I rubbed at my neck where I could still feel his breath hot against my skin. I trod carefully to the bedroom and shut the door behind me waiting for the nightmares of a child's face and a past lover I could not let go to grip my unconsciousness.

TOM

I know I am drunk, but Nick's initial line of questioning this evening has gotten me thinking. About marriage. About Cate. About how happy I am. Probably for the first time in my life I can say I am truly contented without half looking over my shoulder waiting for everything to come crashing down or worse, waiting for something or someone better to come along. Because that's what I have always done. Just kind of held onto my 'lot', thinking I could change course whenever I grew bored of the current situation – which I regularly did –feeling like I would never know if what I was doing was the right thing. I guess that's what you do in your twenties and then when you tip over into your thirties, you spend the first couple of years in denial. You find yourself staring at guys a bit older huddled at the other end of the bar, nursing a beer with one eye on the clock because they have to get home to the wife and kids.

Meanwhile you and your mates sink the beers in a steady stream, making slurred pacts that you will never become like that – nodding to the other end of the bar and laughing.

Gradually and inevitably the pattern starts to change. One of your mates finds himself getting very serious about a girl, another one discovers they're moving up in their career so says good-bye to late nights. Little by little, the tight-knit group of six or seven guys begins to fray. Not so much at first, just a few threads around the edges which mean not all of us are at the pub at once. Maybe some of you don't even notice the dropping numbers, there are some instant benefits to this, buying each other rounds of beers gets cheaper, you get more conversation in and girls don't feel so intimidated because you and your mates aren't hunting in packs. As the numbers peel even further and it's tough to get anyone to join you for a drink on a moment's notice, it makes you think you want something different, something more. All the promises of 'never changing' get soaked up in the beer mats and then you catch a glimpse of yourself in the mirror behind the bar, making you a do a double-take that's yes it really is you, just the older version who should know better. By the time you are standing on the edge of the curb hailing a cab, some major life decisions are shaping and re-shaping in your mind. Is the girl you're with the right one? Should I think about buying a house? Have I got enough money if I lose my job?

There and then you find yourself mechanically running through a life inventory, stocktaking what needs replenishing and what needs replacing. This process will usually be pretty harsh, with decisions and meek explanations made over the phone to a confused girl who thought you were about to pop the question, not ask her to collect her presumptuous range of toiletries from your bathroom cabinet.

You breathe a sigh of relief and then get on with your new mid-thirties life, feeling somewhat smug when you see the younger ones huddled together up the other end of the bar. You know what they're thinking and you know what's going to happen to them, just give them a few years.

Unlocking the door to mine and Cate's house after that booze-filled dinner where Nick and I topped up our bodies, already groaning under the pressure of wine, with whiskies in a late night jazz club, a perfect moment of clarity washed over me.

I tiptoed along the floorboards, feeling my way down to our bedroom off the main hallway. The door to our bedroom is half opened and I can see the outline of Cate lying in the bed. She stirs slightly, rolling over.

"It's just me babe," I whisper in case she wakes up suddenly and freaks out.

"Did you have a good time?" Cate replies sleepily.

"Yeah," I say sitting on the edge of the bed to take off my shoes. "Are you awake?"

Cate rolls over a bit further and strokes my back, "I am now."

"How awake?" I ask yanking one shoe off which immediately drops to the floor, echoing as it hits the floorboards.

"Hmm?"

"Are you properly awake or do you think you are about to go straight back to sleep?" I take off the other shoe. I should have undone the laces first, it would have made it a lot easier because now I am falling backwards onto the bed.

"Well if you keep talking to me and rocking around like that I am going to be properly awake," Cate replies, sounding more alert.

"Good," I say, leaning over to switch on the bedside lamp.

"Geez Tom!" Cate scolds me sitting up and rubbing her eyes.

"Sorry, sorry. I'll turn it off again. Hang on," I am blundering around trying to squeeze the switch between my fingers.

"Don't worry about it, the light's on now so just leave it on. Besides I am awake now. What time is it anyway?"

I flip back the cuff of my shirt sleeve attempting to focus on the watch face. The numbers are swimming around the glass so I close my eyes for a second. Opening them again I see that it's nearly three o'clock. "Wow I didn't know it was that late!"

"Oh God Tom, what time is it?"

"It's nearly three."

"Great. You're pissed and I am never going to get back to sleep now. I have a massive meeting in the morning too. Thanks a million."

I try to focus on Cate. Part of her fringe is sticking up like a cockatoo, it makes me smile. I clumsily reach across to try to pat her hair down, but Cate pulls her head away. "Don't Tom! Bloody hell."

"Oh I'm sorry. I was just trying to pat your fringe down because I can't talk to you properly while it's like that."

"Oh piss off," Cate says wriggling back down under the covers. "And turn off the light."

"Oh no Cate. Stop. Listen. Oh please sit up again and look at me. I have something really important I want to talk to you about and I can't do it while you're hiding down there," I say attempting to curl back the covers. Cate's fingers are gripped tightly around the bedclothes. Her knuckles are turning white.

"You're slurring your words," she says muffled by the blankets.

"I am not!" I retort in what I hope is a convincing string of words which sound sober.

"You are so," Cate replies still under the covers. I try pulling them back but she grips her fingers even more tightly stretching the fabric taut so I can see she has flexed her legs straight pushing them against the end of the bed to keep me out. I continue to pull on the covers, but she's not giving in. Cate is pretty damn strong when she wants to be.

"Alright," I say, releasing my grip on the covers and straddling her on the bed. The weight of my body sinking down on her makes Cate yelp and pull back the covers. Her face is all red and she's got strands of hair across her mouth.

"Jesus Tom, you're heavy," Cate stammers pulling the hair strands away from her lips.

I lift myself up so my weight is resting on my knees and smile at her. "Are you listening?" I start to say, but Cate is trying to roll over onto her side to wriggle free of me. "Babe," I try again, "Please. Come on. I am serious."

"So am I!" she practically yells from under me. "I'm really tired Tom and I want to go to sleep. You're pissed and annoying me. Now please get off me and decide whether you are coming to bed – properly – and if you're not, would you please go into the lounge room and stay there until morning."

For a moment I am not sure what I should do, Cate's already decided I am drunk so maybe she won't take me seriously when she finally hears what I have to say. But I know when she finally does hear me out she won't be annoyed anymore.

"Cate," I try again.

Cate flips over onto her back, "What!" she practically screeches in my face. This is not going well at all and certainly not how I had planned it.

"I have a very important question to ask you."

Cate raises her eyebrows.

"Cate, will you marry me?"

"You're drunk," she starts to say, but I am grinning like an idiot, "Please say 'yes'. I love you to bits, more than I can ever tell you. I know you think I am drunk and you do have a point. But drunk or not, I still know how I feel and it doesn't change when I am sober or drunk. So come on what do you say?"

Cate is staring at me. I can't read her expression. "Ask me again in the morning when you've sobered up."

"Will you say yes?"

"Yes," Cate whispers nodding her head for emphasis. I lean down and kiss her on the lips, her lips responding tells me she means what she said.

I continue to grin like an idiot at her, then roll over and switch the light out. Nestling down beside her, still on top of the covers, I hug Cate as close to me as I can.

"You sleeping like that?" she asks.

"Yep," I say into her hair.

CATE

I am sitting on the bus on the way to work. I am watching the traffic stop and start, my body jerking forwards with the movement of the bus. I can't help smiling.

The first thing Tom said when we woke up in a tangle of sheets and blankets was, "So will you marry me?" I was already smiling so broadly in the half light of the bedroom waiting for him to open his eyes that I instantly blurted out, "Yes". I had been awake for over an hour, turning the words he uttered, albeit with alcohol-stained breath, over and over in my head. Half of me was preparing for both of us waking this morning, then dropping into our regular routine of getting ready for work without any mention of the string of words delicately left hanging – maybe forever – in the air above the bed.

So my honest answer, probably tinged with some relief, made Tom spring to life, jumping all over me so the sheets twisted in a complicated knot threading between and around our bodies, rendering it almost impossible to move. For a moment we both lay there, embalmed like two ancient mummies, unable to properly embrace. "I can't even kiss the bride," Tom had laughed.

When we finally freed ourselves and Tom had urgently ripped off the remainder of last night's clothes, our bodies fell into a gentle, easy rhythm that confirmed the sureness of our decision.

Now sitting on the bus, my stomach was fluttering in anxious bursts. It wasn't because I had any sort of doubt that I felt this way, rather I could barely contain my surprise. I wasn't one of those girls who presume a holiday or a romantic dinner signifies a marriage proposal. Quite the opposite really, I was so comfortable with Tom that I just thought there was no point in making any changes to what was a very happy and easy union. I can honestly say I didn't even know he was planning to ask me to marry him. When my mum excitedly screamed down the phone after I broke the happy news while scraping toast crumbs into the bin, excitedly chattering away about whether Tom's proposal was a 'surprise', my answer was honest. I had told her it was more of a shock than a surprise. I hadn't even thought about marriage, let alone expected it. However what was becoming increasingly obvious to me was once the idea had been planted in the early hours of this morning and the longer I had laid tangled in the sheets with Tom's breath steady in my ear, the more the seed flourished, making me want it. So by the time the sun was breaking through the curtains and Tom repeated the question, I felt sure I wanted it too.

Despite this, the anxious pulses of what can only be surprise or shock, are persisting like motion sickness. By the time the lift doors to my office slide open and I am greeted by the smiling receptionist, a new girl called Larissa, I really do feel ill and am not sure how to break the news to anyone.

"Hi Cate, good night last night?" my boss, Garry, asks as he hands me a takeaway coffee.

"Yeah, thanks, I..."

"Great. Listen I have already set the laptop up in the boardroom. They should be here at about nine-thirty so that gives us some time to run through things first," Garry is already walking towards the boardroom, "Of course get yourself sorted first and then come and join me," he smiles over his shoulder before disappearing in the boardroom.

"OK. Well I just wanted to tell you I got engaged last night," I say to the blinking computer screen. I looked down at my ring finger, bare, at least until we go to the jewellers on the weekend.

"Cate, I can't get the thingy to work properly," Garry calls from the boardroom.

"Coming," I reply.

I sit through the meeting, chipping in where I am supposed to, smiling at three suits in varying shades of navy and shiny lapels from over dry cleaning, thinking how strange it is that no one is aware of my life-changing news. When the meeting is finally over, after we have shaken hands and watched as the lift doors slide together on smiling faces, I go back to my desk to see a bunch of flowers overflowing onto the chair.

I slide my finger under the glue of the small square envelope to pull out the card. *For my wife to be. I love you. Tom xx*

ISOBEL

The gallery door opens and in walks Gabrielle, dipping her sunglasses and flashing me the same wide smile she struck in the restaurant bathroom at that dreaded dinner a few weeks ago.

"Hello Isobel," Gabrielle purrs like a cat.

"Hi," I answer sounding surprised, even though I had half been watching the gallery door waiting for Gabrielle to slice through it ever since I had met her. To me Gabrielle was one of those types who easily made people uncomfortable just in the way she held herself, standing poised with her head cocked to one side regarding you with half-interest.

"How are you?" Gabrielle asks, leaning against the antique table which doubles as a counter.

"Fine thanks," knowing my reply is clipped, "What brings you here?" I add, trying to sound more in control.

"I thought it was about time I checked out this gallery of Patrick's. It's not really my cup of tea, but then again Patrick and I never did agree on art," Gabrielle smiles, running her gaze up and down the length of the room before returning her attention back to me with a broad smile.

"So you told me."

"I did?" Gabrielle looks surprised.

"Yes that night at the restaurant."

Gabrielle ignores me. "Mind if I smoke?"

"Not in here, but you can outside."

"Do you want one?" Gabrielle asks flicking open the lid on the cigarette packet.

"I'll join you," I reply, allowing myself a quiet smirk when I notice a light ruffle to Gabrielle's expression before she turns to walk outside, she certainly wasn't expecting me to join her. What is that saying – keep your friends close and your enemies closer?

Gabrielle leans over and lights the tip of a cigarette balancing it between her fingers and those red-slashed lips of hers, deeply drawing her breath in before passing me the lit paper. I glance at the lipstick stain marking the filter in the shape of a grotesque kiss before elegantly placing the cigarette between my lips, I suck my own deep draw of breath to let the smoke swirl down my throat. Gabrielle watches this act while she lights her own cigarette and snaps the lighter shut. We stand on the footpath in silence for a moment. I am trying to decide how to play this visit that I had been waiting for when Gabrielle starts to talk.

"So how are things going with Patrick?" she asks blowing a puffy white cloud of smoke from her mouth.

"Fine," I lie. I had mostly managed to ignore Patrick's calls since that night at the restaurant. He'd only caught me out once when he too had arrived unannounced at the gallery, looking up at me with big, pleading eyes, his confidence losing air like a slow puncture. He had been away for business and was about to head back to London for a couple of weeks but before he went he was apparently desperate to attend to our own personal business and 'fix' things between us. I had told him I wasn't broken so didn't need fixing. Patrick ran his hands through the greying strands gathering at his temples and straightened his shoulders. "I don't understand you Isobel. I don't get you and do you know what I think?"

he paused, staring at me until I had to look away. "I think you don't even get yourself. You're so busy trying to be this unattainable, mysterious figure that no one is allowed to reach, when really you're one dimensional. There's nothing to you. No substance. I think that's bloody sad. You're bloody sad."

Just then the gallery door had opened and two women walked in, their laughter echoing through the space. Patrick continued to stand rooted to the floorboards in front of the counter, staring at me. I looked past him, trying to smile at the women with tears stinging the backs of my eyes. "Can I help you?" my voice didn't sound like mine. Both the women smiled, shaking their heads while they strolled around a statue of a nude at the far end of the gallery.

"Isobel," Patrick hissed.

"Can I help you, sir?" I smiled, fixing my stare to meet Patrick's.

His eyes widened for a moment but this time it was Patrick who broke his gaze in defeat. "Not anymore it seems," Patrick answered quietly, buttoning his jacket and leaving the gallery.

Shading my eyes from the sun, I take another puff on the cigarette and watch Gabrielle draw imaginary circles on the footpath with the tip of her stiletto.

"That's not quite what I heard," Gabrielle answers in response to my lie about how Patrick and I are getting on.

"Look, what do you want?" I say, rapidly losing composure. Her lip marks still wrapped around the end of my cigarette make me feel ill.

"I am worried about Patrick that's all. You can't play with people like that."

"Like what?"

"Like let them fall head over heels for you and then just cut them off like that. Although, I do have my suspicions about why you might have done that." Gabrielle lets the words slide around my neck into a noose.

"Oh really?" I'm intrigued as to how much Patrick may have told Gabrielle about our last liaison in the gallery.

"Patrick thinks you're still pining for someone else. A guy you used to go out with. Tom is it?"

The mention of Tom's name from Gabrielle's lips is so unexpected and out of context it catapults me straight back to being that petrified young woman, nothing more than a girl, speaking a life-breaking lie down the phone to a young man, nothing more than a boy. In an effort to bring myself calmly back to the present, I wrap my fingers around my upper arm, squeezing the blood from the fingernails and slowly flick ash from the end of the cigarette. 'Tom' as a topic is one I actively and consciously avoid, especially around Cate, Laura and current boyfriends, so I was certain I had never brought any topic even close up with Patrick. I had never even exhaled Tom's name from the back of my throat while feigning fervour.

"Tom?" I venture.

"Yes I am sure Patrick said his name was Tom. Apparently you do quite a lot of sleep talking Isobel. Whole detailed conversations of some pretty disturbing stuff. Patrick was quite freaked out by the whole thing. Said sometimes he had to sleep on the couch because he was terrified you were going to strangle him in your sleep."

The noose squeezes tighter around my neck. The nightmares had returned, sure I knew that, my eyes snapping wide open at all hours of blackness, my skin clammy to the touch, my throat constricting as I watched the figure of a man – Tom – disappear around the bedroom door followed by a child – our child. Looking at the sheets all twisted and tangled, wondering if I was still asleep or if these figures were ghosts and I really was finally going crazy. A full night's sleep was a fantasy sifting faster and faster out of the bedroom. The mornings when I had found Patrick in the lounge room with a blanket dangling over the edge of the couch, I told myself the midnight relocation was down to him thinking my bed was uncomfortable. In truth, had I been honest with myself the following morning while I stirred the coffee and listened to Patrick in the shower, I would have shouted and screamed at the top of my lungs that my life was nothing more than an empty facade clinging to the edges of a lie. I knew Patrick was zeroing in on me the same way they all had – Dominic, that other guy I left for London with, what's-his-name. All of them working it out and causing me to get nothing more than fitful sleep snatched in fragments night after night which was slowly and surely killing me.

I rubbed at the dark circles under my eyes, not wanting to look at Gabrielle who had unknowingly stumbled into my lonely secrets.

"Why are you really here?" I calmly asked Gabrielle.

"Have I upset you?" Gabrielle said, dropping her cigarette to the concrete and stubbing the end out with the tip of her stiletto.

"Why are you really here?" I calmly repeated.

"I told you, to see Patrick' gallery."

"My gallery Gabrielle, the gallery is mine. Patrick is an investor."

"So fairly important I would have thought – him investing money in your little..." Gabrielle stopped short.

"Are you threatening me?" I cut in sharply.

"No I'm not. Look I'm sorry I am just very protective of Patrick. He would kill me if he knew I told you this, but he wanted me to talk to you, to see if there was any chance you two might get back together."

"You? Talk to me? Don't you find something slightly absurd in Patrick getting his ex-wife to talk to his ex-girlfriend about getting back together?" I smirked and stubbed out my own cigarette. Now I really had it heard it all.

Gabrielle lit another cigarette and held it out to me. I shook my head, burying my hands deep inside my trouser pockets to punctuate the refusal.

"I admit it's not exactly a conventional approach, but Patrick and I aren't exactly conventional people. You don't seem to strike me as the conventional type either," she said with the cigarette clasped between her teeth.

"What benefit would it be to you if Patrick and I were to get back together anyway?"

"Well hopefully the whinging phone calls and turning up on my doorstep at all hours would bloody stop, and that's just for starters. I guess though..." Gabrielle stopped and gazed up between the sheet of black glossy hair falling in a jagged line across her forehead, "I guess though, if you are still in love with this Tom character then Patrick doesn't really stand a chance, does he?"

Some of life's most defining moments often creep up on you and usually it's only with hindsight that you truly understand the impact of a comment or an observation. Other defining moments don't need to bask in the glory of hindsight, but instead smack your insides and change your course with the world the instant they fall from the kisses of a lover or the lips of an enemy. Had I been fully conscious and aware of this little-remembered fact, would I have stood in the late afternoon sun with the ex-wife of my ex-lover letting the truth of her words collect every last splinter of resistance I had to pretending I didn't love Tom and then burn each splinter in a raging bonfire.

"I'm still in love with Tom," I let the sentence trail off, feeling a total sense of relief that by simply saying those few words out loud to another human being I had at long last released the constant deceit catching and winding on every cog in my body. Now those words and the liberation that went with them were travelling through the air for anyone to hear.

"Well that's that then," Gabrielle was saying.

"That's that," I confirmed, turning to walk back inside the gallery. I watched from behind the counter as Gabrielle paused against the glass, her back to me, slowly and deliberately finishing her cigarette. When she had extinguished the last of the flame with the twist of her heel against the concrete, she slowly slid her back off the glass, and without turning around, walked off down the street. I watched Gabrielle crease into the crowd of people until it was impossible to make out who she was, before I was satisfied that she wouldn't come back and then went into the storeroom to make a coffee.

The sound of my mobile phone ringing louder than the boiling kettle sent me back out into the open space of the gallery. Still feeling strangely light following my earlier admission to Gabrielle, I answered the phone without checking the number.

"Hello Isobel. It's your mother."

I let an uncomfortable pause fill the gap between us. The relationship with my parents, particularly my mother, had remained soured ever since the pregnancy when I was banished to the safety of Aunt Jean's house in the country to save my mother's face, over a decade ago now.

"I know," I said finally.

"How are you?" My mother's voice was strained, but gentler than usual.

"Fine."

Another pause.

"Isobel."

Another pause.

"Sweetheart…"

My skin prickled at her using a word that was intimate and tender, but still I didn't say anything. My mother rarely called and when she did it always felt like it was purely out of duty, to be able to say to her bridge friends that we had spoken and she could keep up the pretence that she was a caring mother, just the same as they were with their stuck-up daughters. My parents had tried one visit to London when I was living there. But the way it was packaged up – as a side-trip on the way to Paris and the rest of Europe – made me so angry that the few days we did spend together were laced with snapped retorts, clenched jaws and bitter silences.

"Isobel," Mum tried to pick up the conversation again.

"Yes, I am still here."

"Isobel, I have some very sad news. It's about your Aunt Jean."

"What, what about Aunt Jean?" I held my breath.

"Isobel, sweetheart, she, she died in the early hours of this morning. I am so sorry…"

"What? How, I don't understand. What do you mean she died this morning? How, how, how can that be?"

"The thing is she had cancer. No one knew. I was as shocked as anyone. I still am. She didn't want anyone to know and when the hospital contacted us this morning, I couldn't believe it. I just couldn't believe it. It still hasn't sunk in. We didn't even know she was ill and it sounds like you didn't either," my mother replied gently.

"What kind?"

What kind of what?"

"What kind of cancer did she have?"

"It was a brain tumour. According to the hospital it had only recently been diagnosed, but her health had deterio-rated so quickly that it had only really been a few weeks.

I mean we just saw her at Christmas, with you, and she seemed like Jean, absolutely fine, it's just so strange. Poor Jean. I, I still can't quite believe it. I know you two were so close. Perhaps I should come to Sydney. I know this is such a blow for you."

"No." I gripped the edge of the table, letting my body rock back and forth listening to my mother ask me over and over again if I was alright and if she should come and get me. She couldn't see me shaking my head and my eyes filling with water.

"Isobel?"

"No. No I don't want you to come to Sydney. It's not necessary, thanks for the offer, though. Just please tell me when and where the funeral is."

After I had scribbled down the details of where my aunt was to be buried, thick blue ink rubbing over the gloss of a gallery card I had fingered from the box on the counter, the other cards scattering across the counter top, I slumped down onto the floor. I didn't care how many people were passing on the street, peering into the window to see my body, limp and sagging on the wooden boards. Tears streaked long lines down my face as I cried, silently, knowing I was now truly all alone in the world if I didn't claw back the family that was rightfully mine. Tom and our child. Our child.

TOM

O ur heads are pressed together, almost touching the glass. My stomach is full of butterflies. I feel so anxious it's really hard to concentrate on the boundless rows of shine and sparkle laid out before us like tins on a supermarket shelf.

"They're all starting to look the same," I say squeezing Cate's hand tighter. She nods her head.

"How do we know which is a good one?" Cate asks.

"The good one is the one you like," I answer.

"But they all look the same."

I watch as Cate drops her forehead right onto the glass of the jeweller's window. "Aaaah, I don't know. I thought choosing a ring would be fun, but it's hard. I'm going to have this thing on my hand forever and I don't ever want to get sick of looking at it, so how am I ever going to choose something like that!" She rolls her head off the glass and turns to face the street.

For a moment I am not really sure what to do, I squint my eyes trying to focus on all the intricate gems adorning bands of gold, silver, platinum, white gold and rose gold. How do you tell the difference between white gold and just plain old silver, or even platinum. They all look to be the same colour to me. We could get really ripped off here and I wouldn't be any the wiser and it's obvious Cate doesn't know any better.

"Do you want to at least go in?" I say turning around to join Cate who is staring at the cars snaking their way to the traffic lights. She makes a face. "Do you want to try somewhere else?" I offer. Cate shrugs her shoulders, still screwing up her face. I start to laugh. "Babe this is meant to fun. You're meant to demand massive diamonds the size of small boulders. You're meant to screw your face up at a price tag less than ten thousand. You're...you're...you're...I don't know what else you're supposed to do because I am just taking my lead off those terrible chick flick things you sometimes make me watch, so I am not really prepared for you being all *normal* about choosing an engagement ring." I am really laughing now as I brush the hair escaping from Cate's ponytail drawing tentacles on her face. She is so beautiful and somehow I love her even more that she doesn't really care about shopping for an engagement ring. I had to ask her twice this morning if that's what she wanted to do today. I had sat on the end of the bed, all salty from surfing, a paper bag with croissants for breakfast clenched between my damp fingers. In her response to the question, Cate rolled over onto her stomach, muttering something into the pillow.

"What? I didn't quite catch that," I said, tickling the end of her feet. Something else was muttered into the pillow sounding much like the first mutterings.

"We could go to the beach," Cate said rolling onto her back.

"Don't you want to get a ring?"

She rubbed her eyes, nodding, "Of course."

Now standing here in front of the jewellery store with Cate gluing her eyes onto the traffic instead of a row of rings makes me love her even more. I kiss her full on the lips. "Come on let's go inside and at least try some on, maybe that will be more fun than staring at a row of rocks through a sheet of glass," I say grabbing Cate's hand and pulling her inside the jewellers.

"Can I help you?" the shop assistant trills, shaking diamonds hanging in large chandeliers from her earlobes. Cate and I look at each before Cate starts mumbling something about *just looking,* but the shop assistant hasn't heard her and grabs onto my very confident-sounding response.

"Yes you can, we're looking for a ring, we've just gotten engaged," I am straightening my back and winking at Cate.

"Congratulations!" The word comes out in high pitch making a couple admiring a tray of rings look up at us.

"Thanks," Cate smiles self-consciously, but blind Harry can tell she is happy – at least that's what I think.

The shop assistant springs into action. Keys are jangling as they unlock glass cabinets from which trays and trays of gleaming colours are being laid out in front of us. The woman with the chandelier earrings is remarking on carat size and clarity while continuing to pull out more trays of gleaming colours. How many can she have in there? She's excited and click-clacking on impossibly high stilettos over to the window to hold up diamonds to the light with Cate and I trailing behind her, looking bewildered. Cate looks over her shoulder trying to conceal laughter. I wink at her again and speed up to join the over-excited assistant who has barely noticed we haven't yet joined her to admire diamond clarity where the light is better. Cate and I are both squinting at a diamond clasped between the fingers of the assistant as she continues to babble on with foreign phrases, seemingly to do with diamonds. We are both nodding our heads in unison, making 'hmmm' sounds whenever we think it's the right moment.

Half an hour later, confused and empty-handed we stagger out onto the street. Both of us are silent.

"If nothing else, I now have clarity," Cate says side-stepping a woman with a stroller.

"Diamond clarity?" I say laughing.

"Oh yeah, I didn't even mean that type of clarity, so now I have two types of clarity."

"Two types? What's the second type?"

"Yes two types. I don't want an engagement ring with a whacking big diamond, with or without brilliant clarity, hanging from my finger!"

"Really?" I ask, cautiously studying her face, but apart from the very faint beginnings of a furrowed brow, there are no clues to pick up on. Cate's eyes are fixed back on the traffic streaming past in a blur of grey and red brake lights. I breathe in deeply, closing my fingers around hers. I know gripping onto her fingers like this is a total act of terror and I am doing all I can to keep calm because what I ultimately think is that Cate is about to tell me she doesn't want to get married. I am putting one foot in front of the other in an effort to walk down the street, our hands break to let shoppers pass between us but all I am thinking is that I have misread all the signs, letting myself swim around in a pool of complete ignorance. I snatch a look at Cate as she side-steps a teenager before falling back into stride with me, absent-mindedly sliding her hand into mine.

"Really," Cate says firmly, picking up the conversation where we had left it. She's totally unaware that she has just opened the flood gates of my ignorance pool and I am treading water at an exhausting speed. My eyes are fixed back on the traffic.

"I have you and that's all I care about. Our love isn't proven with a lump of rock on my left hand is it?" I'm going under. Water is filling my nostrils and now I really can't breathe. Suddenly I want more than anything in the world to marry this girl and any possible thought that it could all slip away scares the life out of me. I watch the traffic slowing, torturing myself that when I climbed out of bed this morning, half-peeled on my wetsuit, grabbed my board and went to the beach I was engaged. When we were eating croissants in bed I was still engaged. Even inside the jewellery store, not more than five minutes ago, I was still engaged to be married and now the reality is that when I pull the sheets back on the bed tonight I could be no longer engaged – un-engaged, is there such a word? Would I even be getting into our bed tonight or are we going to break up because it now seems to be me that we are heading backwards, not forwards. We're meant to be going forwards, this is meant to be about the rest of our lives. Together. Is this the reason why we haven't really told many people about us getting engaged, because she doesn't really want to? Please don't let all the pieces be falling into place and I have just been too blind to read the signs. My mind is running away with me. I know I really want to marry Cate, it's not about *needing* it's about *wanting* and to me that's always the clinching factor. I don't want this scene unravelling and becoming my life's biggest 'what if?' moment. It's now or never.

"Are you saying you don't want to get married?" I manage to struggle out of my throat.

Cate stops dead. A man bumps into her back, jerking her forwards, he mutters 'watch where you're going', and keeps walking. It's like time is moving in slow motion with Cate and I the two main characters in a film that is hanging by a creaking hinge threatening to snap.

"No, not at all," Cate looks mortified. "I just mean you and I should be exactly that, *you and I,* which doesn't mean we have to have a traditional ring. Maybe it shouldn't even be a ring. Maybe our engagement should be celebrated with something totally different, like...umm...I don't know just yet."

God I love this girl.

LAURA

"Oh my God! You're what?"

"Engaged," Cate repeats, bending over to tie up the lace on her trainer.

"Cate!" I scream, yanking her up by the shoulders to hug her. I am jumping up and down while Cate just looks embarrassed, red flowers her chest and neck.

"Aren't you excited?" I say, suddenly feeling very self-conscious as two joggers round the corner of the park, staring at a confused scene unfolding – one figure jumping up and down excitedly while the other looks like a reluctant rag doll being pulled around. We fall silent, waiting for the joggers to pass.

"Cate?" I ask, growing worried that this is not good news after all.

"Oh no it's great Lau," Cate says, dipping her head to meet mine. "No, really. I promise you," she is grabbing at my shoulders now and smiling broadly. "It's just I get so embarrassed about telling people, it's kind of impossible to drop into conversation. I can never find an appropriate way to bring it up…"

"Please tell me you are joking!" I screech, "This is the most amazing news and you're being polite about it. Shit Cate! I just spent two laps of the park harping on about yet another appalling date not having a bloody clue that you have the most amazing news but you can't even tell me because I won't shut up. God you were even asking me

300

questions and offering advice, why didn't you just tell me to shut up?"

"Because I was interested –"

"Saint Cate."

"Oh fuck off!"

I clasp both her hands in mine. "This is fantastic news. I am so happy for you both. You two are perfect. God, was Tom's proposal really romantic?"

"Ah we're talking about Tom here Lau. He was pretty pissed and I thought he was joking, but on sobering up the next morning he was still adamant."

"Oh my God," I say starting to jump up and down again. "The ring?"

"Hideous Lau."

I can't even hide my face dropping. Cate starts to laugh.

"Oh your face is priceless," Cate is still laughing and I know I am still looking mortified. "No, no. I haven't got a ring yet. We tried shopping for one yesterday and the experience was hideous. I don't even know if I want a ring, it's all a bit too traditional for me I think."

"You have to have a ring!" I say, squeezing Cate's hands tighter. "Actually hang on a minute, can we just rewind. How long have you been engaged and why haven't you told me?" I drop Cate's hands and take a step back before planting my hands on my hips.

"A few days and we haven't really told anyone, well apart from our parents. I told you it's really hard to drop into conversation..."

"Cate, I am meant to be one of your best friends."

"And you are! Seriously Lau, I can just never find the right moment to bring it up."

I raise my eyebrows, "How about starting with, 'Guess what?'," I offer.

"It's the truth. Promise," Cate smiles at me, slips her sunglasses back down over her nose and breaks into a jog.

"Hey wait up," I shout to her back as I take off.

"Does Iss know?" I pant catching up with Cate.

"No. Not yet."

"When are you going to tell her?" I ask, jumping over a pothole in the track.

"Tom's keen to have a party or something to celebrate and let everyone know, but of course I will tell Iss before then, if I see her that is."

"Good luck!" I nudge Cate in the ribs with my elbow, speeding up.

CATE

I am buttering toast watching as a pool of creamy yellow sinks into the bread. I am not particularly hungry, just trying to find ways to distract my head from repeating over and over again the conversation with Laura in the park. The conversation keeps snagging on Laura saying '*good luck*' when I told her Isobel didn't yet know about the engagement. Did Laura mean, *good luck* in breaking the news to Isobel, or did she mean *good luck* in managing to see the elusive Isobel to actually tell her?

The logical voice whispering through the replay tells me that it was certainly the latter Laura was referring to. But the other voice which has stripped away most of the words, leaving me with *good luck*, shouts louder and plays on the questions about Isobel's real feelings for Tom which I had silently been turning over in my head or entering in a one-off undated log in my notebook. My paranoia had basically dissolved until Laura's words reawakened them. It worried me even more now that a seemingly spontaneous remark had the capacity to catapult my thinking out of its comfort zone and straight into the gawping jaws of paranoia. This paranoia stuff is just not like me at all.

'Not me at all,' I say out loud into the empty kitchen to punctuate my position on the matter. 'You're being silly,' I add for double effect before spreading a thick layer of apricot jam on top of the toast, picking up the newspaper and making my way to the sunroom.

The house is silent. Tom has gone surfing. I slink into my favourite cane chair by the window, snuggling my back into the cushion and bite into the bread. I reassure myself again that I am being silly and take another bite until I have finished the toast. I dial Isobel's number on my mobile, it rings out until I hear her voice recorded on the voicemail, sounding distant and distracted, like she is in the middle of something and would really rather you didn't leave a message, so I don't. I want to actually say this news to Isobel, not a recording of her voice. Making a promise that I will try again later, I rest my head against the wall, feeling the newspaper falling from my lap in folds onto the floor while I drift off to sleep.

LAURA

I have been tapping the end of my pen against a notepad for the past ten minutes, staring at a bullet point in a client proposal document: *conclusive research suggests, an effective way to reposition Hedges Bank and appeal to a new audience of young cash-rich investors is to align the bank with the arts and cultural sector.*

The client had completely bought into the strategy, but unfortunately for me that's where our strategy recommendations finished. Banking clients were a whole new deal for my agency, we are only a small outfit of six people and tended to specialise in offering PR services to more 'lifestyle' clients, but Will, my business partner knew someone who knew someone at the bank and before we knew it we were drafting PR strategies to reposition Hedges Bank. All I know about Hedges Bank is that Tom works there. I had already quizzed him about it, but Tom is a numbers man and knew next to nothing about why the bank would want to be re-positioning itself. When I asked him what he thought about the arts as an idea for the bank's reposition, he at least gave me the benefit of pretending to be interested, before telling me he really didn't understand the career Cate and I had both worked in since university.

"Any luck?"

I look up to see Will holding out a takeaway cappuccino. "It's already got sugar in it." I smile and take the paper cup, the heat instantly scolds my hand and I drop the cup on the desk.

"Sorry," Will says, "here," he is holding out a napkin with the name of the cafe printed on the corner. I take it and wipe the milk droplets from the desktop. Will plants himself on the edge of the desk and takes a sip of his espresso, squinting from the grit of the caffeine.

"This arts link up thing needs to be interesting and not obvious," he says tapping the document lying on the desk in front of me. "I mean anyone could just get Hedges to sponsor some crazy show at the Museum of Contemporary Art, but that's really boring."

"And really obvious," we both say together, rolling our eyes.

"It can't just be a badging exercise, the association with the arts needs to be more meaningful and give potential new customers a reason to engage not just with the art but with the bank too," Will says, sighing.

"I keep coming back to the idea of 'juxtaposition'. You know, playing on the traditional pinstripe suits and serious business of the bank and setting that against something really modern and 'now'," I say, taking the plastic lid off the coffee and blowing gently on the froth.

Will is nodding. "I like it, that's interesting. I reckon we're getting into the right space with that idea."

"Yeah I think so too. It's just what the hell is it?" I let out a sigh and turn the cup around in my hand, still too cautious to take a sip.

"Well I need to go meet the fashionistas," Will says, dropping his feet to the floor and throwing the disposable espresso cup into the bin. The 'fashionistas' were two over-eager twenty-somethings with a swimwear label, backed by one of their rich fathers, who said 'like' a lot and were more concerned about range launch parties than actually producing any designs which retailers were prepared to sell.

"Oh you're taking one for the team there Will, thanks," I say half-heartedly, rubbing my temples before dropping my forehead onto the keyboard.

"That's very dramatic. Don't worry, we'll crack it."

"Before tomorrow's meeting?" I groan, looking up at Will with the keys pressing into my cheek.

"Yep," he says, sounding anything but confident. "Maybe the fashionistas will *like* have *like* the most *like* amazing idea, *like* that we can use," Will laughs as he zips up his laptop bag and collects his mobile from the desk next to mine. "See you later," Will says. Vibrations shudder through the huge metal door as it shuts behind Will, leaving me all alone in the warehouse space we converted into our office. Slowly I raise my head up off the keyboard, tracing my finger-tip across my cheek to feel the outline of keys pressed into the skin.

Mine and Will's desks are side by side against two windows which hang in an imposing length, running from floor to ceiling, on the far wall of the open plan room. In the winter time the cold shatters through the glass clinging to my nose and fingers as I sit huddled at my desk with an electric bar heater at my feet. Today though, it's warm outside with the sun cutting elongated grey shapes across my desk and stretching onto the floorboards. The heat prickles my nose and I can feel my cheeks flushing. The sun combined with the coffee Will gave me are both making it too difficult to concentrate. I swing around on the office chair, letting the wheels scrape along the wood of the floorboards until I am facing the swollen belly of the warehouse, searching for inspiration. The walls are all whitewashed. We have a few pieces of artwork hanging in the area we use for client meetings, but these are old movie posters box-framed and not really an original idea.

Then I revert to doing what I always do when I am totally stuck on an idea – call Cate for her advice. She picks up on the second ring and sounds distracted.

"I'm on eBay looking at vintage jewellery," Cate informs me after we've said hello.

"Why?" I ask.

"Trying to get some inspiration for something that could be an engagement ring, without necessarily being a ring. Do you think it's weird to wear something that someone else has owned? I am sure my mother would think it was bad luck. Is it?"

"Is it what?" I reply.

"Bad luck to wear a piece of jewellery someone else owned?"

"Don't know. Could be. But maybe that person had really good luck so that would rub off on you."

"Yeah maybe. Anyway, how are you?"

"Desperate for inspiration," I answer, groaning to emphasise the point, "remember that art brief I spoke to Tom about?"

"Oh yes, something to do with his bank?"

"Yes that's the one – well we went and won the business didn't we?"

"That's fantastic. Congratulations."

"Well it would be if we were able to implement the strategy. It's in the art space and shouldn't be too obvious like a straight sponsorship, but more something the bank owns. But of course the bank has no credentials in the art space. We have a meeting tomorrow and we're no closer."

"Have you spoken to Isobel about it?"

"Isobel doesn't really know anything about PR," I answer, feeling deflated.

"True, but she knows a lot about art, doesn't she? Her finger is on the pulse with what's going on, so she should be able to at least give you a steer in the right direction. Support of a new exhibition perhaps? I'm not sure because I don't know enough about art, but Iss will."

"Definitely worth a call. The real challenge though might be getting her to pick up the phone. The last I heard she was going to the country for a few days, something to do with her Aunt, I think, but she was really vague and I had to go into a meeting. That was about a week ago though, so God I hope she's back by now."

"Yeah, she must be back by now because she doesn't really have anyone else to run the gallery. But I would try the gallery instead of her mobile, mind you I haven't really had much success with that tactic, but you might get through," Cate offers.

"You're a genius. Right got to go and crack this brief. Lots of love. Bye." I roll the words into a jumbled stream, literally throwing the phone back onto the hook to dial Isobel's number.

ISOBEL

The customer takes an exaggerated pace backwards regarding the painting from another angle. How I play out these next few minutes or even seconds is crucial to the difference between making the sale and not making the sale. I am walking a tightrope slowly luring the customer to fall in love with the piece or at least feel they must own it, regardless of love. Even the proximity of where I stand in relation to the potential purchaser can have an effect. Too close means too eager, but leaning in to lightly touch their elbow while telling them some fact or other about the work can tilt the purchase in my favour. Especially if the potential owner of the artwork comes to the conclusion they have fallen in love with the piece all by themselves – absolutely nothing to do with the curator taking calculated moves to push the game towards a favourable outcome. It's all a game of manipulation.

I snatch a careful sideways glance at the man considering an abstract I've had hanging on various walls of the gallery over the past few months, it's had quite a lot of interest but no one has ever stumped up the cash. He has rearranged himself from crossed arms (not sure) to hands on hips (will this fit above the fireplace in the living room?). I allow myself a tiny smile.

"How much did you say this was again?" he asks, turning to face me.

I pause before answering, adjusting the level of my voice, "Thirty," I reply catching just the right tone to suggest that of course it's worth every cent.

"Thousand?" he smiles, thinking he has cracked a really funny joke. I smile back to confirm the price, thinking he is a moron. He takes another step back. I start to make a comment about the artist when the gallery phone starts ringing. Fuck it. I continue to watch the man, trying to ignore the phone.

"Do you need to get that?" he asks, nodding his head in the direction of the antique table with the ringing phone intruding in on our game.

I smile tightly, "Be right back," I say, virtually sprinting to the table. As I pick the phone up, I notice his arms cross again. I frown and attempt to be civil. "Pop Gallery."

Laura's voice comes travelling down the line, making me yank the phone away from my ear. "Can I call you back?" I whisper urgently. She is still talking, totally oblivious to what I have just requested. I watch the man take a couple of paces to the right. He lifts his arms from his hips to fold them across his chest.

"Laura, please I will call you back in a minute. I promise. I'm in the middle of something."

The guy scratches his neck – not a good sign. I could just hang up on Laura, but she's so persistent she'll only start calling my mobile. I'm not listening to her because I am trying so hard to read the body language of this guy studying the abstract, but soon the decision is made when he plants his hands in his trouser pockets and turns to make his way to the door, mouthing 'thank you' to me and giving an apologetic wave. "Hang on!" I say into the phone to Laura, but the guy thinks I am talking to him, he looks alarmed. "Sorry, not you," I say to him while pointing to the phone. I shove my hand over the receiver and tell him I will be one second. He smiles, "I want my wife to have a look at it," he says opening the gallery door for what I know will be the last time. They rarely come back with their wives.

Later that evening I am sitting on the balcony rolling a glass of chilled pinot between my hands. The condensation dampening my palms makes me nearly drop the wineglass, I grab the stem just as it slides towards the decking and place the glass on the table beside me. I close my eyes briefly, conjuring up an image of Aunt Jean and I sitting on her veranda watching the sun drop behind the eucalypts. It's my favourite image of the pair of us together and the same one I always drew on when I lived in London and needed a jab of her wisdom. Even now she is gone, for good, she is still so vivid in my mind. I can hear her voice and smell the faint scent of lavender oil she wore dabbed on her neck and wrists. But she's gone and I can't ask her what she thinks anymore. About anything. Ever.

My eyes snap open. I haven't told Cate or Laura that Aunt Jean died, I don't want them fussing over me, I don't need the misguided attention or the sympathy. Right now I need to concentrate on the advice Aunt Jean repeated to me time and time again, to focus on what I need to make a situation better. This time, it's me focussing on capturing what's rightfully mine, *my* family. I need to have somebody in this world who really understands me. I need to re-plug the gap Aunt Jean has left blowing and gaping.

I close my eyes slightly again, drawing up the conversation with Laura on the phone this afternoon. At first I was cross with her for making me lose the sale, but her offer turned out to be much more interesting and fortuitous than she will ever know. Not only have I picked up a project to turn the foyer of Hedges Bank into a pop-up urban art gallery, but I now have a completely legitimate reason to 'bump' into Tom without it looking engineered, suspicious or Cate's physical presence drawing a dark shadow in my conscience. It was too good to be true. Now all I had to do was make Patrick see that the Hedges Bank project would be a fantastic PR opportunity and lead to some impressive price tags hanging from work by artists we could never attract to a small little-known gallery.

When Patrick agreed to the investment to get the gallery off the ground, it wasn't without its conditions. I had been so eager, almost smelling the crisp banknotes, that I had signed the contract after not much more than a glance at the black type printed in neat rows above the dotted line. One particularly quiet afternoon in the gallery, after the space had been stripped and whitewashed with the scent of fresh paint and promise hanging heavy in the air, a steady stream of yawns overcame me. I walked into the back room to make myself a cup of coffee. I was reaching for the kettle wedged between a couple of mugs and a teacup full of crusting sugar, the whole ensemble balancing precariously on top of the bar fridge, when I disrupted the wedge of unopened mail and official documents to do with the gallery lying dog-eared bound in a grubby elastic band I used to tie up my hair with. Switching the kettle on, I leant against the fridge and yanked the envelope containing Patrick's investment contract from the elastic band, which caught and ripped at the edges of the envelope until I finally freed it. The other documents dropped in a heap to the floor which I kicked free of my foot. I flicked to the end of the document to double-check both signatures were still in tact. I'm not sure why I thought they might have disintegrated into the paper in a few short weeks, strangely, nor did that logic stop a wave of relief washing over me when I saw the signatures were both still there. Mine forming big loops across the line, while Patrick's signature bent in tight, jagged lines scratched across the page. I turned to the second page where all the clauses were outlined, my eyes growing wider with every new line. I twisted my lip, staring at what I had agreed to. Patrick basically had full control over everything, he was to be consulted on every single decision during that time, almost right down to what brand of loo roll to put in the bathroom, I thought bitterly. Not only that, he was to retain majority share for a minimum of five years with no new investment partners considered during that period and that included existing 'interest parties' (me) having any power to buy into the business. "You fucking bastard," I breathed out loud. The whistle of the kettle screeched through the tiny room, rattling the coffee mugs and making me jump. I let go of the contract, twisting it into the floor with the heel of my stiletto as I reached across to jam shut the switch on the kettle.

I knew Patrick would never budge before the five-year period was up, so the money Aunt Jean had left me would never be enough to tempt him of a buy-out, and I knew I could never ever sell her house. I checked my watch, almost eight-thirty pm, plus eleven hours made it about seven-thirty in the morning in London. Not too early to call. Patrick had sent me an email yesterday, pleading that I re-consider, he was so, so, so sorry for what he said that day in the gallery...he was angry...he would never want to hurt me...anger and jealousy does cruel things to him...he wants me back...he loves me. There was no mention of Gabrielle. I hadn't replied – that had more to do with the fact I had to play this game with Patrick very carefully, properly considering what my next move would be. But now, given the opportunity Laura has unwittingly presented to me, my delayed response could in hindsight be perceived as orchestrated, with all the pieces of the game standing to attention in a perfectly straight line in my favour.

When Patrick picked up the phone on a crisp London morning to hear my voice, it was startling how effortlessly he gave into the sound of an estranged lover.

Tom

Even though I am running late for a meeting, a light brush at my elbow is all it takes to make me stop and turn around to see Isobel smiling at me. If I didn't know her any better I would say she almost looked shy – definitely not the confident Isobel whose face is so often betrayed by a careless dark shadow falling through her eyes. I must look shocked because Isobel's smile drops for an instant before she readjusts it to be even broader than her first attempt.

"Hi Tom," Isobel says, keeping that smile fixed to her lips.

"Hi," I say slowly, perplexed, glancing around the foyer of the bank. "What are you doing here?"

Her smile stays put as she smooths down the cotton of her white shirt. "Oh I am doing this great joint art project with the bank, here in the foyer," she says, lightly sweeping her arm out to the side.

"Wow," is all I manage to reply while slightly nodding my head, "That's great and...different."

"Yeah, Laura got me the gig. I am just here measuring up some stuff so I can work out how we're going to lay the gallery out."

"Right. Well good for you. I have to go actually, I'm running late for a meeting," I say, pushing my shirtsleeve back to check my watch and then start nodding my head more vigorously.

"It's a pop-up." Isobel says, seemingly undeterred.

"OK, great," I mumble, starting to stride across the polished cement, "I really have to go. It's good to see you Isobel," I look back over my shoulder to see her still standing in the same spot, smiling at me. She raises her palm in a half-wave where only her fingers flutter slowly, before dropping her hand back down to her side.

I push through the double glass doors onto the street, shoving my hand into the waistband of my trousers to tuck my shirt in where it has freed itself. I really am running late now, I need to get moving so I break into a half-jog, my briefcase belting against my thigh. Breathing sharply at the pedestrian crossing, waiting for the lights to change I look back up the length of the street to where the bank sits like a tired grey man smudged into the backdrop of the city. I know I am half-expecting to see Isobel walking down the footpath, following me. When I can't immediately see her, I find myself searching for her in amongst the throngs of city workers rushing in scattered directions up and down the footpath. But she's nowhere I can see and I am actually really looking.

"What the hell is a pop-up?" I mutter, stepping out onto the road as the light turns green.

The meeting dragged on with me spending the last half an hour of it catching glimpses of the sun slowly dropping behind the skyscrapers. I was hoping to squeeze in a surf tonight but we'd hit a snag only fifteen minutes into the meeting and I knew it was going to be a long one. I was finally out of there though and parking the car outside our house. Cate looked up from her book and waved at me from her seat on the veranda. She had obviously been home for a while, her bare legs were resting on the railing and a glass of something set down on the low table beside her.

"The lavender is looking really gorgeous isn't it?" Cate says gesturing to the row of hazy purple lining either side of the garden path leading up to the veranda steps.

"Yeah it looks great," I reply, leaning down to kiss the top of her head.

"Good day?"

"Long. I'm going in to get changed and get a beer. You want anything?" Cate reaches for the glass and gives it a small shake as she holds it out to me.

"Hey, I've been thinking," I say, gripping a freezing glass in both hands as I push my elbow down on the door handle to release it, "we should really hurry up and organise having everyone around for a barbeque to celebrate our engagement."

Cate takes the wineglass from my hand and balances it between her knees.

"Yeah that's a great idea. When should we do it?" she replies, stealing a sip of wine.

"I don't know. Soon. Next few weeks, maybe, while the weather is still warm. It would be really great to have everyone over, all the people we haven't seen for a while. We should invite old mates too, like I could invite Christian from uni. Apart from the odd email, I haven't seen him for ages." I am getting really excited now, starting a mental checklist of people I would invite. "We should invite family too," I announce, moving my brain down the checklist.

"Of course we should," Cate replies, looking at me like I am a crazy person.

"I was just thinking of Damien that's all. Maybe we could go to Europe for our honeymoon."

"I'm sure your brother wouldn't miss our wedding, it's been ages since he's been home so it's a good excuse isn't it? But babe," Cate stops and looks at me very seriously, "maybe don't get your hopes up that Damien will also be able to fly across to the other side of the world for a barbeque in our back garden in a few weeks' time," she says trying unsuccessfully to stifle a smile.

"Cheeky."

"Well he may be very tempted by your sausage skills. What you can't do with a sausage is not worth knowing about it," Cate is really laughing at her own joke and I know she doesn't hear me when I ask her if she wants a red wine instead. "Hey where are you going?" she looks up at me still laughing as I step over her legs on the way to the door.

"It's the interval at the comedy club so I am getting another drink." I can still hear Cate laughing as I walk down the hallway.

"I love you," Cate's voice catches up with my back, I smile before answering with the same words.

LAURA

Isobel has emailed some imagery of a few of the pieces she is thinking of including in the pop-up gallery. The first is a religious image of 'Madonna and Child' spray-painted onto newspaper clippings screaming controversial headlines about abortion and right-to-life. I read the artist's descriptor about the piece pasted into the body of Isobel's email, I don't understand it, then I look at the price tag and the artist's age – twenty-two – and make a face. I am a bit out of my depth, I don't know enough about art to know if this is a really talented piece of work or if it's just basically someone having a laugh. What I do know though, is that we are going to have to let Hedges Bank approve the artwork before making the final cut of what makes up the exhibition. The last thing I want, or need, is for the pop-up gallery to backfire and I spend the next few weeks dealing with negative press. Worse than that, the bank's reputation could be severely damaged, and even worse than that we lose the client.

I click 'reply' to Isobel's email:

Hi Iss,
     Thanks for sending the imagery of the artwork through to me. They look interesting! As this is very new for the bank, I think it would make sense that we let them have a look at

the pieces you are thinking of including in the exhibition before we go any further.

Let's have a meeting with them, so you can talk them through the pieces, as I think this will be more impactful and receive a better result (i.e. getting the pieces you want to show!) rather than sending sample imagery through on email.

Are you OK to do a meeting next Tuesday? Maybe we could do late afternoon and go for a drink afterwards?

Love Laura x

P.S. Have you seen the email about Cate and Tom's engagement barbeque? Do you want to go halves on a present?

I press 'send' and go to make a cup of tea.

ISOBEL

I am staring at the laptop screen, feeling the first surges of vomit creeping to the back of my throat. My eyes are on a repetitive cycle of reading and re-reading the email I have just opened. It had to be true – Tom and Cate really were getting married. Cate's voice dripped like syrup into the voicemail on my phone earlier this morning. I had barely listened to her words before the shaking started to erupt in spasms all over my body. Somehow I shifted my mindset into what I can now see was denial mode, choosing to obliterate what she was saying from my mind, not daring to believe it. Deleting the message without listening to it for a second time sealed the track of denial I had decided to take in only a split second. Then, swallowing hard and holding my breath while I silently counted to ten in a pathetic bid to suppress the shaking, I tensed my shoulders back to appear confident and strode across the gallery to help another customer admiring that damn abstract.

But now, public confirmation of Tom and Cate's engagement had arrived in print. First, reading an innocent 'P.S.' at the end of Laura's email, like it was some casual after-thought, and then me frantically scrolling through the inbox to find the email from Cate that I had rolled the cursor over, without pausing to even read the subject title, only an hour ago. There it was, my worst fears confirmed. My eyes continued to read and re-read the words, slowly but surely the words started to seep in, falling in heavy thuds to the core of my stomach – lying there rotting.

The gallery was quiet now, just me frozen at the laptop with my fingers resting on the keyboard. I'm not sure how long I sat like that for, it could have been two hours, it could have been two minutes, I just don't know. Gradually I peeled each finger up from the keys, letting them hover in mid-air until I pressed them down again, each one pressing on a different key until 'congratulations' appeared as one lonely word on the screen, cursor blinking at me waiting for something more. But there was nothing more to be said.

It's five days later and I am standing on the footpath out the front of Hedges Bank waiting for Laura to join me for a meeting with the Bank's marketing team. I have a folder with boldly printed images of seven pieces of artwork I want to be included in the exhibition wedged under my armpit. Laura was running late, Laura is always running late. Just as I am about to give up and go into the foyer to report to the security guard and then reception, a taxi pulls up. The door swings open and out swings one bare leg, no mistaking it belongs to Laura. She has her hand out waiting for change from the driver and is smiling apologetically at me, before slamming the door and running up to me, pecking me on the cheek.

"Sorry Iss, there is always a crisis as soon as I try to leave the office. How late are we?"

"*You* are about fifteen minutes late," I say and I know the words clip sourly in the air around us. "Come on, let's go," I tell Laura, trying to sound like my comment was only a joke.

The meeting goes OK. The first lot of images – the ones I thought were the tamest – pricks raised eyebrows and long awkward silences. Laura smiles encouragingly and uses phrases that would sit well in politicians' mouths. I have to say, I admire her knack of being able to couch situations so even the toughest critics in the room begin to relax back into the chair upholstery, stretching their arms up behind their heads and grinning. When I see Laura give me a tight little smile, averting her eyes as soon as they meet mine, I know the meeting has swung in our favour. We leave the room to a flurry of handshakes and don't say a word to each other until the lift doors are firmly shut. Laura's reflection in the mirrored surrounds of the lift physically puffs outwards. "Think we deserve a drink," she sighs.

I manage to tweak the corners of my mouth up into some form of smile. Christ, I have been functioning like a robot the last few days, trying to decide what to do about the 'Tom and Cate situation'. Sleep had become an even scarcer commodity than ever before, dark circles ringed the thin skin under each eye. My diet had largely involved alcohol and cigarettes. Thinking about it now, I wasn't sure if I had let any solid particle past my lips since Thursday when the news was sent so blissfully from one inbox to the other.

"Come on Iss," Laura is persisting.

"I don't know, I am pretty tired," I am watching the floor numbers decrease on a small digital screen above the lift doors. Just as I am about to emphasise my excuse with a large yawn, Laura delivers another approach.

"I spoke to Tom yesterday and he said if he finishes work around the time we're done with our meeting, he's keen to join us for a drink."

I freeze, desperately ravaging through thoughts of what to do, but my time has run out – the lift doors ping open to release us into the foyer with Laura already hunting through her bag looking for her mobile phone. Seeing Tom is what I need to do, I know that, I need to remind him of me. But this arrangement has happened all too fast; it hasn't given me any time to work through a proper plan. God knows I had mulled over different courses of action over the last few days. Most of them hazy – blurred in a film of vodka and cigarette smoke. Despite not being one hundred, or even fifty, per cent ready, Laura presenting a golden opportunity on a platter seems far too good to miss. If I were to call Tom up and invite him for a drink, he would be completely freaked out by the proposition, the whole thing backfiring and breaking. I also knew I couldn't wait another three weeks when I would see Tom, and invariably Cate, at their barbeque. By that time it would be far too late and any attempt on my behalf would be forever encrusted in a lost game.

"OK," I answer Laura feebly.

"Great!" she mouths to me, already holding her mobile phone to her ear with Tom's number pushed into the keypad.

The pub we are meeting Tom in is only a few doors down the street from the bank. By the time we pull open the stained-glass door emblazoned with the establishment's name, the place is brimming with city-types leaning against high bar tables decorated by beer glasses and rings of condensation from a steady stream of drinks. Laura walks purposefully in the direction of the bar running the length of the room manned by five busy bartenders stopping and starting in perfect formation as they serve the swarm of suits all vying for their attention. There is a sliver of a gap at the far end of the bar that Laura is making for, sliding her body in sideways and popping up on the other side right in front of the bar, I can see she has already caught the eye of the bartender closing the drawer on a till. I stand where I am, knowing Laura will order us both a red wine, and instead begin the hunt for Tom.

TOM

I catch sight of Laura handing money to the bartender. There's little chance she's going to notice me, it's so packed in here. "Shit," I say out loud.

"What's up?" Stuart, my work colleague, asks me as he sets his beer down on the bar.

"My friend who's meeting us is way up at the other end of the bar. She'll never find us in here, it's so packed."

"Which one is she?"

"Up there, blue top."

"What's her name?"

"Laura."

"Easy mate. Watch and learn. Excuse me," Stuart says leaning across the bar to flag down the bartender closest to us who frowns and tells Stuart to wait his turn.

I start laughing, "That was impressive mate. Really impressive."

"Hang on, I'm not done yet," Stuart quips and turns his attention back to the bartender who this time, cups his hand over his ear, nods and shouts out to the bartender closest to Laura. I watch Laura nod, lift herself up onto the bench top with her elbows until she has a view straight down the barrel of the bar, catch sight of me and smile.

Stuart turns to me looking like the cat who got the cream and raises his eyebrows in anticipation of my obvious forthcoming praise.

"Nice one." I mutter.

"Is that it?"

"Yep," I reply, seeing Laura threading her way through the drinkers with a glass of red wine in her hand. Behind her is Isobel. Ah. I didn't think she would end up coming. I thought Laura said she wasn't that keen.

"Jesus, who is that?" Stuart mutters under his breath, as Isobel moves into the spot Laura has just created for them between us and the edge of the bar.

"Stuart, this is Laura and Isobel," I declare like a weird train conductor announcing stations.

"That's all very formal of you, Tom," Laura giggles, leaning over to peck me on the cheek before reaching her hand out to Stuart, clasping his in a firm shake. Isobel half-smiles at us, she looks self-conscious grabbing at the strap on her handbag and tensing her fingers around the stem of the wineglass. I remind myself that I have figured Isobel out. She isn't really layer after layer of the complication and intrigue that she thinks she is. Finally Isobel follows Laura's lead by kissing me on the other cheek and pausing over quite what greeting she should give Stuart. Then she clearly chooses 'Charming Isobel', "Oh you get a kiss too," Isobel says tilting towards Stuart to brush the side of his face with barely puckered lips. Stuart looks very pleased with his inclusion on the kissing greeting and is now rocking back and forth on his heels, the same way he does when we he gets excited on the trading floor.

Stuart has obviously translated Isobel's barely-there air kiss as his opportunity to strike up a conversation and goes about engaging her with a truly original line: Haven't I seen you somewhere before?

I groan internally, while Laura rolls her eyes in an over-exaggerated movement. In truth, I am grateful to Stuart for detracting Isobel's attention away from me. On the whole, Isobel and I seem cool with each other. Apart from bumping into her in the foyer at work the other day, I haven't really seen too much of her. That unexpected little liaison did freak me out a bit, making me paranoid she would follow me, but it didn't take long for my logical side to jump in telling me she was in the foyer for a legitimate reason. My logic quickly got further backed by my remembering of the 'epiphany', a while ago now, that I finally understand what makes her tick.

Cate too, seems to be seeing less and less of Isobel giving me the feeling their friendship might be more out of habit than a mutual like. Sometimes you just out-grow one another, at least that was the advice I used to reassure Cate when she had despaired (countless times I might add) over not being able to get hold of Isobel to tell her the news about our engagement.

God each of us now must be up to drink number four or five. There have been quite a few shouts. Stuart and I have moved on from beer to wine and if we manage to stay for another drink or two, there'll be talk of whisky.

"Another?" Stuart asks the three of us, wincing as he swallows the remainder of wine in his glass and slams it down on the bar. There's a team silence as each of us turns over the consequences of another drink in our minds. *It's only Tuesday…I have a massive meeting in the morning…I was only coming for one or two drinks…I feel quite pissed…I'm starving.* We all look at one another the way you do when you're in a pub, no one has left the fold yet, so you decide (very maturely) the decision of whether you stay for another drink (all night) or go (slightly pissed but not too bad) is utterly based on whatever the first person brave enough to speak up says. Those few seconds of silent contemplation are excruciating for everyone.

"Oh fuck it, let's stay for another. I'm busting for the loo though," Laura breaks the silence and makes the collective decision – not very eloquently, but firm nonetheless.

"That's the spirit," Stuart says, "so we're all in, yes!" Isobel and I nod our heads in agreement. "Why not?" I say, sealing my fate.

"I'm going to the loo," Laura reminds us.

"I need to go too," Isobel says, collecting her handbag from under a barstool and following Laura through the increasingly thinning crowd.

"She's bloody gorgeous," Stuart half-slurs, watching Laura and Isobel.

"Who?" I reply, pretending I hadn't noticed that every single guy in the pub had been shooting looks in Isobel's direction all night. I have to admit, I swallowed hard when I saw her step out from behind Laura when they first arrived. Isobel's hair was swept up away from her face, accentuating her razor sharp cheekbones and crisp green feline eyes. Embarrassingly, I had been snatching quick glances at her lips all night, plump and full, smeared with clear gloss. It was the way those lips moved, when she talked, laughed and took sips of her drink. Those damn lips were taking me back to a whole other place and time when I knew we would be heading home together at the end of the night. I shook my head, physically trying to rid my mind of allowing myself to slide right into memory lane.

"Isobel," Stuart said into the empty bulb of glass, drained of wine, and which he was now slanting his head dangerously near. I shifted the glass along the bar and gestured to the bartender that we wanted another round.

"Bloody beautiful," Stuart tried, straightening himself up. "How do you know her again?"

"She's mates with Cate, well I kind of knew her before Cate. We went to school and a bit of uni together and..." I paused, not sure whether I should admit the full nature of my relationship with Isobel. In the depths of my stomach, some male bravado stirred and before I could fully control what came out of my mouth, I let ego take over, "…and we might have also had something going on."

Stuart stood to attention, his eyes sprouting large and wide, "You did not! No way!"

I was on a roll – merely nodding my head in response and digging the wallet from my back pocket to pay for the drinks.

"Fuck me!" Stuart said a little too loudly.

"Yeah well it's ancient history and you know sometimes things that come packaged up like that are not always so fantastic once the packaging comes off."

"Yeah right!" Stuart came back with.

"No, you're right, she is very, ah, good looking and she does seem to have mellowed. I guess she's grown up a lot since uni, we all have, but let's leave it as ancient history," I say quickly, spotting Laura making her way back across the room.

ISOBEL

I slump my head against the toilet door, breathing short, shallow breaths. Angry tears are starting to bite the backs of my eyes. Tom has barely paid attention to me all evening, a few sentences here and there when he really had to is all I seem to be able to get out of him. That bloody Stuart guy keeps monopolising me with his stupid one-liners and boring conversation about finance. Do I look like the type of girl who would be interested in fucking finance?

OK, getting angry and worked-up is not going to help. I need to think clearly. I stare at the grubby floor tiles, swallowing hard to push the hot, angry tears back inside. What's it going to take to make Tom take more notice of me? Time this evening – actually just generally – is starting to run drastically low, it's getting late and Tom is clearly getting quite pissed so will be starting to think about wanting to go home…to Cate. The thought of her lying in bed waiting for him makes me want to shudder. But he hasn't gone home to her, in fact apart from a brief conversation about their engagement where it took every ounce of decorum not to spit out that I couldn't bear it, Cate has hardly been mentioned. A crack in the seams of urban boredom? Carefully I undo the top button on the crisp white shirt to reveal a hint of cream lace skirting the swell of my chest.

"Iss, you still in here?" Laura's voice comes barging through the door.

"Yes," I answer, quickly checking the undone button and opening the toilet door.

"What do you think of Stuart?" Laura asks, drying her hands on paper towel. I frown, "Nice," I lie. Laura smiles and raises her eyebrows. "Oh no Laura, not for me. He's not my type."

"OK I just wondered if you were interested that's all."

"No!"

"I quite like him," she smiles again, scrunching the paper towel into a ball and throwing it into the bin.

"Go for it."

"I just might, you ready?"

"Just a tick," I can hear my mobile phone ringing inside my handbag. Yanking it out, Patrick's name is flashing incessantly on the screen, "I need to take this, I'll be out soon." Laura smiles again and pushes open the bathroom door. I wait until the door has swung shut before answering the call.

"Hi Patrick."

"Iss! I can't believe I have finally gotten hold of you. Listen I'm at the airport."

"The airport?" I know I sound alarmed.

"Yes, Heathrow. I'm coming home, I thought that's what you wanted."

I shut my eyes, the fluorescent light of the bathroom is stark white and is already giving me the beginning of a headache.

"Isobel?"

I snap open my eyes and see my reflection in the mirror, my features look like they are in an over-exposed photo, "Yes of course," I lie, "When do you arrive?"

"I'm stopping over for a night in Hong Kong for a meeting and then I arrive in Sydney early Thursday morning. Will you come and get me?"

"I can't, I have a really early start with meetings all day. There's so much to do with curating the pop-up gallery at Hedges Bank, it's really hectic at the moment." I can almost feel Patrick's mood slumping. "Sorry," I try.

"OK well what about Thursday evening, can you catch up then?"

"Yes definitely. We can catch up then, OK?" I say, wincing.

"I can hardly wait to see you. We're going to sort everything out and it's going to be for keeps this time," Patrick's optimism seems forced and in response I let out a nervous giggle.

"Listen Patrick, I have to go I am actually out and my friends are waiting for me."

"Alright. I'm really looking forward to seeing you, and Iss?"

I twist my lip, knowing what's coming next, please don't say it, I repeat inside my head, "Yeah?"

"I love you," Patrick delivers the next move in the tangled charade I have created to convince him to agree to the art exhibition with Hedges. Now he's coming back to the country on a false sense of purpose, totally led by me to find excuses to get close to Tom.

"I've got to go," I breathe into the phone and hang it up before he has a chance to respond.

I look back at my reflection in the mirror, 'what have I done?' I ask the stupid girl staring back at me.

TOM

Isobel stands right next to me, smiling she asks where her drink is. I catch a glimpse of lace shifting with the movement of her shirt. Jesus. Stuart is asking who is hungry. Right concentrate on Stuart's question, don't think about lace bras on ex-girlfriends. I need to get home. Laura is slinging her bag over her shoulder and draining the last dregs of wine from her glass. Her and Stuart are going to get a kebab, Isobel hasn't yet answered if she is going with them or not, she is fidgeting with the base of the wineglass, it's now empty. That was quick, I could have sworn she had at least half a glass left only a minute ago. My own glass is empty.

"Thanks guys, but I think I am going to go home, I have a big day tomorrow," I say, patting my pocket to check my wallet is still there. Where's my phone? I can see it sitting in sticky drops of wine on the bar behind Isobel. I reach around her, my arm brushes her back and I can feel the outline of her bra clasped at the back. She leans ever so slightly into me, her perfume drifts into my nostrils. Memories sting hard. God it's the same scent she used to wear, I can't remember what it was, but somehow she always smelt of…what was it… it's a fruit of some sort…apples? That's it, apples. I jerk backwards and nearly collect a barstool.

"Whoa, easy tiger," Stuart laughs. His face is red and his tie is half-knotted dangling down a partly unbuttoned shirt.

The air temperature is still warm when the four of us spill out onto the street. "Sure you guys won't come?" Laura asks, looking at me and Isobel.

"Yep sure," I say, spotting a taxi as I answer, "and there's a taxi, anyone mind if I jump in it?" I stick my arm out to hail the car and because I have had quite a bit to drink, I think it's a good idea to make extra sure the taxi driver knows I want him to stop, so I whistle him down as well. The taxi indicator blinks and the car slows down to pull into the curb. I yell out goodnight to my friends and dive into the back seat of the car. Before I know what's happening the door on the opposite side swings open and two long, bare legs slide onto the vinyl seat next to me.

"Mind if I share, I think we're both going in the same direction?" Isobel asks, shutting the door and tapping the back of the driver's seat indicating we're ready to go. Before I can hesitate, object or agree, the taxi pulls out from the curb and loops into the traffic. I smile awkwardly at Isobel, "Well looks like I don't mind."

We travel in silence for a few minutes. I concentrate on watching the lights of the city pass in multicoloured streams. Weirdly it's not as late as I thought, the clock on the dashboard blinks over to nine fifty eight. Cate will probably still be up when I get in. She sent me a text earlier saying she was working late and then was going to go for a run along the beach.

"Stuart seems like a nice guy," Isobel suddenly says.

"Yeah. Remind me where you live again," I say.

Something shifts ever so lightly on Isobel's face before she answers me, "New Hollings Road."

"Cool, I can drop you off on the way then," I offer.

"OK, cool," Isobel's words clip at the air. Then silence again. The slight aroma of apples weaves around the back seat. I try hard not to think about being twenty at university, Isobel and I having sex in her cramped bed jammed against the corner of her campus room. Me – smacking my head on the bookshelf above her bed. Her – coming up with a very creative way to make me forget about the throbbing pain spreading across my forehead. I shake my head to try and rid the image but it persists like a short film. It's the scent of the apples I am sure of it, scents do weird things to people. Eventually I can't help but smile.

"Anywhere around here will be fine, thanks," Isobel tells the taxi driver. The car slows down. "Oh the wine bar is still open," Isobel remarks casually. "It's a fantastic little place, feel like a nightcap?" She is looking at me as the interior light snaps on. I squint. Under the harsh little block of light streaming above the back seat it's clearly evident my eyes are firmly fixed somewhere in the vicinity of Isobel's cleavage. Realising what I am doing, I quickly avert my gaze to the back of the front passenger seat.

"No it's late I should get home," I start to say.

"Oh, it's not that late. Barely ten o'clock. Come on Tom it would be nice to catch up for old time's sake. I feel like we kind of got off on the wrong foot a few months ago. I want to apologise properly and show you I am not really crazy. It's important for us to be friends, don't you think?"

I turn to look at Isobel. She is now bending forward, the front of her shirt gaping open to reveal much more of the lace bra I spotted the edges of in the pub. "Ah, I shouldn't..."

"It's only one drink Tom, what happened to the Tom I used to know? Come on." Isobel is raising one eyebrow and doing that half-smile thing she always used to do, right when I was about to...Jesus Christ.

"Have you made up your mind mate, it would be good to get home at some stage tonight." The driver's voice comes booming into the back seat.

"Sorry, umm, yeah," I look at Isobel, that smile, that cocked eyebrow, those lips and that bloody bit of lace protruding from her shirt, "I'm getting out here, thanks."

Isobel smiles, "Right decision, my friend," she laughs, handing the driver money for the fare.

CATE

I drop my plate into the sink, I can't even be bothered rinsing the last of the pasta off it or even putting the plate in the dishwasher. I had a shower when I got home from a run and am already cosy in a pair of Tom's pyjama pants and a singlet. I pad my way up the hall into the bathroom, half-heartedly brush my teeth and stand at the basin for a moment deciding whether to do a whole cleansing, toning, moisturising routine. After a quick examination of the condition of my skin in the mirror, I decide I really can't be bothered, all the day's make-up either slid off during the run or gave way to the thick stream of water from the shower head. Decision made, I snap off the bathroom light and climb into bed. Staring at the book lying on the bedside table with the bookmark Tom gave me – years ago now – poking out between the pages makes me smile. The edges of the leather are rolled and cracked. The purple dye is faded where I habitually stroke it while reading, the bookmark resting on the back cover. Tom calls the bookmark my security blanket. I turn over and look at Tom's side of the bed, blank, bare, just me here. Last time that happened, he came in proposing marriage – what would I get this time? Touching his pillow, I click the lamp off and hope Tom will try to be quiet when he stumbles in at God only knows what time. No doubt he will be hung-over and full of regret tomorrow.

"Good night Tom," I whisper into the darkness.

ISOBEL

Tom's hair is flopping into his eyes – in just the same way I remember. The cut is different now though, but still he manages to have strands falling in his eyes. I can't put my finger on exactly when his body language started to tear away from cautious and slightly stiff to almost open, the same way he had treated Laura and Stuart all evening. But now sitting at a table for two in the wine bar, a bottle of red and a cheese plate between us, the shift was obvious and becoming more so with every sip of wine.

He was falling much more easily than I thought he would. I had been carefully handpicking an assortment of memories I knew he would remember with a smile, sprinkling each with subtle nuances of intimacy to trigger a whole other part of his memory to wake up. Maybe that part of Tom's memory never went to sleep. The game being batted backwards and forwards between us was a careful one, with me much more mindful of the rules than my opponent, studying every movement to make sure he didn't tip over into startling, remembering he shouldn't be here and running out the door. All laced with the right measures of alcohol.

The people sitting at other tables must think Tom and I are a couple. The thought of that makes me steal a secret smile to myself.

TOM

Nostalgia has been leaking into the cracks of my memory. Isobel's familiar scent mingled with memories I haven't thought about in over a decade are turning my head upside down and transporting me back to a really simple time in my life. Every bloke I know reminisces and romanticises their very early twenties. It's the time we had the most energy, the most sex drive, no hint of a pot belly and to coin a phrase: 'The world was our oyster.' Falling into your thirties and being snapped back into your glory years does weird things to you. So does drinking a hell of a lot.

I look at Isobel, even though she is becoming more animated there's a coating of calmness I had never really noticed before. Probably because any time spent with Isobel has involved rigorously avoiding eye contact and wishing she would go away. My eyes slip to her mouth, those lips are killing me. The flashes of bra escaping from her shirt, those wide eyes looking up at me from under thick eyelashes, the press of her breast against the shirt…I am going crazy. Suddenly she is leaning over the table, pouting those lips and whispering something to me I can't quite hear. It's too late anyway because her lips are falling onto mine and I am breathing in the aroma of apples. My body has given over to any shred of common sense I might have had left and I think I am kissing Isobel back. Actually I know I am kissing her back because her lips are moving more vigorously and my tongue is pressing at her teeth trying to find her tongue.

As quickly as it started it stops with Isobel pulling away, "Let's get out of here," she breathes. All I do is nod and stand up, oblivious to the stares and stifled giggles of other customers sipping wine around our table.

Out on the street, the kissing starts again, this time more violent and desperate. We move our bodies backwards off the footpath and into a row of bushes bordering a golf course. "Jesus," I mutter into Isobel's ear. She falls lightly backwards into the soft, spongy leaves of the bush. I fall into her and we both start laughing, before she grabs my head and starts kissing me again. A part of me has totally given over to some sort of primeval longing I can't even describe or even begin to understand. I can't remember it being like this with Isobel before.

"We can't stay here. Let's go to my place, it's only across the road," Isobel is still talking in that same breathy voice that is slowly getting me deeper and deeper into trouble.

"Alright," I agree urgently, letting my physical instincts take control of any mental or emotional reasoning. Only once when we're crossing the road does one fleeting, scary thought of how quickly we arrived at this point enter my mind. In truth I wasn't giving my actions much, if any, thought at all – let alone any of the potential consequences. Isobel is unlocking the door and I am already hitching her skirt up, it's leather. "You minx," I mutter into her hair. Then that's it, any particle of sense I might have had left, which might have drawn me back to reality just disintegrates as we collapse onto the couch in a sweaty tangle with both of us pulling and ripping at one another's clothes. Each frenzied second slips me further and further into a familiar ritual that my body and instincts seem to never have forgotten. Now, that really scares the hell of me.

ISOBEL

Tom has rolled over, his back is to me and I study the tan marks created by his wetsuit. Very lightly I trace my finger where brown meets white on his shoulder, he flinches slightly. I pick my finger off his skin and let it hover above his body. He can't see that I am smiling. I know I have won.

Abruptly, he rolls onto his back, staring at the ceiling, "I have to go," Tom says very quietly.

"No you don't," I begin to pretend to protest, twirling a strand of his sun-bleached hair playfully around my finger.

"Yes I do," he says, going to stand up.

He is obviously not joking and I'm filled with horror as I see Tom is serious.

"What are you doing?" I try to remain calm, but my arm automatically flings across his chest in a bid to pin him back to the floor. We never made it to the bedroom and at some stage slipped from the couch to the floor. Our clothes are in uneven heaps around the room and slung over furniture.

"I'm leaving Isobel. I have to go, OK," Tom says very carefully, staring at me straight in the eyes and slowly picking my arm off his chest. I try to squeeze his hand with my own, but he discards it like a piece of litter onto the floor between us. I watch as he stands up, pulls on his trousers and then his shirt.

"Please don't…" I start to protest in earnest this time, and he stops buttoning his shirt and crouches down to press his finger to my lips. I go to kiss his chest, but he takes my shoulders in both hands, holding me at arms-length and re-fixing his eyes straight into my own, "Listen Isobel," he starts quietly, like a teacher talking to a child, "I really do have to go and you know that as well as I do," he finishes, straightening himself up and walking straight out of the room without even turning around or saying another word to me. I sit on the floor, naked, hugging my knees to my chest, squeezing my eyes shut as I listen to the person who is again my lover opening and closing the front door, leaving me alone. All. Alone.

CATE

Sunshine is creeping in through the curtains, the bedroom is a pool of yellow light. My eyes are only half-open as I stretch my arms above my head, hold them there for a bit and then sink back down into the warm dent in the mattress. I feel myself start to doze off again and then remember it's Wednesday morning and I have to go to work. I try opening my lazy eyelids a bit further, lying very still and loosely focusing on the shapes the sunlight is catching and drawing on.

I feel a stir against my body and turn to see Tom lying on his side, his back to me. Who knows what time he got in, I was so tired I didn't hear a thing. Carefully I ease myself up onto an elbow and look across his body forming a big lump under the sheet to look at the alarm clock. It was blinking at six-fifty, it would go off in two minutes. Tom and his weird theory about setting the alarm clock at strange times in the twisted belief he would somehow get more sleep. I kiss his back, he doesn't even rouse, and then I sit up rubbing my eyes, might as well wait until the alarm goes off. I love our bedroom at this time of day, the soft colour with the sounds of the early morning birds – cockatoos and grass parrots – makes it feel like a cocoon. Two minutes later, even though I was prepared for it, the alarm sounding its distinctive siren makes me jump. Tom is still unstirred, so clearly he isn't going to switch it off or press the 'snooze' button – his usual favourite.

Instead I give up and slink out of bed, tip-toeing my way quietly across to Tom's side and switch the alarm clock to 'off'. I kneel down and stroke Tom's face, his eyes flutter, but don't open. "Tom," I whisper. Still nothing. "Tom," I repeat. This time he peels open one eyelid and half-smiles. "It's time to get up babe."

"Hmm."

"Do you want me to re-set the alarm?" I ask.

"I don't know," he muffles into the pillow.

I start to smile, "Did you have a big night, my darling?" He nods and breathes in very deeply. "Did you have a good night though?" Both his eyes open and for a moment he stares blankly at me. Then Tom grabs me in close and imprints a kiss of stale alcohol on my cheek.

"When are you going to decide what you want as an engagement ring?" he asks, taking me by surprise.

I pull a face, confused about where his train of thought might be stemming from, especially this early in the morning and with a hangover too. "I guess when we find the right thing. The thing that's right for us and says us," I reply gently.

Tom nods and holds me in close, "Please hurry," he says into my hair.

"OK," I reply, kissing his cheek and starting to release myself from his grip to go and have a shower, but Tom keeps hanging on to me. "Babe," I laugh, "come on I am going to be late."

"I don't care," Tom says, his voice cutting and breaking.

"God you did have a big night didn't you? Listen to your voice! Come on let me go so I can have a shower." Slowly Tom unwraps his arms from my shoulders and shuts his eyes tight again. I go into the ensuite and start to brush my teeth, examining my face in the mirror I see a few streaks of black gathered in the laughter lines (wrinkles) under both eyes, maybe I should have cleaned my face properly before getting into bed after all. Rubbing at the streaks with my fingers, I think about the antique ring I saw in a shop window on my way to a meeting yesterday. Laid out in the window were Georgian, Victorian and Art Deco rings of all shapes, sizes and colours. Each ring threaded along ribbons of the deepest purple velvet hung in rich streams from the top of the glass casing. Every loop of gold, diamond, ruby or emerald caught the sun in its own unique way as the rings spun on the ribbon, drawing me to the window like a magpie. About halfway down the thick ribbon closest to the edge of the window, I spotted an Art Deco ring of a square-cut emerald surrounded by diamonds which reminded me of shattered glass. I stared at that ring, holding my hand up to the glass trying to imagine what it would look like on my finger.

Now I am looking down at my bare ring finger resting on the edge of the basin, a drop of thick white toothpaste drops from my mouth onto my hand, reminding me that I am getting ready for work.

As I am leaving the house, I pause outside our bedroom, dipping my head inside the doorway I see Tom is still in bed, lying flat on his back with an arm slung over his eyes. "Are you not going to work today?" No response, not even a stir, "Tom?" I try again.

"Hmm," a shuffle of legs and his arm loosely falling from across his eyes back to rest on the bed.

"Are you going to work or not?" I repeat, walking into the room to squeeze his toes poking out from under the sheet at the end of the bed.

"Yeah, I am. I'll get up in a minute," his voice is still husky.

"Do you want me to give you a call when I get to work to make sure you're up?"

"Nah, I'm getting up now, see…" Tom demonstrates by sitting up very slowly and swinging his legs, one at a time, over the edge of the bed.

"Impressive," I laugh, pulling my handbag over my shoulder, "Right, now that I can see you are alive I am going to go to work. Have a good day my love," I say, collecting my house keys from the top of the dresser. "By the way I could hear your Blackberry going mad, but I couldn't see it, your work might be trying to get hold of you," I say, stepping into the hallway and unlocking the front door. "See you tonight babe," I yell out, closing the front door behind me.

It's a beautiful day, the sun heating the metal latch on the gate that already feels warm to the touch. Closing the gate behind me, I notice a man dressed in a suit hammering a 'To Let' sign into the garden of the small block of four flats across the road. "It's going to be a hot one," he calls out to me. I smile, nodding, "Yes I think so."

Tom

I listen as Cate shuts the front door and takes one, two, three steps down onto the path leading to the gate. Like clockwork, the gate squeaks as its rusty hinges release. Flashes of last night are creeping around like an army of ants deep inside my head making me scratch furiously at my hair until I can feel streaks of scalp and blood welling up under my nails. What the fuck have I done?

My Blackberry is ringing. I can't remember where I put it when I came in last night. Jesus, last night. Gradually I stand up, deciding to go in search of the phone, and finding my suit jacket tossed over the back of the couch in the lounge room, triggers a faint recollection of me dumping it there when I got in last night. Probably before I went to have a shower in the main bathroom. I reach into the breast pocket and pull out the phone, the red flashing light tells me I have a new message. In fact, it appears I have seventeen missed calls, four voicemail messages and six text messages. I frown at the screen, my heart thumping and a wave of nausea rising up. For a few minutes I have to grip the back of the couch, slowly breathing in and out in an attempt to clear my head. Finally I pluck up the courage to select the voicemail first.

'You have four new messages. First new message received at twelve sixteen am'. Isobel's voice erupts in my eardrums: *"Tom. It's me, I'm sorry about tonight. I know you are probably feeling awkward and really there's no need to. Just call me back OK?"*

'Next new message, received at twelve twenty one am.'

"Tom did you get my message? Why won't you answer the phone? Call me back."

'Next new message, received at twelve fifty six am.'

"Tom why won't you answer the phone or call me back. I need you to call me back, it's really important. Tom I need to talk to you tonight. It can't wait. Please. I am begging you to call me back. You really can't treat me like this. You haven't changed at all. Who the hell do you think you are?'

'Next new message, received at one sixteen...' I couldn't bear to listen to anymore and cut the message off before the increasing wildness in Isobel's voice hit an all-too-familiar crescendo. My heart was still thudding against my chest and the nausea had strengthened. The phone shook in my hand until I could no longer hold onto it and I watched as the black square dropped to the floor. How the hell did Isobel get my number? What if she contacts Cate? Oh my God. Cate. What have I done to you? To us? The photo of Cate and I on holiday sitting on the sideboard catches my eye. Look at us. What have I done?

It was impossible to think clearly, but even through the edges of a hangover and lack of sleep, I was going to have to regain my wits. I start deleting all the voicemail messages from my Blackberry, glance sickly at the unread text messages and see the whole lot of them are from Isobel and hit 'delete' on those and then shut the Blackberry off. Next I head into the main bathroom, a damp towel is sitting in a heap on the floor, I kick it into the laundry basket and check the room for any further evidence I might have left in here last night. Cate and I always use the ensuite bathroom off our bedroom, rarely, if ever this one. Even if one of us home late wants to take a shower but doesn't want to wake the other one, we still never use this bathroom. Grabbing the hand towel off the rail, I wipe the water beading around the inner of the basin until the porcelain is dry and then neatly replace the towel back on its rail. Just as I am about to leave the room, I notice fat dots of water forming incriminating splashes on the glass shower door. Shit. Grabbing the hand towel again, I yank open the glass and frantically run the towel up and down the length of the door before dropping the towel on the floor tiles, mopping up even more incriminating water drops. At last, satisfied the bathroom is passable, I head for the shower in our ensuite, cursing myself as I flip on the coldwater tap in the basin. The cold should help clear my head, help me think straight and help me start to make a plan to sort this bloody mess out. Besides, I don't even deserve hot water this morning. The cold bites at my skin, leaving little red blotches. Pouring shaving foam into my palm, I look at myself in the bathroom mirror, looking back at me is the face of a bloody fool. God, what I would give to rewind the clock to this time yesterday morning, doing exactly the same routine, but knowing what the evening would throw at me, and me in all my new-found wisdom being able to avoid completely sabotaging my future with Cate. I'm a bloody idiot.

ISOBEL

I fling the phone across the room, it belts into the couch and lands neatly on the soft cushions like I had thoughtfully placed it there. Streaks of salt stain both cheeks. My T-shirt hangs from one shoulder, the cotton draping loosely to my waist with crinkled folds where I have unthinkingly scrunched at the fabric, twisting it around and around in knots with my finger.

After Tom shut the door behind himself, I sat scrunched in a ball, rocking lightly backwards and forwards in some sort of trance. Water spilled from my eyes. I don't know how long I was like that for, I can't even remember thinking about anything in particular. Then suddenly without the slightest bit of warning my entire body took charge of my mental state, kicking itself into action and becoming a machine out of control. I jumped up and started pacing the lounge room like an animal trapped in a cage. The impact of every single text message or phone call I had made to Tom that he had completely ignored, only swelling my rage until it came rushing out in physical acts. Eventually I grew exhausted, found a T-shirt to put on and relocated to my bed, reforming myself into a scrunched up ball on top of the mattress. Fitful semi-consciousness followed for the next few hours. Sometimes I woke thinking Tom was still beside me, feeling his body heat. Other times I dreamt we were at university in my room on campus – the day I told him I was pregnant. The look on his face. Him leaving the room without even turning around to look at me, in exactly the same way he had done again in the very first hour of today. That's when I woke up, eyes shooting wide open and fingers gripping the edges of the sheet. The bedroom was quiet, just me breathing.

Carefully I get out of bed and walk gingerly into the lounge room. The room is in total disarray. The art glass vase which normally sits arranged in a well-thought style atop of the coffee table is lying on the floor, smashed into three large pieces sticking up ridged and sharp against the backdrop of the curtain they are lying beneath. Books and magazines are strewn over the two club chairs and a bottle of wine lies on its side next to the couch – most of its contents drunk or splattered against the velvet arm. The scene only makes me feel more wretched and hopeless. Tom has made me feel like this for yet another time in my life.

I touch the skin on my hollow abdomen. 'Hollow'. The word drags through my mind, snagging on a lost child. I have to tell Tom about the child – our child – it exists. There's a child out there made up of him and I and as much as I know he is going to try and run away from it, the past can't be erased. He needs to be told, it's just what Aunt Jean would tell me to do, I am sure of it. I can't go on living this lie alone for any longer. We are meant to be a family, together. Tom. Me. Child. Simple.

Very calmly, I pick the phone up from the couch and select 're-dial', I listen as it rings out. One, two, three, four, five rings and then the phone diverts to Tom's voicemail. Again. Still calm, I hang the phone up and select 're-dial' once more. This time, there are no rings and the phone goes straight to Tom's voicemail. Perhaps the phone was still connected to the voicemail from the last call. I wait a couple of minutes before calling again. The phone is immediately diverted to voicemail. Pulling the phone away from my ear, I put it on 'speaker' and listen to Tom's voice asking me to leave a message. When I hear the beep and get ready to say something, I haven't rehearsed exactly what it is that I am going to say, my throat dries up and I can't speak. I think of the messages I have already left scattered across Tom's voicemail at different times in the early hours of this morning. Each one would have sounded more and more needy and if I was honest with myself, incoherent. A swollen bulb of water crushes the soft papery skin under the inner corner of my eye, red and plump from crying. I press the red button to end the call, knowing that all that will be recorded is my breath going in and out.

Suddenly the phone rings, startling me. The name blinking on the screen isn't the one I am desperately willing to appear. Laura is calling. Oh fuck off will you. I switch the phone to silent and feel it vibrate against my hand until it finally stops. Then another sharp vibration indicating Laura has left a message. Seeing the words 'new voicemail' stinging the screen, a spike of panic stabs at my chest, perhaps Laura knows about Tom and me. Perhaps she noticed an energy between us when we were out last night, she was always more loyal to Cate than to me. I chew at my bottom lip, trying to decide whether this could be used to my advantage or if it's verging on the beginnings of a disaster where I have lost all control of the situation.

Why the hell isn't Tom picking up the phone? He can't just avoid me. Controlling my breath, deeply inhaling and exhaling, I turn my attention to the glass doors opening onto the balcony, beyond them I can see the ocean rolling in curls towards the sand. The horizon is a perfect straight line against the blue of the sky with the sun gradually inching higher up into a wisp of cloud. For a while I watch the water, the sky and the sun. Feeling calmer, I decide to listen to Laura's message.

"*Hi Iss, it's Laura. Really fun night last night. So good to see you and hope you got home OK. I certainly did! I am feeling horrendous today though. Listen, can we catch up later today to work out next steps on the Hedges Bank project? OK, speak to you when you're awake!*"

Then I smile, there is one major legitimate reason why I should at least be in the same area as Tom at the moment and that's the Hedges Bank project. I am sure I need to go over there to recce the space further. Besides, I am not sure the new pieces I showed the bank's marketing team are really going to fit in the foyer as part of the current plans for the pop-up gallery. There's no reason for Laura to join me either, the actual layout of the gallery is not her responsibility. I can go alone, but not today. Today I need to get myself together and work out a plan to bring order back to the circumstance so I don't waste my next opportunity.

CATE

"Do you want salt?" No reaction. "Tom?"
"Yeah?"

"Do you want salt?" I ask again, holding out the salt shaker.

"No I'm fine, thanks babe," Tom says even though I know he still hasn't heard the question. I place the salt shaker back on the table between our plates and spike a piece of chicken with the fork. Tom is staring at a spot on the table just above his plate. His hands are resting on the knife and fork which are both still lying either side of the plate. I try to ignore him and continue eating, but it's like I am by myself and I hate eating alone. Finally I give in, "Is something the matter?" I ask, my shoulders slumping into defeat. Tom looks up from whatever it is he is staring at giving me a lop-sided smile, "There's just a lot going on at work that's all." He curls his fingers around the fork and then unwraps them again before planting both hands in his lap, hesitates for a moment and then starts to rub his palms up and down the length of his thighs. "I don't think I'm hungry. I don't feel great, I might go and lie down for a bit," he says quietly and stands up. "Sorry. Dinner is lovely, I just don't feel like eating anything right now." Tom goes to pick up his plate.

"Just leave it," the pitch of my voice rises too high and I know I sound angry, "I'll take it when I finish," I say, spiking another piece of chicken.

"OK, thanks," Tom replies quietly, kissing me lightly on the top of the head and walking to the door. He pauses at the door for a moment, tapping his fingers on the frame, his back is to me, "I'm sorry Cate."

"It's only dinner Tom."

"Yeah," is all he says squeezing the doorframe and then walking down the hallway. I watch Tom's back until he is out of sight and drop the knife and fork down onto the plate in front of me. I'm angry and I don't really know why. Why would I be cross about Tom being ill – apart from the anger being totally illogical it's not like me. But sitting here on my own with two dinners laid out on the table, hardly touched, the feeling that I have been trying to squash back down continues to grow and swell in the pit of my stomach. Tom is somehow unravelling in a different direction to me and in a way I don't understand. This unfamiliar behaviour has been going on for a few days or so now and it is starting to really unsettle me, mainly because Tom and I have never really been ones to fight. We've always been so at ease with one another and it just works, even our disagreements are more like debates. We just tend to respect each other's point of view. I've never really been one to hold grudges and confront things head on, instead I guess I try as hard as I can to try and understand the other person's opinion. When we were first together, Tom would always tell me how much he loved that trait in me. That and my calmness.

Now though, something that I just can't quite put my finger on seems to have shifted. One minute Tom seems completely distant, like he did tonight at the table, hardly hearing me and making me repeat sentences over and over until I snap at him and refuse to talk any further. Then at other times, he is needy, suffocating me with impulsive embraces that crush our ribcages together and fragments of his clothes suck up into my nostrils until I have to pull away and watch Tom's face visibly folding inwards. Perhaps it's Tom reacting to us getting engaged. It's been difficult to keep my own emotions in check, an army of butterflies have been twinkling around inside my entire body ever since Tom asked me to marry him. Feelings of what can only be described as euphoria pass as quickly as feelings of pure fear – wondering how we can possibly know that what feels so right now is still going to feel so right in fifty years time. Usually though, all I have to do is look at Tom, feel his arms wrapping around my waist, his nose nuzzling into the nape of neck and then simply wait for that feeling of calmness to return.

It's OK, everything is going to be OK.

I shove the plate away from myself and cross my arms, staring out into the sunroom. Tom's outline is still indented in the cushion on the cane chair where he had sat down to take off his shoes when he got home from work. Both shoes are under the chair, lying on their sides with the laces still done up and the backs trodden down. In spite of myself, I smile at such a familiar scene and weirdly it helps to make me feel safe. I take a sip of wine before I bend down to untie the laces on Tom's shoes and then lay them neatly together back under the chair with their black patent leather toes perfectly aligned.

TOM

I am sitting on the edge of the bed, my head in my hands, knowing what a sorry figure I cut. Cate is somewhere else in the house and I know she didn't eat dinner either because the sounds of dishes being rinsed in the sink started up a few minutes after I left her, twisting the guilty knife further into my chest. I don't want Cate to come into the bedroom to see how I am, I need some time to work out what the hell I am going to do and that beautiful face of hers peering at me full of questions and confusion is making things worse.

I know my behaviour towards Cate is inconsistent with 'normal Tom', but the fact is I am killing myself with guilt and I want so much to spoil Cate, taking away the pain of something she doesn't even know about, that I am doing things which I had always promised myself I would but never made the time to do.

Isobel has been ringing and ringing me. Most of the time though, she doesn't leave any messages, I can just hear the outline of her breath against the silence making me feel much more disturbed than when I have listened to her irate, uncontrolled messages. Then she also really spiced things up with a phone call to Cate neatly slithered in somewhere between her thirty-second and thirty-third unanswered call to me.

Cate and I were out for dinner. I had booked us in for dinner at a new restaurant that someone at work told me was very good and I really wanted to surprise her. I'm not sure which part killed me the most, Cate's voice on the phone when I called her at work to tell her to meet me there at six-thirty for cocktails before dinner, or the fact it was a misguided guilt lever.

I had gone to the toilet and come back to the table to see Cate on the phone. Cate mouthed 'sorry' to me as I sat back down, poured more water into each of our glasses and started to look at the menu. The bloody pathetic thing was I wasn't paying any attention to the conversation being played out in front of me. I was deliberating between fresh rock oysters and crab for a starter when Cate leaned across the table and tapped my arm, making me look up. She had covered the receiver with her hand, "Sorry, it's Isobel," she said, her hand still laying on my forearm, "I haven't spoken to her in ages. Do you mind if I quickly go outside to finish the conversation?" Mechanically my head moved up and down, Cate sitting across from me in a surreal wash, smiling and stroking my arm. She smiled. "I promise I won't be long. Order the starter for me, I'll start with half a dozen oysters." Just like that, Cate stood up, still continuing her conversation with Isobel while weaving her way through the tables, opening the door and then standing on the footpath with her back pressing against the glass and the phone pressing against her ear. I stared above the blur of diners, focusing on my fiancée's back and silently going mad with the imagined end of my relationship with the person I love. Her body language was hard to place. She stood in the one position for about a minute, then she turned slightly so her shoulder leaned against the glass, noticing that people were sitting on the other side inside the restaurant, she rocked over to her back and took a step into the middle of the footpath.

At that point the waitress came to take my order and surreal thoughts pushed at the edges of a completely normal moment when I wondered whether I would be ordering a meal for someone who in the next few minutes would no longer be my fiancée. The same way in which my head had moved in agreement to Cate going outside to seal my fate, my mouth moved mechanically ordering a dozen oysters to share and a whisky. The waitress laughed at the whisky order and then seeing I was serious wrote that on the pad alongside the oysters and left the table. The whisky arrived as Cate opened the door to the restaurant. I downed the brown liquid in one go, feeling it hit the back of my throat in a rush of heat.

"I've ordered our starters." It's funny how you cling to the routine of a normal action when you're trying like hell to silently make everything all right again. Cate eyed the empty whisky tumbler and looked at me, "Thirsty?" she asked, sitting back down and slipping the phone into her handbag. One really bloody simple word had bundled up every shred of hope into a gigantic ball which was now exploding inside my chest telling me it was all right – at least for now. My world might be shattered tomorrow, but it wouldn't be tonight. Tonight I still had my fiancée.

"Isobel seems really good. She said you guys all had fun the other night," Cate was talking while she buttered a chunk of bread she had plucked from the wicker basket plonked down on the table by the waitress when she brought the whisky.

"Yeah," is all I managed to cough out. Cate looks up from buttering, "the whisky," I say, belting my chest with one hand.

"When Laura called me yesterday she said the same, and said Isobel was in great form when you were out – back to the Isobel we know and love. I wish I could have made it."

"So do I," I answer, never meaning anything more in my life.

"I am really relieved you guys are all getting on. Things were feeling a bit weird there for a while and I was starting to get paranoid."

There is silence as we both butter our bread. I don't know how to pick up my part of this conversation. All I know is that I don't want it to end up where I think it's leading. Cate had stopped buttering another chunk of bread, but still held the knife.

"Oh it's silly and you will laugh, but I thought I was picking up in some weird vibe between you and Isobel and, well you know, I just started to imagine stuff that was all really stupid. I was being stupid..."

"You're not stupid," I had cut Cate off. Her words were making me feel worse and like a total arsehole. God it was awful that someone like Cate could be feeling paranoid, and as it turns out, I had been making her feel paranoid even before I fucked everything up.

Cate was playing with the top of her water glass, red blotches rising up her neck, too uncomfortable to look at me, but with enough guts to admit out loud what she had been tormenting herself with. I wanted to grab her and never let her go. The truth was bitter and it hurt – what a fucking coward I am.

Cate continued running her finger around the top of the glass, "I know now that I was just being stupid," her finger stops and she looks at me, "this is meant to be a really happy time and I know we want people around us who are important to be part of this, so I am really happy that everything is working out, you know?"

I had nodded mechanically again.

Calls from Isobel to me had been rapid and urgent, that was until yesterday. Since yesterday everything has gone quiet. Not one message. In only a few short days I had managed to work myself into the habit of checking my phone every ten minutes, expecting another missed call to be waiting for me. But now there's silence and I can honestly say there has never been a time in my life when I have felt more vulnerable. The minutes tick over into hours, the hours tick over into days where I am constantly preoccupied with thoughts of my life coming undone. Whether it will come undone slowly piece by agonising piece or whether it will happen quickly like a bandaid being ripped off a gaping cut, I just don't know. All I know is that everything is at stake. The course of my life could be about to take a twist in a different direction and I am clutching so tightly at the threads, trying to knot it all together, that I am going crazy. I have to do something about this, but I don't even know where to start.

ISOBEL

I am unlocking the main door to my apartment block when I hear my name called urgently, breathlessly, but most tellingly in Patrick's commanding tone. Unable to avoid him any longer and sensing the growing threat in messages Patrick left on my phone, I finally caved in this morning and said I would be home this evening.

The key rests on the edge of the hole as I slowly inhale, close my eyes for a moment, fix a smile on my lips and turn around to see Patrick with two suitcases planted either side of him. A taxi is pulling away from the curb.

"Patrick," I say catching sight of the supple chain of bushes Tom and I had fallen into only two nights ago. I rub at the spot on my neck where Tom had punctured tiny dents with his teeth.

"Isobel," Patrick says again, collecting the handles on the suitcases to wheel them towards me. I keep smiling tightly and feel my skin tighten when he tips his face towards mine to kiss my mouth, but I deliberately move my head and Patrick's lips land clumsily against my cheek. A faint train of Patrick's saliva feels wet on my cheek, I go to wipe the wetness with the back of my hand, except the look on his face stops me. "Where have you been, you've been impossible to get hold of," Patrick is saying, a bead of sweat trickles down from his hairline, trapping on each crease in his forehead before he swipes the water from the bridge of his nose. Watching the glisten collect on his fingers and his saliva on my cheek repulses me.

"Have I?" I am still smiling, "Are you staying here?" I gesture to the suitcases.

"Well yes," Patrick is replying confidently. "Where else would I be staying?" he half-laughs, searching my face for signs that I am joking. Of course I am not joking. Staring at him, I wipe his saliva from my cheek and turn to unlock the door.

I hear Patrick following me like an obedient dog, the click-clack of the suitcases being wheeled across the tiles in the lobby. "I've been back since Thursday. I knew you couldn't meet me at the airport, and I was happy to let you go to dinner with that artist, or whoever it was, that first night – even though you told me you would be seeing me. But since then you have damn well disappeared, I thought I would have at least seen you before now. It's been five days Isobel. What have you been doing? You haven't been at the gallery. That skinny art student has been there," he is saying to my back.

"Do you want a drink?" I ask Patrick, ignoring him, prizing open the glass doors to the balcony.

"Love one," he answers coming up behind me to slide his arms around my waist.

I stiffen and shake myself free from his grip, "Well I better get us both one then." Pouring vodka into two glasses in the kitchen, I swing my gaze out to locate Patrick. I don't want him surprising me by coming into the kitchen, or worse going into the bedroom and expecting a welcome home present. I need to get drunk to stomach that – or better still get him drunk and encourage him to pass out on the couch.

"There you go," I place the two glasses down on the table on the balcony.

"Jesus Christ," Patrick says staring at the clear liquid measuring a good two inches in both glasses. "Is that just straight vodka?"

"Yes that's why the drink is called 'vodka straight', it's my specialty, don't you like it?" I ask sweetly, sitting down on the chair on the other side of the table to Patrick.

"Come here," he is reaching out to me.

I breathe in and count to three in my head and then very slowly pick up my glass and down the whole lot. Patrick smiles and mirrors me. "Another?" I say already standing up and taking Patrick's glass from his hand.

On the fourth trip back from refilling our glasses with vodka, my hip catches on the balcony door, slitting the cotton on my light summer dress and grazing the top layer of skin. Small blood beads rise to the surface, seeping into fabric, but the pain is already numbed by alcohol sliding through my bloodstream. I settle down into the chair, fling my shoes off and rest my hand across my hip so he doesn't see the stain.

"Come and sit here," Patrick says patting his knee. The woolly effects of alcohol have done nothing to dampen my feelings of absolute repulse to the thought of physical contact with Patrick. I know I have been prickly and short with him all evening, finding any excuse to avoid his touch. At the beginning of the evening, he looked wounded, but now after downing a considerable amount of clear spirit, Patrick has taken on a determined air. There are streaks of aggression – and frighteningly well-recognised shadows of me – running through his behaviour towards me. Regardless, I had decided somewhere between vodka number two and three that I was going to win this little game bouncing back and forth between us.

"How long are you back in the country for?" I say, ignoring Patrick's pathetic lap-sitting request.

"What do you mean, how long am I in the country for? What kind of a question is that?"

"A pretty reasonable question. You spend a lot of time in the UK so I just wondered if this was going to be a flying visit to check on the Hedges Bank project, that's all I was saying." I take a large swig from my glass and wait for the freezing sting to lace my mouth, the effects of the alcohol making me shudder less and less the more is consumed.

"Right," Patrick matches my swig, but his shoulders visibly shake as the vodka engages with his mouth and then throat. "Do you know Isobel, I have to say I am pretty confused right now. You see, I thought I was coming back here because you wanted to get back together. That was pretty clear to me on the phone when you called me early one morning telling me you had made the biggest mistake of your life. Pretty hard to interpret that any other way I would have thought. Or could it be…" Patrick let the words hang, taking an exaggerated sip of his drink and drains the rest of the vodka from the glass. He places the glass back down on the table beside him and looks straight ahead over the top of the balcony railing and out to sea. "Or could it be…" Patrick repeats, turning his gaze back to me, "could it be that you need me to have your little project with Hedges Bank actually come to fruition? Actually, come to think of it, maybe it's more about the entire gallery – your dream – being kept alive. No one but me to fund it." For the first time this evening he smiles, his top and bottom lips creasing together in a shape I had seen the last day we saw each other in the gallery. His mind set and made up. Involuntarily my body shudders in response. "You must really think I am stupid Isobel," Patrick is clamping his lips back into a determined, sinister form.

I go to protest, but it's like a child pretending they never broke the window even though they have a bat in their hand and glass in their hair.

"But that's OK because two can play at this game. I have something you want, the gallery of course and now this what do you call it, a 'pop-up gallery', is that right?"

I remain silent, gripping the glass in my hand and pushing it down into my leg. I glare at my bare thigh through the base of the glass.

"Yes, and you know that without me, both can't really exist because I am the one with the money and you need that to have your little dream. Do correct me if I am wrong, but I don't think you can survive without me. But that's OK because, as we've already established, it works both ways. You have something I want too don't you Isobel?"

My grip on the glass becomes so intense that I feel cramps forming in my fingers, my hand looks like a claw strangling the edges of the glass. I so desperately want Patrick to shut up. The familiar spikes of anger pierce my insides and for a brief moment I fantastise about him falling over the edge of the balcony. How easily it could look like an accident. I gulp down the remainder of the vodka, trying to shake the image from my head.

"Yes, you most certainly do have something I want Isobel. Something I want very much and unfortunately no one else can give me that. As I think I made it perfectly clear on the phone, I want you and only you. I'm not going to compete with a faceless person whose name is yelled out in the middle of the night, do you understand?"

The warm whirl of cicada song erupts into the evening air, the same mournful tune that scratched at the walls of Aunt Jean's house while I was waiting to have Tom's baby. Maybe this evening the cicadas had already been singing long before Patrick dealt his final card.

The next morning, I stuff the piece of paper into my handbag, checking over my shoulder to make sure Patrick is still sleeping. His chest rises and falls with heavy breath spelling a deep sleep. The sheet is twisted around one leg, the rest of his naked body lying bare and exposed on the mattress. My eyes fix on where the skin meets the white, crisp cotton of the sheet, pinpointing the place where my naked body was crushed against his. I clench my teeth, push the piece of paper, folded into a small square, down into the pocket of the bag and pick up a pair of red high heels in each hand, tip-toeing to the front door. On the street, I hail a taxi and give the driver the address of Hedges Bank.

Tom

"Thanks mate," my takeaway espresso is handed to me over the head of a short woman standing in front of me. I drop three one dollar coins on the counter and walk out onto the street into the stinging sunshine. Taking a quick sip of the scorching drink, I wait for the green light to cross the road. I spot Nick, the not-so-new-guy from work, standing amongst the crowd of pedestrians all waiting for the lights to change.

"Morning mate," I say sidling up beside Nick.

"Hey Tom, how are you?" Nick answers turning from staring blankly at the traffic lights, to me.

"Good thanks. It's bloody hot enough though I haven't even made it to work yet and I already need to change my shirt, I'm sweating like a pig."

Nick laughs, "Yep, I never thought I would say it, but I am getting pretty sick of summer."

We both step off the curb and fall into step on our way to the office, filling the gaps with small talk about the heat and the coffee quality. Stepping through the glass doors into the foyer of Hedges Bank, I let Nick go through ahead of me while I gulp the rest of the coffee down and follow Nick.

"I need to get one of those myself," Nick says, pointing to the crumpled coffee cup in my hand.

"I could do with another," I start to reply when the throb of the voice I had been doing everything in my power to avoid came echoing through the foyer, chased by the clatter of heels spiking on the tiles. Sickly, I turn to see Isobel striding towards me and Nick. A folder is tucked under one armpit and a tape measure clutched in one hand. My mouth is dry and looking at this figure – alive and real – pushing through the throng of suits all heading towards the lifts sends the caffeine pumping in short, sharp spurts through my body. My pulse is racing.

"Tom," Isobel is standing looking expectedly in front of Nick and me.

"Hi," I finally manage to scratch out of my throat. I am staring at this girl, looking for signs of total mania about to be lashed on me. She looks completely normal – balanced even – dressed in a tight skirt with red heels and a face finished off with a thick smile. My eyes dropped to her toenails painted blood red and peeping through the keyholes in her shoes. I know I need to take control of the situation – fast.

"Nick, this is Isobel. Isobel this is Nick," I say.

"Hi Nick," Isobel shifts the tape measure to the other hand and goes to shake his hand. Nick is smiling at Isobel and gripping her hand. I think they are talking to each other I am not sure. The perspiration gathering under my armpits from the heat of the morning intensified and I could feel trickles of water rolling down the side of my torso.

"I'm just measuring the space for the temporary gallery we are putting in here, you know the one babe," Isobel is talking to me with a tone suggesting we are definitely intimate. My stomach churns. Nick watches both of us.

"I thought you did that the other day," I am saying.

"Oh I did," Isobel is chirping cheerily, "but things keep changing so I need to keep coming and re-measuring the space. You know how things keep changing Tom." The churning in my stomach steps it up a notch. "You got time for a quick coffee, babe?" God she's talking to me. Isobel is fucking crackers.

"No…" I start to say.

"Oh come on," Isobel cuts in, letting her act fractionally slip.

"I'm going to head up mate," Nick says, nodding towards the lifts. Thank God for Nick.

"Yeah, I better too. Sorry," I say turning towards Isobel.

She is moving towards me, standing too close to me. "Oh come on," she repeats, smiling up into my face. I want to slap her.

"Nice to meet you," Nick says to Isobel. Her act drops another tiny fraction as she has to acknowledge Nick and that means physically stepping away from me to shake Nick's hand again.

"I'll catch you later OK," I go to follow Nick, but Isobel grabs my elbow. I watch Nick who is now at the lifts, he turns around and raises his eyebrows at me. Smiling in response like I have everything under control, I switch my look back to Isobel. My heart is thudding and I am angry now.

"Please let go of my arm and I am *not* coming for coffee with you. Not now. Not ever. Do you understand?" My voice is shaking.

"You don't understand…"

"I fucking do understand. It was a mistake, that's it," I say in a loud whisper, one of the receptionists looks up from the computer screen.

"You don't understand!" Isobel's voice pricks at a desperate note. I can feel the receptionist still watching us.

"Not here," I snatch at Isobel's hand, still wrapped around my elbow and literally drag her behind me through the glass revolving doors onto the street out of view of three sets of eyes peering from the reception desk.

"Right I will meet you for coffee. I can't do it right now because I am meant to be at work right now, which I think you might be aware of." The words spitting out in quick, angry spurts visibly take Isobel by surprise. It's obvious she was prepared for me to start refusing her again. Her mouth opens and then it half closes.

"Did you hear me?" Even though I am feeling physically ill, my future slowly rotting in little strips, I am relishing watching Isobel too stunned to speak. Somewhere between the door and the street I decided I couldn't live like this anymore or I was going to end up as mad as Isobel.

CATE

"No, it's the one right at the front. No, no, not on the ribbon. It's in its own box. One of the opened boxes." I watch as the man leans further into the window, his hand hovering over the brightly coloured gems, awaiting my instructions. "Yep, the one right at the front of the window. There, in the corner. I think that's it, that's the one." He plucks up the open navy blue lid between his thumb and index finger, twisting his wrist until the ring is in his sight. He smiles, "Oh it's this one. It's lovely this one. Had it for a while now, not sure why because it's very striking indeed."

Slowly he takes the ring out of the box and shuffles over to the counter where he switches on a lamp and drags the lit bulb down closer to the ring. He turns the gem around under the light. "Hmm," he says crouching down to retrieve a square piece of black velvet that he lies on the glass top of the counter, smooths the fabric with one palm and adjusts the position of the lamp with his other hand. "Ah, that's better, it's much easier to see now. Yes it's beautiful and good quality too. See, look here." He motions for me to come nearer to the counter. "The clarity is good and the colour is exceptional, see how the colour looks…well…just like an emerald really. That's perfect emerald green. Not too sure how to describe it otherwise," he produces a small laugh at his own joke. I smile in response; I have no idea how an emerald is supposed to look.

"It really is lovely," I say in response.

"Would you like to try it on?"

I hesitate for a moment. I should be trying on what could become my engagement ring with Tom. Not on my own in an obscure little antiques store on a Tuesday afternoon between meetings. "Umm, I'm not sure," I answer fiddling with the strap of my handbag. Suddenly I feel a bit stupid. I haven't even told Tom about finding this ring and he's been so intent on us finding a piece of jewellery because I think he thinks it will make our engagement official. I'm probably only looking for pieces of jewellery to make him happy. The way he was so desperate, the only word to describe it, the other morning, hanging onto me and there was a hint of something in his voice that has stayed with me ever since. I want Tom to be happy, I want to help him find his level of balance again.

"It's very difficult to tell if it's the right ring for you if you haven't even tried it on. They can look totally different on you know? Mind with your colouring I think we won't have any problems with it not looking right," the shopkeeper holds the ring out towards me.

"I'm not sure I should. I would like my fiancé to see it first before I try it on."

"Oh it's an engagement ring?" he looks surprised. It had never occurred to me that he might think I am just interested in buying a ring I like the look of. "We have lots of engagement rings – did you see the diamond ones hanging on the ribbon?"

"Yes, but I really like this one. In fact I love this one," I say, looking longingly at the shimmer of green clenched between his fingers.

He smiles at me. "Why don't you just hold the ring in your hand then, you don't have to put it on any fingers, just hold it. Get a feel for it and make sure it is the right one for you before you go to the trouble of bringing your fiancé back to look at it."

I'm still hesitating, I know when I touch the ring and I happen to like it, I will have to slide it onto my finger, just for a look, just to see. But I guess it couldn't hurt to just hold it. "I guess it can't hurt," I say, clasping my hands together in a prayer, folding my thumbs one over the top of the other and really not sure if I have made the right decision.

"Well I am going to need at least one of your hands to take the ring from mine," he says looking from my hands to my face.

"Yes, right," I answer, releasing my hands. He places the ring in my palm where I look at it for a moment before delicately picking up the loop of gold to take in the colour of the green stone. It really was beautiful and the size looked about the right fit for my finger. I breathe in deeply and quickly hand the ring back. "Too tempting. I'll be back though, next time with my fiancé," I grab at the strap on my handbag and start to walk out of the shop.

"Do you want to know the price?" he calls after me.

I pause with one hand on the door handle, "No not this time. I'll find that out when I come back with Tom."

ISOBEL

I am sitting at a table by a wall in the coffee shop Tom has told me to meet him in. The place is tiny – only four round tables inside with a couple of low stools scattered around each one. The barista is cleaning the coffee machine while a waitress totals money from the till, flicking coins into her palm with an index finger as she counts. I've ordered a double espresso that I have only taken a small sip from, the bitter coffee sticking to my tongue. My handbag is perched on my lap, unzipped. Glimpsing at the gaping metal teeth with the leather sagging down reminds me of a wide, grotesque mouth. I slip my hand inside the mouth reaching into the side pocket, feeling for the folded paper, satisfied it's still there I wait for Tom.

TOM

It's after five, I told Isobel I would meet her at five o'clock at *Lopresti's*, the Italian coffee shop I buy my coffee from every morning on the way to work. I know they will be closing soon and I figure that will prevent us dragging this whole bloody thing out. I need to say what I need to say, somehow put a stop to all this and then get out of there – fast. *Lopresti's* has hardly any tables inside, and at that time of the day it shouldn't be busy, so I know that I am hedging my bets that the quiet will help to keep things controlled. As will the absence of alcohol in this equation.

Even though I felt backed into a corner by Isobel springing a surprise visit on me this morning, clarity has certainly come with the day's progression. I rub at my head – my pep talks to myself are sounding more and more like the crap you sprout in a business meeting. But I have decided I need to take action, sort this mess out and get on with getting my life back to where it's supposed to be heading, marrying Cate.

Taking the jacket off the back of my chair, I shove my arms in the holes when I notice Nick swinging out from his desk on his chair. "You off?" he asks. I do a quick look around to see if anyone is paying us any attention. Lowering my voice, I reply, "Yeah, I've got to do something so need to take off a bit early. We're not too busy, but cover for me will you?"

"Sure. I'll see you tomorrow then," Nick winks at me.

"Thanks," I say, already halfway to the lift and checking my watch, six minutes past five. Shit.

I get to the coffee shop and stand in the doorway and spot Isobel straight away. She is the only one in the place. An espresso cup sits on a saucer on the table in front of her. Her back is to me.

"Hey, what can I get you my friend?" Vince, the owner shouts out to me from behind the coffee machine. Instantly Isobel swings around in her seat. Her lips are coated in glossy red and her face is expressionless. Our eyes lock and I go to say something, but she doesn't even show a flicker of recognition. Instead she turns back to the table and raises the cup to her mouth.

"Not long till we shut shop but I am sure I can rustle up something, you want a coffee?" Vince continues, ignoring the silent exchange between me and Isobel.

"Yeah, coffee would be great, thanks. The usual please," I reply walking over to where Isobel is sitting. Vince watches me clearly intrigued that I have chosen to sit at the same table as Isobel. "And some water too please," I say to Vince, breaking his stare and shifting him into reaching for an espresso cup.

"So," I say to Isobel, "we need to sort some stuff out I think."

ISOBEL

Tom is sitting across from me like he owns the place. When he tells the guy at the coffee machine, 'the usual', it makes me cringe. It is now obvious he has chosen this place because it will somehow give him a misplaced sense of security. He should know by now that I am not one to be controlled by public places. I give the paper in the pocket of my handbag a reassuring press between my fingers.

"Let's go and sit at one of the tables outside," I say, watching Tom's face slightly cloud. He gives me a nervous glance before standing up and brushing down imaginary lint from the front of his trousers, an anxious reaction I remembered from years ago. I smile inwardly, pick up my cup, drink the rest of the coffee and stand up too.

"Could I have another one too please?" I say to the barista.

"We're going outside," Tom explains to him.

"Sure, I'll bring everything out to you," the barista smiles at us both, obviously trying to catch Tom's eye.

I follow Tom to one of the tables on the street, they are the same low round tables with stools plotted around them as the ones inside. Out here, it's a lot noisier with traffic pushing up the one-way system and people finishing work and rushing past on their way home or to the pub.

"Here?" Tom says, motioning to a table closest to the door of the coffee shop and still in Vince, the barista's, eye line.

"No, let's sit at that one," I say, already walking towards the table at the end of the row and sitting down with my handbag resting on my lap. Tom joins me looking very awkward; sitting down across from me he takes one of the tubes of paper filled with sugar from an old jam jar on the table and starts twisting the paper between his fingers. Instantly, he launches into what is obviously a rehearsed speech.

"The other night was a mistake Isobel. A massive mistake. I think you understand that and you know that I am in love with Cate. I am going to marry her. I am really sorry if I upset you because I didn't intend to, but the best thing for both of us would be to put it behind us."

I keep quiet and just stare at Tom. He looks expectantly for a response from me, then starts to fill the silence with another tack, trying to keep his voice steady, "I understand if you don't care about me, but what about Cate, she's meant to be your friend for God's sake."

"And she's meant to be your fiancée," I retort, my face is stone straight as I feel the all too familiar hardness gnawing away at the soft edges to help me cope.

"Here we go," Vince plants two espresso cups and a glass of water down on the table from a tray.

"Thanks," Tom says, not looking at me or Vince.

"I am sorry if I hurt you," Tom whispers when Vince leaves.

"Are you?" I answer curtly.

"Yes. Yes I am. I never meant for the other night to happen. I really didn't. I would never want to do anything to hurt Cate. Now I can't take it back. I am sorry to you too, Isobel, I really am. But you know as well as I do that the best thing to do is put it behind us and just move on."

His face is colourless as I begin to laugh bitterly, "Oh yes, let's just put everything behind us, it's that simple isn't it?"

"What?" he fires the word out between half-clamped lips, twisting the tube of sugar more tightly.

"You don't get it, do you?"

"Actually no Isobel, I don't bloody get it. I don't think I ever have and I am a bloody fool for going there again. A bloody stupid idiotic fool," Tom's voice trails off.

I try to take his hand, but he yanks it away with such force that he knocks the glass of water over. "Shit," Tom scorns, flipping the glass over to stand upright and brushing water from the edge of the table. I watch as the water slides in uneven streams off the wood.

"Just don't touch me, OK," he says like he is looking straight through me.

My eyes snap up from staring at the water to Tom, "There's something you should know," I say, touching the paper.

"Really?" Tom says sarcastically.

His tone only triggers the bud of hardness to grow larger and all I want to do is wipe that look of self-righteousness from his face.

"Yes there is," I say gripping the paper and pulling it from my handbag. The folds are so neat and sharp, perfectly concealing the information inside to nothing more than the size of a postcard. I lay the paper down in front of Tom, careful to avoid the water stain.

"What is this?" Tom looks at me questioningly.

"Open it," I reply, wary of showing any emotion.

Tom stares at the paper folded before him. He picks up the cup and drinks all the coffee in one mouthful and replaces the cup back down onto the saucer. Slowly he looks at me and keeps his gaze on my face while lifting up the paper. Still watching me, he starts unfolding the document with both hands. When the paper is fully open, he casts his eyes down to look at it. I can see his eyelids moving back and forth as he reads and re-reads the official type lined in neat, short rows down the page. Then he just freezes.

"What the fuck is this?" his voice comes out, broken.

I don't say anything.

"Isobel, what is this? Is this some kind of sick joke?" Any trace of colour that was left in Tom's face has now drained. The bottom corner of the paper is scrunched inside his closed fist. "Tell me what the hell is going on. You…you can't do this. What the hell are you doing? This is not a game Isobel, we are not at university anymore playing *crazy girlfriends,* this is real life. This is *my* life. What the fuck…" Tom's voice trails off for a second time.

"That," I say thrusting my hand over the top of the paper to point at the type, "*is* real life Tom."

Tom's head sinks into his hands, the birth certificate still gripped between his fingers. Eventually he looks up between his fingers, crushing the paper into his forehead. "You told me you had an abortion. You lied…you lied about that? How the hell could you lie about that, something as big as that? God, who the hell does that? What kind of person are you?"

His words hit me, and the way, the way his eyes are searching, almost ripping at my face makes my whole body tense up. I watch in horror as the full consequences of the lie I let slide off my tongue all those years ago seeps further and further into Tom's face.

"Where is it, where's the kid?"

"He was adopted," my words are cracked and broken. Water is pushing at the backs of my eyes and the hardness is slowly slipping and giving way.

"Adopted," Tom repeats quietly, his eyes sinking away from my face. "Do you…" Tom stops and shuts his eyes. I watch him, growing petrified at what I have done, "do you know where he is?" Tom finishes the sentence.

I shake my head, blinking hard to stop the water spilling, but it comes anyway. I urgently wipe at my face with the back of my hand, smearing damp across my cheeks and biting my bottom lip.

Tom reads the birth certificate again, "How could you lie about this Isobel, how?" his voice is no longer angry, instead it's sadness stinging at my ears.

"I don't know," I whisper.

"You don't know, that's great, just great," Tom folds the paper in half and places his palm on top of it.

My mind is racing, all I know is I have to work out a way to retrieve the situation, make Tom see how much I love him, that we can work everything out. Together. Once Tom and I are together that will push Patrick squarely out of the picture, Patrick won't have any hold over me anymore. I'm sure Tom will help to finance the gallery. Maybe once the initial shock has passed, Tom will see that we have a future. Together. He has to.

"Tom…" I start to say, reaching for his hand still covering the birth certificate.

"Isobel, don't OK. Just don't."

"Tom, please!"

"Please what Isobel, huh?"

"We can work this out Tom, I know we can."

"We *have* to work this out Isobel," Tom says firmly, pressing down on the folded paper.

"Yes I know. I know we do, and we can. We can be a family. Tom, we could find him and we could start again together as a family…"

Tom jerks back on the stool, gripping the edges of the table with both hands, "What?" he spits.

"We could be a family Tom, we could…"

"What the hell are you talking about? Listen to yourself. Listen to what you're saying," he picks up the glass of water takes a large gulp, sets the glass back down on the table, trapping the birth certificate underneath, and goes to stand up.

"What are you doing?" I practically yell, looking at him mortified that he could dare leave now. He can't leave.

"I'm going Isobel. I think I have heard enough for one day," Tom answers, kicking the stool under the table.

"Tom, wait. Please wait!" I shout, standing up and snatching at his arm. He instantly rips the limb out of reach and takes a step back, staring at me.

"Please you can't go like this. We have to work this out together. I want us to be a family Tom, why don't you understand that?"

"You're fucking crackers," he reaches his hand inside a trouser pocket, pulling out a handful of coins which he drops on the table. "You haven't changed, you're still bloody crazy," he drops another couple of tarnished gold coins on the table and walks away.

Through the pools of water smudging at my eyes I see the birth certificate laying on the table, still partly trapped under the water glass. I grab the paper and run after Tom shouting his name to his back that refuses to turn around. Breathless and crying huge streams of water, I pull at his elbow to make him stop, but he shakes me off and speeds up his pace. People are looking at us and I don't care. I keep yelling his name until, out of pure embarrassment at the scene I am making, he snaps his body around like a spring being uncoiled to confront me.

"Please just leave me alone Isobel," he hisses.

"Please take this," I cry, holding out the birth certificate, now a crumpled mass in my hand. Tom pushes my hand away.

"Please," I plead, trying to force the paper into his hand.

"Oh for fuck's sake," Tom hisses, pulling the paper from my hand and shoving it in the breast pocket of his jacket. "Happy?" the word slaps me, "now just let me go." I watch Tom take hurried strides down the footpath, weaving through the traffic to the other side of the street. Before he steps up onto the footpath across the road, he snatches a quick glance over his shoulder to see if I am following him, but I am still standing in the same spot he left me, sobbing.

CATE

I look at the time before trying Tom's mobile one more time. It's after eight, I called him as I was leaving work at about six-thirty and left a message. I haven't heard anything from him, poor thing is probably working late again. He was going to cook tonight so I don't know if I should start dinner anyway, I'm hungry.

Pressing Tom's name into my mobile and trying him again, there's still no answer. Spotting half a bottle of red wine on the counter I decide to pour myself a glass and sit in the sunroom with the windows flung open to let the sea breeze in. The evening has brought no respite from the heat of the day, relentlessly drilling into the buildings and concrete of the city.

I lean out the window, looking at the garden. Neat rows of tomato and grape vines along with the lavender all planted by Tom are now standing proud and tall in the half-light of the evening. Like me, the plants are also relieved the sun has disappeared behind the buildings and will soon melt into the horizon slicing between the ocean and the sky for one more day. As I take my first sip of wine, the cicadas wind up their evening song and I listen to the steady quiver floating across the summer evening with a smile on my face.

I am contemplating refilling the wineglass when I hear the front door open.

"Is that you, Tom?" I shout with my head still half out the sunroom window.

"Yep, I am just going to change out of my suit and will be down to see you. I haven't forgotten I'm cooking," his voice sounds hollow as it echoes off the hallway floorboards.

"Great, I'm starving," I yell back and go to get another glass from the kitchen cupboard to pour him some wine too.

TOM

I slide the knot from my tie loose and let the silk drop on the bedroom floor behind me as I make my way to the bathroom to splash cold water on my face. I have been walking around and around the city, trying to make Isobel's words produce some sort of engagement with my emotions that's not just straight and pure disbelief.

I feel numb and I know it's the shock, once those words and that damn bit of paper sinks in, I know I am going to go into meltdown. What the hell am I going to do, everything is such a bloody mess.

How can there be a kid, my kid, out there somewhere and me not know about it for all these years? How the hell can Isobel lie about something like that? Oh God, the shaking has set in again. I twist the cold water tap on full blast, shoving my hands in the stream of water. The water is lukewarm, the pipes must still be hot from the heat. I leave my hands in the water waiting for it to cool when I suddenly remember the piece of paper hidden in the breast pocket of my jacket. Hastily I shut the tap off, dry my hands off and stare at myself in the mirror wondering where the hell I am going to put it.

In the bedroom, I kneel down looking under the bed, there's nothing under there. I stand up brushing the dust from my knees, frantically searching the furniture in the room for somewhere suitable to hide this damn bit of paper that could seriously fuck my life up. Totally.

I pull open the top drawer of the dresser, scan the socks inside and then slam the drawer shut – too obvious. In a drawer full of my T-shirts I find a cigarette packet which I must have hidden there in an attempt not to be tempted. I flip open the lid and see I must have smoked a few, I can't remember when. Nestled between the remaining cigarettes is a lighter. I pull the lighter from the packet, rolling it around in my hand, for a brief moment I consider burning the birth certificate. The flame sparks and goes out. I try it again and this time it burns an orange glow with a shock of transparent blue. My hand digs into the breast pocket and slides the document out, holding it close to the flame. But I can't do it. I can't burn something like that, that's my kid for God's sake. I've got a kid. I've got a kid. I've got a kid. Jesus.

Right get it together Tom. Pull yourself together.

I return the lighter to the cigarette packet, close the lid shut and jam the box under layers of multi-coloured cotton. Breathing hard I slam the drawer shut, disgusted that I could ever consider doing such a thing.

The paper scrunches in my hand as I look around the room in despair. I can't put it in any of my drawers, it could easily fall out with something and Cate often rummages around looking for my T-shirts and thick socks to wear when she is getting cosy for the evening. It would be too risky to stick it in a pocket of one of my suits and the drawer of my bedside table is so bloody obvious.

The wardrobe door partly open catches my eye. It's going to have to go in there for now until I find a proper place for it. Walking carefully over the floorboards, I slide the door back so it's fully open and quickly scan the clothes hanging in different lengths from the wooden hangers, Cate has always hated wire hangers. On the shelf above the railing, Cate's handbags are stacked neatly on top of one another. It can't go up there.

Squatting down, I trail my fingers back and forth across rows of shoes when finally at the very back of the wardrobe I touch cardboard and remember the shoebox I left in there from the new brogues I bought a couple of weeks ago. Just as I am about to yank the box out, I hear Cate coming up the hallway. Shit. For a split second, I freeze and then something else takes over spurning me into action. Pulling the box out, I lift the lid and drop the paper inside just as Cate arrives at the bedroom doorway. Her footsteps stop, she doesn't come the whole way into the room.

"What are you doing?" Cate asks, leaning on the doorframe. I look up at her and smile weakly.

"I'm, umm putting my shoes away," I murmur, looking at the shoes still on my feet.

"They look like they are both still on your feet," Cate laughs, "what's in the box?"

"Nothing," I choose the word most over-used when someone gets caught red-handed.

"Really?" Cate's not giving up.

"Yeah really," I reply while crushing the lid back on and replacing the box to the back of the wardrobe behind my rows of shoes. Standing up I brush my trousers down.

"Come on, what's in the box?" Cate teasingly comes towards me, draping her arms around my neck, "you can tell me," she breathes into my ear, half-biting my earlobe.

"None of your business," I answer, trying to sound playful, like I don't care if she knows or not, like there's not a secret locked in the box that is only the tip of destroying us.

"Is it for me?"

My body tenses. "Could be," the sound from my throat is more like a scratch.

"Oh, I'm even more intrigued now. Come on, what is it?"

I'm growing nervous about being pushed into a corner because where this conversation is now heading I am going to have to add yet another layer to the lies I have been forced into telling Cate. I really don't want to have to lie again. "Babe, you have your secrets, like whatever it is you write in that book you keep in the drawer under your knickers, so just let me have mine," I say steadily, pulling away. Cate unlocks her arms from my neck and looks confused. Seeing her hurt sends prickles racing across my skin.

"Babe," I go to pull her back to me, but she stands rigid on the spot, "It's nothing. It's not important. Come on let me go and make us some dinner."

I try again to pull her body in close to mine and this time she lets me. Leaning into her, I kiss Cate's mouth, resting my lips on hers for longer than I probably need to. Her brows knit together as I tightly clutch at her ribcage. 'I'm so sorry' are three words said silently inside my mind.

"I think we're up to about forty people on Saturday," Cate says, handing me a glass of wine.

"Saturday?" I look up from dicing an onion.

Cate lightly frowns, "our engagement party, at our house" she cocks her head to one side and raises her eyebrow.

"Of course. Of course. God forty people, I'm going to be on the barbeque all day," I laugh unconvincingly, sliding the onion with a knife down the chopping board and into the wok, instantly sending fizzing steam up out of the pan as the onion hits the hot oil. I carry on pretending everything is normal by moving the onion around the oil with a wooden spoon and trying not to think about the total mayhem that is silently killing my life.

"Isobel is bringing her boyfriend."

My grip on the wooden spoon tightens and I stop moving the onions around the metal. "Isobel has a boyfriend?"

"Apparently. His name is Patrick I think. First I have heard of him. But you know Iss, she does tend to keep herself to herself. She must really like this one if he has gotten an invitation to our party and is obviously going to meet all her friends," Cate continues sipping her wine, oblivious to my stomach silently dropping to my feet. "Watch out, that'll burn," she says, taking the wooden spoon from my hand and giving the wok a shake.

ISOBEL

"Tom?" says Patrick thrusting my mobile phone at me as I come out of the bathroom, drying my hair with a towel. "What?"

"Your phone was ringing, it's *Tom*," Patrick spits out Tom's name. "Is it *the* Tom, the one who seems to be such a big feature of your sleep talking?"

I narrow my eyes at Patrick, pretending I have no idea what he is suggesting, but my chest is buckling and my hand shakes as I grab the phone from Patrick's hand. Tom's name is emblazoned across the screen. I wait for a few seconds, desperately willing a message to be left but the phone is silent.

"How long ago did he ring?" I cautiously ask Patrick who is watching me carefully.

"Expecting his call were you?"

"Oh fuck off Patrick."

"You can give it up with the little game, Isobel. Gabrielle told me that you confessed to her that you're in love with Tom. I was hoping that little phase was over with when you begged me to have you back, but clearly it's not is it?"

"I don't know what you're talking about," I spit back at him, checking the screen again for a voicemail message, still nothing.

"Well is it?"

"Is it what?" I continue staring at the blank phone screen.

"Over Isobel. O.V.E.R," Patrick roars, making me flinch. A shadow falls across his eyes.

"Just leave me alone," I whisper.

"What?"

"Nothing," I drop the phone into the pocket of my dressing gown and tighten the gown's cord firmly around my middle and go to make my way into the bedroom, but Patrick blocks my path, seizing my wrists. "Answer me," he smiles with his lips pressed together.

"Just let me go."

"I'm not going to be made a fool of Isobel. Do you understand?" he very slowly loosens his grip on my wrists, leaving streaks of red knotted through the skin. The veins in my hands have risen into a deep blue.

"Bastard," I mutter.

He follows me into the bedroom and sits on the end of the bed, watching me comb the tangles out of my wet hair. I am silent and don't protest when he starts to rub my shoulders. "I'm sorry baby, I am just very protective of you that's all, and I like to win."

"It's not a competition, Patrick," I turn and press my lips on his, even though it repulses me. I don't know how I am going to get through this evening, with Tom lying to everyone through his little show of public love for Cate. It makes my stomach churn, but I know the truth and so does he. So. Does. He. "Good," Patrick bites my bottom lip, hard. "What should I wear tonight?"

"How about the blue shirt?" I offer, 'That one looks nice on you." Satisfied Patrick walks out of the room.

Looking in the mirror I see a bead of red forming on my lip. I brush it with my finger and watch blood smear down my chin.

LAURA

"Is Isobel here yet?" Cate is asking me as she breaks bags of ice into the bathtub and then grinds bottles of wine and champagne down between the cubes. I am perched on the lip of the bath, squeezing an empty plastic cup in and out. Each time the cup cracks at it's sucked inwards, Cate winces.

"Not yet, I don't think. Well I haven't seen her anyway. She might be here now though I haven't been in the garden for a while," I answer.

"I thought she would have arrived by now, we've been going since mid afternoon, it's nearly nine o'clock."

"Maybe she's had a fight with the new boyfriend and old Iss Fizz has come out to play," I try to joke, but I have no idea where Isobel is. I have already left her two messages, neither of which she has bothered responding to.

"Here," I say, fishing my hand into the bath and pulling out a bottle of champagne and clasping the bottle between my knees. I peel off the silver aluminium in short coils and unwind the cage wire. "You ready?" I look at Cate who is scooping handfuls of ice over the wine bottles she has just slid into bath. She stops and laughs. "Here we go!" I shout, pulling the cork out of the bottle. White foam comes spilling out in great shoots, covering my hand in sticky bubbles.

"Congratulations," I say, handing the bottle to Cate.

"Are there any glasses in here?"

"Who cares, drink it straight out of the bottle. It's your party and you only get engaged once."

Cate laughs again and takes a mouthful of bubbles, spilling champagne down her chin and passes the bottle back to me.

"Thanks Lau, I love you."

"Ah you're pissed and so am I. Cheers," I tip the bottle to my lips.

"Right, I am going back outside. You coming?"

"Yeah in a tick."

"OK, well bring that with you," Cate points to the bottle and kisses me on the cheek.

I wait until I think Cate has gone back to the party and then tiptoe up the hallway and into Cate and Tom's bedroom to find my handbag which I left on their bed when I arrived. Dabbing at the sticky liquid still on my chin, I dial Isobel's number for the third time today. I listen to the phone ring out, getting ready to leave another message, but the phone is answered and Isobel's voice sounds distracted, all she says is, "I'm on my way now Laura," and then hangs up.

I stare at my phone. Not quite believing that Isobel has actually hung up, so press the phone against my ear again. Dead silence.

I find a discarded plastic cup on the dresser in the hallway and go into the bathroom, filling the cup with the bottle of champagne I opened for Cate. Opening the back door I spot Tom and Cate under the light glowing through the windows at the back of the house out into the garden. He has her face in his hands and is kissing her. I smile at my two friends, "Here's to you two," I say out loud, tilting the cup to my lips.

TOM

A ll day I have been on teetering on a knife-edge, switching my attention between the door and the garden gate, waiting for Isobel to breeze through and fuck everything up.

I tried calling her today to persuade her not to come. Tell her it was a massive mistake, I was even prepared to broker a deal with her where I would meet her next week and work this out between us. But not tonight. Not at my engagement party. And Cate, Cate, Cate. She looks so beautiful, her face coloured from the morning at the beach with a light dusting of sunburn on her nose. She had scratched at it when we got home, groaning from the bathroom that she looked like a clown. But I think she looks beautiful.

I've had so much booze, I am getting sentimental and growing more and more paranoid that Isobel is about to perform the final twist of the knife.

"Tom." It's Christian my friend from university, "It really is so good to see you mate," his words are slightly slurring.

"And you mate, and you," I really mean it. We drape our arms over each other's shoulders. "Ah I love this song," I shout into Christian's ear as the Manic Street Preachers strike the opening chords to *A Design for Life*. With our arms still across one another's shoulders we start swaying and singing. Other people start linking their arms across our shoulders until we have made a swaying, singing (badly) knot in the back garden. Cate ducks in under my and Christian's arms, wriggling her body between us and throwing her arms over both our shoulders. Christian smiles at her and kisses her forehead. I too smile at her and kiss her mouth, tasting sweet alcohol. In this light, the sunburn has darkened and I kiss her nose too. Her eyes are shining and my insides are crumbling and breaking for this girl I love.

We don't talk about love, we only want to get drunk. And we are not allowed to spend as we are told that this is the end. I'm designed for life. We all yell with great gusto, gripping harder onto each other's shoulders. Each word shuddering through me with more impact than anyone swaying and yelling around me will ever know.

And that's when I spot her. Isobel is standing at the back door, her figure outlined by the light illuminating from the sunroom.

"Is that Isobel what's-her-name?" Christian yells in my ear. I nod and Cate's gaze follows Christian and mine to the back door, she breaks free of the knot and before I can pull her back Cate is already running up the back steps.

I watch as Cate and Isobel hug. Then I see the outline of someone else coming up behind Isobel. She steps to one side and after a brief pause, the guy kisses Cate on both cheeks. That must be the boyfriend. OK if she has brought him, maybe it will be all right after all.

"You guys still in touch then?" Christian says above the din of the chorus.

"Yep," I breathe the word out of my mouth and decide to unwind myself from the knot, now fraying as people lose interest to return to drinking and talking. With deliberate steps I make my way to the back door. Isobel has seen me coming but pretends she hasn't noticed me until I am standing on the step below Cate.

"And this is Tom, my fiancé," Cate tells the guy with Isobel, stepping to one side so I can join her on the same step. The guy stares at me to the point where I get uncomfortable and have to look down. Cate makes a face, "Tom this is Patrick, Isobel's boyfriend."

"Tom?" Patrick extends his hand to shake mine and at the same time gives Isobel a look I can't read. "Congratulations. I apologise I thought Isobel and I were just going out for some quiet drinks before going along to a party – I didn't realise it was an engagement party, otherwise I would have brought some champagne," he says tightly.

"That's fine, there's plenty here anyway. It's great you could make it. What would you both like to drink?" Cate is saying, smiling broadly at Patrick, but I can see she is hurt Isobel hadn't explained the reason for our party to him. Another drop of pain for my beautiful Cate slides down my spine.

"What have you got?" Patrick replies.

"Come with me, the bar is in the bathroom," Cate smiles shaking the hurt off and first takes Patrick by the hand and starts to take Isobel's hand as well, but Isobel quickly puts her hand behind her back. I wince, but I don't think Cate has noticed.

"Just get me a vodka, if you have it?" Isobel says, smiling at Cate.

"Of course we do, we knew you were coming," Cate answers, laughing. Another tiny piece breaks off my heart.

When Cate and Patrick have left for the bathroom, I drag Isobel into the sunroom to stand behind the only closed shutter on the window. "What the hell are you doing here?" I hiss at her.

Casually she takes a packet of cigarettes from her bag and goes to light one.

"Not in the house," I say, pulling the cigarette from her mouth. She takes another cigarette from the packet. "Jesus Isobel," I mutter, yanking the packet from her hand.

Isobel moves closer so I can feel the heat from her body and leans her face into my ear. "We had to come Tom, what would Cate think if I didn't show up, hmm?"

I press my fingers against my eyebrows and deeply breathe in. The smell of bitter oranges floods my nostrils. I exhale a disgusted breath and wipe at my nose with the back of my hand. Isobel's scent makes me feel ill. She moves in closer still and I step backwards as I catch sight of Patrick coming through the door back into the sunroom. He gives me a look like the one he gave Isobel when we were introduced. Fuck, maybe he knows what's going on and is part of her little act of turning up here tonight. Another wave of nausea hits me. Cate is behind Patrick with a bottle of vodka in her hand. I remember the packet of cigarettes in my hand and slip them into the drawer of the art deco dresser we found on the street coming home from dinner one night last summer.

Cate is in the kitchen looking for plastic cups. She comes out with two wine glasses she's retrieved from the cupboard and gives one each to Isobel and Patrick.

"You get the real stuff, I think we're out of plastic," Cate declares.

"Congratulations," Patrick announces before drinking the entire contents of the glass.

Cate raises her eyebrows at me, "Another?" she asks.

"Please," Patrick replies, holding his glass out to Cate.

ISOBEL

The gate creaks on its hinges as I shut it. Muffled sounds from the party drift from the garden and slowly grow fainter as Patrick and I take drunken steps down the street.

"What the fuck are you playing at?" Patrick stops walking. I keep walking.

"Isobel!" my name fizzes and cracks into the night air. He doesn't care that I haven't stopped walking and starts shouting after me, "You didn't tell me it was a bloody engagement party we were going to. You said we just had to show our faces at some barbeque," he jeers, mimicking my voice. I speed up, the sound of my high heels slicing through the empty street. "That's *the* Tom isn't it? Have you noticed he's marrying someone else? But I don't think that stops you, or him for that matter."

I stop and swing around to see Patrick storming after me. Half his shirt is untucked and he stumbles over a patch of cement on the footpath raised by a tree root. "Or him?" I ask.

"No or him. I saw the two of you huddled together when I came back from getting our drinks. What, you don't think I saw your little tête-à-tête? You may as well have started fucking each other there and then, it was that bloody subtle. He's meant to be marrying someone else you lunatic."

Patrick's final word slashed a hot band across the back of my neck, stirring the familiar feeling that has always risen

401

and swollen inside me each time a boyfriend ever uttered that name or something like it to me. Right at this moment, I wanted to punch and hit and hurt Patrick.

A light goes on in a room of the house I am standing out the front of. As the curtain flutters, I turn around and start walking, more quickly this time. Behind me Patrick's steps are gaining pace and his shoes are matching the rhythm of mine as he comes up behind me and heaves my arms backwards. His body bears down onto my back and his chin juts into my collarbone. I stay perfectly still, hardly breathing.

"I told you Isobel I am not competing with anyone for you. Not Tom, not anyone. So stop playing this little game you can't win. End whatever pathetic little thing you have going with him or I will do it for you."

My arms are still throbbing when I get into bed beside the man I am despising more and more each second.

TOM

"You look rough," Nick says to me while we stand in line waiting for our coffees to be made.

"Thanks," I smirk.

"Big weekend?"

"Something like that," I reply.

Nick's coffee is handed to him, "I'll wait for you outside, it's too crowded in here." I nod at Nick who disappears out the door.

Vince calls my order, "You alright mate?" he asks, handing me my takeaway espresso. I nod. "Have a good day, hey?" he winks at me and turns to the next customer.

Out on the street Nick is sitting at the same table Isobel and I sat at. He has taken the lid off the paper cup and is blowing at the froth on his cappuccino.

"It's a beautiful morning, why don't we just enjoy our coffee before we join the rat race in the office. It's Monday morning and I sure as hell can't cope with that," Nick looks up at me squinting from the sunlight.

I look up at the sky. "Yeah why not," I reply, pulling out the stool opposite Nick and sitting down.

"God this is good," Nick says taking another sip of coffee.

"Hmm, that a cappuccino?" I ask while I twist open the paper on a tube of sugar to pour into the espresso.

"Yep."

I smile to myself, remembering that cappuccino is Cate's favourite way to drink coffee.

"God I am knackered," Nick starts talking again after taking another sip of coffee. "I was house-hunting most of the weekend, so boring, especially when you don't find anything. Just want somewhere by the beach, that's it. Just within easy distance for me to get to the beach to go surfing."

"Really. There's a place up for rent across the road from our place. It's a flat I think, if that's what you're after. We're really close to the beach, I just walk down with my board."

"Sounds good, I will have to check it out."

"Yeah, I'll give you the details when we get to the office," I offer.

We sit in silence for a moment, just watching people rushing past us to get to work. It's a nice feeling just sitting still in amongst all the zigzagging mayhem.

"So, do you want to talk about it?" Nick says carefully.

"Huh?"

"Whatever it is that's bothering you, do you want to talk about it?"

Then before I can even protest, or brush it off as nothing important, I am spewing jumbles of incoherent sentences out of my mouth and I can't stop myself. The whole sordid mess comes out and is swirling around Kent Street. When I finally finish Nick is looking at me. He goes to say something and then stops. I notice his cappuccino is still three-quarters full, the milk bubbles have flattened into a thin film. An overwhelming sense of relief lifts from my shoulders, I am even sitting up straighter.

CATE

The alarm splinters the early morning light falling into the bedroom. I startle and then relax when I realise what it is. Tom stirs next to me, thumping the flat of his hand blindly on the bedside table. Finally he manages to hit the snooze button and we are left in relative peace for another few minutes until the alarm triggers again at some obscure time like six fifty nine.

Tom rolls over and cuddles me in close. Both of us drift off into a light sleep and pull open our eyelids just as the alarm goes off for the second time.

"Morning," Tom breathes into my hair, kissing me on the cheek. "Sleep well?"

I nod and rub at my eyes.

"I'm going to jump in the shower."

"OK," I reply sleepily, nestling back down into the part of the mattress Tom has just vacated. I listen to the sounds of the shower running, all the usual familiar sounds that mark a weekday morning in our house until I muster up enough effort to climb out of bed and pad into the bathroom.

Tom turns off the water and pulls open the shower door just as I start brushing my teeth. I roll his towel off the railing and hand it to him. "Thanks," he smiles, kissing my shoulder. I smile at him in the mirror with toothpaste sliding out of the corner of my mouth.

"Hey ghessh what?" I say through a mouthful of white foam.

"What did you say?" Tom laughs.

"I shound the rhing," I keep talking through a mouth of foam.

"A lady shouldn't talk with her mouth full. Spit, then speak," Tom says drying his back.

I spit out the toothpaste into the basin, "I said hey guess what, I think I found the ring."

Tom stops drying his back, "As in the engagement ring?"

"Yeah," I nod, "I think you will love it. I haven't tried it on yet because I wanted to wait for you."

"That's bloody fantastic." Tom is squeezing me, "let's go try it on at lunchtime today then."

I click my tongue, thinking about how to fit a trip to the antique store into my day. "Well I am working from home today to finish that pitch off. The ring is in the city, so why don't we go tomorrow. I could ring the guy and ask him to hold it for us."

"It's a deal. That's bloody fantastic babe. I am so happy I was starting to get a bit worried for a bit there."

"Why, did you think I wasn't going to marry you?" I giggle, pulling the singlet over my head and turning the shower taps on. Tom grabs my shoulders and pulls my body into his, kissing my face repeatedly making it hard to breathe.

After I've had a shower, I pad back into the bedroom, still damp but I can't be bothered to dry off properly. It's already feeling warm. I'm sliding a T-shirt over my head when Tom comes back in, a tie is hanging loosely around his neck and his briefcase is slung on the bed.

"Cate?"

"Yeah," I reply, opening the cupboard in search of a pair of jeans.

"I really want us to go out to dinner tonight."

"OK."

"Great. Well we can, umm, go through stuff…"

"For the wedding?" I reply, pointing my foot through one of the denim legs. Tom is scratching his neck, "Yeah for the wedding," he confirms.

"OK," I smile, dragging the zip up on the jeans.

He comes over to me, hugs me and kisses me. A long, hard kiss that would normally lead to us doing other stuff, but I am pulling away and telling Tom he will be late for work. "I love you," he says into my hair before picking his briefcase up from the bed.

"Me too sweetheart. Have a good day."

"You too babe."

Tom pauses at the door for a second and turns around, looks me straight in the face and tells me he really means it. If I didn't know better I thought his eyes looked extra bright, just at that moment, like there was moisture building. But he turns his back to me before I can say anything and I hear the front door open and close, followed by the front gate and then a long pause before Tom's car starts up and pulls out from the curb.

Tom

I look at our house before I drive off to work, picturing Cate moving through the rooms. The back of my hand moves up to wipe the water from my eyes. My head drops on the steering wheel and I let my eyes close. Eventually I take a deep breath, lift my head from the wheel and start the car.

I can hear the Blackberry ringing in my briefcase which I've thrown into the foot well of the passenger seat. I let it ring knowing it will be Isobel. Her calls started again the day after the party, she called me all day yesterday, all of the calls I ignored. I know what I need to do now.

ISOBEL

I hang up without leaving a message. Tom has gone back to not answering any of my calls.

Patrick comes into the bedroom and asks me who I am calling. I falter and he knows straight away. He grabs my car keys from the dressing table. "I'm stopping this once and for all," he yells at me as the front door slams behind him. I flinch at the hollow bang of the wood against the doorframe and dial Tom's number again. This time I leave a message, *'Tom it's Isobel. You have to pick up the phone. I need to talk to you for God's sake. Just call me back.'*

Hot angry tears are welling up in my eyes and I scratch at the skin on my forearm until four hacked red lines appear.

Tom

I turn right at the bottom of our street and follow the road to the beach, turning the radio up to drown out the sound of the Blackberry ringing again and again in my briefcase. As I turn onto the main road leading up to where the road winds up above the sea, I turn the radio right down to listen if the ringing has stopped. For a moment there is silence in the car, just the sound of the engine as I change gears. I watch the traffic moving in front of me and take in quick glimpses of the ocean. I'm so bloody tired, but I know what I have to do.

Then the ringing starts again. I wait for the traffic to slow before leaning across the gearstick, grasping for the handle of the briefcase with one hand, while trying to concentrate on the road. My fingers are sweating from the heat and the leather slips from my grip. "Bugger," I curse out loud and put both hands back on the wheel. Stopping at the traffic lights, I take the opportunity to again lunge across the gearstick and plunge my hands into the foot well, until finally I grab the briefcase and toss it on the passenger seat next to me.

Instantly the phone starts to ring again. I flip the lock of the briefcase with my fingers, while still watching the road and find the Blackberry in my bag. Just as I go to answer it, it shuts off but I see seven missed calls – all from Isobel. My stomach turns. I am coming up to the best strip of road to check the surf so I toss the phone back on the passenger seat, it slides straight down over the lip of the seat and lands on the floor, falling out of sight.

I duck my head down to catch glimpses of the surf through the low railing. The phone starts ringing again and as the car climbs higher up the cliff, it occurs to me I can just throw the damn phone out of the window, let it catch on the rock face on its way down the cliff and into the sea. I start to laugh and lean across once more to try to locate the phone on the floor. I wave my hand across the carpet but can't quite reach it, the seatbelt is cutting into my chest and has locked up. The ringing is driving me crazy, so I unlatch the seatbelt to stretch a bit further until my fingers finally feel the little box vibrating.

I can see it's Isobel and in that split second I decide I am going to answer the call and then toss the phone out the window. Isobel's voice is immediately maddened and high-pitched scratching into the receiver. With the phone wedged between my ear and shoulder I try to re-latch the seatbelt. But I've just played a fool's game, dealing myself my final card. Taking my hand off the wheel to desperately pull the seatbelt across my body, I am forced to change gear with the other hand and that's when I lose control of the car. In the confusion and panic of watching the car in front of me draw closer and closer, I plunge both hands back on the wheel and over-correct. My car accelerates straight through the low guide railings, clipping and snagging on the rock face until it falls to its final resting place in the water.

I will never know that Isobel was still on the other end of the phone listening to me plunge to my death, screaming white fear, followed by a deafening silence.

I will never know that Patrick was on his way to Hedges Bank to threaten to blackmail me. Isobel had told him everything.

I will never know that when the police arrived at our front door to tell Cate what had happened, she collapsed. Since then she sleeps in my favourite T-shirt and still talks to me all day long, even though she inevitably finds out the truth, fragment by fragment, but there's nothing she wouldn't do to see me for just one last time.

10850420R00245

Printed in Great Britain
by Amazon.co.uk, Ltd.,
Marston Gate.